KING OF THE HOBOS

Also by Jeff Dennis:

When the Sandman Meets the Reaper: 12 Tales of Magic and Terror (1996) . . .

"With these stories Jeff Dennis proves he's a writer who can wear many hats; from the battered fedora to the astronaut's helmet to the bloodied ski mask. A richly varied mix of fantasy and phantasmagoria, dream and dementia from a writer who cares about his characters and his readers."

> — **Jeffrey Thomas** . . . author of more than 30 novels and collections, including *Monstrocity, Letters From Hades*, and *Punktown* —

The Wisdom of Loons (2009) . . .

"Welcome to Loon Mountain fishing lodge: A refuge from life's corporate insanity, where the Cherokee past is flawlessly interwoven with the present, where falling in love is as natural as not acting one's age—where little is as it first appears. It's an honor to introduce Jeff Dennis—a truly imaginative and innovative voice—to the realm of literary fiction."

> — **Jedwin Smith** . . . author of *Fatal Treasure and Our Brother's Keeper*, and two-time Pulitzer Prize nominee —

"A lovely and involving book about very real people with ordinary but universal human concerns . . . love, loss, regrets, hopes, the relationship between the past and present, our relationships with our families, self evaluations and spiritual ponderings. Think *On Golden Pond* with ghosts. The supernatural elements in the novel are portrayed in a fantastical way, rather than being horrific. *The Wisdom of Loons* is understated fantasy, is intensely but gently real, and I hope it receives the attention it deserves."

> — **Jeffrey Thomas** . . . author of more than 30 novels and collections, including *Monstrocity, Letters From Hades*, and *Punktown* —

King of the Hobos . . .

"A millionaire superhero. Derek Parnell can outfight you
and out-think you. He's equally at home in a boardroom or
a hobo camp. And he's on our side! A fun read about a
fantasy crusader in a very real world. Great character for a
series: a millionaire riding the rails, paying cash to stay
anonymous, spouting libertarian ideals and hunting
criminals . . . it's a great hook."

— **Heywood Gould** . . . bestselling author of *Cocktail,
Fort Apache The Bronx,* and *The Serial Killer's Daughter* —

KING OF THE
HOBOS

Jeff Dennis

Nightbird
Publishing

2012

KING OF THE HOBOS

FIRST EDITION

ISBN: 978-0-9819572-8-9

Nightbird Publishing
P.O. Box 159
Norcross, Georgia 30091

Website: www.nightbirdpubs.com

e-mail : info@nightbirdpubs.com

PRINTED IN THE UNITED STATES OF AMERICA

First Printing: October 2012

10 9 8 7 6 5 4 3 2 1

KING OF THE HOBOS

an off-the-rails thriller
by Jeff Dennis

PART 1: The World According to Parnell

PART 2: Mad Max and Maid Marian
See the World

THE WORLD
ACCORDING TO PARNELL

Riding the Rails

PARNELL AWOKE WITH A START. A hulking, disheveled man stood over him, knife in hand, weaving, either from the lurching of the train or too much moonshine.

"I told you to clear out, mu'fucker!" the man screamed, slashing the knife through the dank, fetid air. "This is *my* boxcar! How many times I gotta tell ya?"

Parnell gathered his wits, sized up the guy. Another delusional blanket stiff riding the rails. Too many of them around these days.

"Show me your deed, then," he said calmly.

"Huh?" A confused look crossed the giant's oafish face.

"You say this is your railcar . . ." Parnell said, carefully reaching behind him, to his waistband, feeling the slick cool steel of his gun. "I want proof of ownership."

The train thundered over the tracks below, wheels slamming the rails with a rhythmic *clackety-clackety-clack*.

The giant paused to consider this request, then blurted, "You some kinda wiseass or somethin'?"

"I just have this thing about legalities." Behind his back, Parnell looped his finger around the trigger. "I'm not giving up my space to some asshole who doesn't have proof of ownership."

"Man, you one crazy dude," the giant said, before springing forward and slashing downward with the knife.

Quick as a cat, Parnell rolled left, leaped to his feet, wheeled the gun around. Knife met gun with a metallic clank. Both weapons skittered across the floor.

Parnell felt a stinging pain in his right hand where the knife cut him, saw blood oozing from the slash. The bleeding wound enraged him. He went after the giant, threw a shoulder into him, the action like tackling an industrial size bag of cement. They stumbled across the boxcar, entangled, doing a herky-jerky tango, slamming into the far wall. The giant's head cracked against the steel wall. Parnell felt the guy's lungs deplete. The giant's massive arms dropped to his sides, defenseless.

Parnell had stunned him. Time to put him down for good.

He tried the Adam's apple crush chop, but the giant seemed to regain his composure, dodging Parnell's punch with surprising agility. Parnell's bleeding right hand hit the wall with a metallic thud. He cried out in pain, a couple of fingers surely broken.

The giant jumped on him. They went down on the floor in a heap, rolling, body over body, sliding from one side of the car to the other. Parnell had the giant in a bear hug, flames of pain shooting up his arms as he held on. The son of a bitch was strong as an elephant. The giant got his arms free, began taking punches at Parnell's kidneys as they rolled across the floor. They crashed into the wall, a ball of human flesh and blood, the impact separating them with a chorus of grunts and groans. The giant got to his knees and reached to retrieve his knife. Parnell took advantage, kicking out and connecting solidly with the big man's chin. The giant went sprawling, arms flailing, backpedaling toward the open side door . . . backward, backward, backward . . .

The giant screamed as he tumbled out the train car, arms wind-milling frantically.

Parnell rushed to the opening. Wind whipped at his face as he looked down the line of trailing cars, saw his attacker flopping and bouncing like a rag doll alongside the tracks. He watched with a fascinated revulsion as the man got sucked under the train. A spray of blood stained the tracks. A severed leg shot down the hillside as though launched from a cannon.

And then, from a dark corner of the train car, Parnell heard the owl.

Hoot . . . Hoot . . . Hoot . . .

He turned and walked toward the sound. Looked up and saw the glowing amber eyes staring at him with an intensity that unsettled him. Huge shimmering orbs, like twin moons on an early summer night.

Derek Parnell knew it was an omen.

The winged harbinger of death had spoken.

Nurse Annie

PARNELL HOPPED OFF THE TRAIN at the Albuquerque yards, his right hand on fire, the pain nearly unbearable. His broken fingers throbbed with every beat of his heart. He needed to find a clinic downtown. Some small out-of-the-way Doc-in-the-Box kind of place. Fewer questions.

He walked along the tracks, the familiar scent of tar and cinder touching his nose. Parnell found 1st Street and crossed over, picked up Stover Avenue, shielding his bloody hand so as not to attract attention. He felt the fatigue in his legs. Exhaustion sapped his soul. Waves of dizziness washed over him. Several blocks down, he found the HealthFirst Clinic on the corner of Stover and 4th.

"Insurance?" the bored receptionist asked him.

"I'm paying in cash," Parnell grimaced through the pain as he pawed through his backpack with his left hand.

The receptionist looked at him dubiously, taking in his ragged, unkempt appearance, his grotesquely swollen right hand, the blood trickling down his wrist. "This could be quite expensive," she said.

Parnell stared at the crone. Bluish-gray hair, hands liver-spotted and gnarled. Her nametag announced her as Hilda Mortensen, Office Manager. "Don't worry about it, Hilda," he said. "I've got it covered, however much it comes to."

She stared at him through her half-glasses, then pushed a clipboard to him, said, "You'll have to fill out these forms."

"Uh, no can do. Even if I could hold the pen, I doubt my penmanship would be legible."

"Very well," Hilda Mortensen said, staring at Parnell's ruined hand, the blood dripping all over the lobby carpeting. "I'll get one of our nurses to help you."

Soon, a young nurse dressed in a crisp white uniform entered the lobby. Her stockings swished as she approached him.

"Annie, please get Mister . . ." she glanced at the computer monitor, ". . . *Parnell* back in one of the exam rooms."

Nurse Annie ushered Parnell into an empty room, handed him a towel and an ice pack. "Keep this on the wound. It'll help until we can get you stitched up."

Parnell wrapped the ice pack to his hand with the towel. The stinging burn turned to a soothing cool numbness.

"So how'd this happen?" she asked, gently examining the broken fingers on his bruised, pulpy hand.

"I, uh . . . I fell down."

"Yeah, sure," she said, looking up at him, green eyes glittering with mischief. "And I'm Joan of Arc."

"Okay then. I was in a fight."

"That's better." She went back to examining his damaged hand. "Aren't you a little old to be getting in a scrap?"

"Not when someone is threatening to kill me," he said, grimacing as she moved his fingers.

"What were you fighting about? A woman? Money?"

"You ask a lot of questions."

"I'm a very curious girl," she said. "It was a woman, I'll bet."

Parnell thought about the guy on the train, the giant with the homicidal stare. "No, nothing quite that pedestrian."

"Well, whatever it was, looks like you got the worst of it."

Parnell envisioned the giant flying off the train and bouncing along the tracks, getting crushed under the huge steel wheels. He wanted to say, *You should see the other guy,* but decided it best to keep his mouth shut.

"Okay," she said, grabbing a clipboard and tapping it with her pen. "Can't get you fixed up until we have all of your personal data."

She walked him through the usual litany of questions. Parnell answered honestly. He had nothing to hide. However, as usual, his legal address was a showstopper.

"I need a street address," Annie said. "A post office box in Millford, Pennsylvania doesn't cut it."

"What the hell does it matter? I'm paying in cash."

"We have to have a complete data sheet before we can tend to a patient. It's the law."

"Personally, I think you're making that up, Annie. I think you're bullshitting me."

"It's *not* BS. We have to have a legal address on file in case a patient brings a malpractice lawsuit against us."

Parnell chuckled. "Is malpractice a common occurrence around here?"

"No, but—"

"There's no way I'm going to sue you, Annie. Too much

paperwork and hassle, and I'm not a big fan of lawyers." Parnell peeled back the cold compress on his hand, saw the wound was still oozing. "However, I might have to reconsider if I bleed out here in this exam room. Wrongful death and negligence. I know a nice girl like you wouldn't want that on her conscience."

Nurse Annie studied him for several long moments, then said, "I'm really not all that nice. In fact, I can be downright naughty. Especially with mysterious men like you."

Parnell smiled. Another small-town girl, bored with her mundane existence, looking for a little excitement in her life. This Annie was bolder and more direct than most.

"Sorry, darlin'," he said, "You'll have to get naughty with somebody else. I'm already spoken for."

She turned defensive. "You think I—?"

"Could we get this hand stitched up? We wait much longer and the morgue will be my permanent address!"

Annie huffed out of the exam room, then returned with a stainless steel tray containing hypodermic needles and stitching implements.

"Okay," she said, removing the towel and ice pack from his hand, "I'm going to numb you up and then inject something that will reduce the swelling. Then I'll sew you back together."

"Wait a minute," Parnell said, pulling his hand back. "I thought a *doctor* would do this."

"Give me your hand, you big baby! I'm a registered nurse. First year Med students can do this in their sleep."

He felt the sting of the needle just above his wrist.

Annie had his right hand stitched up and the broken fingers splinted within five minutes. She definitely knew what she was doing.

"Do you need a prescription for pain meds?" she asked.

"Absolutely," he said, standing.

"Wait here. I'll get Dr. Jernigan to write you one for Percocet."

Five minutes later, Annie was back, signed prescription in hand. As she gave it to him, she said, "I never did ask what you are doing in New Mexico. Vacationing?"

"Yeah, something like that."

"I have a couple of weeks saved up. Want some company?"

"No. I travel alone. Besides, I'm old enough to be your father."

Her green eyes taunted him. "What's the matter with you? I thought all older men fantasized about having an affair with an exciting young Lolita."

Parnell sidestepped her as he moved out into the hallway. "You're just a kid, Annie. Young enough to be my daughter."

She turned huffy. "What does *that* have to do with anything?"

"Everything. If I wanted to travel with somebody, it wouldn't be with a child."

"Child? That's how you see me?"

He turned on her. "Look. I *don't* see you, okay? I don't *know* you."

Her tone softened. "Sorry, Mr. Parnell. What I really had in mind was me being your chauffeur. It'll be a little difficult to drive with your injuries."

"I don't have a car."

"So how do you get around?"

"Public transportation."

"Well the buses only go so far. And taxis are a rip-off. Why don't you let me drive you?"

"I said no!" Parnell barked, losing his patience. Now I appreciate the fine job you did of sewing me up, but I'm going to be on my way. *Alone*!"

Echoes of Jennifer

H E WANDERED THE STREETS of Albuquerque until he found a pay phone. Damn cellular technology had made pay phones almost as extinct as the T-rex. Parnell never carried a cell. Too easy to trace his whereabouts. Little homing devices for Big Brother is all they really were.

He stepped up to the phone kiosk, fumbled with the receiver, finally got it to his ear. With his splinted index finger, he punched in the number for Blanton Miles, the guy who ran the nerve center of Parnell's operations.

"This had better be you, boss," Parnell heard Miles say.

"Yeah, it's me. Any messages?"

"That's it? You've been AWOL all this time and that's all you've got to say? *Any messages?*"

"I've only been incommunicado for five days, Blanton. Not exactly an eternity."

"It is in our line of work, amigo. You okay?"

Parnell watched a gust of wind pick up a spindly tumbleweed and carry it to the far side of the street. "Yeah, I had a close encounter with a Boxcar Willie who fancied himself as a land-lord." He looked at his bandaged right hand, tried to flex it, nearly passed out from the pain. "Got a little scratched up, but I'll live."

"I'm assuming the Willie didn't, however?"

"Correct. I red-lighted the son of a bitch."

"Ouch! Remind me to never hop a train with you."

"Shit, Blanton, the day you ride the rails is the day I run for Congress. You're too soft . . . settled into the pampered life. The Willies out here would eat your candy ass for breakfast."

A slight hesitation, then, "If it wasn't your signature on my paychecks, I'd have a witty comeback to that accusation."

"That's never stopped you before. Look, I'm not feeling all that spiffy at the moment. Don't want to hang on the phone. Any messages for me?"

"Yes. One in particular I think you'll find most interesting. Some woman called here day before yesterday. Claims her name is Jennifer Parnell. She said she has information as to . . ."

Parnell didn't hear any more. The name Jennifer Parnell hit him in the chest like a heart attack. Somebody was messing with him. His head spun. He felt his blood pressure spike.

". . . are you still there, Derek?"

"Yeah, uh . . ." He felt dizzy and off balance, wondered if it was a reaction to the Percocet or hearing the name of his long-dead daughter.

"This Jennifer person wants you to call her immediately, boss. She claims she knows things about what really happened to your Jennifer. She sounded like someone you should take seriously. My read is that she's on the up-and-up. Definitely not some deranged whack job. I deal with enough gonzo chumps to know she's not in that cuckoo's nest. You've got nothing to lose by calling her."

Parnell felt the sweat trickle down his back, razor-hot pain slicing through the fingers of his right hand. "All right. What's the number?"

Blanton Miles recited the woman's number and Parnell committed it to memory. He wasn't sure, but he thought the area code was Arizona, maybe Utah.

He thanked Miles and hung up, stood there in the shadows of the phone kiosk, thinking. *Jennifer Parnell?* Who was toying with him? And why?

He dropped a quarter into the slot and punched in the long distance number. An operator came on the line and told him how much to insert for the first three minutes. Parnell did as instructed. A woman picked up on the third ring.

"Hello?" A mellifluous voice. Young, eager.

"Are you Jennifer Parnell?"

"Depends. Who wants to know?"

"Somebody from this number called claiming to be Jennifer Parnell."

"Derek? Derek Parnell?"

He knew he had to be careful here. "I'm a friend of Derek's," he said into the phone. "He gave me this number."

"I know that's you, Derek," the woman said without hesitation. "You sound very stressed out."

Parnell felt the anger climb into his throat. "Is this some kind of a sick joke?"

A long silence, then, "I don't know what you mean."

"The hell you don't!"

Parnell could hear her breathing on the other end, could hear little pops and clicks on the line. Was the call being recorded?

Finally she said, "Look, I realize you must be terribly confused. I'm someone who has your best interests in mind. I'm Jennifer . . . Jennifer *Parnell.*

Parnell thought he detected a slight Scandinavian accent, a Nordic linguistic slant to the woman's words. Perhaps Danish or Swedish? Before he could think of a snappy comeback, or hang up, she said, "I have answers to the questions you've been asking."

"What questions might those be?"

"The questions your associate, Blanton Miles, has been trying to find answers to."

"I don't know anyone by that name."

"Don't lie to me, Derek. I have no patience for liars."

Parnell felt his spine go rigid, his face flush. "Who *are* you? What do you want?"

"I could be your worst nightmare, Derek. Or I could be the sweetest dream you've ever had," she said, cooing and soothing, while at the same time, maintaining a threatening tone. "It's totally up to you."

He felt his composure fraying. "I'm in no mood to be played, lady. What's your game?"

The woman ignored his observation. "I know you've been wandering the country like a gypsy the past six years, Derek, searching for something. I'm one of the few people on this planet who knows what that is. And I know where you can find it."

"Listen, bitch!" he yelled, "If you think you're going to extort money from me, it won't work. Racketeering is a federal offense. I know a criminal come-on when I hear one."

"You're a fine one to be calling someone else a criminal, Derek. I've got a long laundry list of your misdeeds in front of me here . . ." Parnell heard the shuffling of papers. ". . . murder, assault, blackmail, bribery, Internet fraud, forgery—"

"Forgery? You've gotta be—"

"Yes, forgery," she continued. "We got a little greedy a few years back, didn't we, Derek? You could probably buy and sell Croesus, and yet you wanted more."

"That's a lie!" Parnell said, trying to keep his voice even. He wondered if there was any significance to her reference of Croesus, whether she knew the relevance of that name to him.

"Look, Derek, we're playing on the same field here. We're both products of The Crash. You know it and I know it. If it hadn't been for the greed that brought down Wall Street and the corruption and incompetence of our elected officials, you and I would probably be flipping burgers in a fast food joint. We've profited from our country's misery—"

"Speak for yourself, *Jennifer*."

"No, I'm speaking for the both of us, and you know it. Now let's get down to brass tacks. You have a lot of money and I have information you've been seeking. I want your money and you need my information. There you have it. Supply and demand—the twin pillars of American capitalism."

It was so ludicrous Parnell almost broke out laughing. "Man, you are one seriously twisted *puta madre*!" he said.

"Oh, I don't deny that," she said, with an assurance that startled him.

The operator cut in and told them they had another thirty seconds before Parnell would have to drop more coinage.

When the operator cut out, Parnell said, "You haven't told me anything that convinces me you have anything worth paying for."

"Okay. I understand your reticence. How's this for a teaser? You believe that your wife and only daughter were both killed in a house fire seven years ago. You're partially right. Your wife—maiden name, Barbara Stevenson Logan—did indeed perish in that fire. But your daughter Jennifer survived. She's alive. A fine looking eighteen-year-old young woman, if not a bit damaged."

"You're insane . . . a complete bobblehead!"

"Am I? I don't believe I am. But then I'm biased. Do you know where Sedona is, Derek?"

"Of *course* I know where Sedona is, but—"

"Good. I want you to go to Sedona and have your fortune read by Madame Crystal. She's on Inspirational Drive, and she's expecting you. I'll be back in touch with you soon after."

Parnell was furious. "Listen, you conniving witch! I'll have your head for playing me this way!"

He heard a sharp click. The bitch had hung up on him! Then he heard the operator's unruffled voice, "Your three minutes are up. Please insert more money now or kindly hang up. Thank you."

Parnell slammed the receiver into the hook, pieces of the shattered plastic earpiece ticking against the Plexiglas cowling of the phone kiosk. His broken fingers throbbed.

He made a mental note to get Blanton to trace the number he'd just called. But he was pretty sure the effort would be futile.

Parnell turned and headed south, back to the Albuquerque rail yards. Even though his bandaged hand pulsed in stinging pain, there was a spring in his step. The woman on the phone who had so brazenly used his daughter's name had filled him with hope.

The hope that the real Jennifer Parnell was still alive. The hope that Derek Parnell had clung to throughout his travels of the past six years as he'd searched for elusive answers.

The woman on the phone was probably full of shit—just another hustler after his money—but he had to check it out.

Tombstone Eyes

PARNELL HOPPED A TRAIN HEADING WEST, slipping into a boxcar that contained scattered bales of hay. He sneezed, the overpowering scent of animal hide and dusty straw getting to him. Horses or cattle here recently, probably delivered to ranchers in central New Mexico. He lay nestled in a bed of hay. The Percocet numbed him. Two Ambien chasers sent him to dreamland.

The drugs scattered his thoughts like leaves in a strong wind. He drifted, the buzzing of flies sounding more distant. He heard the steel shriek of another train entering the yards outside. A train whistle. A man shouting something unintelligible. He drifted . . . Parnell traveled to weird places in his dreams. Shadowed, threatening places.

 . . . *trapped inside a flaming structure, the heat intense, pressing in on him from all sides. Windows shatter, exploding with deafening concussions, showering him with glass shards. He hears a sharp cracking sound, then the roof crashing through to the floor above. The foundation shakes beneath him. A heavy curtain of smoke stings his eyes, burns his lungs. He gets down low to the floor, feeling like a fish out of water as he gulps for oxygen. He slithers snakelike along the floor, looking for escape routes, panicking when he realizes there are none.*

Frightened screams from a distant room—high-pitched wails of female distress. Twin screams in tandem, increasing in volume to horrific levels. The terrified shouts for help slam his brain like hammer to anvil. He wants desperately to help but knows all is futile. He curls into a tight ball on the floor and waits for the fire to take him . . .

 . . . Parnell came awake, shaking, jittery, his shirt soaked through. He felt feverish. His recurring fire nightmare. As always, excruciatingly vivid and real.

"Bad dream, Mr. Parnell?" he heard a familiar female voice say.

He looked up from his bed of hay. After a few confused seconds, he recognized the nurse who had stitched up his hand a few hours earlier. She looked different with her hair down, the tight-fitting acid-washed jeans. High-topped black sneakers. No makeup. She looked more tomboyish but it was definitely Nurse Annie.

Parnell thought he was still dreaming, her appearance here in this reeking railcar having a stunning surreal quality.

"What the hell are *you* doing here?" he asked.

"Nice to see *you*, too," she replied with sarcasm. "I figured you might want some company on your way to Sedona. Probably take us seven, maybe eight hours to get there. You can't sleep the whole way. Especially if you keep having those nasty nightmares."

Parnell's guard went up. "What makes you think I'm headed to Sedona?"

"It's either Sedona or Flagstaff. Those are the next pockets of civilization on this route."

Parnell stared at her, thinking about that Danny DeVito movie, *Throw Mama From the Train*. He battled his temptation.

"Pockets of civilization?" he said to her. "You make it sound like we've been wiped out by nuclear Armageddon and reduced to a Mad Max kind of existence."

She smiled at him, her grin mischievous. "I'm thinking maybe it *is* a Mad Max world, the way you tote that gun around. The way you worship it like it was your cock or something."

Parnell felt his anger rise. "Are you still stuck on—?"

She cut him off, saying, "You really *are* an interesting man. I'm glad I followed through. This is gonna be quite the adventure."

"No it's *not*!" he said. "First time this train rolls to a stop, you're getting off, young lady. I travel solo. I told you that."

"Well then, I guess you're stuck with me for a while, Mr. Parnell. Next stop is Winslow, Arizona."

"Not if I toss your pretty little ass off this train."

She gave him a coquettish pout. "You wouldn't do that."

"Oh no?"

She twirled a loop of hair around her index finger. "Do you really think I'm pretty?"

Parnell had to laugh. "You are *so* young."

"I'm not *that* young. I'm pushing thirty."

"Oh wow, definitely on the brink of senior citizen status."

"Just because I'm not ancient like you doesn't mean I don't have a lot to offer," she said, her petulant tone making her seem even younger. "I'm smart. I've been around."

He looked at her, studied her, which seemed to make her nervous. "So, you followed me here," he said. "Why?"

She moved closer to him, plopped down on a block of hay, facing him. "Do you have any idea how dreadfully boring it is to be a nurse?"

"Can't say that I do."

"Well, it is. All day long, dealing with people's infirmities and weird viruses. Exposing myself to all kinds of potential health risks. Listening to people whine about their ailments. Being cooped up all day in a windowless office with sicko people. I'd had enough of that place long before you strolled in with your busted-up hand."

"Please don't tell me you quit your job."

"Yeah," she said, looking away. "Time to move on."

"Wonderful," Parnell said dully.

"Look," she said, her eyes shining, "I desperately need some adventure in my life."

"And you think riding the rails with me will give you that?"

"Yeah, I do. There's an element of danger about you that I find exciting. I figure you're the kind of man who can show me some fun."

"You've got the wrong guy, sister. Look, Annie. Do yourself a favor and—"

"How many people have you killed?"

"What?"

"You heard me. How many human beings have you snuffed?"

"What makes you think—?"

"Because your eyes are like tombstones. They give you away."

"Tombstones? Annie—" he began, thinking of the best way to handle her.

"I really don't mean to be presumptive, but—"

"Look at me," he said, waiting until she turned her head toward him. "I don't want to hear about your career problems. I don't want to hear about your unexciting life. In fact, I don't want to hear one more word out of you. If I do, I promise you'll end up as rail kill for the vultures. Not a fun way to die."

"Jesus!" Annie said, getting to her feet. "You've got *issues*."

Blessedly, she moved to the far side of the boxcar and left him in peace.

Triskaidekaphobia

PARNELL HEARD ANNIE SCRATCHING AROUND behind a bale of hay on the opposite wall. She sniffled a lot. Probably a crack addict or meth-head, he thought.

He lay back against a pillow of straw, drowsy, contemplative. He thought about Crazy Annie's allegation. That he was a killer. She was right, of course. That bitch on the phone had him pegged, too. But how? The last thing people who met Derek Parnell ever suspected was that he was a killer. Too clean-cut, most would say. Too personable. Too sharp. The quick wit and slow smile. He came across more like a financial adviser than a cold-blooded killer. But Nurse Annie had seen through the facade. *Your eyes are like tombstones*, she had told him. *They give you away.*

The drifter he'd killed on the train this morning was number 13 in his hit parade. A baker's dozen. A trail of 13 bodies, none of them ever linked to him. He was careful that way. He planned his hits with precision and skill. Parnell didn't think making people disappear permanently was such a difficult thing. Not if you thought it through. Not if you planned for every conceivable scenario, for every possible thing that could go wrong. After all, it was a big planet with an infinite number of safe dumping grounds.

Thirteen kills spread out over 25 years. Parnell hoped he didn't have to hang on *that* number long. He knew bad things happened when the number 13 was involved. Parnell had looked it up once, this inordinate fear of the number 13. Discovered the name for it—*Triskaidekaphobia*. His triskaidekaphobia was rooted in reality. Parnell's father had been murdered on the thirteenth of the month when Parnell himself was 13 years old. Two years later, his older brother, Ron, had drawn the number 13 in the Vietnam draft lottery and was shipped off to Southeast Asia, only to return home later that year in a polyurethane body bag wrapped in an American flag. As if all that wasn't enough proof of the dangers of the number 13, his mother had also passed away on Friday the 13th. Parnell wore his superstitious nature like an ill-fitting suit. Omens and portents and superstitions—he paid close attention to them all. They were the language of karma.

Parnell received his education in killing some 27 years ago, when he was a grunt sweating through boot camp at Fort Jackson in South Carolina. The Army had taught him how to kill efficiently and without conscience. They had drilled it into him until it was a mantra—your enemies must be eliminated at all costs. Your enemy doesn't deserve to live and breathe the same air as you. Kill or be killed. The only good enemy is a dead enemy. His military experience had transformed his young self into a killing machine, had torn out his heart and replaced it with the dark soul of a killer. The brass at Jackson were training his unit for a hush-hush engagement in Syria, but they never shipped out. So, there they were, twenty-four of them, all fired up for the hunt with no place to go. Twenty-four trained killers with no one to kill.

After Basic Training, Parnell took his newly-learned military skills out into civilian life. His first target was his father's murderer.

His father—Louis Parnell—had been a middle-class wage earner with a heavy gambling addiction. He threw money around like the federal government. First problem: Louis couldn't print his money when he needed it the way the government could. Second problem: Derek's father never considered the odds. Louis would place bets with big-time bookies that made absolutely no sense. Before Derek's mother passed away, she'd told him about some of Louis's more outrageous wagers. He once put 25 grand on a long-shot horse in the Kentucky Derby. How big a long-shot? Try 240-to-1 odds. The horse rode the rear the entire way around the track. Never climbed out of last place. Twenty-five-thousand dollars gone in a matter of minutes. Another bet: Twenty thousand on an early Super Bowl game where he took the points and a huge underdog. No way would the Dolphins lose by 9 points to the Cowboys, Louis had said. And he was right. His Dolphins lost by *21* points. Another twenty grand gone. Another bookie owed. That's when things started getting dicey. Strange men showing up at all hours, making threats. Phone calls in the middle of the night. Parnell's mother filed for divorce and took young Derek to live with his grandmother. "Lou always said all we needed was one big score, and the best way to do that was to take astronomical odds," Parnell's mother had told him at one point. "Your father never understood that the odds were astronomical for good reason."

To finance these monumental lapses in judgment, Derek's father got in deep with loan shark scum Grant Pickett. Pickett didn't have the patience to wait on his money, and when he realized that Louis Parnell would never be able to make good on his loan, he'd ordered a hit on him. Shot through the back of the head, execution style. Parnell remembered the day as if it were yesterday and not 36 years ago. Being called into the principal's office at Arnold Junior High, a scared eighth grader greeted by a policeman, a plainclothes detective, Parnell's guidance counselor, and his very tearful mother, who were all seated around Principal White's desk. When they broke the news to him, Parnell remembered feeling violated, feeling the rage of injustice swell up in him until it was difficult for him to breathe. Sure, his old man had been a weak and pathetic loser, but that was no reason for someone to murder him. Parnell always saw that situation—his father's life for the cash his dad couldn't pay back—as twisted street economics that he just couldn't get his head around. It wasn't an equitable settlement in Parnell's mind. Even less equitable was the fact that Pickett had skated on a technicality after framing one of his underlings, Clyde Pasco, who was doing life at Lewisburg Federal Penitentiary.

So, after boot camp, Parnell tracked down Grant Pickett, surprised to find him not only still alive, but thriving. The creep was operating a string of adult movie theaters around Philadelphia, running a prostitution ring out of one, and a numbers racket out of another. Parnell made quick work of Grant Pickett as he notched his first kill. Left him dead of nicotine poisoning sitting up in the back row of one of Pickett's own movie theaters, with an orgy of naked bodies writhing up on the big screen. Moans of ecstasy booming from the huge theater speakers drowned out Pickett's death cries. It wasn't as easy to get your hands on liquid nicotine back then as it was now. But the Army had taught Parnell to be resourceful. Liquid nicotine made the perfect untraceable weapon, a toxic poison that was tasteless and colorless, and only a small amount needed to be administered. Death was quick and violent. Justice had finally been served.

Parnell had not been in a movie theater since. That was perhaps his weirdest phobia, this fear of cinemas. He couldn't find the scientific name for it, and was sure one did not exist.

He thought about the other dozen lives he'd snuffed. None of them deserved to live. All were extremely bad people who had done horrendous things to others. To Parnell's way of thinking, he was taking care of business in a way that America's legal system could not. *Would* not. The laws were written by Casper Milque-toast liberals to favor the rights of the criminal, victims be damned. Parnell saw himself as The Great Equalizer, tipping the scales of justice back in the proper direction.

He rolled over on his side, the action hurting his bruised ribs. His hand hurt, too, which pissed him off since he couldn't do his daily pushups and sit-ups. It was part of his self-discipline routine—300 of each every day, without fail.

Parnell lay there, the rocking of the railcar lulling him into a fitful sleep. He didn't know how much time had passed when he came awake to a strange chanting sound. He leaned on an elbow, listened. Nurse Annie. He couldn't make out the words, but it was definitely her.

"What the hell are you mumbling about over there?" he called out to her.

"I'm praying," came the response.

"Praying for what?"

"I'm praying for you. Anyone who thinks the number thirteen is dangerous needs some direction from God."

Parnell felt his gut clench. Could this crazy nurse read his mind? "What are you talking about?"

"You know damn well what I'm talking about. You fear the number 13. I believe they call your affliction triskaidekaphobia."

Parnell's heart skipped a couple of beats. Just who was this woman?

The Lone Ranger and Tonto

H E SAW HER CLUTCHING A FRAYED BIBLE to her chest. Her backpack lay beside her, opened, the contents spilled out across the hay—lipstick, cell phone, hairbrush, a silver gun with a snub-nose wide-mouth barrel. Parnell saw the bold black lettering running the length of the pistol grip—**MACE**—and knew the gun was a serious pepper spray weapon. He knew about these MACE guns, had seen one of them take down a strong six-foot man from 25 feet away.

She looked up at him with a glance that was challenging yet vulnerable.

"So what's your deal?" Parnell said to her.

"My deal with what?"

"How'd you know about triskaidekaphobia?"

"I read a lot. I have a gargantuan vocabulary."

"You know that's not what I mean."

"Yeah, I know." An awkward silence, then, "I know the number 13 isn't your only fear."

Parnell studied her. Annie's all-knowing expression unsettled him. He decided to take the bait. "Please tell me my wise and astute seer, what else am I afraid of?"

"Fire."

Parnell felt something catch in his throat. "Well of course. *Everybody's* afraid of fire."

"Not like you," she said. "Your fear is unnatural. Like it's personal or something. I didn't notice any burn scars on you, but I'm thinking maybe you lost somebody important in a fire. Am I warm?" she said, rolling her eyes and chuckling. "Pardon the pun."

Parnell stared down at her where she lay. He pointed at her Bible.

"You believe in those fairy tales?"

She glanced at the tattered binding of her Bible. "Fairy tales? You're wonky! It's the Old Testament. An eye for an eye. God's vengeance. The way I like it. The way I think *you* like it, too."

He started to say something, but then realized Annie was reciting scripture.

" 'There appeared to them tongues like flames of fire that parted and rested on each one of them. They were all filled with the Holy Spirit and began to speak in other tongues, as the Spirit gave them to utter.' Acts two, verses three and four," she said, snapping the Bible shut and looking up at him.

"Yeah? So? You care to translate that for me?"

"It means that fire has divine properties."

"Sure, whatever you say. Look—"

"God touches each of us with fingers of fire. Fire is a celestial energy force, capable of both burning and healing. Depends on how you interpret God's meaning."

"God's meaning?" Parnell blew air through his cheeks. "Do you really think there is some grand benevolent deity looking over us, watching out for our best interests?"

"Absolutely. Don't you?"

He wanted to tell her no, that in his world view, evil had won out far more often than goodness. In Parnell's experience, Satan had the upper hand. But he sidestepped his skepticism and said, "It doesn't matter what I think." Doesn't matter what any of us think when you get right down to it."

"You are *so* cynical," she said, hugging the Bible to her chest. "Maybe that's why you're afraid. Maybe that's why you're so sad and lonely. When you accept Jesus Christ into your heart and mind, your fears and loneliness vanish. When you love Jesus unconditionally, Jesus smothers your fears, eliminates the dark-ness . . . leaves you standing in the light."

Parnell glanced at her MACE gun. "If you're so tight with Jesus, why carry that pepper spray around with you? Seems to me you wouldn't need it with God as your bodyguard."

Embarrassed, she scrambled to stuff the pistol and other items into her backpack. Then she looked directly at Parnell and began reciting the Lord's Prayer: "The Lord is my shepherd; I shall not want. He maketh me to lie down in green pastures: he leadeth me beside the still waters. He restoreth my soul: he leadeth me in the paths of righteousness for his name's sake . . ."

"Save it, lady!" Parnell barked as he backed away from her.

But she kept on with her prayer. ". . . Yea, though I walk through the valley of the shadow of death, I will fear no evil: for thou art with me; thy rod and thy staff they comfort me. Thou preparest a table before me in the presence of mine enemies . . ."

Parnell got back to his makeshift bedding of hay and plopped down just as Annie finished up her prayer. He called out to her from where he lay. "If you're finished it would please the court if you'd shut the hell up. What does it take to get it through that pretty little head of yours?"

"You called me pretty again!" he heard her chirp from the other side of the boxcar. "Flattery will get you everywhere, Mr. Parnell. And despite your stubborn male pride, you *do* need me. Very much. You just don't know it yet. I mean, shit, even the Lone Ranger had Tonto. I figure if a cowboy could rely on an Indian, then certainly, I could be useful to you. Everybody needs somebody to watch their back."

This nursing chick was the last person Parnell wanted watching his back.

He had a very simple plan for ditching Little Miss Bible Thumper. Once they hit the Winslow yards, Parnell would take her to Shangri-La.

Shangri-La

P ARNELL ESCORTED ANNIE through the Winslow train yard, knowing they had to keep a low profile to avoid detection by rail security. He wanted no part of the bulls. They had a reputation for being sadistic when dealing with vagabonds. He knew that carelessness had caused many a hobo to be roughed up and thrown in lockup for the night. Railroad officials took trespassing seriously, especially in these days of terrorist threats. The Winslow freight yards—a major switching hub on the Burlington Northern-Santa Fe line—warranted additional security.

Parnell preferred to move under cover of darkness. No such luxury today. In the late-afternoon daylight, he and Annie sprinted through the receiving yard, between lines of cars, taking pains to remain well hidden. Coming up on the engine house, he noticed several bull cruisers parked nearby, so they took the long way around.

They exited the train yard on a high promontory overlooking I-40. Down below, rumbling 18-wheelers made their way east. Car windshields reflected the day's low-lying sunlight in sparkly spangles.

Parnell had ruled out going to Sedona. Madame Crystal and her gypsy fortunetelling services could wait. He desperately needed to get to Flagstaff to see Elaine. That's where he was headed before he got sidetracked by Nurse Annie.

Parnell's world revolved around Elaine Leibrandt, and had since he began his nationwide wandering six years ago. She was his ballast, his emotional gyroscope. He missed Lainey terribly. They'd been apart for close to a month, though Parnell had called her regularly. The past few days, he'd found himself hallucinating over the perfume she wore—Obsession. Last week up in Colorado he had taken a detour to visit a department store in Boulder, where he spent the better part of an hour at the perfume counter, spraying the sample bottle of Obsession and sniffing the air.

Parnell laughed every time he thought of Elaine's favored fragrance. Early in their relationship, he'd spied the tiny egg-shaped bottle on her vanity, and looked at the ingredients, wondering what concoction could possibly create this sensual scent that excited him so. Vanilla, orange blossom, oakmoss, and assorted Oriental spices. Lainey had walked in on him as he was sniffing the bottle. She'd stood behind him, silent, observant, waiting, watching, then clearing her throat when she'd seen enough. Parnell had been embarrassed, offered a lame explanation. She listened to him quietly, and then burst out laughing. Through the years, Obsession perfume from Calvin Klein remained a long-running joke between them.

Nurse Annie brought him back to reality. She turned to face him, a brisk breeze lifting her hair off her shoulders. "So when are you going to tell me where we're going?"

"When we get there. We've got a two-mile hike down the other side of the highway."

"Two miles? My feet are already killing me. I don't understand why we had to leave the train."

Her whiny tone irritated him, but Parnell kept his thoughts to himself. He started working his way down the hillside, toward the zooming traffic. He couldn't wait to unload this ball-and-chain who huffed and puffed behind him. He could only hope that Harvey would be at the camp. Either Hopeful Harvey or Buttonhead. They would watch the girl. Keep her occupied long enough for Parnell to escape. But they wouldn't hurt her. Either man would scare the shit out of her, but neither had a mean bone in his body.

And both of them owed Parnell a few favors.

An hour later Parnell and Annie broke through a curtain of trees and entered a large clearing. Birds chattered all around them. The hard-packed dirt floor showed a crisscrossing of footprints. On the far side of the clearing, Parnell spotted a small target propped up against a pile of brush. Difficult to see in the fading light, but he could make out an enlarged photograph of Bernie Madoff pinned to the center of the target. His eyes had been shot out, but it was definitely Madoff. Parnell smiled. Harvey Henshaw had been here recently. Parnell was privy to the fact that Hopeful Harvey had been reduced to Homeless Harvey, thanks to the fraudulent wiles of Bernard Madoff, the Wall Street Ponzi-scheme scam-artist extraordinaire.

"Here we are," Parnell said.

"Where is *here*?"

"Shangri-La."

"Shangri-La? You mean like in Hilton's book?"

"Hilton's book?"

"*LOST HORIZON*."

Parnell frowned. "A little before my time, perhaps?"

"You are so illiterate!"

Parnell ignored the barb. "Come on," he said, "let's go make contact before they start shooting at us."

"Nice friends," he heard her say as she followed behind him.

King Midas

THEY HIKED ALONGSIDE A GURGLING CREEK, coming upon the enormous drainpipe the breezers (hobos) called The Orifice. Parnell knew this stainless steel pipe to be an aqueduct belonging to a flash-flood relief system constructed by the state of Arizona after World War II. When Parnell's search for the truth had first brought him out west, he'd been dubious about the possibility of floods in the desert. But then he'd witnessed a couple of flash floods and learned respect for Mother Nature when she went on a rampage—the quickly darkening skies, the rain off in the distance, the increasing rumble that shook the ground like an oncoming freight train, the force of onrushing water so sudden and so great that it ripped huge saguaro cactus from their roots and knocked out bridge struts as the great mass of water swept away everything in its path. During his second experience, Parnell had seen two men gobbled up and swallowed by the rushing water, never to be seen again.

As they entered The Orifice, he chuckled as he thought about what the long-timers had dubbed this massive drainpipe—The Vagina To Shangri-La—the entrance to one of Parnell's favorite hobo camps.

He entered the duct, quickly gobbled up by the darkness. Annie followed close behind, bumping into his backpack and keeping up a nervous chatter, her voice echoing off the steel walls: "Are there snakes in here?" she kept repeating. "Are you sure this is safe?" and "What if we get trapped in here?" To which Parnell finally said, "According to you, we've got Jesus watching over us. So quit your yappin'."

Their footsteps echoed loudly as they clopped forward. It hadn't rained in these parts for some time, making the silt that had washed into the pipeline hard-packed and dusty. When they had walked fifty yards, they came to a bend. Parnell caught a whiff of something cooking over an open fire, could hear the faint strains of an out-of-tune guitar. He guessed the dinner fare was either rabbit or squirrel, and that Fingers Johnston was the man behind the discordant music.

They exited the pipe into a small clearing. A wide creek ran along the eastern side. Down a small hill and through a grove of trees stood Shangri-La, one of the larger hobo camps. He saw the familiar cardboard signs etched with crude symbols tacked to trees.

"What do they mean?" Annie asked, pointing at the cardboard artwork.

"It's hobo-speak for 'Welcome to Shangri-La,'" he told her. "Nothing to worry about."

"Hobos? You're taking me to a camp full of bums?"

The comment rankled Parnell. "Certainly not very Christian of you, is it, Annie? They aren't bums. They're people with hopes and dreams. Just like you."

They stood together, examining the half-dozen signs drawn by his Shangri-La friends: An upside-down triangle with eyes indicated safe camp; a large 'U' meant visitors could sleep here; a circle with a line over it meant good people gathered here; a long oval with lines slashed across it announced that bread was available; a triangle with two arms warned of men with guns. Parnell smiled. Good people who would share their food, but who remained armed and cautious. That summed up his Shangri-La friends perfectly.

Darkness had almost descended, but he could make out the ragtag spread of sleeping quarters—torn bed sheets and dirty pieces of canvas draped from the limbs of tall oaks, makeshift plywood constructions nailed to their trunks. Tattered hammocks strung between smaller trees. Even a dilapidated Port-O-Let that looked like it might have been used by the Army Corps of Engineers when they had done their flood plain work out here in the late '40s.

A gruff male voice came out of the darkness behind them. "Well, if it ain't King Midas himself. And I'll be damned, the king even has a 'bo-ette. Quite a looker, too, if these old eyes don't deceive me."

Parnell turned and saw Weasel Bethea cradling a sawed-off shotgun, the stubby barrel pointed at the ground. Weasel got his moniker from his narrow face, elongated torso, impossibly long neck, and wispy mustache that consisted of several silver strands standing straight out like whiskers. Some of the older hobos still called him Catfish, but "Weasel" had caught on in recent years.

Parnell gave him a bear hug, ignoring the man's body odor.

"Hey Weaser!" he said, slapping at his back with his good hand. "They still got you doin' sentry duty, huh?"

"Right on, bro! Nobody fucks with me and old Bessie here," Weasel said, holding up his intimidating weapon. "And who might this be?" he said, looking in Annie's direction.

"I'm Annie . . . Annie Finnegan."

Weasel smiled, revealing gaps where teeth once resided. "Welcome to Shangri-La, land of the down-and-out and disenfranchised. Any friend of King Midas is a friend of ours."

Annie smiled demurely and thanked him. "Why does he call you King Midas?" she said to Parnell.

"You don't know?" Weasel implored.

"No. Don't tell me whatever he touches turns to gold because—"

"Nothing like that," Parnell said, wanting to end this conversation. "Weasel here lives with the warped fantasy that I'm wealthy."

"You *are,* dawg! You're richer than the Sultan of Brunei. Don't go denying it, you got a portfolio that would do Warren Buffett proud."

Parnell knew that not too many years ago, Greg "Weasel" Bethea made an exceptional living as a fast-track Wall Street executive. He had been a high roller who wore custom-tailored suits and entertained rich clients on a generous expense account. But that was before The Crash—what many historians referred to as "the day the Wall came tumbling down for good"—the second deadly Wall Street crash that plunged the U.S. economy into darkness, bankrupting the nation's middle class and poor, and rendering millions homeless. Back before the feds started printing more money to bail out banks and mortgage lenders and all the rest of the criminal element that made up the corrupt American military-industrial complex. Back before the American Dream had turned into America's Nightmare. Like many once-proud Americans who had lost their jobs, homes, health insurance, and retirement savings, Weasel Bethea had seen both the best and worst of times.

And Parnell knew these were indeed the worst of times.

Unemployment hovered near 40%. An increasing number of drifters crisscrossed the country in search of work, food, shelter, friendship, two pennies to rub together. Many had lost all hope, unsure of what they were searching for. Suicides were a far-too-common occurrence. Gangs of bandits roamed the countryside preying on the migrating homeless like buzzards feasting on carrion. Hobo camps similar to Shangri-La had popped up across the country like mushrooms sprouting after a heavy rain. The camps offered vagabonds safe haven, a hot meal, and friendly human contact. Strength in numbers and all that. Each time Parnell visited Shangri-La and saw Greg Bethea, he was reminded of how this once-great country had been pushed over the side of a cliff.

"What happened to your hand?" Weasel asked, pointing the shotgun butt at Parnell's bandages. "Been jerkin' off again?"

"Nice!" Parnell said, his tone sarcastic. "We have a lady present."

Annie smiled nervously. "Thank you," she said, never taking her distrusting eyes off Weasel.

Parnell held up his wrapped hand. "This is the price I paid for dealing with an asshole who thought he belonged on my train."

"He didn't have a ticket to ride, then, I take it?"

Parnell nodded. "The guy's road kill now. And my hand would be in a lot worse shape if not for the excellent care provided by my nurse friend here."

"You're a nurse?" Weasel asked Annie.

Parnell answered for her. "An *unemployed* nurse, as of today. The fool quit her job to follow me out here—"

"I didn't follow—"

"—and Annie here is also quite an evangelist. Aren't you, Annie?"

She shot him a look of disgust.

"Well, what does it matter?" Weasel asked rhetorically. "You guys are just in time."

Parnell said, "For what?"

"Buttonhead's back in from the desert, back from the land of the magic cactus. He got quite a harvest this time. This new batch puts the silly in psilocybin."

Parnell laughed, knowing Weasel referred to the thing that earned Buttonhead his nickname: peyote button, the powerful hallucinogen derived from the tops of mescal-producing cactus. Good chance the entire camp was strung out, he thought. Good chance the Shangri-La residents were seeing kaleidoscopic colors and talking to unseen spirits.

Weasel led them down the hill, the gamey scent of sizzling mystery meat getting stronger. Parnell spotted Fingers Johnston,

sitting on a thick stump near a roaring fire, plinking out accomp-
animent to a spirited sing-along on his battered acoustic guitar. A
small group of scruffy people sang along with him:

> *"Ain't got no place to call my own,*
> *Can't call nobody on the phone,*
> *Ain't got no money for the rent,*
> *Thanks to the U. S. government!"*

Parnell got a kick out of the song that had become the unoffi-
cial protest song of the new American hobo. He had heard slightly
different versions in his travels, but the sentiment always remained
the same.

> *"Ain't got two quarters to rub together,*
> *My pocket's light as a goddamned feather,*
> *So tired of this rainy weather*
> *Time for a revolution, for now and forever"*

Parnell stood outside the circle of firelight—Annie hanging on
his arm—listening as the voices rose in volume for the chorus:

> *Uncle Sam did us wrong,*
> *And we all went along,*
> *A tax for this and a fee for that,*
> *Till we're fuckin' busted flat, flat, flat*
> *And now we know our Uncle's bent*
> *So fuck the U.S. government!*

The gathered sang the last line repeatedly until the music
finally petered out. Parnell stepped into the ring of light, careful to
stay well away from the roaring fire.

"King Midas!" came the greeting in unison. Soon, he and
Annie were surrounded by a handful of Shangri-La residents.

"Hey, Fingers, where's your tip jar?" Parnell asked Fred Johnston, who laid his guitar against the stump and stood to embrace
Parnell.

"Where it always is," Fingers replied, pointing to his dilapidated guitar case before wrapping his bony arms around Parnell.
"Good to see ya, Derek. Where you been hiding lately?"

"Here and there," Parnell said, stepping back from Fingers and removing his backpack. He laid the pack on the ground near the fire and fumbled through it, finding his money clip, then peeled off a hundred-dollar bill. Parnell stood and flipped the bill into Fingers Johnston's guitar case. "Buy yourself some fresh strings," he told the guitar player. "Any protest song worth its salt should be played on new strings, don't you think?"

"You *are* rich," Annie said in a disbelieving voice, looking down at the hundred lying in the guitar case, Ben Franklin's face staring back at her.

Fingers nodded. "Really, Derek, a new set of strings will only cost me fifteen bucks."

"Sorry," Parnell said. "Don't have any smaller bills. Use it to stock up on strings. And while you're at it, buy yourself a tuner, too."

Fingers eyed Parnell warily, the flickering firelight casting shadows across his face. "Are you dissin' the way I play?" he said.

Parnell smiled, hefted his backpack and strapped it back on. "No, you play beautifully, Fingers. It's just that someone with your talent should be playing *in tune*." He sniffed the air. "I'm starved. Let's go get us some grub, Annie."

Parnell heard Fingers Johnston start in on a rousing rendition of Dylan's "Blowin' in the Wind" as he led Annie to a second campfire, a large pit in the ground with a makeshift grill sitting on top. Laid out across one side of the grill were stringy strips of meat he knew to be squirrel. The other side contained greasy-looking blobs he thought might be rabbit. Parnell greeted Chef Alice, a longtime resident of Shangri-La and the acknowledged camp cook.

"What's on the menu tonight at Alice's Restaurant? Smells delicious," he said, noting the look of disgust on Annie's face as she observed the wild game cooking on the grill.

"Tonight, in honor of our wonderful peyote harvest, we have a bounty of delicacies," Chef Alice said as she poked at the sizzling meat with a whittled branch. "Over here, we have squirrel, but not your normal gray tree squirrel . . . it's black-bellied Kaibab squirrels. Much more tender than the everyday, run-of-the-mill squirrel. And over here," she said, stabbing one of the large pieces of meat and turning it over on the grill, "is Gila meat. Hooper and Speck bagged a couple of them this morning. We ain't had Gila meat in many a blue moon. Soooo tasty!"

"Gila monster?" Parnell said, knowing about the cold-blooded venomous lizard. "Surely you know Gilas are protected by law in these parts, Alice."

She laughed. "Since when do you care about the law, Mr. Midas?"

"Good point," Parnell said. "Let's eat."

They sat by themselves—he and Annie and Chef Alice—eating off of shiny hubcaps that Parnell knew Alice brought out only for special guests. *The good china*, is how Chef Alice referred to the strange dinner plates. They sat and ate the slimy strips of meat with their fingers, Annie complaining continuously as she fought to keep the greasy fare down.

"You'll get used to it, darling," Alice told her. "A week or two out here and you'll appreciate how good wild game can taste."

Annie said, "We won't be out here that long. We've got a train to catch, don't we, Derek?"

Parnell didn't answer. Instead he pulled three more hundred-dollar bills from his money clip and handed them to Chef Alice. "Consider this a donation for Alice's Restaurant. Go into town and buy a few steaks and fresh vegetables."

"Thank you, sweet man!" Alice responded, stuffing the money into her apron, which was adorned with a faded image of folk-singer Arlo Guthrie's album cover for ALICE'S RESTAURANT.

"You're welcome, Alley Cat," Parnell responded, calling Chef Alice by her more familiar hobo name. "Where's Hopeful Harvey been hiding?"

"Ah, Harvey," Alice said. "Old Hopeful caught a cow crate out of Winslow a couple weeks back. Heard about some work all the way up in Fresno, in one of the logging camps. America's in a tough way, but she still needs wood pulp for paper."

Parnell nodded. "Anybody else go with him?"

"Yeah, Broadway Bling and Oshkosh Moss."

Parnell watched Alice return to her grill pit, barking out orders to a man he didn't know.

"She's cool," Annie said. "But does she really think this crap is any good?" she said, pointing at the greasy slop sliding around on her hubcap.

"No she doesn't. But it's all they have, so they make the best of it. You know, Annie, this will be your future too if you don't go back to your job."

"No way! I hate that clinic."

"I'm just saying," he said between bites of the stringy meat, "your life would be a lot simpler if you went back."

"So why do *you* do it, then?" she asked. "I mean, you're obviously wealthy. You throw hundreds around like you're printing them yourself. They call you King Midas for Chrissakes. You could be living in style and comfort. But you don't. You ride trains and stay out here in the wilderness. Why?"

"It's a long story."

"Looks to me like we've got nothing but time."

Parnell continued to chew, keeping his thoughts to himself.

"Where do you get all your money, Derek?"

Parnell decided to turn the tables, ask her a question. "How did you know about my triskaidekaphobia and my, um . . . *discomfort* with fire?"

Annie snorted out a laugh. "Simple. You talk in your sleep. Quite clearly, too. You should watch that. It can get you in trouble. Now, how about an answer to my question. How is it you're so loaded, Mr. King Midas mystery man?"

Parnell was saved from answering as Buttonhead Murphy, the resident drug baron, approached them. Buttonhead wore a porkpie hat that was frayed around the brim, his bushy red hair springing out underneath in a kind of fright wig, clownish appearance. Every time Parnell saw him, he thought of Harpo Marx.

"King Midas! You old dog, you!" Buttonhead exclaimed, clapping Parnell on the shoulder. "What brings you back around?"

Parnell could see Buttonhead was flying high, his eyes dilated big as flying saucers. "I heard a rumor you stumbled across some new strain of peyote button that puts the silly back in psilocybin," he said, quoting Weasel Bethea.

"You got that right, bro. This shit'll send you on a magic carpet ride to the end of the universe, man! Half the camp is down at the creek, higher than Everest, naked and chanting at the moon. Here," he said, reaching into his shirt pocket and pulling out a small glassine bag containing a half-dozen peyote buttons. "Don't do more than one at a time. These things are pretty juiced-up, my friend."

"Thanks," Parnell said, taking the buttons from him, knowing he would wait until he got to Flagstaff and Elaine's before doing them.

Parnell reached into his backpack and pulled out another hundred-dollar bill. "Here, Buttonhead. Hope this covers it."

Buttonhead stared at the large bill in his hand. "I can't accept this. Peyote doesn't cost anything to grow. It's Mama Nature's gift."

"Keep it," Parnell said, closing Buttonhead's fingers around the bill. He nodded at Annie. "How about a few trips for my friend here?"

Buttonhead handed a glassine bag to Annie, who said, "Far out! What's the best way to do these? Swallow them? Smoke them?"

"If you ingest them," Buttonhead said, "your ride will be a thing of beauty and it will last longer. But I'll remind you—don't do more than one at a time."

Parnell watched as Nurse Annie dry-swallowed one of the bigger buttons.

Within the hour, she had floated down to the creek with Buttonhead to join the rest of the trippy campers. Parnell assumed that she was probably naked and chanting along with the crowd.

Before he left Shangri-La, Parnell found Weasel, and gave him a crisp hundred-dollar bill, the last of his money in his clip.

"What's this for?" Weasel asked.

"You know that woman who was with me? Annie?" he said, pulling a small pad of paper and pen from his pack, scribbling hurriedly.

"Of course, the nurse."

"Yeah . . . here," Parnell said, tearing off a sheet and handing it to him, "I want you to get Annie back to Albuquerque safely. I don't know where she lives, but here's the address of the clinic where she works. She doesn't belong out here with us."

"Yeah," Weasel agreed. "She seems pretty green. Real bourgeois. This place would probably be the death of her. I'll get her to Albuquerque. You can count on it."

"Thanks, Weaser. I know she'll be in good hands with you."

"You have to leave so soon?"

"Yeah. Gotta catch out in Winslow. Things to do elsewhere."

"When will you be back?"

"Sooner than last time."

As Parnell made his way back through The Orifice, he could hear the chanting from down at the creek. People laughing and water splashing. Folks taking that magic carpet ride to the end of the universe, as Buttonhead had so eloquently put it.

And he had laid a total of six-hundred dollars on key members of the camp. Money very well spent, he thought.

As he hiked back up the ravine and across I-40, he saw the lights of the Winslow rail yard. He quickened his pace.

Here I come, Lainey, he thought as he walked. I want you like never before!

Westward Hobo

E CAUGHT A MIDNIGHT FREIGHTER TO FLAGSTAFF, riding in the open air on a flatcar, down inside the huge shovel of large backhoe. Parnell was tired and sore, but relieved to be away from the pesky scripture-quoting young nurse, Annie Finnegan. He could actually hear himself think now.

He lay back in the protective womb of the big steel scoop, the two enclosed sides funneling the cool wind against his face. He watched the stars speckling the big sky overhead as the train raced through the dark Arizona countryside. A full moon hung above, mysterious and bright orange. Parnell wondered if the Shangri-La peyote disciples were still gazing up at this same moon from the river, doing their moonshine act, chanting at it like it was some orange-complexioned god.

The wind buffeted his face as the steel wheels below clanked and rumbled. The expansive sky overhead suggested infinite possibilities. Purple-black mountaintops on either side rushed past like dark, stumbling giants.

His mind meandered. He thought about Elaine, about the small network of employees who kept his day-to-day business operations going. But mostly he ruminated over what Annie and many others had asked him: Why did he live like a hobo when he was obviously wealthy? Well, his answer—if he felt inclined to tell anyone other than Lainey—started with his intense passion for trains. For Parnell, there was no better way to see the country than riding the rails. Railroads went places cars could never travel, and when he rode as a hermit catter (a solo hobo traveling on an open flatcar) the way he did now, the beauty of the world opened up before him and came alive.

But his fascination with the railroad went much deeper. As a young boy, Parnell shared his train obsession with his late father, Louis. Parnell remembered his seventh Christmas, when Louis had given him his first model train set, a Lionel. It was bright and shiny and colorful, had a track that ran through the living room, over bridges, through tunnels, passing a miniature Alpine village with fake snow. The set even had railroad crossings with operational gates, street lights that worked, and a train switching yard. Very elaborate and sophisticated. His father had stayed up all night Christmas Eve assembling the thing. Parnell would never forget that Christmas. His father had been animated, seemingly much more in love with Parnell's mother, much happier than usual as Louis regaled young Derek with his train stories. Parnell recalled the couple of years after—*good* years—when he and his father had immersed themselves in train history and railroad operations, discussing their findings with each other as they enjoyed that miniature Lionel set together. Those were good years and Parnell cherished them. But then, Louis started drifting away from young Derek and Parnell's mother as he moved into the murky world of sports gambling and loan sharks that eventually brought his life to a violent end. Parnell still had most of that Lionel train set, which he'd erected in Elaine's spare bedroom in Flagstaff, along with quite a few new components he'd added over the years. It remained his most valuable possession.

As his father continued his downward spiral, Parnell dove even more deeply into railroad lore, as if keeping up with it for both of them. In fourth grade, he wrote a book report on trains, the history of the locomotive, from steam-powered to diesel-fueled. He got his first ever A+ grade. His teacher had been impressed with Parnell's research skills, and told him so, asking him at the end of his oral presentation what he wanted to be when he grew up. Parnell had responded without hesitation, "A train engineer." He'd been so sure of himself at that young age. He laughed every time he thought about it. Riding the rails as a freeloading hobo was the closest he would ever get to fulfilling his childhood dream.

As the train approached Flagstaff, Parnell's thoughts turned to more current events. Who was the young woman on the phone who called herself Jennifer Parnell? How did she know him? And who was this Madame Crystal in Sedona? Was she just your everyday New Age flake, or was she a genuine player? Parnell felt an unsettling shift in his psyche—things turning end-over-end. Somebody was onto him. He needed to find out who. But there was a bright side to this new information that had come through the mysterious phone call. Something registering on his internal radar told him he was getting close to his prey. All signs pointed that way. Arson had been the executioner's choice. They'd burned his house to the ground, cremating his wife and daughter.

He began to shake, the familiar black rage welling inside of him.

He shifted his thoughts to Elaine, tried to relax. He couldn't wait to see her. He knew he couldn't stay with her long. As usual, she would be disappointed, but he had a killer to catch and bring to justice.

Parnell was determined to make sure his family's killer went down in flames.

The School of Hard Knocks

PARNELL'S TRAIN ROLLED INTO FLAGSTAFF just before dawn. He spent a couple of hours lingering over breakfast and endless cups of coffee at an all-night diner on East Phoenix Avenue, reading the *Arizona Daily Sun*, one of the few U.S. newspapers still in operation. He shook his head at notices of yet more manufacturing plant closings, a couple of big corporate bankruptcies, another multi-billion-dollar loan from China, further swelling the already ludicrous national debt. He read about the three wars the U. S. waged in the Middle East, all lost-cause efforts. The unemployment rate stood officially at 41% and the nation's GNP had now dropped 59%, lower than even the first Great Depression of 1929. It seemed the only Americans who were thriving were defense contractors and politicians.

Parnell laughed every time he heard the president or a congressman claim they were doing something "for the good of the American people." He thought: If so much is being done for the benefit of the American people, why has the country crashed and burned? He was amazed that the American public continued to buy into The Big Lie. He often thought of American voters in terms of circus impresario P.T. Barnum's infamous comment— *There's a sucker born every minute.*

He slugged down the last of his coffee and folded up his newspaper, left it on the table with a generous tip. His waitress showed surprise as she slid the bills into her apron pocket. *No dirty, unshaven drifter should have that kind of cash*, her expression said. Parnell had seen the look many times before.

Next, he performed his usual Flagstaff ritual—restocking his money clip—which involved visiting a number of ATMs. At each, he withdrew just enough to make the exorbitant foreign transfer fee worthwhile, careful not to exceed amounts that would send up a red flag. When Parnell had first come into his wealth, he'd studied the American financial structure and learned how money flowed through the system. He educated himself on the series of checks and balances incorporated by financial regulators, the reporting structure of the U.S. banking system, and how it all differed from European banking. He'd educated himself on legal loopholes and tax shelters and investment schemes long employed by the rich. Parnell had been meticulous in laying out his financial world, setting up dummy corporations within shell companies nestled within shadow organizations, all embedded within a bureaucratic maze so deep and complex nothing could ever be traced directly to him. Classic smoke-and-mirrors stuff. A financial three-card-Monte game with huge stakes. The same game the feds and big corporate America had been playing for decades.

He visited a total of seven ATMs around Flagstaff. The banks were offshore financial institutions in locales like Luxembourg, Belize, and the Caymans. When Parnell first started out on his never-ending road trip, he'd had all his money deposited in Swiss accounts. However, a few years back, one of the big Geneva banking executives had been indicted for fraud, and, through a plea deal, blew the whistle on thousands of American businessmen who were doing illicit things within the Swiss banking system. Parnell had been on top of that and immediately transferred all of his assets out of Swiss banks.

His method of cash collection posed an expensive, time-consuming way to do his banking. But it was sealed-up private and extremely mobile. And using his offshore ATM cards instead of bank credit/debit cards made it even more difficult to track him. Parnell preferred to live "embedded in the grid," rather than "off the grid." To be off the grid was to not exist. No Social Security number, no birth certificate, no passport, visa, or legal identification of any kind. He knew many people who lived this way. Especially now that the U.S. economy had plunged over the cliff so many had to partake in borderline illegal activities to make ends meet. These "off-gridders" thought they were safe, that the government didn't know who or where they were. But he knew better. He'd seen too many of these folks rounded up and shipped off to prison for tax evasion and fraud.

So Parnell lived his roaming lifestyle embedded in the grid. He used his real name, which appeared on all legal documents. He paid taxes, albeit greatly reduced. He reported all dividends and income from his investments. Everything above board, everything legal. But Parnell controlled Big Brother's view of his activities. The feds couldn't nail him for things they couldn't see.

And Parnell knew they were watching him, with interest.

They didn't teach this stuff in public school systems. Public education these days prepared people for very little in the Real World. Today's high school graduates didn't learn much that would adequately prepare them for survival over the long run.

And that's what it's all about, really, he thought. Survival.

Elaine described Parnell's education as *The School of Hard Knocks*. She often told him he was the smartest man she'd ever known. But then she always followed it up with "You're also the *craziest* man I've ever known."

Parnell's hard knocks had made him into a wealthy man. But it had been a long hard stretch of road getting there. He had dropped out of school on his sixteenth birthday and began riding the rails. Saw a lot of the country from between the slats of box-cars and stretched out on flatcars. Learned the ways of the new American hobo. Of course, back then, the economy was still healthy, so Parnell didn't cross paths with too many other "night riders." After a couple of years of criss-crossing the country, he realized the futility of his life—that there was no future in his aimless wandering—and he headed back east to enlist in the Army.

It had been strange, really, Parnell's metamorphosis from pauper to King Midas. After his Army duty, he took a job as a pest exterminator near where he grew up in eastern Pennsylvania. He figured killing was the only thing he was qualified to do. Miller's Pest Control seemed like the obvious career path.

He hated it. Eight long years of running around Pike County and into upstate New York, keeping the insect and varmint population at bay. Eight years of listening to rich people rail about the injustice of disease-ridden insects invading their homes, of listening to poor fools with unnatural fears of the critters he chased acting all hysterical. He exterminated cockroaches, fleas, rodents, and hornets, even raccoons and a snake or two. Parnell would have liked to exterminate old man Miller himself, the way the owner constantly rode him, pushing, pushing, pushing for him to bring in more business, to work more hours. Eight long years of breathing in toxic fumes, of strange skin rashes and an arthritic back from crawling through low-ceilinged attics and dark, damp basements. At one point, he became so depressed he actually entertained thoughts of re-enlisting in the Army.

And then he met Barbara Logan, who turned his world around.

Parnell remembered their meeting as if it happened only yesterday, and not 18 years ago. Barbara was a high-society semi-celebrity who had just gone through a bitter divorce with her husband, banker extraordinaire, Willis Logan III, a young jet-set CFO of a major U.S. bank. Parnell got the call that morning. Mrs. Logan, complaining of squirrels banging around in her chimney. Off he went, driving deep into upstate New York, arriving at her Tudor-style mansion around noon, thinking it looked more like a lavish hotel than someone's private residence. Sprawling verdant-green grounds that looked like a well-manicured golf course. Sweeping arched doorways and gabled windows. Intricately designed roof spires. A cobblestone Italian marble driveway. The inside was even more impressive. A two-story foyer with a pair of spiral staircases leading up to the second and third floors. Shined and buffed mahogany floors and beams. Eight bedrooms, four fire-places. An indoor pool and sauna. Bronze and marble statues everywhere, with framed oil paintings brightening the walls. Par-nell remembered thinking he'd entered a museum, what with the luxurious dark interior and the obviously high-priced artwork all around him. Attached was a four-car garage that housed a Bentley, Ferrari, and a Lamborghini. In all, 20,000 square feet of house stuffed with expensive antiques.

Parnell recalled that first meeting with Barbara Logan as one of those weird chance encounters that happen without warning, but seem to be a part of some mysterious bigger plan. He remembered poking around in one of the chimneys, finally locating the unruly squirrels. As he walked out to his truck to get some needed tools, she intercepted him.

"What's the matter?" he had asked her.

"You do good work," she said, leaning into him, touching his arm.

He smelled the faint scent of booze on her breath. Her hazel eyes shone with excitement. She tugged at his arm as he tried to move past her.

"Look," he said, "I've got to get those squirrels out—"

"Screw the squirrels!" she snorted, "I've got far more interest-ing work for you."

He held her gaze for a long moment, feeling something shift within him. Her need was palpable, no denying it. Her eyes bore into him, seeking, searching, requesting, *demanding* that Parnell take her right there on the hardwood floor. A woman accustomed to getting her own way. A woman with a serious need.

She continued rubbing his forearm.

Why does this well-connected woman want me? he wondered. She can have any man she wants. Parnell had been hit on by women in the past, but this was different. Barbara Logan had to be in her late-30s, probably had at least eight years on him. And she was a rich, gorgeous, society woman while he was just a lowly pest exterminator who smelled of boric acid and insecticide spray.

As he debated whether to take the plunge, she leaned in and kissed him on the mouth, gently at first, her tongue probing tentatively, then kissing him more passionately as their mutual heat grew. Parnell felt his erection straining against his cotton work pants. He felt her hand snake its way down there, her expert fingers fondling him through the thin fabric. She moaned as she tugged his zipper down. This woman knew what she wanted and how to go about getting it. He thought he might combust as she kept working on him.

The next thing he knew, they were rushing up one of the spiral staircases to the master bedroom, awkwardly stripping off clothing as they went. They spent the rest of the afternoon in Barbara's solid brass Queen Anne canopy bed, rocking the four posts until Parnell thought the entire bed would collapse and fall through the floor. They had even knocked the crown on top of the canopy askew. Absolutely the best sex he'd ever had. The older woman had shown him a few new tricks.

Barbara Logan became Parnell's lustful addiction.

Little known to both of them, they'd made a baby that afternoon. A daughter, Jennifer, who came into the world nine months later. Something her eunuch ex-husband could never give her, Barbara had told Parnell. Something she'd always wanted—a child. And so they did what they thought was the right thing: they got married. Barbara became Barbara Stevenson Logan Parnell in a civil ceremony attended by more than 200 family and friends by the big swan fountain on the front lawn.

The sex continued to be great for the next few years, but the marriage had no legs. As Jennifer grew to school age, Parnell felt more and more like a kept man, like a play toy for a rich woman. Like a *babysitter*. As Barbara continued to live the high life with her snooty, shallow friends, Parnell became the primary caregiver for Jennifer. It was Parnell who fed their daughter, Parnell who read Jennifer bedtime stories and tucked her in every night. Parnell who got her up in the morning, fed her breakfast, made sure she got to school on time. Barbara meanwhile escalated her partying, staying out later and later, sometimes not coming home at all, finally arriving at the point where she viewed their daughter as just another possession, a ball-and-chain that cramped her social styling.

The great sex became routine, then monotonous, then not at all. The arguments escalated. But somehow they remained married, for little Jen-Jen's sake. And they remained a married couple up until the blackest night of Parnell's life, the night when a still unidentified arsonist had torched the mansion, trapping Barbara and Jenny inside. Investigators found only charred bones and ash. ATF investigators ruled it as arson as they discovered traces of acetone and carbon disulfide around the foundation, highly flammable accelerants used by professional torch men. The killer made sure the job would not fail.

But who? And better yet, *why*? These were questions Parnell had been chasing for seven long years.

Initially, Parnell had been the primary suspect. But detectives cleared him as he had an airtight alibi during the time of the fire (he'd been working out at the fitness center as he did every Tuesday night). And if there were any lingering doubts as to Parnell's involvement, they were put to rest after discovering that he was not a beneficiary on Barbara's life insurance policies, nor did he appear in her will. He didn't stand to make a dime off of his wife's death; everything went to Barbara's three sisters. Barbara was 50 years old while Jennifer had been all of eleven.

After the smoke cleared, Parnell had moved back to Millford, where he rented a tiny one-bedroom apartment. He spent the first month vacillating between grief and rage. Then he summoned up his old resolve and began mapping out his future. Finding out who was responsible for the heinous act became his obsession. Eliminating them became a necessity.

As he began digging into the details of the double-murder, strange things occurred. He remembered getting a call late one night on his unlisted phone. A deep, gruff male voice telling him to stop looking into his wife and daughter's deaths, informing Parnell he would be rewarded if he backed off. That he would "suffer serious complications" if he didn't.

Parnell tried to trace the call. No success. The phone number did not exist.

It only made him more determined to find his family's killers.

A couple of weeks after the late-night call, Parnell ate dinner in a burger joint near his apartment and was approached by a slight young man who wore an expensive three-piece suit and carried a leather briefcase. Everything about the man screamed fed, from his cool, calculating, borderline paranoid demeanor to his dark Rayban sunglasses. Secret Service maybe? NSA?

"Mind if I join you, Mr. Parnell?" the man said in a high, reedy voice as he slid into the booth across from him.

Sounded like the guy just inhaled a lungful of helium. No way this was the guy who'd called him on the phone. "Yeah, I *do* mind," he responded sourly.

"Well, I'm sure you won't when I tell you I'm about to make you a very rich man."

Parnell was in no mood. "What?" he said, "Did I win the Publisher's Clearinghouse Sweepstakes or something?"

The man smiled humorlessly. "Funny guy, aren't you, Derek? You mind if I call you Derek?"

Parnell stared him down, wishing he could see the man's eyes, seeing instead his own reflection in the two dark lenses. "You can call me anything you want, but I refuse to communicate with a man whose eyes I can't see. Tells me you've got something to hide."

"Derek, Derek," the man scolded in his whiny voice. "No need to get cynical on me. I come bearing gifts. Consider me a friend."

"I've got all the friends I need, Squeaky. Take off the shades or I'm out of here."

"That would be the biggest mistake of your life, Derek," the man said, setting his briefcase up on the table in front of him, snapping open the latches and lifting the lid. He fumbled through a stack of papers. "Allow me to introduce myself. My name is Croesus."

Parnell snorted. "Croesus? That's quite the code name. Which branch of the government do you work for?"

Croesus didn't flinch "I understand that your late wife, Barbara, didn't leave you a thing in her will. Is that correct?"

Parnell didn't answer.

"I take that as a Yes," Croesus squeaked. "You were married for, what was it, ten years?"

"Eleven," Parnell corrected.

"Don't you find it odd that your spouse of eleven years would cut you completely out of her will?"

Parnell felt his adrenaline kick in, could feel his heart pounding in his temples. He wanted to reach across the table and strangle this asshole. Instead, realizing his cooperation might teach him something, with great difficulty he said, "It wasn't a normal marriage by any stretch. My wife also cut our daughter out of the will."

"That's gratitude for you."

Parnell held back his anger. "Just what are you trying to stir up here?"

Croesus pulled a sheet of paper from his briefcase and slid it toward Parnell.

Parnell squinted at it. "What's this?"

"I believe it's the routing and transit number of your bank in Millford. And right below it is your savings account information. Tomorrow, you will receive your first wire transfer payment. Then, providing you continue to cooperate, you will keep receiving payments."

"Cooperating how?"

"I think you know the answer to that, Derek. Have a great day." Croesus closed the lid on his briefcase and stood, pointed down at Parnell's greasy half-eaten cheeseburger. "You won't have to eat that crap much longer. Think choice cuts of filet mignon washed down with expensive champagne from now on."

And then he was gone.

Sure enough, Parnell checked his savings account the next day, and a huge payment had been wired in. Blood money. A payoff from the upper echelons of the U.S. government. And the wire transfers kept coming, one per week like clockwork, until he sat on top of a small fortune. The payments were all tied to, and referenced by, some vague trust fund in the name of Humpty Dumpty Industries. Parnell had tried to trace the payments back to the source, but couldn't. He tried to find something on Humpty Dumpty Industries, but couldn't. The company never existed. They had covered their tracks well. Stealth and precision. No one was talking. Parnell was left to try and figure out who and why.

He had never felt right about spending much of this tainted blood money on himself. Instead, he used it to help out others in need. There were so many who needed it—so many wandering homeless cast adrift by a system gone terribly awry. And he also used it to finance his quest of finding his wife's and daughter's killers.

Finishing up at his last ATM, Parnell stuffed the cash into the false bottom of his backpack, and went in search of a pay phone.

He got hold of Blanton Miles on the third ring.

Parnell could hardly believe what Miles told him.

Locomotion Enterprises

"COULD YOU REPEAT THAT, BLANTON?" Parnell asked. "I don't think I heard you right."

"I said there have been arrests in the murders of your wife and daughter."

"Don't toy with me," Parnell warned, thinking that Blanton Miles had changed his businesslike stripes and was putting him on.

"I would *never* make light of your situation, Derek. You know that."

"Yeah, but it's been *seven* years. All this time, nothing, now suddenly, an arrest?"

"Not just one arrest, but *two*! The authorities caught a break on the case."

"What kind of a break?"

"A lucky one," Miles said. "Your wife's first husband, Willis Logan? Sir Moneybags?"

"Yeah, what about him?" Parnell said, feeling his gut clench.

"He's been indicted on three counts of interstate fraud and two counts of embezzlement. Five major felonies. Got caught with his hand in the till. Quite a huge till it was, too. And those alleged crimes are opening up other cans of worms. Authorities are also investigating Mr. Logan for possible illegal campaign contributions and associations with the Genovese family."

"Imagine that," Parnell muttered as he tried to digest this information. After a long moment he said, "Surely you don't mean Willis Logan is the killer."

"No. But he said he knows who did it and named names. Used it as leverage against his own sentence."

"Jesus, another friggin' plea deal," Parnell groaned. "Why the hell do they even bother with a justice system in this country? How long have you known about this, Blanton?"

"This all went down last week, and—"

"And you're just getting around to telling me now?"

"Let me remind you I've had calls in for you and you haven't gotten back to me."

"I've been busy."

"If you would carry a cell phone once in a while—"

"Don't start! You know how I feel about cell phones."

"You okay, Derek? You sound a little uptight."

"Ah . . . I've just been away from Elaine too long, that's all."

"Are you going to be seeing her soon?"

"Yeah, I'm in Flagstaff now."

"Wonderful. Stop by your post office box. I mailed you a report that gives you all the particulars."

"Thanks, Blanton."

Parnell thought about the days following the fire, when the New York State Police had questioned Willis Logan III with regards to the torching of his ex-wife's mansion. Interrogators had spent two intense hours trying to break the banker in the same claustrophobic interview room where they had first questioned Parnell. They'd aggressively braced Logan but had gotten nothing. Parnell wasn't surprised. Willis Logan III was a cool-as-a-cucumber master sociopath.

He said into the phone, "So how was Logan involved?"

"Behind the scenes. No accelerant chemicals on his hands, no blowtorches in his possession, if that's what you mean. But if you trace the money back far enough, you'll find Logan's fingerprints. He knows about all of it."

Parnell scratched his head, thinking. "Are they all still being held? Any of them make bail?"

"Bail was no problem for Logan. He's out and about. The two alleged arsonists, however, are behind the iron at Broome County Correctional in Binghamton."

"Who are they? What can you tell me about them?"

"Too much to cover in a phone call. It's all in the report I prepared for you."

"Well, keep someone on them," Parnell said, frustrated. "I want to know if and when they leave that facility. I want to know what they eat for breakfast and when they take a crap. I want to know the names of any visitors. Do these two pyromaniacs have a court date yet?"

"Yes. Both have lawyered up. Both got public defenders. They're being tried together. Jury selection starts next week. And I'm two steps ahead of you, Derek. I've got Spottswood and Delancey watching the two jailbirds."

"Good," Parnell said. Spotts and Del were superb shadows.

He thought about what it would take to get back east for the trial, then dismissed it as an impossibility. He needed to spend time with Elaine. He needed to regroup, to recharge his jets, let his damaged hand heal. His people could keep a watch on things in New York.

"What about Logan?" he said to Miles. "Where is he?"

"Everything's cool. I've got Sanchez tracking him."

"Julia? You think she can—?"

"Willis Logan has a weakness for fast women," Miles said, cutting him off. "Especially those of Hispanic persuasion. Julia Sanchez is perfect for this assignment."

"Touché," Parnell said, smiling. "What else you got for me?"

Parnell heard papers shuffling on the other end, the clicking of a computer mouse, then Blanton Miles's voice, "We keep hearing from this Madame Crystal in Sedona. She says she has important information concerning your daughter."

"*Madame Crystal*? Are you serious, Blanton? What's that all about? That young woman you put me in touch with? Claiming to be my Jenny? She demanded I speak with this Crystal flake."

"Well, maybe there's something to it, Derek. I'll dig deeper, see what else I can find out."

"Great. You're top drawer, Blanton. Now let's get on with our usual business."

Parnell spent another ten minutes on the phone, approving or rejecting various business transactions. He approved checks to two burn wards, two more to VA hospitals and a large donation to Gamblers Anonymous. Several more payments to private practice physicians who specialized in treating ex-military personnel diagnosed with Post Traumatic Stress Disorder. He also approved a stock purchase, a move of three mutual funds, and the redistribution of some of his securities within his portfolio. Next they reviewed earnings and expenses, capital gains, losses that could be written off. In all, Parnell was pleased. His net worth was up. His investments were doing well. His staff of financial advisers had steered him in the right direction. Parnell made a mental note to approve bonuses for each of them.

And then, just as quickly, he felt shame. So many people were in dire straits, so many folks starving and homeless and destitute, and here he was, feeling good about his blue-chip portfolio.

But then he knew he should be proud of the organization he'd built, and the way he was using it to help as many as he could.

Parnell had painstakingly put together a streamlined team of professionals, all of whom were considered the cream of their chosen fields. He certainly had the money to attract such talent. Currently his payroll stood at 42 strong, and included a dozen private investigators, four attorneys, a CPA, and a pair of investment consultants. Also, a congressman lurked deep in the folds of their payroll. This particular congressman had proved to be most valuable to the organization.

Yes, Locomotion Enterprises had become a well-oiled, efficient machine. Parnell intentionally kept himself detached from day-to-day business, relying on Blanton Miles to keep things running smoothly. In fact, Blanton Miles was the only Locomotion employee he had actually met. When Parnell first started mapping out his plan, he knew he wanted to remain low profile, even within his own organization. So he set about finding the one person qualified to be Parnell's chief operations officer. This executive needed to be trustworthy and intelligent, possessing that special competent savvy required to skillfully manage people, money, and missions of a dubious nature. Someone who remained cool under pressure, someone who enjoyed stealth and working with forensic intelligence. Parnell spent three months conducting dozens of interviews before he found Blanton Miles.

Miles came with a high pedigree. Law degree from University of Pennsylvania, graduating third in his class. A Masters of Science in Finance from Villanova. A list of top-notch references a mile long. Parnell didn't hire him that first meeting. Instead, he spent two weeks looking deep into Miles's history, turning over every stone, even testing him at one point. The man had nothing to hide. And Parnell had been even more impressed when the man called him and asked why Parnell was checking up on him through the Chester County court system.

Parnell remembered Blanton Miles saying to him, "If you want to know anything about me, Mr. Parnell, all you have to do is ask. I'll always be straight with you."

"So how did you know I was doing a background check on you, in, of all places, Chester County, Pennsylvania?"

Long hesitation, then, "Sorry, but I never reveal my sources."

Parnell recalled thinking this guy was plugged into some widespread informational network. And he was discreet. Certainly well educated and capable. "Mr. Miles, you have passed every one of my tests," Parnell remembered saying, "but I just have one more question."

"What's that?"

"Well, I'm thinking you could make a good bit more money going to work for a big corporation. Why Locomotion Enterprises?"

Parnell recalled thinking Miles would come back with some rehearsed response designed to impress him, but instead Blanton Miles said, "Because big corporations are too sterile for my tastes. I don't want to spend my days working with yuppie pinheads in suits. The position you've described convinces me that you need me. And I have no qualms about telling you that I have researched you thoroughly and I know I can trust you. *That's* why Locomotion Enterprises, Mr. Parnell."

Parnell couldn't believe his good fortune. This guy was prepared. Blanton Miles had turned the tables on him and checked him out. Parnell liked the guy's moxie. He liked the way he operated.

"One more thing before we close it down, Derek."

"What's that?"

"It's the Liberty Dogs again."

"Jesus! Don't they have anything better to do?"

"It's a growing movement, as you know, Derek."

"They're all a bunch of bomb-happy idiots," Parnell said, thinking about the anti-government militia that had formed a few years ago up in Colorado and Montana. The Liberty Dogs had been building forces, allegedly preparing to launch an attack on Washington D.C. "They still planning on driving their armored vehicles up Pennsylvania Avenue, guns blazing?"

"That, and more, I'm afraid."

"Morons! They'll end up a tiny grease spot on the map. The feds will annihilate them. Don't these whack jobs know what they're up against? Don't they remember the way the FBI handled the Weavers at Ruby Ridge? Aren't they familiar with how the ATF crushed David Koresh and the Branch Davidians in Waco?"

Miles replied coolly, "I don't think history is their strong suit, Derek."

"Well, they are *not* getting any of my money. No support from us. I don't want our fingerprints on this thing once it gets started."

"I know. The only reason I bring this up is that reports coming in from the field tell me things are heating up. The Dogs are getting much more bold and dangerous. One of our field ops reported a confrontation with them last week."

"Which op? What happened?"

"Pettigrew. A half-dozen Liberty Dogs confronted him in Des Moines. They threatened to kill him unless they receive a hundred grand from us."

"How'd they know Pettigrew is one of our employees?"

"Don't know. I'm looking into it. In the meantime I've got Carlson watching Pettigrew's back."

"Good. Get someone else up there in Iowa, too. Maybe get a few of our guys up along the Continental Divide to see what these trigger-happy clowns are up to. And please see that Pettigrew stays safe."

"You got it, boss. Top priority."

Parnell hung up and walked to the post office to pick up the report Blanton Miles had prepared for him. The package he pulled from his box was slim. He opened it as he rode in the back seat of the taxi to Elaine's house.

Parnell smiled. Blanton had burned the report onto a compact disc. He had hand-printed the label to read: *The Three Stooges Do Jail Time.*

The man actually possessed a sense of humor.

The Synchronicity Model

E LAINE LEIBRANDT LIVED in the gated community of Forest Highlands on the perimeter of the Coconino National Forest. Her modest three-bedroom house overlooked five acres of stately Aspen trees. A thicket of white birch lined the eastern border of the property, standing watch over a rolling meadow of heather. The San Francisco Mountains loomed behind the tree line, its impressive snow-capped peaks stretching all the way to the North Rim of the Grand Canyon, 80 miles away.

Parnell paid the cabbie, a young Navajo man wearing a frayed Phoenix Suns ball cap. The Indian's dark eyes glimmered like twin oil slicks as he watched Parnell count off a large tip.

"*Ahéheé*, kind sir!" the cabbie nearly shrieked as he accepted the large gratuity. "Thank you so much! For this I would gladly drive you all the way to the moon!"

Parnell slung his backpack over his shoulder and smiled at the driver. "So you mean your cab can fly?"

"*Aoó*," the Navajo nodded as he studied the bills in his hand, practically salivating. "For this much my cab will grow wings." He fumbled in his shirt pocket and pulled out a business card. "That's me—Naalnish . . . Naalnish Yazzie. Funny name, *aoó*. But you won't find a better driver. Please ask for me by name next time."

"You got it, *akis*," Parnell said, laughing, using the Navajo word for friend.

The morning sun warmed Parnell's shoulders as he walked up the flagstone steps to Elaine's front door. As he reached for the knob, the door swung open. Elaine greeted him with a hug and a kiss.

Her scent—a hint of Obsession and freshly shampooed hair—enveloped him and held him hostage. Dizzy, he stepped back out of their embrace to look at her. "I've missed you, Lainey," he said, rubbing her shoulder with his good left hand.

"I've missed you, too," she said, her expression solemn as she ran a finger over his wrapped steel-shank splint. "What happened to your hand?"

"What, this?" he said, lifting his arm and smirking. "Word of advice: Don't ever get a manicure from an alcoholic with the DTs."

Elaine laughed, that throaty chuckle of hers he loved. "I should know better than to ask. So, other than your butchered manicure, just how is my favorite wandering desperado?"

Parnell stared at her, mute in his admiration of her damaged beauty. Seeing her after a long absence always affected him this way—lungs seemingly void of oxygen, his tongue unable to form coherent words. She wore her lustrous coal-black hair swept over the left side of her face, covering the network of pink scars there. Her eye patch peeked through her thick curtain of hair. The left corner of her mouth was permanently frozen in a twisted grimace. Parnell had seen Elaine Leibrandt's modeling portfolio, photos taken before her horrific ordeal completely changed her looks and her life. She had been a stunning woman. Pale translucent skin like a priceless porcelain doll. Luminous dark eyes. Wide, sexy mouth with full bee-stung lips.

But as gorgeous as she had been, Parnell thought Elaine possessed an even more alluring beauty after the attack that had destroyed one side of her face. She had a quiet inner beauty, an internal magnificence and strength and resourcefulness that he greatly admired.

And just looking at her excited him beyond anything he could describe.

She had been one of Parnell's first official reclamation projects. Six years ago he'd learned of this young department store catalog model who had suffered horribly at the hands of a jealous ex-boyfriend, one Jessie Waltham, a no-account loser from Los Angeles. Elaine had broken it off with him several months prior, invoking a restraining order against him when his stalking had become scary. Waltham decided that since he couldn't have Elaine, no one else would either. His weapon of choice was battery acid, flung in her face when she answered his knock on her apartment door. The surprise assault blinded Elaine in her left eye and burned her skin down to the bone on the left side of her face. She had nearly died from the shock. And after four operations, the best plastic surgeons LA had to offer could not restore the skin or cheekbone completely.

The attack brought Elaine Leibrandt's modeling career to a crashing halt.

Parnell had gone to see her at the Torrance Memorial Burn Center in LA. He'd walked in to find Elaine propped up in bed, her face swathed completely in bandages after her third round of surgery. He remembered sitting next to her bed, conversing with her about everything but the attack, Elaine talking through the heavy gauze wrap like a come-to-life mummy. It took all of ten minutes for Parnell to fall in love with her. He couldn't see what she looked like that day, but he fell for her lovely soft voice and her passion for life. She could converse intelligently on a wide range of subjects, and did so with zeal. She had surprised him with her intelligence and indomitable spirit. Before that meeting, Parnell had assumed models to be little more than empty-headed narcissists. Ten minutes with Lainey had changed his stereotypical perception.

He had no idea what was happening between them that first meeting in the burn unit. He just knew that the more he listened to Elaine talk, the further he fell for her. Though it might have been sympathy that drew him to her initially, he knew quickly that Elaine's pride would never permit any kind of sympathy from him. He remembered seeing the look in her good right eye, peeking through the white gauze wrap with a determined steadfastness that said she could take anything life threw at her. Elaine Leibrandt was tough. She was a survivor. Just like him.

The most amazing thing about Elaine was her lack of bitterness toward her attacker. To this day, Parnell didn't understand. *Couldn't* understand. In her only reference to Jessie Waltham, Elaine had told him: "He's not as far along the path of enlightenment as some of us, Mr. Parnell. And who knows, Jessie might have done me a favor. I really never liked modeling all that much. This means I was meant to do something else."

Elaine understood her misfortune as destiny, as in her words, "an opportunity borne out of coincidental synchronicity." She loved Jungian psychology and relied on the principles of Carl Jung to explain nearly every facet of her life. She later told him that "a perfect synchronicity" had brought her and Parnell together.

Elaine might have seen her dire situation as an opportunity or some twisted sense of synchronicity to be easily sloughed off, but Parnell had other thoughts.

Darker thoughts.

The law hadn't been able to locate Jessie Waltham. Parnell did, however. He found Waltham in San Francisco with a little help from his hobo network. Jessie Waltham became victim number 7 on Parnell's growing hit parade. Certainly one of his more gruesome jobs. The big sharks in San Francisco Bay between Alcatraz and Angel Island got a very tasty treat on that full-mooned Saturday night. Shark chumming had never been so interesting. Remarkable creatures those sharks. Nature's most efficient predators. Parnell loved to watch the big creatures eat. And even then, he felt like Jessie Waltham got off easy.

"Earth to Derek," Elaine said. "What's the matter, baby? You're a million miles away."

"Sorry, E. I'm exhausted."

"Well, come on in, nature boy," she said, gingerly taking him by the forearm. "I bought you a present and I can't wait for you to see it."

"Wait . . . me first," he said, removing his backpack, pulling out the perfume gift set. "Sorry, I didn't get the opportunity to wrap it."

"Oh, Derek, you're so sweet," she cooed, caressing the box. "Obsession. And with so many stores closing and all. You went to a lot of trouble."

"No trouble at all, Lainey. And that's not all," Parnell said, reaching down into his backpack. "Look what else your favorite wandering desperado has for the sexiest woman on the planet." Parnell showed her the glassine bag containing the peyote buttons. "It's party time, babe!"

"Oh, sweetie!" she exclaimed, her good eye shining. She opened the baggie and took a sniff. "It smells potent."

"It is."

"You've tried it?"

"Not yet. Not without you."

"So how do you know it's strong?"

"Because Buttonhead Murphy gives it his highest rating. And if I needed further proof, when I left Shangri-La last night, a dozen or more swam naked in the creek, singing their praises to the full moon."

"Wow. If it's anything like the last crop, you and I will be spacing out on the Cartoon Channel the next couple of days." Elaine had never visited any of the hobo camps, but knew most of the residents by name from Parnell's road stories. "Now it's my turn," she said breathlessly. "I can't wait to see what you think of my gift."

She led him through the house, up the stairs to the large spare bedroom where he kept an office. He could sense her excitement by the way she literally ran up the stairs, pulling him along as if he were a reluctant child. As they entered, Parnell saw his extensive model train layout, thousands of feet of track winding across the floor and up two elevated tiers through the spacious office. Familiar smells tickled Parnell's nose: the rubbing alcohol smell of the track lubricant; the burnt electrical odor of the transformers; the greasy petroleum smell of the gear oil he used to keep the trains running squeak free. He called this room his office, but apart from the desktop computer and filing cabinet, this was Parnell's train room. This is where he came to think and plan. More importantly, this is where he came to relax.

He scanned the room and didn't see anything new or out of place. "What?" he said, turning to her for an explanation.

"Just wait," Elaine told him. "I want you to close your eyes and don't open them until I say so."

Parnell started to protest, but she cut him off, telling him this would all be worth it if he would just try a little patience. So, he obeyed, wondering just what the hell Elaine was up to. He heard her shuffle across the room, heard her flick on the power booster followed by the hum of the power packs engaging. Then he heard the whine and swish of a model train gaining speed on the tracks. He had to fight to keep his eyes closed. "What's going on, E?" he asked finally.

"Hold on, Mr. Impatient," she said, barely able to contain her glee. "Here it comes . . . two more seconds . . ."

And then Parnell heard a long whistle from a tinny horn, followed by Elaine telling him to open his eyes. There, coming around the nearest bend on the colossal track was a Santa Fe Super Chief passenger train, complete with headlamp and interior lights. He counted the cars as they passed. Fourteen in all—two locomotives and a dozen passenger cars. This was the real deal, the collector's edition of this Lionel model. The replica diesel locomotives had the classic red-and-silver war bonnet livery. Six sleeper cars, the famous pleasure dome car with its accurate straight-shaped dome, the equally heralded sleeper-lounge observation car, the diner car populated with miniature diners and wait staff. Each car had detailed lighted interiors. And even better, each car had the red striping that Lionel had produced for only three years (1959 – 1961). Parnell had been looking for a set like this for years. The cheapest one he found ran close to five-thousand dollars.

"And this is the icing on your cake, babe," Elaine said, moving close to him and plopping a new train engineer hat on his head. "You are now an official H-O scale conductor of the Santa Fe Super Chief." She leaned in and gave him a quick peck on the mouth.

"Jesus, Elaine, this had to cost a small fortune," he said, watching as the model train moved away from him, the illuminated Super Chief tail sign glowing as if it were winking at him.

"Don't worry. It didn't break the bank. I got it online from somebody in Illinois. They were selling off a bunch of their fun stuff to pay their mortgage. I got it for a song. Are you happy with it?"

"Happy?" he said. "Try *ecstatic*! I love you so much, E."

He went to grab her around her waist, trying to rope her in to kiss her, but she stepped back. "Slow down, Derek," she said, pushing him away. "You smell a little ripe. I'm up for anything you want to do. But only after you get that three-week hobo stink off of you."

"Well," Parnell said, "with my hand in this condition, I don't think I can do it alone. Don't believe I can hold onto the soap."

Elaine let out a mock sigh. "Any excuse in a pinch, right? I guess I can help out an old man in need."

Dead-Eye Elaine

THE SPRAY FROM THE SHOWER NOZZLE pelted his skin like warm little acupuncture needles, the tiny pin-pricks massaging his tired muscles and achy joints back to life. Parnell watched three weeks of road grime circle the drain at his feet. Elaine stood facing him, her soapy fingers kneading the soreness out of his chest and arms. She had an artist's hands, deft and sure, creative. As she worked her hands over his body, she rubbed her scarlet-painted toes against his feet and ankles with a slippery sensuousness.

He leaned into her—his erection rubbing against her thigh— and brushed the thick knot of wet hair away from her face. He planted a light kiss on her glass eye, the tiny café-au-lait-colored orb slick and cool against his lips. She smiled demurely at him through the swirling steam.

Elaine had been against the glass eye at first, claiming "I don't want to look like some taxidermy experiment gone bad!" But in time, Parnell convinced her that prosthetics had come a long way and that the glass eye would be a more natural look than wearing the patch. He had paid for her prosthetic eye and the instructional fitting sessions. In time, Elaine learned to accept the glass eye. But she was never comfortable with it. Especially out in public, where she imagined everybody to be staring at "the mannequin with the dead eye."

She moved around behind him, used the oversized sponge on his shoulders and back. He luxuriated in her touch.

"So tense . . . so tight," she cooed as she worked him with the sponge. "It's not healthy, babe. You feel like a rubber band all twisted up."

"Yeah," Parnell mumbled. "Hobo accommodations aren't all they're cracked up to be."

He felt her fingers sneak down between his legs and gently stroke his testicles from behind. Parnell sucked in his breath as Elaine's feather touches brought him close to the edge.

"Ooh, we've got some real serious tension here, babe," she moaned while sliding her hand the length of his erection. "Sure feels like something I might enjoy taking care of." She turned him around and dropped to her knees, took him in her mouth. Parnell nearly lost it. Three weeks on the road without any sex and now this. Elaine's warm, wet mouth and the way she flicked her tongue drove Parnell to delirious heights. He tried to think of things non-sexual so he wouldn't come. No use. It was impossible to think much at all.

He fondled her soapy breasts the best he could with his left hand, rubbing her large nipples the way he knew she liked it done. Elaine's head bobbed up and down, soft little moans escaping her throat as Parnell continued stroking her.

Suddenly she pulled away from him and stood, leaned back against the tile wall. "Come on, babe. I want you! Right now!"

Parnell entered her, slowly, gently, teasingly, until he was deep inside her. He didn't dare move for several long seconds, remaining stock still for fear of climaxing too soon. He waited like that, frozen in place, buried deep in her, on the precipice of losing it, feeling her muscles grip him, squeezing the fullness of him.

And then he bucked furiously, thrusting into her with a reserve of energy he didn't know he possessed. She returned his heat, their hips crashing together in a violent ballet. Elaine shouted "Ride me!" over and over as Parnell groaned and held on for dear life. The shower filled with the sounds of wet bodies slapping against the wall. Steam swirled around them like a cottony cocoon.

Their voices rose to a crescendo as he exploded, the release intense, making his knees buckle. Elaine shuddered with a series of extended orgasms that seemed to go on forever. She clung to Parnell as they tumbled to the floor, sliding along the slippery tile.

They lay there entwined, drained but satiated, the water from the shower nozzle continuing to pelt them from above.

"I love you so much, Derek," she said after a time. "It's great to have you home."

"I love you, too, Lainey," he said, his voice hoarse from his sexual grunting.

After a time, Elaine separated herself from him and stood, turned off the shower and began twisting the water out of her hair. "Now that we're clean, how about dipping into that peyote treat you brought with you."

Parnell stood and kissed her shoulder. "Great minds think alike!"

Five Days on the Peyote Train

PARNELL AND ELAINE SPENT the next week ingesting peyote, making love, and enjoying each other's company. Both knew the time they had together was limited, so they made the most of it. They spent the first 48 hours in bed, spacing on peyote buds, alternately having spectacular sex, watching movies on Elaine's high-def wide-screen television, eating junk food, followed by more sex.

Parnell loved watching his favorite movies on that 55-inch display—*The Godfather*, *Raging Bull*, *Gangs of New York*, *Easy Rider*, *Chinatown*, *Bullitt*, *Fort Apache The Bronx,* the first Indiana Jones flick. All so real Parnell felt like he could leap into the screen and actually exist in those worlds. Maybe take a few swings at De Niro, or ride a chopped hog next to Fonda, Nicholson, and Hopper. That LCD-screen world became even more vivid when the peyote buzz kicked in. Elaine had her favorites, too, which changed depending on the altitude of her high. *Titanic, Thelma and Louise, Gone with the Wind, Steel Magnolias, Beaches, The Valley of the Dolls* . . . most not Parnell's kind of thing. But hey, everything was entertaining when indulging in the magic cactus button with a woman like Elaine. The hallucinogen put a supernatural sheen on everything, made the colors more psychedelic, adding incredible depth to the visions on the screen. And he found great enjoyment in observing Elaine's reactions to certain scenes. He loved listening to her throaty laugh during the funny parts, the way she would scrunch her brow and bite the inside of her cheek as she concentrated on the screen during the dramatic scenes.

He loved being with Elaine Leibrandt. When he was here, Parnell couldn't imagine ever leaving her again. But he always did, usually getting restless and feeling the need to move on after a few days. Every mournful toot of a train whistle in the distance awakened the vagabond in him, telling him he had much to do. Telling him he'd better get out on the rails once again, that his hobo friends needed him.

And every train whistle served to remind him to get back to his first priority—dealing with the murderers of his wife and daughter. He finally knew who they were. Blanton Miles had supplied him with two names, both being held at Broome County Correctional back east awaiting trial.

THE THIRD DAY PARNELL AND ELAINE got outside, feeling the need for fresh air and sunshine. They spent the afternoon flying a box kite Parnell had assembled from a kit. He was so high the kite's tail morphed into and out of snapping snake-like creatures with rows of jagged teeth. In his stoned state, the kite resembled a flying coffin, with a skeletal figure waving from inside. He'd had the kite aloft for fifteen minutes, floating easily on the thermals when either the wind shifted or Parnell lost his concentration. He watched as the kite crashed into the tops of the aspen trees. And there it sat, stuck in the upper network of branches, one side collapsed, looking like a shattered pterodactyl sneering down at them. Parnell, of course, blamed the accident on his wounded hand, which Elaine quickly called him on.

"Your hand?" she exclaimed. "What a lame excuse!"

"Hey, I can't help it if I'm messed up."

"You want to see messed up? I'll show you messed up!" She grabbed the ball of string out of his hands and began tying him up with it, binding him with the thin strands as they laughed maniacally. Soon they were on the ground, bound together by what seemed like miles of string. Which of course led to a long makeout session, the two of them bound to each other, tumbling around in the grass like a couple of hormonally-crazed teenagers.

LATE THAT SAME NIGHT Parnell awoke from a disturbing dream to find he was alone in bed. Elaine's scent wafted from the sheets. The television was on, some cable huckster peddling a cure for baldness. The glassine bag with the cactus buttons lay on her pillow. Bleary-eyed, he reached for the tiny baggie, held it up in the shivery light of the television, realized they were almost out of their drug of choice.

Parnell got out of bed, his leg muscles rubbery from the peyote hangover. He donned his terrycloth robe, cinched the belt, and went downstairs.

He found Elaine in her converted dining room studio, working on a new painting. He stood in the doorway, quiet, watching her work with her back to him. He breathed in the bitter smells of turpentine and oil paints, heard the soft scrape of her pallet knife against the canvas.

She had started a fresh painting. Lots of red and gold slathered across the surface in thick globs. Too early to tell what it might turn into. Parnell watched her graceful movements, the sweep of her arm, the tilt of her head, the way she jiggled her ass as she leaned in with the brush to daub and pat. She had her hair tied back in a long ponytail, and it bobbed like a squirrel's tail as she worked.

Parnell marveled at her resourcefulness, the way she had re-made herself from a catalog model into a painter who was now showing and selling her work in several local galleries. During her recuperation period following the attack, Elaine had rediscovered her childhood artistic talent. She'd started with charcoal and pen-and-ink sketches. She would sit for hours at a time, drawing on her sketchpad, fully engrossed in her craft. She started small, recreating bowls of fruit, vases of flowers, birds who visited her feeder outside her workshop window. Then she graduated to portraits. Parnell had framed the sketch he had posed for, and it now sat on his desk in his office/model train room. He couldn't get over how much it looked like a black-and-white photograph. Elaine was that good. Every nook and cranny in his face rendered authentically. Every follicle of hair on his head reproduced with painstaking care. She even had the small scar on his neck just right. After six months she had churned out close to a hundred sketches, became a bit bored, and moved on to oil paints, never looking back.

She continued to work, blissfully unaware of him standing behind her. Parnell looked around the room. Nearly a dozen paintings sat on easels in different stages of completion. One was a canvas she had just finished as a commission job, a very detailed depiction of a lion leaping over a fallen tree trunk set against a jungle backdrop. One of her best, he thought. Another was an expansive panoramic view of the San Francisco Mountains as seen from the window of her studio. She'd told him yesterday that she still had work to do to get the snow-capped peaks just right. When it came to painting, Elaine Leibrandt was a fussy perfectionist.

She turned to throw her brush into a jar on the credenza when she saw him. "Jesus, Derek!" she exclaimed, bringing a hand to her paint-smattered smock. "You scared the shit out of me! Don't ever sneak up on me like that."

Parnell smiled, and moved toward her. "What's the matter?" he said, grabbing her around her waist and reeling her in. "Feeling guilty about something?" He loved the feel of Lainey in his arms, the solid warmth of her body next to his.

"I got this crazy idea for a new painting," she said, shaking her head, ponytail flapping. "I had to get started on it before I lost it."

"What's it going to be?" Parnell said into her neck as he planted soft kisses there.

"It's a surprise," she said, stepping out of his embrace and reaching to pull the elastic from her ponytail. She snapped the band loose and her hair cascaded down to her shoulders. She shook her head, her thick black mane flying about.

Parnell stepped closer, took the ponytail holder from her hand, and, best he could with his clumsy left hand and injured right, tried to bunch her hair and put it back on.

"Don't, Derek," she said, grimacing, fighting him, grabbing his arm, giving him her wounded bird look.

"I love seeing your face, E."

"But I'm so . . . *ugly*—"

"Please don't start with this again. You are absolutely *gorgeous*, darling." He pulled his face back from hers, studied her. "I thought we were past this."

She looked down. "I know," she said. "But there are still times when . . ." She let her answer trail off.

Parnell felt his rage at Elaine's attacker returning, even though Jessie Waltham had been shark food for years. An event that happened more than six years ago continued to haunt their relationship, and it pissed him off.

He lifted her chin, spoke to her, his voice strained with emotion. "Look, Elaine. We can't go back and change time. We can't undo the attack. What's done is done. It changed the picture in huge ways, yes. But I don't want to hear this ugly duckling stuff anymore. When I look at you I see the world's most beautiful woman. No, you are not a model anymore. So what. That's a shallow world populated by superficial airheads. You've said so many times yourself. Now you're a hot painter, with showings in top galleries. I'm really proud of the way you bounced back and I'm happy for your success. You have to believe that, Lainey."

Though he didn't say it, Parnell wondered how Elaine could be so quick to forgive a psycho like Jessie Waltham, yet struggle with forgiving herself.

He continued. "Just know that Jessie Waltham will never be able to hurt you again. Nobody will, as long as I'm around."

Her good eye became heavy with tears. "That's just it, Derek. You're *not* around much. In another couple of days you'll hear your vagabond siren call and you'll ride the rails again. And here I'll be, alone, worried about you, scared sometimes . . . sometimes late at night I hear things, I *imagine* things. And I have no way of getting in touch with you—"

"You can always call Blanton Miles," he responded, telling her the same thing he always did when this discussion came up. "Blanton always knows how to find me."

"No he doesn't, Derek. Sometimes it's days before you get back to him."

He pulled her chin up with his splinted hand. "What about your sister, Gina? She comes to visit on a regular basis."

She backed away from him and crossed her arms defiantly. "You just don't get it, do you? We've been playing this game for what? Six years now? You, the gallant knight in shining white armor, out doing lord-knows-what in the big world . . . me, the damsel in distress waiting patiently in the castle for her man to come home and pay her some attention."

Parnell groaned. "What are you saying, Elaine?"

She turned her back to him. "I . . . I don't know," she sighed. "Everything's really confusing right now."

"How so?"

She turned back to him, her pale skin flushed with anger. "Did you hear any of what I just said?"

"I did, but—"

"Well then you know I speak the truth," she said, looking him straight in the eye. She shook her head in dismay. "I've been doing a lot of thinking recently. This is likely to hurt you, Derek, but it's something I have to say."

"Go on," Parnell said, dread in his voice.

Elaine stared at him for long seconds, and he wondered if she would say anything. Finally she said, "You have to be one of the most selfish men I have ever known. There, I said it. And I *mean* it."

Parnell stared her down and she looked away. He could feel the adrenaline coursing through his veins, the pool of anger bubbling in his throat. After all he had done for this woman—the thousands of dollars he'd spent on her medical bills, buying this house for her, all the hours of tender loving care he'd provided helping her through her many insecurities . . . the revenge murder he had committed for her—and this was how she showed her gratitude?

He grabbed her by the arm, pulled her close. "What is it you want from me, Elaine? You want me to stay here with you 24-7?"

"No. I know that's not possible. I wouldn't ask that of you."

"What, then?"

She moved away from him, stood in front of the big picture window staring out into the opaque blackness of night, her back to him. Parnell could see their reflections in the window. Their images wavered ghostlike in the glass.

"I want you to take me with you," she said finally.

"No! Absolutely not! We've been down this road before."

She turned on him, her face tight with rage. "I'm not a god-damned invalid, Derek!"

"I . . . I never said you—"

"Don't even go there," she literally screamed at him.

What is her problem? Parnell wondered. Peyote hangover? Runaway hormones? Something else?

"Look," he said, "I've told you before how dangerous it can be, cattin' trains. Hell, E, just last week I had to, um . . . *take care* of some dude who was causing trouble. Happened right on the boxcar as we were rolling. How do you think I got this bum hand? Some asshole tried to slice me to ribbons."

She studied him for some time, then said, "And this is exactly what I'm talking about. Your injuries. I ask you what happened and you give me some smartass frat-boy shit like you got a mani-cure from a drunk or something. I worry about you incessantly, Derek, and you continue to shut me out."

"Okay, okay," he said, softening. "You're right. I have been self-centered. I'll try to do better."

Elaine still looked troubled. She said, "As long as we're coming clean here, I have something else to tell you. I probably should have told you sooner, but . . ."

"What?" he said, bracing himself, not liking the sound of that.

"I got a visit from a couple of federal agents last week."

"What? Who? What kind of feds?"

"One was from the FBI. The other man was from the Arizona Criminal Investigations Division."

He felt the anger coursing through him in fiery waves. "Jesus, Elaine! I've been here five days and you're just telling me this now?"

She gave him her demure look. "I'm sorry. I . . . I just didn't want to spoil our time together. I should have known you'd react this way."

"What'd they want?" he said, trying to keep the annoyance out of his voice.

"They wanted to know where you were. The younger one from the State kept mentioning organized crime activities. He claims you're up to your neck in it. *Mobbed up* is how they kept referring to it. Anything you want to tell me about, Derek?"

"Mobbed up? You gotta be shittin' me! Do I look like a gangster to you, Lainey?"

"I wouldn't know. I've never met one."

"Come on," Parnell pleaded. "You know me better than that."

"Do I?"

"Elaine, I'm a lot of things . . . some of them not so good. But I absolutely despise the Mafia . . . the Cosa Nostra . . . whatever else they call themselves these days."

She stared at him, bewildered. "Funny," she said. "They gave me the impression that your organization was like a Mafia family. They even called Blanton Miles your *consigliere*."

"They mentioned Blanton by name?"

She nodded. "Yes. The FBI man kept referring to Miles as the consigliere and you as the don. Said your operation is structured like a Mafia family, just without all the wops. His words, not mine."

Parnell exploded. "Just where do a couple of federal agent cowboys get off looking down their noses at organized crime? The Mafia and the feds are both peas in the same pod. The federal government is the biggest organized crime syndicate on the planet! Hypocrite bastards!" He started pacing. "Christ, E, this is bad. Did you let them inside? Did they go in my office?"

"No, they didn't get past the front door. Not without a warrant. I'm far from stupid, you know. I told them to wait outside while I went and got my cell phone. When I came back, I asked for their identification. They flashed me their badges and photo IDs. While they waited, I entered their information into my phone, then called both of their district offices to confirm they were who they said they were. I'm well aware of my rights." Elaine jutted her chin out at him in a challenging stance.

"Okay, good," Parnell said, somewhat placated. "I'm going to need those names."

She stood her ground. "I'll think about it."

"Look, Elaine. I don't think you understand how serious this is—"

"I know *damned* well just how serious this is! I'm so tired of your condescending tone. I've had enough, Derek. I can't go on living like Robin Hood's kept woman."

"Robin Hood? Cute, E."

"Christ, you're impossible!" she said, then stormed past him out of the room.

"Hey, where're you going?" he yelled behind her.

He heard her trudge up the staircase and slam her bedroom door shut.

Parnell felt his heart deflating like a tire with a slow leak.

Robin Hood and the Sherwood Forest

HE LAY ON THE FLOOR of his bedroom office, watching his model trains zoom around the tracks. Parnell had taken the last of the peyote and retreated here after his spat with Elaine. As the psychedelic began to work its magic, his thoughts vacillated between his lust for freedom and the burdens of commitment.

Intellectually, he knew Elaine was right. He had been extremely selfish. It wasn't right the way he left her here all alone while he spent weeks riding the rails, doing his thing. Robin Hood she'd called him. He shook his head over that one. Completely wrong analogy. Robin Hood was anything but selfish. And the grand archer of Sherwood Forest was a fictional character, nothing more than medieval British folklore. An awkward metaphor, yes, for Parnell's world wasn't anything like what Robin and his Band of Merry Men experienced.

But Elaine had hit home with her point. She was drowning in loneliness while he was out gallivanting on his adventures. After six years of frequent abandonment, she wanted him to fix things. She wanted—no, *demanded*—that he take her along on his travels, despite the obvious dangers. Parnell knew he would never be able to forgive himself if he led her into his dark jungle world only to have something catastrophic happen. Elaine Leibrandt was a domesticated housecat while many of the creatures lurking in his Sherwood Forest were vicious predators and desperate con artists. They would trick an innocent like Elaine, lull her into a trap and feast on her before she'd ever know what hit her. Elaine's safety was a burden, a responsibility he didn't want to take on.

But, crazy as it seemed, Parnell had entertained thoughts of taking Elaine with him next trip out. He thought about her constantly on his sojourns, always missed her. During his more reflective times, he reasoned this was no way to live—being away from the one human being who made him whole. There was the health of their relationship to consider. Maybe he should give up the vagabond life and remain here in Flagstaff with her permanently.

But then, Parnell realized he was letting the heat of his emotional side take over his cooler analytical instincts. The peyote always affected him that way. His gut told him that Elaine would surely be a liability out on the rails. He knew that firearms were an alien concept to her. Guns terrified her. The noise they made hurt her ears. She'd said many times that guns were "instruments of the devil and good only for two things—killing and maiming." Once, Parnell had stirred up trouble by responding, "Obviously, so what's your point?" Elaine had retreated to her bedroom for a full day after that one. And he knew the closest she ever got to a knife was filleting fish or slicing tomatoes and cucumbers for salads. Just about everyone Parnell encountered out on the rails carried razor-sharp blades, and never hesitated to use them. And then there were Elaine's physical attributes—tall and rangy, willowy in the tradition of most models. She didn't have the muscle required to defend herself in hand-to-hand combat situations that often arose.

But the biggest factor that told Parnell she would be way out of her league was that Elaine Leibrandt was just too damn trusting of her fellow human beings. Too quick to forgive. Christ, she had even forgiven the asshole who had blinded her in one eye and permanently disfigured her face. *"He's not as far along the path of enlightenment as some of us,"* Elaine had told him about her attacker as she lay in her hospital bed, wrapped up like a mummy. How could anyone be that damned forgiving?

And then there was Elaine's muddled view of the world outside her windows. Back during her modeling days the country hadn't devolved into the lawless frontier it had now become. Back then, on a typical day, she would drive herself to work in her shiny new sports car, do photo shoots for people who pampered her and adored her for her physical beauty. Then Lainey would retreat with friends for a few drinks and dinner at an expensive LA restaurant. Maybe catch a concert or a stage play. She had led a charmed life. The money was fantastic. She was young and gorgeous and invincible, surrounded by people who claimed to love and admire her. Elaine's life might as well have been wrapped in colorful gift paper and topped with a bushy golden bow. She had it all. But this was before that psycho Jessie Waltham attacked her. Before she spent nearly six years living here in the foothills of the

San Francisco Mountains of Flagstaff as a virtual recluse. Before another Wall Street crash had plunged America into a second Great Depression. Elaine had been holed up here in her safe little cocoon as millions of Americans lost their homes and became rootless wanderers, riding the rails and traversing the land in search of food and shelter and an honest day's work. Crime was rampant throughout many of the hobo camps and shantytowns, even worse in sparsely-populated areas where there were few witnesses. Parnell had seen so much of it. *Too* much of it. He had seen the worst of human nature in action—robbery, murder, rape, torture, sadism—he had even witnessed cannibalism on more than one occasion.

And he was quite certain that no matter how often he'd warned Elaine of the dangers that lurked behind every tree or boulder in his Sherwood Forest, she still viewed the world as it had been during her modeling days. She refused to watch any news programs on TV, saying the negative reporting depressed her. She didn't subscribe to any newspapers or news magazines (the few that were still publishing). Every time he returned from a rough road trip, bearing wounds from his encounters, she tuned him out, refused to listen to the gory details. She refused to accept reality. The outside world had turned into a Mad Max Road Warrior kind of survivalist existence while Elaine subsisted here in her safe little time capsule.

And yet, she demanded that he take her along with him on his journeys. Said she was too afraid to stay here alone anymore.

If she's afraid here, Parnell thought, she'd be freaking mortified in the outside world. In short, his Elaine was a lamb, and he didn't want to be the one to lead her to slaughter.

But still, he had to do something to save this relationship. She had made that quite clear.

He was really flying now, the peyote jump-starting his synapses.

He stretched out, dropped his head against the cool slick surface of the oak flooring, positioning himself at the end of a long straightaway where the trains clicked down the tracks. The hardwood floor felt like a sheet of ice against his face. His new Lionel passenger train came directly at him, the locomotive's headlamp blinding, throwing snaky trails across his retinas. He heard the imitation steam whistle, sounding like an out-of-tune fairground calliope. He flinched as the train rushed by, the passing cars a kaleidoscopic blur of color and light. As he usually did when playing with his trains, Parnell thought of his late father. The Lionel miniatures brought back memories of the one good year they had together, sharing their mutual love of model trains . . . the year Parnell felt he actually *had* a father.

Suddenly, he heard his dad's voice, a spot-on scratchy baritone with the slight lisp caused by a few missing teeth. "That's a beautiful piece of craftsmanship, Derek. They got all the detailing absolutely right. Just look at the wide-door baggage car and the extruded stainless steel construction of each car . . . and that war bonnet livery, that's pure genius, son!"

Parnell sat up, alarmed, looking around the dimly-lit room. He swore his father's ghost was in the room with him at that moment. Parnell could *feel* his presence.

"Dad?" he said. "Are you here?"

As if in response, the Santa Fe Super Chief tooted its steam whistle as it rounded the bend on the far side of the room and ascended up the trestle to the second level, into the papier-mâché mountains.

Parnell slumped down on the floor, feeling foolish. *I'm losing it*, he thought dejectedly. *I need to get back out on the road. I need to cleanse my system of these hallucinogens and get back to work.*

But right now he was so tired . . . he had a bone-weary ache in his soul. Parnell closed his eyes and drifted off . . .

. . . He dreamed he stood in a clearing surrounded by thick woods. A small stream gurgled nearby. A quick glance down showed him to be dressed in an olive green woolen outfit that overlaid thin cloth leggings. High buckskin boots made his calves sweat. A nickel-studded leather belt encircled his waist. He held an archer's longbow in his right hand, could feel the weight of the quiver on his back that held the arrows. He couldn't believe it. He was *Robin Hood*!

He looked behind him, saw a few of his trusted Merry Men— Little John, Friar Tuck, and Will Scarlet . . . a few others whose names he didn't know. Little John poked his lethal-looking staff in the dirt and offered him a grim smile. Will Scarlet caressed his belt of daggers as he gazed off into the distance.

Friar Tuck spoke. "Shall we go after her, Robin?"

"Who?"

"Why, Maid Marian, of course," he said, pointing to the creek.

He looked to where Tuck pointed, saw Maid Marian being

accosted by three grungy men splashing around in the shallows. He heard her shouts for help as the men struggled to get her under control, saw them ripping her blouse, tearing her vest from her shoulders. Suddenly she broke free and lunged for the slippery bank, falling back into the creek. She had Elaine's face, complete with the scarring along the left side and her glassy left eye. He had never seen her looking so panicked.

Quickly, he reached over his shoulder, removed an arrow from his quiver, notched it into his bow, took aim. *Thwack!* A perfect gut shot, taking down the closest assailant.

Hands a blur, he grabbed another arrow and notched up . . . aimed. A direct hit on the second attacker, this one producing a sickening *thwock* sound as the arrowhead hit bone, lodging deep in the scoundrel's skull. He heard a chilling scream as the man splashed in circles, trying desperately to pull the arrow from his head. After several long minutes of cursing and splashing, the guy collapsed into the blood-red water.

He reached behind him for another arrow, but saw he was too late to get the third man, who had grabbed Maid Marian and disappeared with her into the trees.

He screamed a cry of frustration as he heard Maid Marian's yells for help become more faint . . .

Parnell came awake with a start, his heart hammering in his chest. His phone was ringing. He scrambled to get to his feet. Awkwardly, he tumbled toward his desk and the jangling phone.

Teflon Justice

C ALLER ID SHOWED it was Blanton Miles.
Parnell picked up, looking at the digital clock on his desktop: 1:37 AM. That would make it 4:37 back east.

"The goddamned rooster hasn't even crowed yet, Blanton," he said, irritated. "Don't you ever sleep?"

"Plenty of time for that later, when I'm ashes in an urn."

Parnell tried to clear the peyote cobwebs from his mind. His head swirled in a maelstrom of thoughts, bouncing around without finding purchase.

Miles broke the short silence. "I've got some important news that can't wait. You okay, boss?"

"Yeah, yeah. I'm just . . ." One thought finally did register. Elaine's house had possibly been compromised by the government agents. "Uh . . . Blanton, uh . . . I'm not sure this phone is secure right now, so—"

"Sure it is," Miles said. "I had Grabowski sweep the house last week before you arrived. Elaine called me about the visit from the feds. She told me what went down. That's a very sharp lady you have there, Derek. She handled things superbly. Rest assured, this is a safe call."

"Okay," he said, still trying to recover from his Robin Hood dream.

"Your two alleged arsonists—Tico Samuels and Jerry Ray Allenson? They've been released."

It took Parnell a few long seconds to process this information before he realized Miles was referring to the murderers of his wife and daughter. "Whaddaya mean *released*?"

Blanton Miles remained cool, professional. "Both of these mutts got slick defense attorneys who got the Broome County DA to overturn the case based on lack of sufficient evidence. The judge deemed all collected evidence to be circumstantial. Something about extreme violations in the chain of custody protocol. Apparently the prosecution was incompetent in presenting the solid evidence they had—the fire accelerants they found in Allenson's basement, the credit card records showing the purchase of those chemicals, Tico Samuels' previous arson conviction in an insurance fraud case four years earlier, both men's lack of airtight alibis the night of the crime. In short, the prosecution blew it. The judge dismissed the jury this afternoon and acquitted both Allenson and Samuels."

Parnell could not trust his ears. "Jesus, Blanton! You're telling me these dipshits walked? How the hell can that be?"

"What can I say? The prosecution team redefines the term *weak*. They make the O.J. Simpson prosecution look competent. But my gut tells me this all goes much deeper than that, Derek."

"How so?" Parnell silently cursed himself for putting off a trip back east to deal with these killers.

"My instincts tell me these two worms dropped the dime on Willis Logan. I think they made a deal—their immunity for details of Logan's involvement in the murders of your wife and daughter."

"What makes you think that?"

"Some very powerful people would like to see your wife's ex finally take the fall for something. Willis Logan has been engaged in criminal activities for years. But so far, he's made of Teflon. Nothing sticks to the man. And a related fact: credit checks on Tico Samuels and Jerry Ray Allenson show that neither has any money. Both are unemployed. Neither could afford to pay for their crackerjack defense team. Somebody's financing them. Somebody with a grudge against Willis Logan."

"A grudge against Logan?" Parnell said. "Hell, that could be any of a hundred different people. Maybe a thousand. What else you got?"

"Well, Tico Samuels' history would lend credence to this theory. Four years ago, he walked on his arson indictment by pulling the same stunt. He turned state's evidence in an insurance scam in Pennsylvania. He was arrested for burning down a warehouse for a failed retail business. He squealed like the rat he is, saying he had been paid by the owners to burn their biggest storage facility to the ground. Said they stood to receive a cool two million insurance payoff by collecting on their ruined multi-million-dollar auto parts inventory. Tico Samuels got himself a blue-chip defender and worked a plea deal, turning the owners over to the authorities. He walked away with nothing more than a year's probation and a fine. You've seen photos of him in the files I sent you. The man is a lot sharper than he looks."

"Yeah . . ." Parnell said, feeling his blood begin to boil. "Too bad our justice system isn't as sharp."

"Indeed," Miles said. "Creeps always walk in these plea deals. One more thing that tells me I'm right about this, Derek."

"What's that?"

"Willis Logan . . . He's gone missing."

"What? Missing how?"

"Vanished . . . up in smoke . . . gone without a trace. Nobody's seen him the past 48 hours. Even those in his inner circle can't get in touch with him. The FBI has made it a top priority to find him."

"But I thought Julia Sanchez was—"

"Julia lost him."

Parnell felt his frustration turn to fiery rage. "Shit! I told you she wouldn't—"

"Settle down, Derek. Julia had everything under control. She did a great job seducing him, getting him to talk to her. Like I told you before, Willis Logan can't resist Hispanic pussy. He took her to Philadelphia on a business trip where they checked into a large penthouse suite on the top floor of the Four Seasons Hotel. The first day, they never left their room. She screwed his brains out, even got him to confess his part in hiring Samuels and Allenson to do the hit on your wife and daughter, which we've got on tape."

"How'd he get away?" Parnell said with disgust.

Blanton Miles told him that Logan slipped out a door in the back of a master closet into an adjoining suite, which exited on a hallway on the other side of the floor. They'd had backup posing as a room service waiter watching the door to Logan's suite around the clock, backed up by a camera setup, but there was no way to catch this. A check with hotel management indicated that Logan had stayed in this room many times before, always with a different woman.

"I'm betting he actually owned this room, and had the secret closet door installed himself while hotel management looked the other way," Miles continued. "Don't blame Julia Sanchez for this, Derek. She did everything in her power to keep him close. She got us some very valuable information . . . evidence that will stand up in court and nail the Teflon Don once and for all."

"Only if he's found. Jesus, Blanton! Please tell me Spottswood and Delancey are still tailing our two arsonists. I don't want to hear that Samuels and Allenson have given them the slip."

Miles' voice turned more cheerful. "You'll be happy to know

that Spotts and Del are still tracking them. But our two firebugs have split up since their release from jail, and the shadowing has become more difficult, so I have assigned backups for each."

"Who?"

"Corrigan and Hartwell."

"Excellent," Parnell said, taking a deep breath. "Now, here's what I want you to do, Blanton. I want both of them—I'm talking about Tico Samuels and Jerry Ray Allenson—rounded up and brought to me—"

"Out there?" Miles asked. "In Arizona?"

"Yes. To a location of my choosing. I plan to be their final judge and jury. There won't be any chain of custody problems with evidence when I'm through with them." Parnell could feel his heart thumping in his throat. His hands shook.

"I don't think that's a good idea, boss."

"Why not?"

"Because every available east coast fed is watching these two clowns right now, thinking they'll eventually cross paths with Willis Logan. Spottswood told me yesterday it's like a paparazzi feeding frenzy surrounding Tico Samuels. Spotts says the last time he's seen anything like it was years ago, when he did a stint working on Michael Jackson's security detail. The feds have never been very good at covert operations, you know that, boss. Christ, they're all white dudes who wear the same aviator sunglasses and Brooks Brothers suits. They all drive dark blue Crown Vics and chain-smoke cheap cigarettes. They might as well be wearing uniforms that say FEDERAL DICKS across the front."

Parnell smiled in spite of his anger. "Yeah, well, I still want a piece of Samuels and Allenson."

"We'll get them to you in due time, but you're going to have to be patient. The last thing you need is half the agents in Quantico out there breathing down your neck. A couple of western-based Fibbies are already sniffing around for you. Best thing you can do right now is keep a low profile . . . get back on the move. No sense making things easier for them. It's not safe for you to stay at Elaine's much longer. You planning on hitting the road again anytime soon?"

"Yes . . . yes I am. Day after tomorrow."

"Why not tomorrow?"

"Because tomorrow's the thirteenth. You know I never travel on the thirteenth of the month."

MAD MAX AND
MAID MARIAN
SEE THE WORLD

Landing on Mars

THE WIND WHIPPED AT PARNELL, his shirt flapping with a machine-gun staccato. He sat next to Elaine on an open flatcar, their backs against the giant tires of an anchored road grader. They'd jumped this moving freighter a mile out of Flagstaff to avoid the many bulls policing the switching yards this time of day. He and Elaine had hopped at one of Parnell's favorite jump-on points—a narrow meadow, two football fields long, surrounded by thick stands of birch, coming out of a steep bend where trains had to slow to half-speed. The site provided jump-catters a good hiding place and a long level runway to "work the fly." Elaine had surprised him with her speed and agility. She'd "flown" better than he had in fact. She caught out first, running alongside the train like an Olympic track star, hooking on and swinging her lithe body up on the flatcar with an athletic ease that would do a circus acrobat proud. Then she laughed at him as he had difficulty hooking on with his splinted hand. Called him an old man, kept on with her barbs, calling him a "geriatric basket case." Couldn't stop laughing.

Maybe this would work out yet, Parnell thought, smiling. Elaine was a gamer, that was for sure.

The sweet scent of juniper pine permeated the crisp mountain air. Early morning sunlight threw vast shadows across the canyons. Parnell never tired of this beautiful 30-mile jaunt from Flagstaff to Sedona. Northern Arizona was a spectacular landscape, perhaps the most breathtaking real estate he'd seen anywhere in his extensive travels. From the aspen-shrouded high country of Coconino County to the burnished coppery beauty of the desert below, Parnell thought this land to be Mother Nature's masterpiece. One of the many reasons he'd decided to call this area home, inasmuch as a drifter like him could claim anyplace to be "home."

He spotted a bald eagle soaring majestically over a crimson butte in the distance. To the east he saw several pronghorn antelope scampering across the scrub-brush plain. Elaine saw them, too. "Hey, look at that!" she said, nudging closer to him and pointing. "They're so fast. Weird looking, too."

He turned, stealing a glance at her, returned her smile. She looked like a pirate hobo, with her black eye patch and black-and-white polka-dot scarf covering her head, the frayed baggy jeans, the soiled cotton shirt, the paint-spattered sneakers. Parnell thought she would fight him on the clothing when he'd told her she would have to look the part out here on the rails. But as much as Elaine loved her expensive designer clothes, she didn't object to slumming it. She had been agreeable to every one of his requests, with the exception of having to leave her iPhone at home. Her entire existence was wrapped up in that damn phone. It was her organizer, her mobile entertainment, how she stayed connected to family and friends. Parnell had explained to her the dangers of remaining "connected" out here in the real world, especially now that the feds were looking for him. Reluctantly, Elaine left her precious phone at home.

She had been ecstatic when Parnell told her she would be coming along. One would have thought he'd just given her the Hope diamond the way she carried on. Immediately, their relationship improved. They hit the sheets for the best sex Parnell could ever remember. She had been frisky, playful. He hoped she would be as happy after they'd been out of pocket for a week or two, when the road grime clung to them like a second skin and their backs hurt from sleeping on the ground.

"It's gorgeous out here, Derek," she said, laying her head against his shoulder.

They took it all in—monolithic cliffs of brilliant red rock towering over bronzed tumbleweed plains. Sprays of colorful wildflowers. The prickly-pear and yucca cactus that created a thorny carpet across the canyon floor. The way the light and shadows played across the earth, creating dazzling spectrums of amber, scarlet, and burgundy.

"It's a whole other world," Elaine said into his ear, shouting to compete with the shriek of the steel wheels below. "Like landing on Mars. I'd forgotten how inspiring it is. It motivates me to paint a few new landscapes."

Parnell nodded, threw his arm around her. He had encouraged her to bring along her oil paints, brushes, and a few small canvases, which she'd stowed in her backpack. It was his one concession to her wishes. He knew better than to deprive her of her art.

Parnell hugged her close and rubbed her shoulder. Silently they watched the panoramic scenery flash by as they approached Sedona.

His mind drifted. Tico Samuels and Jerry Ray Allenson had been released, a fact that perturbed him. And because of the situation with the feds, the two arsonists couldn't be rounded up and brought to him. Parnell ached for justice, itched for revenge. No way should the killers of his wife and daughter be allowed to walk. But Parnell would have his day, he just knew it. It was his fate to deal with the killers. It was karma, and he knew the only real justice was karmic. He also realized that sometimes karma had to be pushed along. He'd nail the bastards, oh yes he would. Samuels and Allenson would fry for their crimes.

Even more frustrating was that they'd lost Willis Logan. Now that Parnell's late wife's first husband had been implicated in her murder, Parnell wanted Logan, too. Badly. Wanted him to pay for his crime every bit as much as Samuels and Allenson. He'd get all three of them, but right now he had to be content to fantasize about what he'd do to them when he had them.

As the train approached Sedona, they rounded a bend and passed through a steep cut-through, plunging them into dark shadows. Parnell grabbed the cool iron of the lading strap anchor beside him that held the grader in place.

Elaine hung on to him as they swerved into the turn. "It's like a thrill ride," she shouted with glee.

Parnell always enjoyed visiting Sedona, but he had to wonder if this trip was the best use of his time. Blanton Miles had been on him about going to see this fortune teller, Madame Crystal. Sedona was full of these characters, these New Age hippie-dippies—the spiritual kooks and quasi-religious nuts and goofy metaphysical flakes trying to center their vortexes and get their auras into sync. Sedona attracted them like mosquitoes to a brackish pond. Parnell thought it was all a bunch of hooey. But if Blanton felt so strongly about him seeing this Madame Crystal, there certainly was something to it.

He wondered just what it could be.

He grabbed his backpack and nudged Elaine. "Get your stuff together," he said. "We're about to our jump-off spot."

Fortunes and Fables

"YOU HAVE THE WRONG IDEA about me, Mr. Parnell." He and Elaine sat facing Madame Crystal, a woman in her mid-thirties with coal-black hair and a dusky amber complexion. She wore gypsy clothing—lacy renaissance blouse with billowy sleeves, sequined olive-green shawl draped over her shoulders, purple Turkish scarf around her neck. She leaned forward, elbows up on the desk, staring at Parnell over tinted granny glasses.

Parnell found her intensity to be unsettling. "How so?" he asked.

"I don't tell fortunes. I don't predict the future . . ." She paused, reaching down to pick up a plump cat, pulled it into her lap. "Good boy, Zeus," she cooed as she stroked its humped back. Parnell could hear it purring from where he sat.

He was losing patience with the woman. She had kept them waiting in the lobby more than an hour where they'd been subjected to piped-in elevator music that reminded him of the Moody Blues on Thorazine. Even worse, the only available reading material was spiritual healing magazines.

"So if you don't tell fortunes, what the hell *do* you do?" he asked her.

"I'm a certified intuitive clairvoyant."

Elaine said, "You want to explain that to us mortal earthlings?"

Parnell couldn't help but laugh.

"My work is serious business," Madame Crystal said without emotion. She brushed Zeus from her lap, her silver hoop bracelets jangling. "I'm able to see into someone's soul and ascertain what is ailing their psyche. Once I get to their center, I begin work on the healing process. Like I said, I'm certified to practice. I have a long list of satisfied clients if you want referrals."

Parnell observed the gypsy woman as she talked, the way she moved her hands, the way her purple nail polish and crystal rings adorning each finger flashed in the overhead light.

When she finally paused, Parnell said, "Save your spiritual

mumbo-jumbo bullshit for the rubes. Drop the act and give me the information you're supposed to have for me."

Madame Crystal seethed. "They warned me that you might be difficult, Mr. Parnell," she said, attempting to maintain her dignity. "What I do is anything but *spiritual mumbo-jumbo bullshit*, as you so inelegantly claim. You might be interested to know that I have helped the police solve many felonies over the years. I've managed to get some very self-deluded individuals to confess to the most heinous of crimes. I have found stashed murder weapons that the authorities couldn't. Once I even located a kidnapping victim—a girl who had been buried alive, given just enough oxygen and water to keep her going. I probed the suspect's mind and was able to find the burial site. I saved that poor girl's life. I can see into the darkest corners of the human mind and soul . . ."

Parnell listened to her ramble. Was she trying to convince them or herself of her qualifications? When she finished her spiel, he said, "Wow, David Copperfield has nothing on you. I'm surprised you don't have your own TV show. I'll bet you even have your own publicity agent."

Elaine laughed, a husky chuckle.

Madame Crystal frowned, her granny glasses sliding down her beaked nose. "You know, Mr. Parnell, skepticism is nothing new to those of us who work in this field. But I find your arrogance to be especially offensive."

"Listen," he said, "I'm only arrogant when I think people are jerking me around—when they're wasting my time."

Madame Crystal stared at him, saying nothing, keeping her expression neutral. Parnell held her stare. He wasn't about to let some New Age flake play him.

Finally, the gypsy woman turned her attention to Elaine. "Is he this difficult with you, sweetie?"

Elaine's smile evaporated. She leaned forward in her chair. "Don't call me *sweetie*," she said. "It's demeaning, especially coming from a charlatan. We're on a tight schedule. You've been incredibly rude by making us wait well beyond our appointment time, so tell us what you have for us or we'll be on our way."

Madame Crystal attempted to collect herself, shaking her head. "Two peas in the same pod," she said, glancing back and forth between them. "Very well, I'll tell you what I have and I know you will be most interested. But first, we need to discuss payment—"

"I'm not paying you a dime until I know you're giving us something real," Parnell said. "Something of value. Let's hear what you've got. I'll determine how much it's worth."

"Mr. Parnell, I have a standard hourly rate for my work and I always get payment in advance. This work—getting this information for you—has not been easy. I've had to go through many layers of bureaucracy and deal with some very unsavory characters . . ."

Elaine huffed. "You just went on and on about your genius at reading people's minds. Shouldn't be too difficult to get information when you can do that."

Madame Crystal blinked. "Um, you don't understand—"

"Oh I understand *plenty*," Elaine countered. "I understand a flim-flam hustler when I meet one."

The gypsy woman studied Elaine, then finally said, "What's with the eye patch and do-rag, *sweetie*? Halloween's four months away."

Parnell could see Elaine clench her fists in her lap, could hear the rage in her voice as she countered with, "Listen, *bitch*! I could say the same about your ridiculous gypsy getup."

"Ladies, *please*," Parnell mumbled as he rummaged through his backpack. "Put your claws back in. No need for a catfight here." He pulled out his money clip, peeled back the big bills, holding them out in front of him, fanning them like a magician asking a mark to pick a card. He spoke to Madame Crystal. "I'm paying in cash, in case I forgot to mention it. No bank fees for you. Financially speaking, I'm being considerate, so talk to me!"

The gypsy woman's eyes dilated above her granny lenses as she viewed the cold hard cash. A handful of hundred-dollar bills. It always amazed Parnell, the hypnotizing power of these little green rectangles of paper.

"Very well," Madame Crystal said, her eyes never leaving the cash in Parnell's hands. She reached into her desk drawer and pulled out a leather-bound ledger, placed it on the desktop in front of her.

"Okay," she said, opening the ledger but not referring to it. "Seven years ago you began receiving some very large payments from an unidentified source. It was all set up for you and communicated to you by a man calling himself Croesus. The payments started soon after you lost your wife and daughter in a house fire in upstate New York. You lost everything in that fire. Heartbroken, you moved back to Pennsylvania . . . Millford, to be exact. There you regrouped, began to invest your newfound money. You also began building your organization—Locomotion Enterprises—starting with employee number one, Blanton Miles, your legal and financial wizard. Do I have this right so far, Mr. Parnell?"

Parnell nodded. "Yeah, but it's all information you could get from public records."

"Granted. But hear me out. I'll get to the juicy stuff." She gave him a knowing smile. Parnell wanted to slap it off her face.

"Those payments stopped three years ago," she continued. "But thanks to your innate business savvy and some good fortune, you have built that initial nest egg into quite a remarkable financial empire. And to your credit, you have done a lot of good work for the, ah . . . shall we say, *homeless* sector?" She glanced at Elaine. "And your man took good care of you, too, didn't he, darlin'? I know why you wear the eye patch. I was just messin' with you. I understand why you're so angry and bitter. God knows I would be, too, if I walked in your shoes—"

"Look, I'm not—" Elaine began to protest but was cut off.

"It's okay, sweetie," Madame Crystal said soothingly. "I understand your pain. I can *feel* your pain. It's more palpable than you think. But getting back to you, Mr. Parnell. You have spent the better part of the past six years searching for two things: the source of your original financing, and the people responsible for the deaths of your wife and daughter. I have information that will lead you to your benefactor. And I have the, um, dare I say . . . *intuitive* feeling that your financial donor will lead you to the truth behind the murders of your loved ones."

Parnell met her stare, getting the uncomfortable feeling that she was reading him somehow. He was impressed with her knowledge, as she hadn't once looked down at her ledger. All of this was from memory. She was very well schooled, he'd give the woman that.

"Now we're getting somewhere," he said. "Does this information you have about my benefactor have anything to do with a phone call I got from a young woman claiming to be Jennifer Parnell?"

"Yes, it does," she said, writing something on a pad of paper, then tearing the sheet off and sliding it across the desk to Parnell.

"What's this?" he asked.

"The name and phone number of your contact. Up in Colorado. The southern part of the state. Durango to be exact."

Parnell looked at the note, saw the name *Thor* with a long-distance number printed carefully beside it. "Is this a joke?" he said, leaning to the side and showing it to Elaine. "Thor? Do you take me for a fool?"

"I guarantee you this is the real deal, Mr. Parnell. Thor will lead you to your mystery financier . . . and a few other things I believe you'll find of interest."

"Okay," Parnell said, folding the note and stuffing into his shirt pocket. The phone number didn't match the number he'd called to talk with the young woman claiming to be Jennifer Parnell. "I'll leave you a down payment of two-hundred—"

"Two *hundred*? Be serious, Mr. Parnell. Your guy, Mr. Miles? He promised me five grand for this information."

"Okay, then," Parnell said, peeling off five Ben Franklins and sliding them across the desk to her. "There's a ten percent down payment. I'll be back to deliver the balance if and when this Colorado trip pans out."

"Fair enough," the gypsy woman said, flinging the bills into her desk drawer. "I'm absolutely sure that Thor will lead you down the right path. Please give him the remaining payment when you're satisfied with the results. Notice I said *when*, not *if*."

"And if I don't pay the balance?"

A dark look crossed her face. "I really don't think you want to know that, Mr. Parnell."

"Okay, then," he said, standing. "I guess we'll be on our way."

As they exited Madame Crystal's office, Parnell heard her say, "My skills. You're not convinced of my psychic abilities . . . my clairvoyance."

"No, not in the least."

"Well maybe this will convince you. I have divined several things about you that are not available in the public domain."

"Oh yeah? Like what?"

She smiled. "You have a passion for model trains and you fear the number thirteen. Triskaidekaphobia I believe is the technical term for it."

"Not bad," Parnell said, getting a bad feeling in his gut.

"I see I hit a nerve, Mr. Parnell. Do you need more proof?" she asked. "Would you like to discuss the murders?"

"I don't have a clue what you're talking about," he said a little too quickly.

"Oh, I believe you do. I'll spare you and your lady the details right now. But just remember this. There is no statute of limitations on murder."

As a general rule, Parnell wasn't easily spooked. But this woman somehow had the goods on him. If he didn't know better, he'd suspect a mole in his organization. But that wouldn't explain how this evil woman knew about his model train obsession. Didn't explain how she knew about his triskaidekaphobia. Or the murders . . . Jesus!

"Have a nice day, Mr. Parnell," Madame Crystal said with false cheer. "It's been a pleasure chatting with you."

Razzmatazz

BEFORE LEAVING SEDONA, they dined at the Red Rock Café, feasting on grilled trout and black beans. *Hiking stamina fuel,* Parnell called it. While they ate, Elaine admired the paintings done by local artists, making editorial comments about technique in a rambling monologue while Parnell remained lost in his thoughts. He wrestled with how this Madame Crystal had known so much about him. Personal things. He refused to believe the gypsy woman was actually clairvoyant. There *had* to be a mole in his organization.

He and Elaine now hiked along a bramble-strewn trail, headed for the Sycamore Canyon hobo camp, northwest of Sedona. Parnell hadn't been there since early spring, and wanted to catch up with several of his old friends before embarking on the 300-mile trip to Colorado. As he walked the trail, Parnell replayed the phone conversation he'd had with his Durango contact, Thor, from a pay phone after lunch. The guy had a deep, scratchy voice and conducted business in a straightforward manner.

". . . Sorry, Mr. Parnell, but I cannot hook up with you until later in the week. If you'd called last week—"

"Yeah, I know," Parnell interrupted, "I got sidetracked with, um . . . other business concerns."

"Yes," Thor said, "I understand you're a very busy man. As am I. The earliest I can meet with you is Friday afternoon. Does that work for you?"

"Sure," Parnell said, disappointed that it was five days away. "Where?"

"Mesa Verde National Park. Southwestern Colorado, near Durango. You know where I'm talking about?"

"Yes, I've been there."

"Excellent! Meet me at the Cliff Palace Overlook at noon. We'll take the ranger-guided tour . . . kind of lag behind the group, do our talking as we walk."

Parnell thought the site of the Ancestral Pueblo cliff dwellings a strange place for a meet, and told Thor as much.

"Best to do the tourist thing for our first get-together," the man replied, "in case we're being watched."

"And just who might be watching?"

"You don't need to know. Trust me, you don't *want* to know."

"How the hell do you know what I want and don't want?"

He heard Thor sigh on the other end of the line. After a slight pause, the guy said, "Mr. Parnell, I know more about you than even your pretty traveling companion does. Is Elaine Leibrandt with you now? If so, please tell her I said hi, and that I'm looking forward to meeting her. I'm sympathetic to her plight. She's had a difficult time of it. It's got to be tough to have a successful modeling career derailed by some pinhead toting a Mason jar full of battery acid."

Parnell was too stunned to respond. What the hell was going on here? This Thor guy knew about the attack on Elaine, even knew that psycho Jessie Waltham had carried the acid around in a Mason jar. And just this morning, a self-professed clairvoyant shocked him with her knowledge of his model train obsession, his triskaidekaphobia, and his string of murders.

"Who *are* you, Thor? What's your real name?"

A long silence.

Just when he thought the man might have disconnected, Thor said, "Save your questions for our meeting, Mr. Parnell. Everything will come into focus then. Just make sure you show up. You'll be very sorry if you don't. If you fail to show you'll never know the truth behind . . . well, let's just leave that for Friday, shall we? See you then, Mr. Parnell. Don't be late."

The line went dead.

Parnell shook his head as he shuffled along the trail. His life had quickly become wrapped in a strange synchronistic shroud. Events and players danced just outside his circle of comprehension. No matter how much he analyzed recent happenings, he couldn't see the big picture. Things seemed to be happening in a predestined way, but he had no idea how it all fit together. And now he'd have to wait almost a full week before he got more answers. He hated this lack of control, this lurking around in the dark.

They were out in true red rock country, down in a canyon in an untamed and remote place. Weathered cliffs towered on either side of them, the late-afternoon sun painting the rocky façades in flames of fire. Shadows moved around outcroppings like ghosts. They passed several caves, their entrances adorned with Navajo paintings that depicted alien-looking animals and stick-figured humans in sun-faded splashes of color. The cave paintings told stories of ancient times, and Parnell was always struck by their similarity to the hobo signage of today.

To get where they now hiked, he and Elaine had hopped a freighter. They rode a side-door Pullman (boxcar) for the first 15 miles, then jumped off to hike these final couple of miles through rugged wilderness. Deep gorges and the thin air made the hiking difficult. They crossed over a switchback and came to a small creek. Wild blackberry brambles grew thick along the bank. Parnell noticed bear tracks around a trampled bush. Two or three big black bears had been feasting on berries here recently.

"Hey, look at this, E," he called out to Elaine, who stepped up beside him "Looks like Bigfoot's been through here." He pointed down at the smattering of paw prints.

"You're so full of it, Derek," she said, slapping his arm playfully.

"Really," he said, doing his best to maintain a serious expression. "There've been quite a few sightings of good old Sasquatch in these parts the last few years. You'd know that if you paid attention to the news once in a while."

"Give me a break, Derek. I've seen bear tracks before. I'm not a complete idiot about nature, you know."

"I know you're not, but personally, I've never seen bear prints like these. These are twice the length and width of those of the largest bear. Deeper, too."

"The only thing deep here is the amount of shit you're slinging. To use your lingo, Derek—save it for the rubes!"

That got both of them laughing.

Parnell twisted off a bunch of berries from the vine. "Here, Lainey, try some, they're really sweet," he said, smearing the gooey berries against Elaine's face. Elaine shrieked, then retaliated, and soon they were involved in a blackberry food fight.

After their juvenile outburst, they cleaned up in the creek, Parnell keeping an eye out for returning bears.

Thirty minutes later, they walked through an arbor of giant cottonwood trees, emerging into a small clearing. Parnell pulled up short, knowing immediately something was amiss. He motioned for Elaine to stop, drew his finger across his mouth in a zipping motion, indicating for her to remain quiet. He crouched and looked across the way, pulled his gun from his waistband holster, Elaine taking a knee behind him. He saw no sign of activity in the camp. The place was eerily deserted. The preternatural quiet weighed on him with a crushing gravity.

Something terribly wrong here, he thought with growing apprehension.

They faced the remains of the old fire-charred cabin and the toppled stone chimney that served as "town square" of the Sycamore Canyon hobo camp. The stacks of burnt rocks stood alone, silent, looking like a scorched Stonehenge nightmare. Usually a couple dozen hobos congregated here, some of them Parnell's closest friends. Surely they couldn't have all found work elsewhere.

Parnell signaled for Elaine to follow him. Carefully, he took the long way around to the dilapidated cabin, keeping to the tree line, his gun out in front of him. Elaine nervously dug through her backpack, finding her little derringer, emulating his shooter's stance as she stayed glued to his back. He hoped he had taught her enough in their firearms crash course that she wouldn't accidentally shoot him in the back.

Cautiously, they made their way to the tumbledown chimney, ducked behind it.

Still no sign of anyone.

An owl hooted from the forest.

Great, Parnell thought. An owl active in the daylight hours was the worst of omens.

He and Elaine remained crouched behind the remains of the chimney, quiet, on alert.

And then a voice from nearby, harsh and threatening. "Flip yer gats and throw yer feet real slow or my hogleg will torch ya."

Parnell couldn't place the voice, but knew the message was hobo-speak for *Throw down your guns and come out slowly or I'll shoot you with my rifle.*

"It's okay, we're cool," Parnell cried out. He stuck his head above the chimney, attempting to see the man. "We're fellow breezers," he said, using the hobo term to let the guy know they were friendly and part of the train-hopping tramp fraternity. "Just a Willie and a 'bo-ette," Parnell added to make sure the guy understood.

A shot rang out, the bullet shattering stone near Parnell's face. He ducked quickly, his heart racing.

"I'm not fuckin' around! Now flip 'em an' get out here where

I can see ya."

Parnell crouched low, realizing the man had a high-powered rifle and wasn't afraid to use it. He glanced at Elaine, could see the fear etched in her good eye. His mind scrolled through options.

A second shot boomed like a howitzer across the canyon. Parnell heard the bullet rip through the treetops behind them.

"Come on outta there, goddammit!" the man screamed. "Show yerselves."

"Not until you tell me who you are," Parnell said, wanting to keep him talking. "Are you a cop?"

"I ain't no town clown! Don't insult me."

This was the last place Parnell expected trouble. For years this hobo camp had been a safe haven for train jockeys. Now somebody he didn't know was playing ghost town sheriff. "Look, I'm here to see Aubrey . . . Aubrey Fenton," he yelled out, trying to establish some common ground. "Either Aubrey or Frank McNeil. They were both here a few months back."

"You know Aubrey n' Mac?"

"Sure do."

"Well, if'n you know 'em, then what's their camp monikers?"

Parnell expected this. "They call Aubrey *Abracadabra* . . . Frank is known as *Muffin Man*."

A long silence, then "Okay, you're good. But I still want you comin' out nice and slow. No tricks."

Parnell smiled at Elaine, who exhaled in relief. He stood slowly, scanning the area carefully, pulling her up behind him. He raised his bandaged right hand high above his head to show he wasn't holding a weapon while keeping his left near his belt where he could draw his gun quickly if needed. They stepped out from behind the chimney, Elaine cowering behind him like a frightened child.

Fifty feet away stood a grungy, disheveled black man wearing a battered fedora with a snakeskin band. Long white chin whiskers gave him the appearance of a black billy goat. He gripped a hunting rifle, the barrel pointed at Parnell's breastbone. "Stop, right there," he instructed. "Who are ya and whaddaya want?"

Parnell stopped in his tracks. "Name's Derek," he said, quickly sizing the man up. The guy had the rugged outdoorsy look of a longtime drifter, but his stance and demeanor told Parnell he wasn't going to kill them.

The man thought this over a minute, then said, "You the one

they call King Midas?"

Parnell felt himself relaxing. Somebody in the camp had told this guy about him. "That would be me, yes."

The man lowered the rifle. "And who's the blinky twist hidin' behind ya?"

"This here is E," Parnell said, pulling Elaine around to his side. "We're just a couple of boxcar tramps come to visit."

"All right, then," the man said, walking toward them. "Cain't be too careful after what happened here."

"Guess not," Parnell said, still on alert. "You always shoot before you know what your target is?"

The man moved closer, revealing the ragged scar on his cheek—a jagged pink slash across dark chocolate skin. He tipped his head at them, said, "I'm a helluva shot, Mistah Midas. I can shoot the eyes out of a mosquito at three-hundred yards. If I meant to hit ya, I woulda."

Parnell said, "So what did happen here? Where is everybody?"

"Old man Perkerson—the rancher who owns all this land—he went on the warpath coupla days ago. Guess he got tired of us homesteadin' out here. Practically called out the National Guard. No skin offa his rich-ass nose, this bein' probly five miles from dat mansion he calls a farmhouse. But he done it anyway. Dis place was crawlin' with pigs and immigration asswipes. Craziest shit you ever did see . . . helicopters n' Jeeps n' badges everwhere. Complete chaos, I'm tellin' ya—mass hysteria. Rounded everbody up n' hauled 'em off to jail. Deported the illegals. You know how dis state is about illegals."

"Yeah, I sure do," Parnell replied, thinking about his friends sitting behind bars. "So, who are you, my friend? How do you fit into all this? I've been coming here for years and never saw you before."

"My apologies for my rudeness," the man said, removing his hat. "They call me Razzmatazz . . . Razzy for short. Been stayin' here 'bout six weeks now. I was out huntin' when the roundup shit came down. Got back to camp just in time to see the bastards cuffin' my brothers and haulin' 'em off. It disgusts me, I tell ya Mistah Midas. We wadn't hurtin' no one out here . . . jest mindin' our own bidness."

Parnell knew the landowner, Carl Perkerson, to be a multi-millionaire with major interests in the oil and pharmaceutical industries, as well as being a big-time corporate rancher. If the man had cared that much about this part of his expansive property, he would have repaired the cabin that had burned more than twenty years ago. Rounding up Parnell's hobo friends had been nothing but a power play by a self-absorbed asshole.

"Yeah, I know what you mean," Parnell said to Razzy. "Hardly seems right, does it?"

"Lotsa things ain't right in dis world, Mistah Midas. I done learned dat when I was a young un."

Elaine spoke up. "So where are they keeping your friends, Mr. Razzmatazz?"

"Please, call me Razzy, Mizz E. An' as to yer question, I believe they bein' held down to the Yavapai County Jail, south o' here a ways. Least the ones not headed back to Mexico."

Parnell knew that Yavapai was the only facility nearby large enough to house a roundup like this. "Okay," he said, "we'll sleep here tonight. Bright and early tomorrow we'll hike down and catch a freighter on the fly, head to Yavapai and bail our friends out. Care to join us, Razzy?"

Razzy nodded, returned his fedora to his white-haired head. "Wouldn't miss it fer the second comin', Mistah Midas. Gets awful lonely out here at night widout 'em."

"Good. Got any grub?"

Razzy smiled. "I'm a helluva hunter. Been huntin' fer the camp since I got here. On de menu tonight we got fresh-kilt coyote. A big un, too. Mighty tasty when they cooked up right."

"You bagged a coyote?" Parnell said, impressed, knowing how cagey and intelligent the creatures were.

"Yesiree, I did. I nail one a them dirty dawgs ever coupla weeks. Ya just hafta know how to track 'em."

"You hear that, E?" Parnell said to a very pale Elaine. "We're having a gourmet dinner tonight."

Elaine had a green look about her.

Midnight Train Confessional

TWO NIGHTS LATER Parnell and Elaine rode the rails, headed north to Colorado. They sat snug in the corner of an intermodal shipping container amongst pallets of computer equipment, which occupied most of the available space. They had broken into the huge container under cover of darkness in the Burlington-Northern switching yards, lucky to have avoided detection by train yard bulls.

They hunched close together in the pitch dark, listening to the rhythmic *clumpety-clump* rumble of steel wheels traversing the tracks below. Over the clatter, Parnell heard Elaine sneeze. The cloying plastic smell of the shipping covers and polyester strapping got to her. It bothered Parnell, too, even though he found it preferable to the usual livestock and coal dust smells of open boxcars. Much cleaner riding in a container unit lashed to a flatcar like this.

He and Elaine had spent the past two days dealing with the Yavapai County sheriff, bailing eleven of Parnell's hobo friends out of jail. The charges ranged from loitering and vagrancy to trespassing and even public indecency. Parnell had wanted to deck a couple of the smartass deputies who had little use for the homeless, but knew unless he wanted to join his friends behind bars, it was best to maintain his cool.

When Sherriff Dunleavy and Judge Holton discovered that Parnell—contrary to his ragged appearance—was a man of wealth, they set bail so high it was nothing short of financial rape. He had visions of Yavapai County officials building a new courthouse with the funds he'd dished out to free Abracadabra Fenton, Muffin Man McNeil, and nine others. Afterward, he and Elaine had helped them get set up in a new camp, south of old man Perkerson's ranchland. Razzy seemed happy to have his little community back intact. But it wasn't all the original Sycamore Canyon camp crowd. Six were illegals and had been handed over to INS for deportation. Unfortunately there was nothing Parnell could do for them.

He had wanted to pay a visit to the wealthy rancher, Carl Perkerson, and mess with his head a little, make him pay for what he had done to his friends. But there wasn't time. He and Elaine had to get on to Colorado for more pressing business. Parnell had called Blanton Miles and told him he wanted a few of his people out there to screw with the rancher a little. He told Miles he didn't want the animals harmed. Maybe just rough up the asshole enough to make him see the light. Of course Blanton Miles—being the voice of reason—warned him it wasn't the best idea. Parnell didn't care about good ideas. He despised these rich scumbags who used their power and influence to harass and harness the less fortunate. And so, in the next few days, Mr. Big-time Pharmaceutical-Oil Baron-Rancher Carl Perkerson would get a midnight visit from a couple of Parnell's more ruthless employees. He'd told Blanton that he wanted a full report when the deed was done and Miles had grudgingly agreed.

"So is that story true you told me? Did you really have a dream about being Robin Hood?"

Elaine's voice pulled him out of his reverie. "Yeah. Why?"

"I just think it's funny, that's all."

"How so?"

"I have trouble visualizing you in green tights."

"What—you don't like my legs?"

"Was I your Maid Marian?"

"Yeah, and I have *no* trouble visualizing you in what you were wearing!"

She laughed and slapped him on the arm. "You're such a tease." She caressed his wrist. "How is your hand? Still sore?"

"A little."

A long stretch of silence, then, "Why do you live this way, Derek?"

"What way?"

She sighed, a long, breathy groan. "*This* way. Like a poverty-stricken bum. I mean, come on. You have the means to drive or even fly to your destinations—"

"Get serious, Lainey!" Parnell interrupted. "No way I can fly into remote hobo camps."

"You know damn well what I mean. You can afford to buy your own plane. You have the money to stay in elegant hotels and to eat in five-star restaurants. But no. You elect to hitch rides on freight trains, bathing only when you're near a clean river or pond. You sleep on the ground or in boxcars. You eat what amounts to fresh road kill. I don't get it. Why don't you enjoy the good life you've worked so hard for?"

Parnell thought for a minute, then said, "I'm sensing my lady doesn't approve of my adventurous lifestyle."

"Why do I bother?" she said in exasperation.

He sensed she was about to go hormonal on him again, and he didn't want this conversation to go there. "Okay, listen," he said. "You deserve to know some things about me, I guess."

"You *guess*? We've been together, what? Six years? And you *guess* I deserve to know some things? Jesus, Derek!"

"Calm down, E. I didn't mean it like it sounded."

"How do you mean it, then?"

"Look, I live this way because . . . well, because I'd feel like a fraud if I didn't. Okay?"

"A fraud?"

"Yeah, I just wouldn't feel right traveling in luxury when so many of my friends have nothing but the rags on their backs . . . when folks actually feel lucky to call a broken-down port-o-let or a cardboard box home. Most of my hobo buds did nothing to deserve their fate. They're good people who've been delivered some bad breaks. They look up to me because of my money and the way I dole it out so freely. That makes me feel like a fraud. They call me King Midas, which makes me feel like an even bigger fraud. I didn't really earn it. Oh sure, I've turned it into a larger portfolio by educating myself about the financial world and hiring the right people to manage it. But I never really earned it initially. I never felt it was mine to spend on myself."

"But I thought your late wife's family was rich."

They had never discussed this—the source of his wealth. Parnell had always just let Elaine believe his money came from his late wife's fortunes. He thought about his relationship with Barbara and her family, felt the anger bubble up in his throat.

"They're disgustingly filthy rich," he said with disdain. "But I never saw any of the Logan money. Barbara didn't leave me a dime in her will. She and her snooty family and pretentious yuppie friends always looked down their aristocratic noses at me. To them I was the blue collar redneck pest exterminator who reeked of insecticides. No better than a bothersome little cockroach. A second-rate human being. Babs always bragged to anyone who'd listen what a stud I was in the sack. Said I was the only guy who ever could scratch her itch. It was degrading the way she treated me . . . the way *they* treated me. I hated them . . . I despised my-self."

"But you were married to her for what? Twelve years?"

"Just short of twelve years, yeah. A dozen *long* years. Felt like twice that long."

"So why'd you stay with her?"

He tried to think of the best way to be evasive, a way to be truthful, yet vague. Finally he said, "It wasn't all bad. Babs and her friends were always talking about their money and material possessions. They were obsessed with the pursuit of wealth. They thought I was just a stupid bumpkin who couldn't possibly under-stand all the lofty financial concepts they discussed, so they talked freely around me. Like I was a retarded child. But I listened to every word and picked up a lot—Offshore banking regulations, setting up shell corporations, using float to your advantage, laun-dering questionable revenues, shadow loans, marketable securities, hop-scotch investing. I learned the best place to invest was in American green technology startups operating in China, mainly because the Chinese realize what green technology can do for their economy while the U.S. politicos continue to line their pockets with oil money. I learned all that and more from these arrogant snits who thought they were so above me. I felt like a kept man, but I got one hell of a financial education."

The train rattled onward, the car swaying side to side.

Elaine said, "The sex must have been pretty hot . . . I mean, to stay in a situation like that."

Parnell chose his words carefully. "That's all it was between Babs and me . . . flammable pheromones or something. There was nothing more to it than that."

"But then, there was your daughter. You've never talked much about her before. I'm sorry to bring her up, Derek, but—"

"No, it's okay," he said, surprised that he felt like talking about Jennifer. He and Elaine had only danced around the issue of his deceased daughter to this point in their relationship, never really getting to the heart of it. The words seemed to spill from his mouth freely, easily. "My marriage to Barbara was crazy . . . a loveless mistake. But it produced a wonderful daughter. Jennifer— my little Jen-Jen. That girl was the light of my life. I miss the hell out of her." Parnell thanked the opaque darkness that prevented Elaine from seeing the tears pooling in his eyes. "She would have turned eighteen last month. I would have given her the biggest

birthday bash ever thrown—a celebration to end all celebrations."
He quit talking, not trusting his voice as tears slid down his
cheeks.

Elaine rubbed his arm. "I'm so sorry."

"Yeah, me, too. My little Jenny was all I had. I used to read
her bedtime stories when Babs was out partying with her friends.
Jen-Jen loved *Cinderella* and *Jack and the Beanstalk*. All the fairy
tales. And she made up her own stories. She was so creative. She
used to make me laugh when she would act out all the parts of her
kiddy tales, doing different voices for each character. Jenny was a
little ham. I'm telling you, Lainey, my little girl was destined for
Broadway. My favorite was the one she did about Woofy the Dog,
where she would bark out the dialogue. She was adorable . . ." He
stopped, feeling himself perched on a shaky edge, the tears flowing. He snuffled back a sob.

"Are you crying?" Elaine asked in the darkness.

"No—I'm . . . I'm just tired, that's all."

"It's okay to cry. It's good for you to let it go. I like seeing
you like this. You don't show this side of you enough."

"What side? Wounded? Weak?"

"Why do men think crying is a weakness?"

"Because it is."

"No, it's not, Derek. Look, you can't be a tough guy all the
time," she said, running her hand through his hair. "You suffered a
terrible loss. You're entitled to get emotional about it. In fact, if
you'll permit me some blunt honesty here, I'll say I've long felt
the reason you live the life of a wandering hobo is because of guilt
. . . guilt over the fact you weren't able to prevent what happened
to your daughter. You weren't able to help her and that's why you
keep having those fire nightmares. Please don't be mad at me for
saying that."

Parnell felt an alien emotion wash over him. He couldn't
define it exactly, but he felt a great burden being lifted from him.
He leaned into her, draped his arm across her shoulders, taking in
her warmth, her softness, her scent.

"I'm not mad at you, Lainey," he said, feeling closer to her
emotionally at this moment than he ever had. "I actually agree
with what you just said."

"You do?"

"Yeah. I've thought about it a lot the seven years Jen-Jen's
been, um . . . gone."

"What? That maybe you've been beating yourself up over it? Punishing yourself?"

"Exactly."

"So it's more guilt than fraud that drives you," she said, a statement, not a question.

Parnell thought for a moment. "Actually, it's more than that," he said. He laid his head against her shoulder. "This nurse I met on my last trip through Albuquerque—the one who fixed up my hand—she thought I was a real hard case."

"You *are*, Derek. That's a side of you that gets me totally hot—your dangerous side. I've told you that before."

"Oh yeah?" he said, thinking if she really knew how dangerous he was she would probably leap off this moving train in a heartbeat. "This nurse—Annie was her name—she said I had tombstone eyes . . . the eyes of a killer."

A long silence ensued, the only sounds the rattle and hum of the container car as the train pushed northward.

When Elaine didn't respond, he continued. "I've got a confession to make," he said, feeling her stiffen a little next to him. "I've had to, um . . . I've had to . . ."

"What? Just say it, Derek. You've had to kill a few people? That's what Madame Crystal was talking about, isn't it? That's what she meant when she mentioned the murders, isn't it? About there not being any statute of limitations on murder?"

He searched for the right words.

"How many, Derek?"

"I don't think it's necessary to go into—"

"*Tell* me," she demanded. "How many notches have you got on that gun belt of yours?"

Parnell was amazed at how little they really knew about each after six years. But then, they'd spent a goodly part of those years apart, thanks to his wanderings. "Thirteen," he said. "How unlucky is that?"

Elaine let out a long, slow whistle before saying, "Unlucky for who? You or the victims?"

"They all deserved to die, Lainey."

"Oh, I don't doubt that," she said. "Jessie Waltham was one of them, wasn't he?"

"Yeah."

"How?"

"I went shark fishing in San Francisco Bay. Near Alcatraz.

Used that psycho for bait. Look, Elaine, I had to do some—"

"Say no more. I'm glad you got rid of that piece of trash."

"You are? But I thought—"

"I know what you thought," she said. "Keeping my feelings repressed about Jessie made it easier to get through each day. But I knew when I never heard from him again that you had taken care of the problem somehow."

They sat in silence for so long, Parnell became uncomfortable.

"What are you thinking?" he said.

A long pause before she answered. "You have always thought me to be naïve and innocent, especially when it came to your . . . shall we say, violent activities? I never thought you were a choirboy, Derek. Several times you've come back to Flagstaff worse for the wear. Blood on your clothes. Bruises, cuts, broken bones."

She stopped, collecting her thoughts. The silence dragged on. In the distance Parnell heard a muffled train whistle. Coming up on a crossing, he thought.

"I'll let you in on a little secret," she said finally. "I have always had a thing for dangerous men. Shit, it cost me my left eye and a lucrative modeling career. But before Jessie Waltham I had a couple of relationships with guys from the wrong side of the tracks, men who made Jessie look like a Boy Scout. One was a Death Row inmate at San Quentin. It started out innocently enough. Just occasional correspondence. Frank had seen several of my bra and panty layouts I had done for Maidenform and he contacted my agent. Said he wanted to meet me. Frank Jarshick was his name. He had been convicted eight years earlier on a double-murder charge. Killed two people during a botched drugstore robbery in West Hollywood. Frank was housed in the North Seg barracks of the prison where he got more privileges than most. We wrote each other letters for a while. I would include sexy photos of myself. The letter writing led to phone calls, which finally progressed to visitations. It was wild and risky—a real thrill ride—and it turned me on something fierce. But like your relationship with your ex, it ended up being just a physical thing. I was young. *So* damned young."

"What happened to him?"

"He ran out of appeals and was executed. They stuck him with the needle about a year before I met Jessie."

"Christ, E, you really know how to pick 'em."

"We all have our crosses to bear, don't we?"

"I reckon."

"I don't have any regrets, if that's what you're thinking, Derek."

"No—I'm the last one who should be judgmental," he said, hearing the *ding-ding-ding* of the railroad crossing bells whoosh by outside, the different timbre of wheels meeting tracks as they passed through the intersection.

"You know, all this talk has got me horny," she whispered, her warm breath tickling his ear. "How about you?"

He felt her hand tug at his zipper, her fingers flutter along the edge of his erection, teasing him with slow feathery touches.

"I'm getting there," he said as she continued to work on him.

Soon they were naked and Elaine straddled him.

"Ohhh—goddamn, honey, I love the way you fill me up!" she breathed, rocking in his lap in time with the movement of the swaying train car. "Fuck me, Derek! Show me how dangerous you can be, baby!"

Soon Parnell fell over the edge, dropping into paradise.

And then, a sonic boom ripped a hole in the night.

The concussion slammed them against the wall. Momentarily dazed, Parnell grabbed a pallet strap and hung on, pulling Elaine close with his other arm. Gravity pinned them to the side of the pallet as the anchor cables snapped and their container uncoupled from the railcar, scraping across cinders and gravel. They held on tightly as they jounced over railroad ties with a deafening *thump-ety-thumpety-thump* sound. A series of pops like automatic gunfire rent the air as their shipping container separated from the flatcar. Parnell felt his stomach fall away as their container left the tracks and plunged downward, sliding down a steep ravine.

Slip-Sliding Into the Heart of Darkness

E LAINE SCREAMED IN HIS EAR. She clung to him, arms around his neck, choking him. The rampaging container flattened bushes and small trees on its long, sliding descent.

Their container sideswiped a rocky ledge with a grating, screeching scrape, the blow peeling back the siding and knocking the wind out of Parnell. He gasped for breath as Elaine held on to him with a vise grip. His arms ached, but he held on. They slid another twenty yards before slamming into a rock outcropping. The runaway shipping container finally came to a jolting stop.

A whirlwind of dust and gravel swirled through the ripped-open sidewall. Parnell could feel Elaine's sweaty naked body next to his, trembling in his grasp.

"You okay?" he asked her.

She nodded her head against his chest. "I think so," she murmured in a weak, shaky voice.

Muffled gunshots exploded in the distance. Parnell heard screams, clips of conversation.

"What's going on?" Elaine whispered.

"Train robbers," he answered, knowing they needed to make a quick escape.

Parnell knew of the recent rise in train-jacking incidents but had never witnessed one during his travels. In these desperate times, a new type of piracy had evolved. Freight trains carrying valuable cargo were hit in the middle of the night in remote areas. Explosives were used to derail trains, followed by the search for—and execution of—train security personnel and witnesses.

"Find your backpack, E," he said, fumbling around in the dark, searching for his pack and shoes. "Hurry! We've got to get out of here. Get some shoes on. We're going to have to make a run for it."

More gunshots. Closer now.

Laughter. A pleading voice. Another gunshot.

Silence.

He located his backpack and gun, strapped the gun belt and holster around his naked waist, quickly grabbed a pair of boots from the pack and slipped them on without tying the laces (hobo rule number one: always carry a second pair of shoes). No time for his clothes. They'd have to run in the buff.

"You got everything, Lainey?" he said, watching her hurriedly strap sandals to her feet.

"Got my pack, yeah, but we're naked, Derek."

"Better to be naked and alive than dead and clothed."

Cautiously Parnell peered out, searching the area. The moonlight cast a silvery sheen over the hillside and the destruction up around the tracks. Most of the railcars remained bunched up. Parnell realized they had been lucky that their container had separated from their railcar and slid down into this gully. He could see the outline of the path they had taken—a giant gouge running straight down the hillside. He could see a couple of other, more jagged, scars on the hill, at the end of which sat shipping containers that had come to rest on their sides or upside-down. Seeing that destruction, he realized how lucky they'd been that their container hadn't flipped end-over-end on its descent. He and Elaine most likely would have been killed had their container flipped out of control like that.

It would take the train pirates a while to get down here to investigate. But as Parnell thought this, he saw two men carrying rifles carefully making their way down the hillside.

"Come on!" he urged Elaine. "Time to run."

They hopped down from the wrecked container. The burnt metallic odor of scraped steel stung Parnell's nostrils. The heavy scent of ammonium nitrate told him the robbers had used a cheap fertilizer-based explosive to derail the train. He saw several small fires up along the tracks. The two trainjackers cradling rifles were maybe a hundred yards down the hill, headed toward them.

He and Elaine ran. He let Elaine lead while he covered the rear in case the men spotted them and opened fire. She sprinted ahead of him, several hundred yards downhill, Elaine losing her bandana do-rag, her hair coming loose and flying wildly about her face as she ran.

After what seemed an eternal run, they made it to the edge of the forest where they hid behind a pair of huge boulders.

"Talk about explosive sex!" Elaine said, huffing and puffing, trying to catch her breath.

Parnell laughed—a nervous chuckle. He could sense her fear as he watched her rummage through her pack and pull out a change of clothes. She stepped into a pair of shorts and pulled on a T-shirt.

Parnell quickly pulled clothes out of his own pack while taking a cautious peek over the rock, up the slope to where the two men with rifles stalked the wrecked container. He watched one of the men climb up into the container while the second guy searched the perimeter.

"I doubt they'll venture too far into the woods at night," he said, pulling on a pair of pants.

Elaine turned and looked behind her, into the dark maw of the thick forest. "We're going in *there*?" she asked.

"You got any better ideas?"

Suddenly, a long, low caterwauling sound came from nearby, sounding like a woman in distress.

"What the hell was that?" Elaine whispered.

A similar, high-pitched call came from deeper in the forest.

"Bobcats," Parnell said, knowing the distinctive sounds of the small cats to be either mating calls or territorial communications.

Elaine said, "Please tell me you're making that up, Derek."

"Don't worry," he said, pulling on a long-sleeved shirt. "They don't eat much. Come on. We need to make ourselves scarce."

A bobcat wailed again, closer this time.

"No way I'm going in there," she said, backing away from the edge of the forest.

"Look, it's either disappear in the woods or deal with those psycho train robbers out there. I'll take my chances on the bobcats."

He was twenty yards into the forest when he heard her whisper-shout, "Hey, wait for me!"

They trudged onward through the thick brush, the gunshots and shouts fading behind them as they moved deeper into the forest. Bushy treetops cut out any trace of moonlight and Parnell used the thin beam of his pencil flash to lead the way. Not great navigational lighting, but it beat total darkness.

Nocturnal creatures made noises all around them. He felt Elaine behind him, grabbing hold of his belt loops to keep him close, her breath tickling the back of his neck. The bobcats cried out a few more times before they faded away completely.

By Parnell's estimation they were in the heart of Navajo

country, maybe 30 miles northwest of Chinle, in no-man's land due north of the Canyon de Chelly national monument. He checked his compass, knowing that if they kept heading north, they would eventually pick up rail lines that would take them on up to Durango.

They continued on through the night, hiking through the dense forest, taking the path of least resistance, making their way through the twisted underbrush. About two hours in, they came upon a well-traveled path that meandered in a northeast direction. They stayed on the path, Parnell thankful for the easier navigation.

Near dawn, as the skies above them paled, their adrenaline all used up, exhaustion began to sap Parnell. He wanted nothing more than to lay down and catch some sleep, and knew from Elaine's huffing and puffing and slowed pace that she was also exhausted. Gotta keep moving, he told himself. Too dangerous to pass out in these woods. He kept up a whispery banter as they walked to keep Elaine alert and with him.

An hour later, they came to a clearing. At the back of the clearing sat a dilapidated shack with a weathered tin roof. Parnell figured it was a hunting lodge. The place didn't look like it had seen any activity recently. Nonetheless, he drew his weapon and approached cautiously. Elaine drew her small pistol and walked close behind.

They approached the sagging porch that held a rotted wooden bench and an old rocking chair. Bushy vines snaked over the railing. Parnell stepped up on the porch flooring, a board squeaking underfoot. He tried the front door, which pushed open easily. He stepped into the dim interior, leading with his gun.

He waved the penlight around the room, dust motes dancing in the beam. A battered sofa sat against the far wall. A scarred table sat in front of the couch, several beer cans and a half-filled bottle of Wild Turkey on top. Next to the whiskey sat an ashtray overflowing with butts. A bearskin rug covered a quarter of the floor. Animal heads were mounted on the walls—mule deer, elk, bighorn sheep, antelope. Parnell focused the light on a bear head that sneered at them in frozen rage.

Definitely a hunting lodge. But when was it last used?

They checked out the rest of the cramped shack—the walk-in kitchen, the small room in the back with a stained mattress on the floor, the closet-sized bathroom, really nothing more than a glorified privy, the small shower stall rigged to use rainwater collected in an overhead cistern. It didn't appear that anyone had been here recently, but it was difficult to tell. Clearly the place was deserted now.

"You know," Elaine said pointing down at the mattress on the floor, "as grungy as that thing is, right now it looks like a cloud in heaven. Are we gonna be here long enough to get some sleep?"

"Yeah," Parnell said, seeing the nasty bruise on her arm. He wondered how many bruises he'd picked up from the tumbling around they'd done inside the runaway container. He felt like he'd been run over by a truck. Weariness held him captive. His knees and ankles ached. Every joint screamed in pain. He knew Elaine was battered and bruised, too. She was being a trooper, trying to prove to him how tough she was, and Parnell appreciated it. "We both need to rest up," he said. "You take the mattress. I'll grab a nap on the sofa out front."

"You think we're safe here?" she asked.

"Yeah, I do," he told her, though he wasn't sure. Something about this shack didn't sit right with him, but he wasn't going to show those doubts to her. He touched her shoulder. "Go on. Lay down and get some sleep. You deserve it. We'll both need our energy to get up north later."

He left her in the back room and went out front, stretched out on the musty-smelling sofa. A spring kept poking him in the ass and he moved around to get comfortable. He smelled stale cigarette smoke, yeasty beer, the sharp medicinal tang of whiskey. The place reeked like a bar at closing time. He picked up a beer can—cheap stuff, Pabst Blue Ribbon—an unopened can amongst many empties. The bottle of Wild Turkey was half full, the amber liquid at the top of the turkey's legs on the label. Two sticky shot glasses sat nearby.

Somebody had been here recently, maybe as recently as yesterday.

He didn't like it. Didn't like it at all.

Though he was exhausted, his adrenaline surged. His senses were on alert. Best if he stayed awake and kept guard while Elaine caught a few winks in back. He sat up, shook his head, tried to clear the fog. Stretched. His tired muscles and joints protested.

As the sun began to peek above the treetops, the room brightened, the animal heads on the walls looking less threatening. Parnell dug into his backpack, pulled out his canteen and a vial of pills, shook two white tabs out into his palm and washed them down with hefty glugs of water. Nothing like caffeine pills to trick the mind into staying awake.

Soon he was infused with new energy and couldn't sit still. He decided to get up and move around, do a little exploring. He checked out the cast-iron fireplace, poked around the ashes. A faint heat rose from underneath the charred logs. Yet another clue that the shack had been occupied recently. He strolled out onto the front porch and looked around, noticing something they had missed on the way in. Propped in a dim corner was what looked like a rifle with camouflaged stock. Closer inspection revealed it to be a high-powered crossbow with a multiplex scope. A couple of Parnell's old Army buddies were crossbow hunting enthusiasts, and he knew this weapon was capable of bringing down the largest of game from a good distance away. A very serious weapon. Parnell knelt and reached into the lock-on quiver mount, pulling out an arrow. He held it up, the sunlight gleaming off the aluminum shaft, dried blood crusted on the serrated broadhead tip. He shivered, knowing the damage one of these suckers could do.

Parnell slid the arrow back into the quiver and left the crossbow in the corner. He decided to scout the property. He walked slowly around the side of the shack, tried without success to see in through the two grimy windows on that side. The roof sloped low on the back side for drainage, orange fingers of rust staining the tin. A huge hawk's nest sat in the shade of the chimney, vacant and silent.

He walked around to the rear of the property, noticing a makeshift walkway of smooth river stones leading away from the structure. He followed the stones, wondering where the path would take him. He passed through a crowded arbor of pine trees, the air redolent with a sweet-sap evergreen smell. Soon the pines thinned out and Parnell walked into a small clearing.

What he saw stopped him in his tracks.

He had entered Satan's playground.

Instinctively he reached for his gun.

Garden of Grotesqueries

A NIGHTMARISH PARADE OF OBJECTS surrounded him. Shrunken heads.

A dozen or more mounted on top of long wooden poles, which were sunk into the ground and spaced evenly around the airy glen. *Human* heads. A ring of macabre fence posts, a ghoulish collection of desiccated heads facing him like mummified sentries.

An icy creepiness traveled up his spine.

Slowly, carefully, his sweaty hand tight on the gun, he moved in for a closer look. He examined two heads positioned close together. Their facial features were distorted by the ravages of the shrinking process—eyelids sewn shut, jaws seriously distended, lips pinned together, foreheads collapsed, cheeks sunken. Most were bald, but a few had wispy strands of hair that blew in the gentle breeze like straw on coconuts. They reminded Parnell of emaciated scarecrows.

But they were definitely human. Or at least had been human at one time.

He turned in a slow circle, taking in the gruesome sight. What the hell kind of a hunting lodge is this? he wondered.

Each head was stained brownish-orange, a tint matching the rust streaks on the shack's tin roof. Parnell assumed the strange coloration was the result of tannins used in curing the skin for shrinkage. He reached out and touched one on the cheek, felt the tight leathery skin stretched over the smooth hard surface of whatever was used to replace the skulls underneath.

He had seen some weird shit in his time, but this was another level of gonzo altogether.

Who were these unfortunate souls? Had they been fellow hobos with whom Parnell had shared a meal? Old friends who had exchanged stories over an open campfire? Maybe fellow peyote poppers? Difficult to tell. The facial features were indistinguishable.

How long had these people been dead? Who killed them? Why had they been decapitated with their heads mounted on poles out here in the Arizona wilderness?

In search of answers, Parnell walked out of the circle of death, further away from the shack, returning to the deep woods. If there were heads, there might be bodies somewhere nearby. Maybe he could find the discarded skulls.

He followed a narrow path that had been carved through the ponderosa pine, looking for signs of body parts or a blood trail. He stopped periodically to look behind rocks or to pull away twisted underbrush. Nothing. But he figured the path was there for a reason, and so he kept on.

Soon he came upon a small creek. Instantly he was overcome by a feeling of déjà vu so strong it made him lightheaded. He sat on a boulder near the bank and observed the scene, trying to determine why this setting looked familiar. Parnell knew he'd never been here before, but something about the gurgling creek and the layout of the trees beyond spoke to him in a language he couldn't remember.

And then it hit him. This was the identical setting from his Robin Hood dream.

Which set him to thinking that maybe this was another of his fevered dreams. Was it possible that Little John and Friar Tuck would appear from out of the trees momentarily? Could it be that Maid Marian was up around the bend? For the sake of those unfortunate souls who'd lost their heads back in that ghastly garden, Parnell hoped this was all just one of his patented warped dreams.

He got to his feet and followed the path along the creek until it stopped, looked around. Saw a flash of white in his peripheral vision, something on the other side of the creek, behind a tangle of brushwood.

He craned his neck, trying to get a better look. He stepped into the creek—leaving his hiking boots on to protect his feet against sharp rocks—and waded across the shallow stream. Reaching the far side, it took him several tries to negotiate his way up the slick bank. Muddied, feet numb from the ice-cold water, he finally traversed the bank and approached the twisted underbrush where he'd seen the white flash.

Parnell peeled back the thick tangle of vines and felt his heart leap into his throat.

He saw dozens of human skulls and bones, all stripped clean and sun-bleached a bright white. It looked like photos he'd seen of the killing fields in Cambodia. Leg bones and arm bones and rib cages littered the forest floor. The skulls had been thrown into a wide pit. Further back sat a large bloodstained rock with a flat top—unmistakably the processing slab. Against the rock leaned a saw, the teeth of its serrated blade blood-encrusted. A swarm of flies buzzed around it in a gray cloud. Several rawhide bags containing ivory-handled knives hung from tree limbs. A couple of large machetes lay on the ground, their curved blades reflecting glints of sunlight. Nearby a squat cast-iron cauldron sat in the shade, dark and ominous. No telling what gruesome ingredients it contained.

He caught a putrid smell on the light breeze—the death-knell scent of decaying flesh—and he fought to control his gag reflex.

And then he heard the screams.

Elaine! Panicked and urgent. Coming from the shack.

Each scream hit him like a bullet to his brain.

Hurriedly, he splashed back across the creek and sprinted through the woods, his legs numb and uncooperative.

Elaine's shrieks became more urgent. He heard her screaming his name.

He bolted down the path, low branches slapping his arms and shoulders as he ran. He tripped over stones and underbrush, his boots soggy and squishy.

He reached the grisly garden in full stride, hitting one of the poles with an elbow, knocking it flat, the head separating and bouncing across the hard-packed dirt.

He kept running, Elaine's cries chilling him to his core.

Midstride, he checked his gun to make sure the safety was off. His legs and lungs burned. His breaths came harder, faster. His wet boots felt like concrete blocks. Parnell's mind seethed in a black rage. He'd kill anyone who touched Elaine. Without hesitation.

He broke through the woods, the rear of the shack coming into view. Parnell slowed his pace and approached carefully, visually scanning his surroundings for any interlopers. It appeared he was alone.

He heard Elaine's muted cry from inside the shack, "Get away from me! Please don't hurt me! Oh, Jesus . . . not that! Oh mother of God! Derek! Help!"

Parnell moved quickly, stealthily, making his way around the side to the front porch. He entered the front room, both hands on his gun, keeping it out in front of him, maintaining a shooter's stance, ready to fire at anything that moved.

He heard sounds of struggle in the back room—Elaine's protests, something being dragged across the floor, bodies thumping against the flimsy wall. Parnell moved down the dim hallway, finger tense on the trigger, hearing Elaine calling his name, his nerves about to short circuit. Fury surged through him like a sinister venom.

He stood to the side of the doorframe, peeked in, saw the backside of a big guy in camouflage hunting togs with shoulder-length salt-and-pepper hair. The big man had Elaine pinned against the far wall. Thrown on the mattress was a large crossbow and a quiver full of arrows. Parnell could only see Elaine's right arm and a tangle of her hair from this angle. He knew he would be endangering her if he opened fire. His Walther semi-automatic would blow holes through his target, the bullets striking Elaine. *Got to hold my fire,* his mind screamed. *Got to separate them somehow.*

Then he saw the hunter swing his right arm free, saw the big blade of the hunting knife in his hand. Heard him say, "Time fer me to fuck yer other eye out, bitch!"

Parnell had to act.

He shouted out to attract the hunter's attention just as Elaine took matters into her own hands. Literally. It took Parnell several long seconds to realize what he was seeing—the guy doubling over and shrieking in pain, backing away from her, knife clattering to the floor. The hunter whirling, bringing his hands to his crotch and yelling, "You fucking bitch! You *hurt* me!"

As the man fell away, Parnell could see Elaine's flushed face, the scarring on the left side a bright crimson, her eye patch twisted up on her forehead exposing her shriveled eye socket. Her shirt was ripped open to her waist, a single naked breast exposed. She was roughed up, but she wore a thin triumphant smile as she watched her attacker struggling. She had grabbed him by his balls and twisted. That's my warrior princess! Parnell thought proudly. But then he noticed the blood running down her neck.

The scumbag had cut her.

The hunter recovered quickly, reaching down for his knife and rising up.

He came at Parnell in a blur of camouflage and flash of blade.

Parnell didn't hesitate. He fired—once . . . twice . . . a third time, watching his shots rip into the hunter, the first shredding his shoulder, the second and third nailing him in the chest and forehead. The man jerked spasmodically with each hit, then slumped against the wall and dropped to the floor, clutching the knife like it was his lifeline.

Parnell looked at the surprised far-off gaze on the guy's waxy face, the pool of blood spreading out beneath the body. No doubt he had left this world.

Parnell rushed to Elaine, who—sobbing and shaking—collapsed into his arms.

"Are you okay?" he asked while holding her close, rubbing her back, feeling her body shaking against him.

"The bastard tried to rape me," she blubbered into his shoulder.

Parnell could feel her tears and blood wetting his shirt. He pulled back from her, examined her neck, ran a finger along the wound, wiping the blood away, checking the severity of the cut. "Is it bad?"

She shook her head no, tears streaming down her cheeks. "He, um . . . he just held the blade there while he threatened me. It's not deep." She looked past Parnell, at the dead man on the floor, at all the blood that now resembled a small oil spill. Another tremor ran through her. "Shit, Derek, five more minutes and I'd have been like . . . *him*. Where *were* you?"

"It's okay, Lainey, everything's okay," he said, pulling her back into his arms, whispering into her hair, "I'm here. Nobody's gonna hurt you now."

Parnell held her and consoled her, whispered assurances in her ear, thinking how close he'd come to losing her. He brushed the tears from her cheek and kissed her, her lips quivery and stone cold as they met his.

"How touching," he heard a voice say from behind them.

Elaine let out a shriek. He whirled around, saw another hunter in camouflage training a lethal-looking crossbow on them. Parnell scrambled for his Walther he had dropped on the floor.

"Don't try it!"

Parnell knew he wouldn't be able to retrieve his gun and get a clean shot off without serious consequences.

Crossbow Man said, "This baby will slice your head clean off with the efficiency of a guillotine. Now kick that gun over to me, and no horseshit!"

Parnell's mind worked at warp speed. The black steel broadhead arrow tip was as wide as his hand and honed to a razor-sharp edge. He felt closed in, cut off. There was no room to maneuver in these close quarters. No chance for escape.

"C'mon, dipshit, move it!" the hunter spat. "Kick that gun in my direction, now!"

Parnell saw the guy was shaky and feared the arrow being launched. Slowly, he toed the Walther, gave it a shove with his foot, watched the gun slide across the floor, hoping he'd get his opportunity when the guy bent over to pick it up.

No such luck. Crossbow Man just stomped his muddy boot on the gun, continued to stare at Parnell and Elaine over the top of his weapon. "You kill't my brother," he said, glancing at the bloody corpse slumped against the wall.

Electric currents of rage raced through Parnell. He clenched his fists and said, "Yeah, well, look at the bright side. You've got another head to add to your collection out back."

The hunter's eyes narrowed to angry slits. "You just signed yer own death certificate with that comment, wiseass." He turned slightly, toward his brother's body. "I'm sorry they done this to you, Skeeter," he said with more anger than remorse. With his free hand, he crossed himself. "May God have mercy on yer soul, my brother."

"Skeeter?" Parnell said. "As in bloodsucking insect skeeter?"

"That's it, you cocksucker!" Crossbow Man roared. "Time fer yer funeral. Both you and yer sleazy shanty queen there. Let's go," he said, nodding toward the door and the hallway beyond. "You two first. One wrong move from either of ya and heads'll roll."

"Where're we going?" Parnell asked as he moved toward the door, being sure to keep himself between Elaine and the head-hunter.

"Out back. Time fer you and the one-eyed twist to join the menagerie."

Elaine bristled. "Listen you mangy creep, I'm not—"

Parnell silenced her with a look as they made their way side-by-side down the hallway, his expression telling her *Let me handle this*. He knew their best hope was to keep up the chatter, keep the yahoo thinking, hopefully knock him off his focus and gain the advantage.

Without turning his head, he said, "Menagerie, you say? That's a pretty fancy word. Big word, too. Four syllables to be exact. Sounds odd coming out of your mouth. You have any idea what it means?"

Crossbow Man huffed behind them. "What're ya sayin'? That I'm stupid or sumpthin'?"

Parnell smiled inwardly. The fool had taken the bait. "Well, it's been my experience that stupid people tend to use big words trying to convince others they're smart. I'm just sayin'. . ."

"I should shoot you right here where you stand, asswipe!"

Parnell stopped, turned and faced the menacing crossbow. "Go right ahead," he said, seeing the look of horror on Elaine's face. Parnell was playing the odds that the guy wouldn't kill them here, in the yard in front of the shack. Too much incriminating evidence left behind. Too much work to drag their bodies away. The guy was too lazy and paranoid. Crossbow Man would want to get them out back, closer to the bloody rock and their processing site across the creek.

"Turn around and keep walkin', both of ya," Crossbow Man said after a staring match with Parnell.

Parnell did as he was told, winking at Elaine in reassurance, letting her know he was in control and knew what he was doing.

As they were marched around the side of the shack, he went back to his chatter to hopefully open up an opportunity. "So just what is this operation you and Skeeter have going out here? This *menagerie*, as you so quaintly put it."

"You don't know? And you call *me* stupid? Unreal!"

"So enlighten me, then."

They were now entering the trees and the short walk through the woods to the garden of heads.

"You really don't get it, do you?" Crossbow Man said, impatience in his raspy voice. "No, you wouldn't. Yer just a smelly old hobo. You an' yer blinky bitch. Just a pair of clueless rail-ridin' scum ain't got a pot to pee in. People in the know like me an' Skeeter, we know folks with money. *Lots* a money. And these folks has got some peculiar tastes—things they're willin' to pay fer. They got a burning need fer one-of-a-kind things so they can brag to their friends about 'em. Makes 'em feel special. Me an' Skeeter, we deliver what they want. Supply and demand, ya know. Basic economics. It ain't easy what we do. These rich pricks pay us handsomely for our efforts. You understand that, wiseass?"

Parnell glanced at Elaine, saw the mixture of fear and confusion on her face. "Yeah, unfortunately I do," he acknowledged, thinking the time for him to make his move was getting short. "So tell me," he said, as they were marched into the woods, "who are the victims?"

"You sure are an inquisitive bugger."

"There's that vocabulary at work again. Any idea what *inquisitive* means, partner?" Parnell scanned the stone path ahead, looking for an opportunity.

"I've had enough of yer mouth! Shut yer pie hole and keep walkin'."

"Tell me who the victims are," Parnell persisted. "Consider it my final request." He snuck Elaine a look to reassure her there would be nothing final about it.

"Final request, huh? Okay, they're nobodies . . . just like you an' yer bitch. Hobos . . . hikers . . . hunters . . . anybody who strays into our territory. That's what they get fer trespassin'."

"Oh?" Parnell said. "You own all this land out here, do you?"

"I'm not answerin' any more of yer questions," he said, poking Parnell in the small of his back with the crossbow, prodding him along the path.

Only another fifty yards to the shrunken head cemetery. Parnell knew he had to make a move. The only thing he could do on this narrow trail would be to turn and kick the guy's weapon from his hands, hope the arrow didn't launch. Crossbow Man had only one shot, but he had the distinct advantage of positioning. Parnell knew if he misjudged his kick, he (and possibly Elaine) would be killed, or at the very least, badly maimed.

Suddenly, a series of gunshots echoed through the forest.

Chaos ensued.

Parnell heard a sharp intake of breath behind them, followed by a string of curses. He turned to see Crossbow Man going down, blood blossoming from multiple wounds in his camouflage hunting gear.

Parnell quickly shoved Elaine into the bush and pounced on her, kept her beneath him as he raised his head, checking the trail. The hunter—from his down position and bleeding profusely—fired the crossbow in desperation. The bow fired like a shot from a .22 rifle, the catapult mechanism releasing with a *swish-boing* sound. The arrow zipped down the path, striking the base of a tree with a heavy *thwonk* and a small explosion of wood chips. Return gunfire peppered the downed hunter, his body dancing with each strike.

What the hell? Parnell thought, looking up the trail and seeing nothing but a thick cloud of smoke. Elaine whimpered beneath him. He whispered to her, told her to stay down.

The forest returned to its previous calm. No bird sounds from the trees. Even the chittering insects had gone silent. The burnt-gunpowder stench of cordite fouled the air.

Parnell heard footsteps crunching in the packed dirt and he lifted his head, wishing like hell he had his Walther. A rangy black man wearing a dusty black fedora and snakeskin boots broke through the wall of smoke, walking slowly, cradling a high-powered rifle with a monstrous scope. Long platinum-white whiskers sprouted from his chin.

Parnell smiled. No need for his gun. Their guardian angel had returned. It was the black billygoat, Razzmatazz.

Parnell stood and called out, "Razzy? Is that you, my friend? What the hell're you doing here?"

"I could ask you the same thing," Razzy said. He approached them, stopping to nudge the downed hunter with the toe of his boot. "Looks like my trusty hogleg did the trick once again."

Shakily, Elaine got to her feet and stared slack-jawed at the aging black drifter. "Oh my God! It's *you*! Did you follow us here or something?"

"Yes'm, I sure enough did, Mizz E. I'm a tracker. That's what I do. Like I done tol' you before, I can track a flea on a coyote's ass across three continents." He reached around to his back pocket and pulled out the black-and-white polka-dot bandana she had lost on their run down the arroyo, fleeing from the train bandits. "Here, I think you forgot something."

Elaine took the scarf from Razzy. "You *tracked* us? I mean, I'm glad you did and everything, but . . . why?"

"Had a hunch you folks might need my help." Razzy looked down at the body sprawled across the path, the crossbow pinned under the right arm. "Turns out, I was right."

"You're smooth, Razzy," Parnell said. "I never picked up your shadow. You were on that train that got jacked?"

"Sure was. Nasty mess, that was, Mistah Midas. Got a bit tied up there dealin' with them pricks. That's what kept me from gettin' here sooner."

Parnell thought about the gunshots he'd heard after the train derailed. "You get into a shootout with them?"

"Sho' enough did. Quite an operation they had goin'. Musta

been fifteen of 'em an' they had a coupla moving vans to haul all the loot they rounded up. I nailed three of the bastards—winged a coupla more of 'em—before I made a run for it. Picked up you an' Mizz E's trail down the hill where your cargo container ended up."

"Well, you've got our thanks," Parnell said.

"Weren't nothin', Mistah Midas. You'da figured somethin' out if'n I hadn't come along."

"Maybe," Parnell said, thinking. "Still, though . . . What you did wasn't exactly a walk in the park."

Razzy propped a boot up on a rock and lay his rifle across a knee. He removed his fedora and wiped his head with a handkerchief, his white hair glistening like light frost on asphalt. The scar across his cheek pulsed with a pink neon glow. He spoke, his words measured and heartfelt. "Well, after you an' Mizz E bailed our friends outta jail an' got us set up in our new campsite, I started thinkin' about what was ahead. Nothin'—absolutely nothin' is what was in my future there." Razzy placed his kerchief in his shirt pocket, returned his hat to his head and adjusted the brim. "I got the itchy feet like I do so often. Couldn't sit still. Had to hit the trail again, go in search of somethin' different. An' lawd a mercy, didn't I find a whole shitload a *different* here!"

Parnell gave Razzy a grim smile and nodded. The man said it well. This was a hell the likes of which even Parnell had never before witnessed.

Razzy asked him, "Where you two headed next?"

"Up north to Colorado."

"Want some company?"

"Sure," Parnell said, understanding Razzy's restlessness. He shared the affliction, what some referred to as *the hobo's hotfoot.* "The more the merrier," he said, reaching out and clapping Razzy on the back. "And thanks for saving our asses, Mr. Razzmatazz."

The Legend of a King

THEY WERE A TRIO NOW.

Late that afternoon they had found the Burlington Northern-Santa Fe tracks well north of the hunting shack, and hooked onto a freighter. They rode in an empty livestock car, the vacant quarters reassuring Parnell that this was a freighter bare-backing on its return to Colorado after delivering stock in Arizona. Much less chance of train bandits pirating a bareback freighter.

They were all exhausted after the horrific events of this morning and the difficult hike through hardscrabble mountain country. Parnell worried about Elaine, who remained quiet. She had obviously been affected by what had gone on at the hunting shack. The experience had left Parnell rattled as well. Visions of shrunken heads floated through his subconscious like decapitated demons, smiling at him through their sewn lips, taunting him. He'd promised Lainey they would check into a nice hotel once they hit Durango. But the promise of a hot shower, modern conveniences, a soft bed, and a clothes shopping expedition did little to cheer her. She continued to slouch in a corner, lost in her silent stupor.

The train rumbled over the tracks with a hypnotic *thumpety-thump-clack*, *thumpety-thump-clack*, the railcar sashaying side to side in a sleep-inducing rhythm. Parnell felt drowsy, on the edge of sleep.

After a long silence, Razzy spoke. "You gonna get me a room in that fancy hotel up Durango way, Mistah Midas?"

Parnell grinned. "Shit, Razzy, after the way you saved our asses, I'll rent the entire presidential suite for you."

Razzy harrumphed. "No disrespect intended toward your fine offer, suh, but I don't wanna stay nowhere some stinkass politician done stayed!"

Elaine emitted a quick, throaty chuckle from her dark corner.

Parnell smiled. "See there, E?" he said to her. "You gotta like a man who shares our political sensibilities." He turned back to the old tracker. "I definitely like your ethics, Mr. Razzmatazz."

Though Parnell smiled at Razzy, he was still bothered by

nagging uncertainties about the man. What would possess anyone to track them alone through miles of wild forestland at night? Why would anyone take on that risk? Money? Working for someone with an unhealthy interest in Parnell or Elaine? Something else?

"If you don't mind my asking, what's your real name, Razzy?"

"My real name?" He seemed surprised at the question. "I was born Lucious Jones—Luke for short—more'n sixty-four years ago in a run-down tenement slum in the projects of Detroit. My childhood weren't pretty, if'n you know what I'm sayin'."

Parnell nodded, surprised the man was giving up information so easily. Most hobos didn't trust anyone, suspicion being their nature. Most drifters Parnell had known were extremely secretive until long-term bonds were forged.

Razzy seemed to sense this and said, "I know what you're thinkin' but by-gawd, that's my real name—Luke Jones. What I'm tellin' ya is the unvarnished truth. I'm the youngest of four kids. Both my parents is gone. My two older brothers and younger sister is all dead. My wife . . . well . . . she gone, too." Razzy paused to wipe at his eyes, then continued. "Me an' Eugenia, we never had no children ourselves. Just me now, fightin' the good fight. They's lots of wrong in this world, Mistah Midas. I just wanna make some things right before I shuffle on."

Parnell nodded, appreciating his candor. It seemed as though their new traveling companion was a fellow vigilante, one who shared Parnell's need for personal law enforcement. But still, something about the man unsettled him.

Parnell said to him, "What I'm not clear on, Razzy, is why you tracked us all those miles through rough terrain at night. What gives? You don't know Elaine and me from Bonnie and Clyde."

"Oh, but I do, suh, I really do," he said eagerly, dragging gnarled ebony fingers through his billygoat beard. "Leastways I know of your deeds. Let me explain. I've wanted to meet ya for a long time, Mistah Midas. You been like a legend to me. Last five years or so I traveled around to the camps where I heard the stories about ya. Stories 'bout how you always helpin' out your 'bo friends, how you spare no expense to make their lives better. How you even killed to protect 'em. So I tol' myself, Luke ol' boy, that there's a man I gotta meet, shake his hand. That's King Midas, a man I can respect. A man I could be proud to pattern what's left of my life after. I made it my mission to hook up with ya. So I kept travelin' around, hittin' the 'bo camps on your route—from down Tucson way all the way north up to the camps in southern Idaho, across Utah and Nevada, on out to the West Coast. Sometimes I'd pull into a 'bo village, and they'd tell me you just been there and left. Other times, they'd tell me you was comin' soon, so I'd stick around but you wouldn't show. Got frustratin', I gotta say, Mistah Midas. I done two tours in Nam back in the day, fightin' the god-damned politicians' war for 'em. Gotta say, that wasn't near as frustratin' as tryin' to track you down. An' I'm the best tracker this side o' Lewis and Clark.

"And then, strange twist o' fate, I finally run into ya at Syca-more Canyon. I seen first-hand how you help people in need, how you bailed 'em all outta jail and found a new home for 'em. You gotta unnerstand, this is like a dream come true for me—travelin' wit you and the missus . . . doin' good in the world. Ain't a whole lotta heroes left in this sorry ass country, but I think you're a bona fide hero."

Parnell digested this. He was flattered, but surprised and a little embarrassed for the man's naked idolatry. "Why didn't you just ask to come along? You had plenty of chances while we were resettling my Sycamore Canyon friends."

Razzy didn't hesitate. "Cuz I knew you wouldn't have no part of it. Was I right?"

Parnell nodded. "Yeah, probably so."

"I figured I had to prove myself to gain your trust. My best bet was trackin' you an' waitin' for an opportunity. Thought I mighta lost ya at the train wreck. Took somma my best tracking skills to pick up your trail again. After that, didn't take long to get my opening. Jesus, what the fuck was with them headhunters, man? That's some evil shit goin' on there."

Parnell glanced at Elaine, who hugged herself and visibly shivered. "Yeah," he said to Razzy. "What we witnessed back there was the dark side of capitalism, my friend."

"Dark don't begin to describe that mess. That was pitch black voodoo—the devil's work, Mistah Midas. Lucifer lives and breathes in that sorry place. Thought I saw some twisted shit in Nam, but—"

"Look, Razzy," Parnell said, shifting gears, "I don't mean to burst your bubble or anything, but I'm not King Midas . . . I'm not the king of anything. I can barely take care of myself, let alone preside over a kingdom. And I'm certainly not a legend or a hero.

I'm just a screwed-up guy with an incurable case of wanderlust. Elaine'll tell you that."

From Elaine's corner came, "The man *does* love his travel. I'm a Burlington-Northern train widow."

"Ouch," Parnell said, feigning hurt, though secretly he liked that Elaine was still tuned in.

To Razzy he said, "I'm flattered you find me so fascinating, but please, no more King Midas or Mr. Midas or talk of my so-called legendary status. I'm just Derek. Plain and simple. Let's leave it at that."

"Sure, okay . . . *Derek*," he said, trying out the name, looking uncomfortable with it.

Parnell wanted to know particulars, what it was that made Razzy think he was a legend or hero. Razzy Lucious Jones responded with an astounding encyclopedic knowledge of Parnell's past activities. He knew about Parnell meeting Elaine Leibrandt at the burn center in LA more than six years ago and paying her medical bills, then buying the house in Flagstaff for her, getting her set up in her new life. He even knew about several of the murders Parnell had committed. The home invasion sociopath who had tortured and raped a housewife and her young daughter before mutilating them and setting the house on fire to destroy all evidence. The mortgage banker who performed financial rape on his clients by setting up fraudulent loans, ensuring huge profits for his bank and guaranteeing foreclosure and eventual homeless status for nearly a dozen of Parnell's friends. The pedophile responsible for the grisly murders of seven children. Razzy knew about these murders in great detail, as well as several other dark deeds carried out by Parnell and his organization.

Surprisingly, he also possessed a strong working knowledge of Locomotion Enterprises. The tracker expounded in great detail about some of the elaborate legal burns Parnell and his employees had carried out. There was the shady financial consultant, cut from the Bernie Madoff mold, who scammed thousands out of their life savings using investment Ponzi schemes. The consultant—Richard Zarnovsky—was probably responsible for more homeless drifters than any other single entity. Parnell figured death was too easy for this guy, and so he went to work destroying the man. Parnell and several of his trusted key employees put a plan together that stole Zarnovsky's identity. Over a period of months they ruined him, wiping out his vast fortune literally overnight. When Parnell and his organization were done with him, Zarnovsky couldn't even rent a room in a roach motel. The last Parnell had heard, Richard Zarnovsky was drifting throughout the Southeast visiting hobo camps under the 'bo alias of Biggie Zee.

But perhaps the biggest and most complex sting Parnell had pulled off was the Colorado drug case four years ago whereby he had framed two DEA agents and a police chief after they busted three of Parnell's farming buddies for growing marijuana. Razzy seemed to know all about this one, too. All three farmers had been indicted on drug trafficking charges. They were facing up to 20 years in Trinidad Correctional. They would lose the land that had been in their families for four generations. Parnell and his associates went to work. A search of the two DEA agents' Crown Vics revealed bales of freshly cut marijuana in each trunk. A subsequent search of the police chief's home found bales of grass from the same harvest in his garage, and for good measure, rocks of cocaine and crystal meth in the chief's cruiser. The federal agents and police chief got ten-year prison sentences while the farmers had their slates wiped clean.

Parnell was stunned at the accuracy and breadth of information in Razzy's head. He asked him, "So how do you know all these things?"

Razzy looked at him through jaded eyes, "There ain't no secrets, Derek. If'n ya know the right questions to ask and *who* to ask, you get answers. You get enough answers an' ya learn people's secrets. It's simple really."

"What makes you think you're right? Those are pretty hefty accusations . . . calling me out for murder."

"Oh, I *know* I'm right, suh. I got what they call unimpeachable sources to back me up on each of 'em. I know a lot more'n what I told ya, too, but you don't have to worry none. I applaud what ya done. You been cleanin' up the environment, You an' me, we got more in common than you might think."

Parnell thought about the vicious, coldblooded way Razzy had gunned down the headhunter in the woods near the shack and the sympathetic way the tracker had talked about Parnell's deeds, like the man took every injustice as a personal affront. A man with a personal philosophy very close to his own.

But Parnell's suspicious nature gripped him tightly. He was uncomfortable being around someone who knew so much about his checkered past. He wondered about those anonymous unimpeachable sources Razzy Lucious Jones had cited. He questioned the man's true motivations. The guy was a sly old fox.

So what was he after? What did he want?

Parnell realized that if Razzy had meant any harm to him or Elaine, he'd had plenty of opportunities to act. And if he didn't have their best interests in mind, why did he blow away the head-hunter, saving them from a violent end?

But still, Parnell's suspicions nagged at him. As he watched Razzy drift off to sleep, he vowed to keep an eye on him. And when they hit Durango, he'd call Blanton Miles and ask him to dig up all he could on their mystery man.

Thumbelina

EXHAUSTION CARRIED HIM OFF TO DREAMLAND. Parnell knew he was dreaming because it made no rational sense to be sitting on his sofa in his house in upstate New York reading a children's story to his long-dead daughter. This house had burned to its foundation seven years ago and eleven-year-old Jennifer Parnell had gone with it . . .

. . . The oversized picture book lay open on his lap as he reads to five-year-old Jen-Jen. His daughter cuddles up next to him, leaning on his every word, her sweet warm breath tickling his arm. She loves the fairy tale of Thumbelina, the adventures of a little maiden named Tiny who lives inside the petals of a tulip. Jen-Jen gets scared when the ugly old toad shows up to wreak havoc on Tiny's tranquil little tulip world, then is held spellbound as Tiny floats down the stream on a leaf and encounters the good little field mouse. She boos when the deceptive mole—who shuns daylight and has a negative view of everything—enters the story, then cheers when Tiny revives the dying swallow and sets it free. When the swallow returns to save Tiny from her dreadful arranged marriage to the obnoxious mole, Jen-Jen bounces around on the sofa, singing "Tweet-tweet, Tweet-tweet," mimicking the happy chirps of the swallow.

"I wanna live in a tulip like Tiny does, Daddy."

"Well, you'd have to be a lot smaller for that to work, princess."

"I'm small."

Parnell laughed, pulled her close. "Yes you are, sweetcakes. But tulips are even smaller. And besides, you wouldn't want to mess with that nasty old toad or that creepy mole."

"Oh, I'd sock that gooshy old toad and make him go away and I'd sock that bad old mole, too."

Parnell laughs again, thinking: *She's certainly a Parnell.* He plants a kiss on her cheek. "Okay, c'mon, it's getting late. Go get ready for bed."

"Aw, do I have to, Daddy? Just one more story, *please?*"

"Not tonight, sweetie. You have to get up early tomorrow for school." Jen-Jen has just started kindergarten, and is not accustomed to the new routine.

"Can I tell *you* a story then?" she says with the innocent smile and eager expression he could never resist.

"Okay, but it will have to be a quick one."

Jen-Jen climbs off the couch and gets down on all fours. Parnell knows this to be the start of her Woofy the Dog story, where she acts out the parts of all four characters and barks out the dialogue of Woofy. Parnell has seen the performance too many times to count, but he never tires of the show.

When Jen-Jen finishes her little production, she takes a sweeping bow and Parnell applauds wildly.

She beams her wide smile and hugs his neck. "I love you, Daddy."

Parnell feels his heart swell, thinks it might explode. "I love you, too, Jen-Jen," he says, cherishing the feel of her small wiggly body in his arms, never wanting to let her go. "Okay, time for bed, sweetie."

He watches her scamper out of the living room and up the winding staircase to her bedroom.

In his dream, Parnell lays back on the couch and closes his eyes, drifting off into a dream inside of a dream. He hears Jen-Jen speaking to him, but this time her voice isn't the high-pitched squeak of young Jen-Jen, but rather the more confident, evenly modulated tones of the older Jennifer.

"How do I look, Dad?"

From within the fuzzy cocoon of his dream, Parnell opens his eyes to see the eleven-year-old version of his daughter standing before him. Her eyes are dark smudges, highlighted by sloppy application of eyeliner and heavy green eye shadow. Her mouth is two slashes of glistening pink lipstick. Her heavily rouged cheeks, large hoop clip-on earrings, tight halter top, and short miniskirt give her the appearance of a young hooker.

He gasps as he sits up to examine her.

"You don't like it, I can tell," Jennifer says with a pout.

"Jenny, we've talked about this before. It's inappropriate for girls your—"

"Why not?" she says, cutting him off. "Mom looks like this when she goes out. And a couple of girls in my class dress like this."

"I don't care!" he bellows, rising off the sofa and approaching her, silently cursing wife Barbara yet again for her irresponsibility and lack of parenting skills. "You get upstairs right now and wash that crap off your face! And put on some decent clothes."

"But Mom says . . ."

"Mom says what? That you should dress up like a little whore? That you should go to school looking like a cheap tramp the way she does when she goes out with her friends at night?" Parnell regrets it as soon as the words leave his mouth.

Jennifer's painted face turns ugly. "You're mean and I hate you!" she yells.

He attempts to take her by the arm, but she twirls away from him, glaring at him, hatred seething behind her racoonish eyes.

"Jenny," he says, holding tight to her arm, "you have to understand I'm just looking out for your best interests. You're a young girl, not a grown woman. Please stay out of your mother's make-up. Don't be too eager to grow up, sweetie. Believe me, being an adult is highly overrated. I love you and—"

"Ow, you're hurting me!" she says, flinging her arm free and twisting out of his grasp. She glowers at him, her mouth set in a pinch of anger. "I hope you die soon so it'll just be me and Mom. Then I can do what I want."

Parnell feels crushed, like all the oxygen has been sucked from his lungs. Why is it always left up to him to handle the tough parenting chores with their daughter?

And then he remembers. He's married to a rich, spoiled bitch who isn't much more mature than their eleven-year-old.

Then, suddenly, Jennifer's head begins to turn color—from a healthy flesh-tone to a sickly bright orange. Her makeup begins to melt and drip down her face. Her cheeks deflate and her forehead caves in. Her lips melt together and her body is sucked away with a whoosh of miniskirt until nothing remains of her but a floating shrunken head.

Her head is joined by dozens of floating shrunken heads, revolving around him, grinning at him with their macabre sewn lips.

One by one, the heads explode, each spilling a fiery gelatinous goo across the floor.

The floor turns into a sea of fire. The drapes flare, then go up in flames. The walls char and buckle.

Parnell stands still, hypnotized by the dancing flames, his face heating up.

Then he hears a faint *Help me, Daddy* from the corner of the room.

He looks in that direction. Hears it again.

Parnell scrambles through the smoke and fire to save his daughter . . .

The Durango Shuffle

"DEREK! HONEY, wake up! Derek—?"

He heard Elaine's voice, muffled, far away.

Heavy smoke and fire surrounded him. He gasped for air and thrashed his arms wildly, took a bounding leap in the direction of Jennifer's shouts. Hit the floor with a jarring thud, grabbing on to what he thought was his daughter.

"Derek? Are you okay?"

Parnell felt her hands on him. He came out of it, disoriented, wondering how the hell he'd ended up on the floor with an armful of drapes. He looked up at Elaine, who crouched over him, a worried frown creasing her forehead. She had abandoned the eye patch and wore her glass eye. The prosthetic orb gave her a robotic appearance—a gorgeous automaton come to rescue him from his terrifying dream world.

It took him a minute to realize they were in their hotel room in Durango. Dazed, his naked body slick with perspiration, Parnell lay clutching the drapes he had ripped down from the large picture window. He glanced up at the curtain rod that was bent at a precipitous angle.

"The fire nightmare again?" Elaine said, rubbing his arm as she separated him from the bunched-up drapes he clung to like a life preserver.

"Yeah . . . the fire nightmare," he said, his voice hoarse with sleep. "Worse this time." The bright sunlight streaming through the window hurt his eyes. "What time is it?"

"Two in the afternoon," she said, helping him up off the floor.

"What? Why didn't you get me up sooner?"

"You needed your sleep," she said defensively. "You were exhausted. We both were. I've only been up an hour myself."

"I've got to check in with Blanton," he said, scurrying around the room searching for his clothes. "And I need to report that crime scene we left yesterday. That can't wait."

He pulled a fresh T-shirt out of his backpack, put it on, then stepped into his pants and zipped up. He grabbed his Walther and held it up, inspecting it.

Looking at the gun, she said, "You're actually going to report those murders?"

He nodded. "Absolutely. It's my civic duty."

"Isn't that a little risky, Derek? They'll find your bullets in that . . . that *monster* Skeeter's body. And Razzy killed the guy who marched us down the trail. I don't know about Razzy's rifle, but your gun is registered. They can trace it back to you."

"Which reminds me," Parnell said, examining the barrel of his Walther. "I need to clean this thing. Get rid of the residue." He shook his head. "Ah—maybe later."

"Did you hear what I said?" Elaine spoke to his back. "I don't think it's wise to report those murders, Derek."

"Look, E, I *have* to report that scene," he said, turning to face her. "If I don't, quite a few missing persons cases might never get solved."

"Missing persons? What are you talking about?"

He forgot that she hadn't seen the Garden of Grotesqueries behind the hunting shack. He stepped back into the room and said, "Okay, fair enough. You deserve to know. Be forewarned that what I'm about to tell you is disturbing."

"Couldn't be much worse than what we've just been through."

"Oh, but it is, sweetheart—it *really* is."

Parnell told her what he'd seen behind the hunting shack—the shrunken heads mounted on poles, the bleached white bones on the other side of the creek, the human skulls in the pit, the blood-ied rock where the processing of body parts had taken place. He left none of it out, hadn't sugarcoated any of it. When he was done, Elaine looked pale and shaken.

"I warned you," he told her.

"I know," she said, sitting down on the edge of the bed, trying to collect herself.

"Are you going to be okay while I go check in with Blanton?"

"Yes, go. I'll be fine."

"I'll be down in the lobby at the pay phones if you need me."

"Just go, Derek."

"Remember, don't open this door for anybody but me. *Nobody*. Understood?"

"Yes, *captain*," she said sarcastically. "Orders received, loud and clear."

Parnell noticed the tiny wound on her neck where her attacker had nicked her. He met her weakly defiant stare, thinking: My wounded angel, trying desperately to soldier on.

He stepped out into the hall, closing the door behind him. He walked down Camino Del Rio to the Doubletree lobby, wanting to report the hunting shack murders to the Arizona Department of Public Safety from a pay phone away from his own hotel. He knew mass murders like these would be quickly escalated to the state Attorney General's office, which would dispatch state investigators to the scene in helicopters. Parnell also knew they would attempt to trace his call.

Reaching the desk sergeant, he altered his voice in case he was being recorded, keeping it short to make the call more difficult to trace: "Yes, officer, I'm calling to report a murder scene—multiple victims—two men shot to death within the last twenty-four hours. There are also dozens more victims of what looks to have been a ritual mass murder, timeframe undetermined. You'll find a grisly scene at a hunting lodge near Chinle in the remote northwest corner of the state, north of Canyon de Chelly. I believe it's on Navajo land."

"Thank you for your call, sir," the agent responded, cool and professional. "Are you at the scene now?"

Parnell ignored the question and gave them approximate coordinates for the location.

"Could I please have your name and a number where we can reach—?"

Parnell hung up.

He left the Doubletree and walked along the Animas River, taking the scenic route back to his hotel. He admired the rugged beauty of the San Juan Mountains, the jagged volcanic summits that towered around him like granite giants. He heard a far-off train whistle. Parnell smiled, loving the plaintive, carnival-calliope sound of it. He knew it belonged to a Durango and Silverton locomotive, one of the last steam-powered narrow-gauge-track trains in operation, a holdover from Durango's gold and silver mining boom days.

As he walked, he kept an eye out for any kind of tail. Seeing nothing to raise his suspicions, he entered the cool, dark womb of his hotel lobby, went to the bank of pay phones.

He inserted a few coins and punched in the number for Blanton Miles, placed a collect call, which Miles accepted.

"Well, well, well . . . if it isn't the Midnight Cowboy."

Parnell laughed. Blanton Miles was the only person in his

organization who could get away with such insolence. "I guess I deserve that," Parnell told him.

"We haven't heard from you in four days, boss. Where've you been?"

"Up to my neck in trouble. Literally."

Parnell heard Miles sigh, then say, "You know, Derek, we need to revisit our discussion about providing somebody to watch your back when you travel. This lone wolf stuff has got to stop. You've been lucky so far, but—"

"I've been *good*, not lucky," Parnell told him.

"Call it what you will. If you don't start taking my advice, I fear your days might be numbered."

"What crawled up your ass and died, Blanton?"

"Lovely imagery, bossman."

"Well—?"

"Willis Logan kicked the bucket Monday. He's deader than the Dead Sea."

"And you belittle *my* imagery!" he said, his mind trying to process the shocking news of his late wife's first husband's death. "Logan dead? How?"

"Run over by a train in Western Pennsylvania, near Pittsburgh."

"What the hell was Willis Logan doing anywhere near railroad tracks? He was no hobo. He was a disgustingly rich banker. The man wiped his ass with hundred-dollar bills."

"I know. It doesn't make much sense."

"So it was a suicide? I could see Logan committing hari-kari. He had a few issues . . . more than a few loose screws."

"No. Not suicide. Authorities are calling it a homicide."

"Logan was murdered?"

"Why should that surprise you?" Miles said. "The man had more enemies than the U.S. government. Apparently Logan was lashed to the tracks, possibly even tortured before the train got him. The crime scene forensics guys found heavy duty nylon rope—the kind they use for boat anchors—attached to one of his severed arms. They also found a loop of it around his body, rope burns across his torso."

Parnell whistled. "Whaddaya know. Somebody finally got the son of a bitch." He shuddered, thinking what it would be like to die that way—hearing the train approach, feeling the rumbling vibrations through the rails beneath you, frantically trying to break loose of your shackles, seeing 150 tons of thundering locomotive bearing down on you, knowing a violent end was just minutes away. "They got any suspects?" he asked.

"Yeah, boss. Your arsonist buddies . . . Tico Samuels and Jerry Ray Allenson."

Parnell remembered that Willis Logan had given their field agent, Julia Sanchez, the slip and that Logan had been off the grid for more than a week. He also recalled that his field agents, Kevin Spottswood and Saul Delancey, had been tailing the two firebugs since their release. "Please tell me that Spotts and Del are still glued to our arsonists."

"They are now. But they lost both men for nearly twenty-four hours—the time during which Logan's alleged murder occurred. Samuels and Allenson found a way to slip not only our tails, but the federal shadows as well."

"How could that happen?"

"Tico Samuels and Jerry Ray Allenson are both crafty, resourceful individuals. They're very slippery operators with well-honed survival instincts. The fact that they're out and about, running around free should tell you that."

"The only thing *that* tells me is our criminal justice system is an unsalvageable mess. But you're telling me that Spotts and Del picked them back up?"

"Oh yeah. Our guys are good. And they one-upped the feds. Spottswood and Delancey checked airline passenger manifests through all airports in the area. Took a while but they found Samuels and Allenson each paying cash for one-way-tickets to Denver. They took separate flights."

"Denver?" Parnell said, getting excited.

"Yes, Denver. I'm assuming you're in Colorado right now, correct, boss?"

"You assume correctly."

"*Southern* Colorado?"

"Quit with the subterfuge, Blanton. What're you trying to tell me?"

"I'm telling you that Tico Samuels and Jerry Ray Allenson hooked up in Denver last night. This morning they rented a car and, as we speak, are driving south to pay you a personal visit. Spotts and Del are right behind them. The feds seem to be out of the picture for now."

"What makes you think they're interested in me?"

"You have to ask?"

"Yeah. Enlighten me, Blanton."

"Okay. According to our intel, they believe you conspired with Willis Logan to rat them out. It's a logical conclusion on their part. It's your house they torched. It was your wife and daught—"

"No way would I *ever* conspire to do *anything* in league with Willis Logan! The man was a festering hemorrhoid. And I haven't been back east in almost a year."

Blanton Miles remained quiet for a long moment, then said, "We've never discussed this, Derek, but I'm curious. And stop me if I'm overstepping my bounds here, but how come you never went after Logan yourself?"

Parnell should have been pissed off at the question, but instead he found himself admiring Miles' insatiable curiosity. "I didn't go after Willis Logan because I was convinced he had nothing to do with any of it. He had an airtight alibi. He also had nothing to gain by killing my wife and daughter—at least financially—and money is the only thing that ever motivated him. His alimony responsibility stopped when I married Barbara, and Logan wasn't getting dinged for child support because Jennifer was my daughter, not his."

"Are you sure about that?" Miles said.

"About what?"

"About Logan not being hit for child support."

"I think I would know about any payments being made of that sort."

"Would you? Seems to me you never had a real good handle on your wife's financial affairs, boss. Isn't it true there could have been a lot of money changing hands that you wouldn't know about?"

"It's possible, yeah," Parnell said, trying to figure what Miles was driving at. "I just didn't think Logan was good for the fire or the murders. He had no real motive."

"Well you know what they say about money being the root of all evils."

Parnell said, "Yeah, maybe money was involved. I don't really know about that. I think it was more about misplaced passions. I believe Logan was glad I got Barbara out of his hair. But still, it was strange. He and Barbara had one of those odd codependent relationships. They enabled each other. Both of them had a need for high drama in their lives. Logan just couldn't seem to stay away from her in the days and months following their divorce. But then, the last eight years or so of my marriage to Babs, Willis Logan remained pretty scarce. I thought he'd gotten over his love/hate relationship with Barbara. But obviously I was wrong."

Miles said, "Well, Logan was a powerful man with a lot of influence."

"Yeah," Parnell agreed, "Logan had his two firebug flunkies in his back pocket. The powerful and influential always hold onto a trump card or two. But let's get back to Samuels and Allenson. How do they know where I am, Blanton? This have anything to do with that Madame Crystal bitch in Sedona?"

"We think so, yes. I sent Grabowski to meet with her yesterday, but I haven't heard back from him yet."

"So you think our killer arsonists have been in touch with Madame Crystal and knew about my travel plans that way?"

"That's what it looks like."

"Do they know where Elaine and I are staying?"

"Even I don't know that, Derek. They only know that you're in the Durango area and that you're hooking up with this Thor fellow on Friday. Where are you staying?"

Parnell gave him the name of the hotel, then added, "We registered as Bonnie Parker and Clyde Barrow."

Miles snickered. "Your wit is unparalleled, boss. How is Elaine doing?"

"Let's just say she's out of her comfort zone, but she's a trooper."

"Good. Spottswood and Delancey are watching your back. Unlike you, they're carrying cell phones and report in to me hourly. If you'd check in with me more often—"

"Save the lecture, Blanton."

"I'm only trying to—"

"So why are these assholes now coming after me? I didn't have a clue of their identities until *after* they were arrested."

"They don't know that, Derek. They're under the impression you were a key confidential informant. Proceed with extreme caution. I believe these guys have vengeance on their minds."

"Excellent!" Parnell said with an evil grin, knowing he was going to finally get his chance to rid the world of his family's killers.

"I don't like the sound of that, boss."

"This news couldn't be better, Blanton. These ass clowns have just saved me a long trip back east."

"I'm warning you, boss. These guys are dangerous . . ."

Parnell barely heard Blanton Miles talking. He was thinking about the abandoned rail spur in Utah, the rail siding with the three dilapidated boxcars out in the middle of God's country that he had set up last year. The perfect place for homicide. An even better place for a warranted double murder.

The site where he would finally get his fiery revenge.

And these two fools were playing right into his hand.

Justice was karmic.

". . . Are you listening to me, boss? I said these guys are stone cold killers."

Parnell laughed at Miles' suggestion. "They have no idea what cold is, my friend. But they will."

Lucious Jones and Karmic Justice

THEY KEPT A LOW PROFILE over the next couple of days as they waited for their Friday rendezvous at Mesa Verde with the man named Thor. Parnell spent much of the time with Razzy in the hotel bar while Elaine, sullen and withdrawn, stayed in their room, watching television and working on a new painting. Parnell worried about her. The attack on her and the two brutal murders she'd witnessed had affected her profoundly. She seemed more frightened and vulnerable than ever. He had tried to console her several times, but she made it clear she wanted to be left alone. Past experience told him she would confide in him when she was ready.

Parnell checked in with Blanton Miles several times. He learned that Tico Samuels and Jerry Ray Allenson had arrived in Durango and were staying in separate hotels. The two arsonists had already visited the local hobo camp at Pinkerton Hot Springs looking for him, and were now making the rounds of hotels in the area. This pleased Parnell. These two mutts had come to him, making things easy for him. Like lemmings to the sea, he thought. After seven long, frustrating years, he finally had the murderers of his family in his line of sight. Soon they would be his. Soon they would experience justice the Derek Parnell way.

He'd instructed Blanton Miles to have Spottswood and Delancey pick them up when the opportunity arose. He wanted to take Samuels and Allenson to the abandoned Utah railroad spur to interrogate them before he did the dirty deed. And he wanted his face to be the last thing they saw.

Currently, Parnell sat in the hotel bar drinking with Razzy.

"Mind if I order another, Mistah Midas?" Razzy asked him over the happy hour clatter.

Parnell looked across the table through a curtain of smoke, seeing Lucious "Razzmatazz" Jones fire up a cigarette and flip his lighter closed. Three empty Heineken bottles and an overflowing ashtray sat in front of him.

"It's *Derek*, not Mr. Midas. Remember?"

"Oh, right," Razzy said. "Sorry, the booze makes me forget." He sucked on his cigarette, exhaled a gray cloud across the table. "But then, that's the main reason for drinkin' ain't it? To forget?"

Parnell looked down at his scotch glass, thinking about all the times he'd obliterated bad memories with alcohol. "Yeah. But shit, Razzy, if I drank like you do, I'd have irreversible amnesia. If I didn't know better I'd swear your mother weaned you on beer and Camel non-filters."

"Naw. It was my Paw done the weanin'. A steady diet of bullets and gunpowder."

"Somehow I don't doubt that," Parnell said, smiling, waving for the waitress.

"It's true. My earliest memories was of my daddy takin' me along with him and his huntin' buddies up in the UP. That's the Upper Peninsula for you folks who don't know raisins from rabbit shit about Michigan's north country. It's God's country, the UP. Thousands of square miles of nothin' but trees and critters. I killed and dressed out my first deer when I was just a wee tyke. The Porcupine Mountains was where I first learnt my trackin' and survival skills."

The waitress came, and Parnell ordered two more Heinekens for Razzy and another scotch for himself.

He had sat in this same seat the past two nights, his back to the wall, chatting with Razzy over the clinking of glasses and classic rock playing softly through speakers suspended from the ceiling. From this position he'd kept a vigilant watch on the entrance to the small bar. Last thing he needed was for Tico Samuels and Jerry Ray Allenson to walk in and shoot him point blank.

He loved listening to Razzy talk. The old drifter had some great stories, and Parnell figured most of them were true, judging by the unrehearsed way he told them. The man's trail to becoming a rail-riding hobo was paved with sadness. His wife of many years died of a rare bone cancer that had gone largely untreated. Eugenia Jones had been diagnosed with the disease six months before Razzy had been laid off from his assembly line job at GM. She had begun her chemo and radiation treatments. Fortunately, a month after his layoff at GM, Razzy found work at the Ford plant. Unfortunately, his new insurance provider wrote off Eugenia's cancer as a preexisting condition, and refused to cover her astronomical medical bills. Razzy said he'd done all he could to help his beloved Eugenia—including using up all of their retirement savings and maxing out the credit cards—but it just wasn't enough. Eugenia Jones left this world at age 46, a bald, skeletal vestige of the woman she had been. Razzy was left alone, shouldering a mountain of debt he couldn't pay off in a lifetime. He obliterated the pain with drugs and alcohol, started missing a lot of time at work.

"That been damn near twenty years ago now," Razzy told him. "But I still think about them scumbag insurance types who sho' 'nuff murdered my Eugenia, clear as we sittin' here. They still get my blood pressure up into the fuckin' stratosphere. After I buried my Eugenia I wanted to go after them smug pencil-necked bastards. My Nam trainin' was heavy on demolitions. I actually drew up plans to bomb the insurance company's home office in Chicago. I was flat-out certifiable crazy with grief. But then I got my head on straight before I went and blew away a buncha innocent folks."

"But you could have gone after the ones responsible," Parnell told him.

"Yep. Thought about that. But then I didn't wanna spend the rest of my days in prison bein' somebody's Nancy-girl bitch, so I swallered my anger and moved on."

"No way I'd have let them get away with it," Parnell said. "You could have eliminated those insurance geeks with a little planning."

"Yep, I know. But back then I was just blue collar labor . . . an assembly line grunt tryin' to survive. But I sho' wish I'd knowed you back then, Derek—"

"Yeah," Parnell said, "I'd have taken them out for you. Without question."

"I know you would. You're the master of makin' bad folks disappear."

Razzy tilted the beer bottle to his lips and took a long swig. Parnell watched his Adam's apple bob as he swallowed, saw him wipe his mouth with the back of his arm.

"You know," Parnell said, "if any of those decision makers in your wife's case are still alive—"

"Naw, I know what you talkin' 'bout, Derek. And I appreciate it. But I'm an old man and I don't have a lotta time left. I don't wanna spend my final days stirrin' up past demons."

"It's just that I feel like I owe you, Razzy. Big time. After what you did saving me and Lainey."

"Pleased enough to do it, Derek. Cleaned up some of the world's trash is what I did. My reward is gettin' to travel with a legend."

Parnell pointed a warning finger across the table. "Quit with that legend shit, I'm telling you."

Their waitress returned with their drinks. Parnell nodded his thanks and took a sip of his scotch, feeling the pleasant numbing burn in his throat. "So, after your wife died you hit the road?"

"After a while, yeah. Got laid off again not long after the funeral. I ended up mopin' around the house, really fuckin' lost, man, so drunk and high I didn't know my own name. And these pain-in-the-ass bill collectors was comin' out of the woodwork like cockroaches, houndin' me, makin' threats. I started puttin' all my monthly bills in a big envelope and mailin' 'em to the insurance company. Kept puttin' a personal note in there to let 'em know they was mostly responsible for my debts, not to mention my wife's death."

Parnell smiled. "I'll bet you were a real big hit in that Chicago insurance ivory tower."

"It wasn't but a coupla months later the bank started foreclosure proceedings on my house. At that point I was barely able to scrape together enough to buy food and enough booze to keep me numb. After my 90 days ran out these banker dipshits plastered my house with foreclosure sale signs, That's when I said screw it and I walked away from it all . . . started ridin' the rails. I ain't looked back since."

"And how has that worked out?"

"Oh, it ain't so bad, really," Razzy said before he lifted the bottle to his lips and drained his beer. He shook another Camel out of the pack and fired it up. "I got me more true friends out here than I ever had in my old life in Detroit. Usually nobody bothers me. But if and when they do . . . well, I just *kill* 'em," he said with a sly wink.

Parnell laughed, a boisterous chuckle that cut through the piped-in Eric Clapton song. "Yeah, I've seen your work, my friend," he said, grinning, feeling a bond with this sad-eyed old man who, like himself, had experienced so much tragedy in his life.

"It ain't a glamorous life or nothin' but it's free and easy,"

Razzy continued. "I can go where I want when I want. And just about ever'body I meet out here on the rails is a kindred soul. Just about ever'body's runnin' from somethin' . . . just like me, so we usually hit it off." Razzy trained his glazed eyes on Parnell. "What you runnin' from, Derek?"

The question caught Parnell off guard. He never really saw himself as running from anything, but rather chasing, and he told Razzy so. "I've been searching for these two killers who're now here in Durango as luck would have it."

"They the ones burnt your house down?"

"Yeah. Been searching for them for seven long years. Strange, but I just recently learned of their identities."

"You're gonna kill 'em, ain't ya?"

Parnell studied Razzy across the table, noticed how the scar across his cheek glowed like fire against a night sky. He wondered how the old hobo had picked up that battle scar. Parnell took a long, slow drink of scotch, wincing with the burn. He set his glass back on the table, then said, "You're one wise man, Lucious Jones."

"Not so wise. Just observant. Like all good trackers. If'n ya need any help in disposin' of them two bastards you just let me know, Derek. It's karma. Some folks just don't deserve to be breathin' the air God put on this great Earth."

Parnell grinned, held up his glass for a toast. "Here's to karmic justice."

Killers and Lovers

PARNELL ENTERED THE ELEVATOR and pressed the button for the fourth floor. The space felt claustrophobic. The air reeked of cheap cologne and cigar smoke. The booze had left him wobbly and woozy and he leaned against the wall for support.

The elevator lurched upward. He thought about Razzy, whom he'd left down in the bar. Parnell had offered to set him up with a house in Flagstaff, and to put him on the Locomotion Enterprises payroll, partly as a reward for Razzy's saving their lives at the garden of shrunken heads, partly as a means of keeping an eye on him. Razzy turned down the house, saying he never accepted handouts. He told Parnell he preferred to live off the grid and travel hobo style. He did accept the employment offer, however. He would do odd jobs, mostly tailing people Parnell wanted watched and working the occasional shakedown. Best of both worlds, a grateful Razzy had told him. His first official job would be traveling with Parnell and Elaine, serving as a bodyguard for the duration of this trip.

The doors swished open and he exited the elevator, made his way down the carpeted hallway, weaving side to side. A fluorescent fixture buzzed above him, annoying him, the bulb on the fritz, creating a strobe effect that hurt his eyes. Parnell fought the temptation to pull out his Walther and shoot the damn thing out of the ceiling. He stumbled along the hallway, hearing sounds from behind closed doors—a baby crying, the waspy buzz of an electric razor, somebody strumming a guitar, a ringing phone, canned laughter from a television set.

He arrived at their room and struggled to get his keycard in the slot. The door kept moving on him. As he fumbled with the card he heard Elaine inside, asking if it was him, her voice full of fear and uncertainty. In a voice much too loud, he reassured her it was indeed him.

Elaine pulled the door open. She wore a paint-spattered T-shirt and jeans. She'd pulled her hair back in a ponytail and had that "otherwhere" stare in her good eye, her serious artist expression that said *I might be looking at you right now but my mind is far away in another world of my own creation.*

He stumbled into the room and she closed the door behind him.

"I see our new friend Razzy has been a *wonderful* influence on you, Derek," she said, her tone accusing. "God, you smell like a distillery."

Parnell flung himself across the bed. The pungent odor of turpentine made him gag, bringing up a bitter gruel of scotch and nachos and stomach acid.

"Why so pissed off?" he mumbled, looking at the brushes and palette knives and paint-streaked rags strewn across the small table near the window. A drop-cloth covered the small canvas she was working on.

"*Why?*" she asked, incredulous. "You have to ask why? We've been here the better part of three days and I've hardly seen you." She glared at him with her good eye, challenging him.

"That's because you've had me out running around Durango picking up painting supplies for you." He knew it was lame as soon as the words left his mouth.

She threw her hand on her hip, gave him her *You've got to be kidding me* expression.

"All right," he said. "That was weak. I'll give you that."

Her voice was shrill. "You spend all your time getting soused with that drunk, Razzy, and—"

"Hey, that *drunk*, as you so inelegantly phrase it, saved our goddamn asses, Elaine."

"I know, I know," she said, looking away, distracted, seeming lost for a moment. She turned back to him, her eye burning with reproach. "But that doesn't mean you have to be his fraternity brother."

"Fraternity brother? Jesus. Is that what you think?"

"Yeah, I do."

"Look, I've invited you to join us, but you keep turning me down. I took it to mean you wanted to be left alone."

She shook her head, disappointed with him, like he was some kind of clueless moron. "You don't know anything about women, do you?"

Parnell felt his anger rising. "Apparently not." He sat up on the bed, leaned back against the headboard.

"The last thing I want right now is to be alone, Derek. Don't you know that?"

That certainly wasn't the signal she had been sending him. Despite his best efforts, Elaine kept pushing him away the past few days. As long as he lived, Parnell would never be able to figure out female logic. He proceeded carefully. "So then, why didn't you join us. I thought you liked Razzy."

"I do. But every time you two get together it's a major testosterone fest. You can cut the machismo with a knife. I want to be with *you*, Derek. Only you. You're different when he's around."

He thought about that. She had a point. *How could you not see it, Parnell?* He reprimanded himself. He'd known Elaine was hurting and he'd run off with Razzy. Abandoned her, left her alone to navigate her own darkness.

They looked at each other for an eternal minute. Parnell was about to apologize when she dropped her aggressive stance and deflated, began sobbing.

"Hey," he said, getting off the bed and going to her. "What is it, Lainey?" He took her in his arms and she folded into him, her tears wetting the front of his shirt. "What's wrong, baby?"

"Oh, I don't know," she said, backing out of his embrace and wiping tears from her cheek. She readjusted her eye patch in an attempt to hide her embarrassment.

"You're shaking," Parnell said, pulling the desk chair over near the bed and offering her a seat, which she took. "Talk to me, please. What's going on, honey?"

She shook her head in bafflement. "I'm so confused, Derek," she began. "I don't know . . . I always thought I was this tough chick. I thought I could handle anything life threw at me. Now I'm not so sure. After what we went through—you know . . . the train wreck . . . the um, well, you know, the uh . . . *incidents* at the hunting shack with those crossbow hunters—I'm just not sure I can handle this kind of rough-and-tumble lifestyle . . . this wild frontier life. I'm frightened all the time. I keep seeing the face of that animal who tried to rape me. I keep reliving the way you and Razzy killed those hunters. All the blood and smoke and noise . . . the terrible violence of it all. I can't sleep more than an hour or two at a time. I'm exhausted and scared all the time."

She smiled at him, a thin, reticent smile. "The only thing I've ever really wanted since we met is to please you, Derek. But I feel like I'm letting you down. I realize now I'm not the tough, steel-hard broad I thought I was. I'm weak and afraid and I feel so—I don't know . . . vulnerable . . . so . . . *fragile*." She looked up at him and he felt a crushing pressure in his chest. "I thought I could handle this, but I can't." She slumped in the chair and started crying again.

"Hey, come on," Parnell said, plucking tissues from a box on top of the dresser and handing them to her. "You are absolutely one of the strongest women I've ever known, Elaine. The way you handled the, uh . . . the premature end to your modeling career . . . that would have destroyed most other women your age. And you stayed right with me through the train derailment, the long exhausting night hike through the forest. And the way you held up during our encounter with those headhunters—wow, Lainey! I don't know many men who could've come through the way you did. Never once did you complain or slow us down. I'm proud of you, babe!"

She snuffled and wiped her nose. "You really mean that?"

"Absolutely," he said, caressing her shoulder.

"I don't want to be one of those weepy self-pitying drama queens. But hellamighty, that's exactly what I've become."

"Look, E, we've been through a lot this week. Your emotional state has been rubbed raw and it's only natural you're feeling these things."

"So how come you're not, Derek?"

"Who says I'm not?"

"You certainly don't show it.," she said. "You're cool as a popsicle about all this."

"Well, I have a lot more experience in these kinds of situations. Keeping my cool is the way I handle it. We're all different."

"Yeah," Elaine said listlessly, "you shot that hunter like he was nothing. You looked so—I don't know—*detached* when you did it. No emotion during or after . . . like you were shooting a rabid animal or something."

So now she's getting to the root of things, Parnell thought, his anger rising again, fueled by the alcohol and her accusatory tone. "That piece of shit *was* a rabid animal, Elaine! You want me to show emotion when I shoot somebody who's trying to rape and kill the woman I love? Okay," he said, angrily strutting toward the full-length mirror by the closet. He saw her reflection, cringing where she sat, cowering, like she expected him to smash the mirror. "*Here's* your emotion." He spat, once . . . twice . . . direct hits on the mirror. "That's what I think of that psycho son of a bitch. I'm delighted I turned that wastrel into worm food, okay?"

He watched Elaine's startled reflection as his two large globs of saliva slid down the mirror.

After a long, stunned moment, she said, "I'm sorry, Derek. What I said came out wrong. But I have to confess something—you scare me right now. Your anger . . . your, I don't know . . . *composure* after killing another human being. The way you and Razzy so easily took the lives of those two hunters really upsets me. I can't deny that. I'm just being honest."

Parnell tried to contain his spiraling wrath. Was she serious? He had saved her from a violent attack and perhaps death, and she was feeling sympathetic toward her attacker? He said: "This from a woman who dated a hardcase con on death row? From a woman who says she has a thing for dangerous men?"

"That's different, Derek."

"How so?"

"I didn't have to witness the murders Frank Jarshick committed. It's different when you see the killing of another human being up close and personal. What I experienced at the hunting shack has affected me in ways I never thought possible."

He looked at her, slumped down in the chair. He could see her trembling. She looked so small and terrified. He wanted to say: *I told you so. I warned you that life out here on the rails wasn't pretty, didn't I? That it could be a nasty, violent existence. I warned you that this life wasn't for you but you insisted on coming . . . even demanded that I bring you along.*

But he didn't tell her these things. Instead, he felt the hard edges of his anger softening. Parnell realized at that moment how much he loved Elaine Leibrandt. He loved her so much it hurt his soul to see her like this. And it hurt him even more that she thought of him as a stone-cold killer, some kind of a sociopathic subhuman life form. He was a killer, yes. Absolutely. Murder was a dark storm cloud he'd had floating over his head since grade school, when his father had been taken down over unpaid gambling debts. Murder seemed to be part of his DNA. Parnell was well skilled in the art of killing—by his count the crossbow hunter made fourteen kills. But did that make him a sociopathic subhuman life form? He didn't think so. Every one of those fourteen hits deserved to die. And yet, even so, Parnell had paid an extreme price for each and every one of them. Just because he kept his emotional scars buried didn't make the wounds any less painful.

He wished he could explain that to Elaine, but he couldn't. She would never understand, no matter how he phrased it.

"So do you want me to take you back home, E?" he said finally.

"No," she said, looking surprised. "No I don't want that at all. I want to be *with* you, not *without* you. I couldn't stand being home alone again, not knowing what was going on with you, whether you were dead or alive." She shook her head, "I couldn't go back to that way of life now." She stood and came to him, took his hands in hers. "I need you more than ever right now, Derek." She steered him to the bed.

Parnell showed his surprise. "You want to—?" he questioned.

"No, not sex," she said, nudging him down on the bed and stretching out beside him. "I just want you to hold me. *Please*. Just hold me."

And he did.

They lay together, Parnell clutching her to him, stroking her hair, whispering reassurances. He was amazed at how this woman managed to have such sway over him. In many ways she was a complete mystery to him, a massive jumble of contradictions. She could be quiet and introspective, but she could also be loud and mercurial. She could be strong and independent, but also delicate and needy. She was a challenge, no question. She kept him guessing from one minute to the next. At times he'd want to throttle her, but most of the time he loved her more than life itself. Perhaps that's what attracted him to Elaine the most—the *challenge* of her, the full range of possibilities she presented.

Finally she fell asleep in his arms. He held her, not wanting to wake her with his movement. As he breathed in the scent of her hair and skin, he recalled clips of conversation they'd had. Elaine telling him about her childhood, how her father had disappeared when she was nine, and about her cantankerous relationship with her abusive, alcoholic mother, her creepy Uncle Walter molesting her when she was thirteen. At fourteen she began experimenting with drugs—Ecstasy and meth mostly, a few acid trips—medicating herself to deaden the harsh realities of her home life. At fifteen she shaved her head and started hanging out with a biker gang. Older guys in their twenties. Walk-on-the-wild-side guys, many of them with long police records. "Two years of my life lost in a wasteland of drugs and chopped Harleys and rowdy boys who thought they were men," Elaine had told him. "I was lucky I didn't end up in prison. Or dead."

At seventeen, Elaine came to the realization that she had to escape her suburban Kansas City hell. She dropped out of school (not that she was attending classes often anyway) and headed west, to Los Angeles. Like a million other young girls before her, she focused on Hollywood and acting. She grew her hair out and took an interest in makeup and fashion, trying to make herself more attractive for her casting calls. But like a million other young girls before her, Elaine received offers only from sleazy men in the San Fernando Valley wanting her to do kinky things on film. She tried a couple of porn shoots to pay the rent, but hated every minute of it. The men all reminded her of her Uncle Walter and the girls . . . well, they were mostly lost souls on the road to ruin. She went back to waiting tables in a sports bar, her spirit crushed and her dignity at an all-time low.

And then, one night, a woman came into the bar and sat at one of Elaine's tables. The woman, expensively dressed and in her mid-forties, introduced herself as Brenda Harksdale of the Mason-Harksdale Modeling Agency. The agent told her she was looking for catalog models for one of their big clients and asked if Elaine would like to come in for a trial shoot. Elaine jumped at the chance to escape the dingy sports bar and the leering male drunks. Things clicked at the audition shoot. Elaine had the look her client was searching for—the perfect willowy body to show off their spring lines, the perfectly sculpted cheekbones and expressive dark eyes for effective close-up work. It took a while, but as Elaine neared her 18th birthday, she was in high demand to pose in expensive designer outfits for major department store catalogs, making more money than she'd ever dreamed possible. The free wardrobes were just an added bonus.

Lainey was in a deep sleep now, and Parnell gently separated himself from her, got up off the bed. He wanted to get a look at the painting she'd been working on so diligently, the one she had refused to let him see.

He moved stealthily to the small table, carefully lifted the drop-cloth from the canvas perched on the small easel.

The painting made him take a step back. Parnell felt a hitch in his throat, a weakness in his knees.

A hunter in camouflage fatigues aimed an oversized cross-bow at him. So lifelike it looked almost like a photograph. The crossbow broadhead seemed to jut out of the painting like a 3-D hologram, it's three-dimensional aspects quite startling. The over-all effect was disturbing, like a nightmarish Hieronymus Bosch vision.

There was something else, something that didn't immediately register as he examined Elaine's warped creation. What is it? he wondered as he perused the canvas.

And then he saw it in the hunter's eyes.

Tiny tombstones where the pupils should be.

PREY
FOR THE
PREDATORS

Crossbow Hunters
and Hell Hogs

FRIDAY MORNING THE CROSSBOW headhunter murders broke in the national news. The story flooded the airwaves and print media like a fast-spreading virus. The sordid reports held U.S. news junkies hostage, replacing the tumbling economy, plant closings, and wars in the Middle East in the public consciousness.

Parnell worked the TV remote, surfing through the cable news channels while Elaine busied herself in the bathroom. He kept the volume low. No need for her to hear this. The script was pretty much the same, channel to channel. Only the reporter varied.

"Authorities came across a grisly scene in Northeast Arizona yesterday at a remote hunting shack north of the Canyon de Chelly national monument. Two hunters, who apparently specialized in the unique sport of crossbow hunting, were found brutally murdered, shot multiple times . . ."

The camera panned the immediate area around the shack as the reporter continued with the voiceover. "The victims have been identified as Steven Kelton Gibbs, age forty-two, from Chinle, Arizona, and Ronald B. Gibbs, age forty-six, from Kayenta, Arizona . . ."

"Victims my ass," Parnell grumbled under his breath.

". . . both men were shot at close range numerous times, their bodies riddled with nine-millimeter semi-automatic slugs and bullets from a high-powered rifle—a thirty-aught-six—suggesting there was more than one killer involved. Federal agents are combing the site for clues."

The camera focused on the male reporter standing on the front porch, a twenty-something actor wannabe with perfect hair, a cheap suit, and an overly dramatic expression. "But what makes this case even stranger," he said into his hand-held microphone, "are the dozens of human heads found out back of this structure. Authorities have cordoned off the area as part of the crime scene and we are not allowed back there at this time. But we are told the heads have been processed—shrunk to a smaller size, and mounted on long poles. This is one bizarre scene here, with all types of law enforcement and crime scene investigative types running to and fro. We hope to be able to—"

Parnell heard the toilet flush and the bathroom door open. He clicked the TV off.

"What were you watching?" Elaine asked, toweling her hair dry.

"Just catching up on the news."

"Anything on the crossbow hunters yet?"

"No," he lied. "I keep looking but there's nothing."

His lie was for her benefit. He wanted to distance Elaine from that nightmarish scene, to shield her from it. But he also didn't want to get into it with her again. She had chastised him for not getting rid of the bodies before they left, for leaving without cleaning up the scene. Parnell had argued he wanted the bodies to be found so families and friends of the shrunken-head victims would have some closure, would know about these evil Gibbs brothers and their atrocious acts. And, he'd reasoned with her, if they had disposed of the bodies they would have left more of their own evidence behind.

"Are you okay, Derek? You seem far away this morning."

"Yeah, I'm fine," he said, checking her out. She had inserted her glass eye and looked stunning in a navy blue Arizona Wildcats polo shirt and cutoff jeans. "Just thinking about our meeting today."

"Do you think this Thor guy will show?"

"We'll find out soon enough."

She went to the mirror over the dresser, flung the wet towel to the floor and brushed her hair in long, sweeping strokes. Parnell couldn't take his eyes off of her ass. The tendons in her shapely calves moved sinuously with each sweep of the brush.

"Thank you for last night," she said as she combed. "For, y'know . . . being so understanding and all. For *comforting* me. I feel a lot better about things now."

"Good, I'm glad," he said, hoping for the best, not knowing what they could expect this afternoon. "Are you sure you want to go with me?" he asked. Elaine had been a hermit the past three days, venturing out of their hotel room only to get ice and vending machine snacks.

She set the hairbrush down and dug through her makeup kit, pulled out her pink powder compact and began dabbing her face with the pad. "I'm very sure," she said, checking herself in the mirror as she worked. "I'm curious about this Thor guy. And if he shows up, you know he's expecting to see both of us."

"I know, lover, but I'm wondering if you're really *ready* for this," he said, thinking about Tico Samuels and Jerry Ray Allenson prowling around Durango, looking for him, lying in wait to eliminate him.

She clicked her compact shut and began applying lip gloss, smacking her lips as she worked. "I've never been more ready, Derek. If I spend another minute in this room I'm going to need scream therapy."

He watched her put away the lip gloss, then apply cheek blush. As he watched her go through the motions with her eyebrow pencil, he thought for perhaps the millionth time just how beautiful Elaine Leibrandt was, damaged face and all. When she finished, she stuffed all of her beauty aids into her backpack, then turned to him, moved closer and kissed him on the mouth.

He smiled at her, appreciating the way she seemed to be ratcheting up her courage. She was regaining her strength; Elaine was on the rebound.

She wrapped her arms around his waist. "Sorry I was a cry-baby last night. I feel like such a fool."

"No need," he said, running his finger along her burn scar.

"I said some really insulting things last night, Derek. About you and Razzy. You sure you're all right with me going with you today?"

"I wouldn't have it any other way, babe," he said, planting a light kiss on her cheek. "Look, Lainey, forget last night. I wasn't in the best of form either." He looked across the room, at the two long streaks of dried saliva on the closet door mirror.

Standing there with Elaine in his arms, feeling the warmth of her body cuddled up close to him, his galloping emotions overwhelmed him. Words tumbled from his mouth as though spoken by a ventriloquist. "I'm not good at saying these things, but here goes—I love you. I *need* you. The best moments of my life are those I spend with you. So, absolutely, I want you with me, no matter how treacherous things might get. After all, you're a proven road warrior now." Seeing the earnestness etched on her face, the sheer, naked vulnerability of her expression, Parnell decided to lighten the moment. He said, "Shit, E, you rode with the Hell's Angels not too many years ago. You've got street cred, babe."

That made her laugh. "They were called Hell Hogs, Derek."

"*Hell Hogs*? Are you serious?"

"Entirely. The Hell's Angels could've eaten those boys for lunch. Strictly minor league. We looked ridiculous. We rode around with a logo on our leather jackets that looked like a label off a canned ham with flames shooting out of it. Looked like a pig farting fire."

Parnell laughed. Elaine was okay now. Her sense of humor had returned.

"Oh, but we thought we were so badass back then. And some of the cops were actually afraid to mess with us."

"That's what I'm saying, Lainey. You've got street cred. You were a biker chick. Not exactly the kind of lifestyle debutantes and good Catholic girls engage in."

"Yeah, a biker chick," she said, smiling up at him.

He pulled her closer, hugged her to him, then released her, held her at arm's length. "Have I told you lately how smoking hot you look?" he said, making a point of examining her from head to pink-painted toenails.

"Not lately, no."

"Well pardon my oversight, milady . . . you look good enough to eat," he said, licking his lips.

Elaine laughed, that randy giggle he hadn't heard in a while. She dropped her hand down between them, brushed her wrist across his crotch. "Ooh, nice!" she cooed, making him want to jump her bones right then and there. "We have time before we have to leave, don't we, Derek?"

"You keep on doing that and we will," he said, reluctantly grabbing her hand, stopping her. "But unfortunately we have to make tracks, sweetness."

"But it's only noon."

"I know, darlin' You're tempting me something fierce. But we need some breakfast and I have to check in with Blanton before we head to Mesa Verde."

"You're no fun," she said with an exaggerated pout.

"Look, I promise. After our rendezvous with this Thor character, we'll come back here and copulate like we're trying to repopulate the planet."

She smiled. "Copulate to repopulate. You're a regular poet

laureate."

"Aren't I though?"

"You promise we'll get some sack time soon?"

Parnell looked at her seriously. "Have I ever lied to you, Lainey?"

"Yeah, you have," she said, tossing her head knowingly. "About an hour ago. When you told me you hadn't looked at my new painting."

Showdown at Cliff Palace

T HE LUSH MOUNTAINS OF MESA VERDE glowed in one of those picture-postcard days unique to southern Colorado in mid-August—bright and sunny, a comfortable 73 degrees, low humidity and a high sky that illuminated everything with a vivid clarity. Parnell and Elaine rode the tour bus along with twenty others, Parnell scanning the ranks looking for someone who might be their contact, Thor. Razzy sat in the back, the brim of his fedora pulled low, silently observing, looking for signs of potential trouble.

After a bumpy 10-minute bus ride, they arrived at Chapin Mesa where the tour turned to foot. They hiked along Mesa Loop Road, listening to their tour guide ramble on about the amazing architectural feats of the Ancestral Puebloans who had inhabited this area 700 years before. Razzy blended in—just another lone tourist taking in the sights. Parnell felt some degree of comfort knowing he watched their backs.

The guide, decked out in his park ranger uniform, took them past monolithic sandstone cliffs, their sheer facings towering above them. Hundreds of crude dwellings were carved into the precipitous sides of the cliffs. Periodically the guide stopped, allowing the group to marvel at the ancient ones' version of contemporary high-rise skyscrapers.

They paused at an archaeological site where their guide informed them: "These cliffs were deposited here during the Cretaceous Period, some 78 million years ago. The alcoves you see here that housed the Ancestral Puebloans' small dwellings were formed by eons of freezing and thawing of the porous sandstone. You can see the way they utilized sandstone blocks, mortar, and wooden beams to build their cliff homes. They made very durable mortar from a local mixture of soil, water, and ash. They also used chinking stones to fill the gaps within the mortar, which added structural stability to the walls. This is why these dwellings still stand today, some seven-hundred years later. And if you look closely you'll see paintings on many of the walls, done with earthen plasters of pink, brown, red, yellow, and white. Our curators here at Mesa Verde have done a superb job of preserving these wall paintings, but the ancient Pueblos' rudimentary paints fade quickly in the brutal Southwest sun. These paintings tell interesting stories about our ancient friends . . ."

"Fascinating, isn't it?" Elaine whispered into Parnell's ear.

"Very," he said absently, his attention focused on the other members of the tour group.

This kind of a blind meet made him nervous. Too many things could go wrong. Too many factors outside of his control. He assumed the guy would be alone, which narrowed the field. He figured the guy would be a pro. He'd be vigilant, overly alert, probably showing signs of paranoia. That eliminated two of them. He finally settled on the slim, tall, man with the giraffe-like neck and longish brown hair who wore expensive aviator shades. He believed the man would make his approach once the tour hit Cliff Palace, as the voice on the phone had stated last week. Parnell was impatient. He wanted to get on with it and get past this charade, find out what the hell the man had that was important.

When they arrived at the Cliff Palace dwellings, their tour guide started his spiel about the significance of the site: "You can see that this alcove is many times larger than the ones we've visited to this point. This is the magnificent Cliff Palace, a gargantuan dwelling that contained 150 rooms and 23 kivas, and had a population of approximately one hundred. It is thought that Cliff Palace was a social, administrative site with high ceremonial usage . . ."

A petite woman with dirty blonde hair and a Nikon strapped around her neck moved next to Parnell and said, "I could never imagine living on the side of a cliff like that, could you?"

Parnell was in no mood for idle conversation with some chatty tourist, so he just shook his head, kept his eyes trained on the tour guide.

The tiny lady persisted. "For one, I've got a bad case of acrophobia. That's a fear of heights if you don't—"

"I *know* what acrophobia is," Parnell said, agitated, looking down at her. She was in her early thirties, around Elaine's age. Very pale Nordic complexion. Freckles splashed across the bridge of her nose, dimpled cheeks. Huge lips that seemed out of place on such a slender face—more like a botched collagen job than genetics. Dressed in a simple white blouse and khaki pants. Comfortable leather walking shoes.

"I'm sorry," she said, crowding him, "I don't mean to insult your intelligence. You look like a very smart man to me. It's just that I'm here all alone and—"

"Hi," Elaine cut in, giving Parnell a quick kiss on the cheek. She extended her hand in greeting, and said. "I'm Jacquelyn. This is my husband, Henry."

"Oh, I see," the woman said, tentatively shaking Elaine's proffered hand. "Don't worry, honey, I'm not hitting on your man." Said like a woman comfortable with authority, accustomed to being in charge.

It pleased Parnell that Elaine was smart enough to use phony names with this stranger. For some reason, this undersized woman set off alarms, her quick, birdlike mannerisms and penetrating stare sending him signals that she wasn't to be trusted. And there was something disturbingly familiar about the woman's voice, the nasal tone of it, her nuanced way of speaking. Some kind of slight European accent seeping into her cultivated American Midwest dialect.

Familiar. But Parnell couldn't place it.

She continued to engage Elaine in conversation. Parnell tuned them out as he returned his attention to the giraffe-necked guy in the aviator sunglasses. He heard the guide instruct the group to move to the next site, and watched people walking away from them as the overly friendly blonde persisted with her overwrought yakking.

"Excuse us, please," Parnell cut into the conversation, his eyes still on the tall man in the sunglasses. "We paid good money for this tour and I don't want to miss any of it, love," he said to Elaine.

Suddenly the woman placed her hand on Parnell's chest. "I think it would be best if we lagged behind the group a bit," she said, her bright green eyes steely and focused.

"What're you talking about?"

"I know your name isn't Henry." She glanced at Elaine. "And you, dear, are certainly not a Jacquelyn. You folks are Derek Parnell and Elaine Leibrandt. And while you might enjoy intimate couplings once in a while, you are not a married couple." She stepped back from them, judging their reaction.

Parnell felt like he'd been slapped. "Who the hell are *you*?" he said, searching for Razzy in the disappearing tour group.

"My name's Jennifer," she said easily.

And then it hit him. This was the voice he'd heard on the

phone, the woman claiming to be his dead daughter. He said: "If you tell me your last name is Parnell—"

"No, it's not," she said. "It's Thorssen. My associates call me Thor."

"You're *Thor*?" Elaine said.

"As I live and breathe."

Parnell was only momentarily surprised. The shadowy types he dealt with often used this type of misdirection. This Jennifer Thorssen was a pro. Regardless of her diminutive stature, he knew he would have to deal with her carefully.

He searched for Razzy in the moving crowd, saw him smoking a cigarette, a plume of smoke trailing his head like a wispy gray tail.

Jennifer Thorssen nodded at the tour group. "Come on, let's catch up. We don't want to draw unnecessary attention to us."

"So you're the one I spoke with on the phone?" Parnell said, moving to catch up with Lady Thor. "The one claiming to be my daughter?"

"That would be me."

"So why impersonate my daughter?" he nearly shouted.

"I had to do something to get your attention." She switched gears. "How much do you know about your family, Mr. Parnell?"

"They're dead. Have been for seven years now."

Lady Thor shook her head. "No, I mean your in-laws . . . your extended family. The Logans?"

"What about them?"

"That's one busy bunch, Mr. Parnell. I know you pretty much walked away from them after the fire . . . and your wife's death. But there's a lot going on there that you might want to look into."

"Such as?"

Jennifer Thorssen came to a stop, keeping a healthy distance from the tour group. "You might want to address that question to your *consigliere*, Blanton Miles. Mr. Miles knows a lot more than what he's been telling you."

Parnell stared at her. "What are you insinuating?"

"You have built up a very lucrative organization, Mr. Parnell. Your trusted Blanton Miles is an extremely ambitious man. Oftentimes the number two man in a successful organization wants very badly to be number one, and will do anything to get there. Perhaps you shouldn't place so much blind faith in Blanton Miles."

He was about to lay into her when she said, "All of that is

really window dressing. My purpose in meeting you here is to let you know your daughter is still alive."

He snorted out a laugh. "Any idea how many times I've heard that over the past six years?"

"Where there's smoke there's fire. No pun intended."

Parnell put his hands in his pockets to keep from doing strangling this strange woman.

"I can reconnect you with her," she said evenly. "But it will cost you. Over and above the fees you agreed to with Madame Crystal."

"You're not getting a counterfeit dime out of me!"

"I'm sure you've heard of the Liberty Dogs?"

Parnell was surprised to hear the name of that radical militia group roll off this Thorssen woman's tongue. He was about to respond when their conversation was interrupted by two loud explosions from the eastern ridge, echoing through the park as if a couple of cannons had unleashed their payloads.

Instincts kicking in, Parnell ducked. Elaine and several others screamed.

People scrambled, knocking each other down in their panic to get to safety.

More shouts, above which Parnell heard the tour guide yelling out, trying to maintain order.

Confusion. A mad blur of jostling bodies, people running for cover. Incoherent screams.

Another series of explosions, sounding like packs of fire-crackers going off.

They were being shot at!

Clods of dirt kicked up nearby; Parnell could hear the dull thuds of bullets striking the hard-packed earth around them.

He saw Razzy running toward them, heard Lady Thor scream in pain and go down, saw the white sleeve of her blouse turn crimson. She had been hit.

And then everything went black as Razzy pounced on him and Elaine, covering them with his body as gunfire peppered the ground all around them.

Rats in a Van

THE SHOOTING STOPPED as quickly as it began.

Razzy hustled Elaine and Parnell down a grassy slope and through a stand of trees. Behind them, Parnell heard a woman wailing in misery.

"What the hell's going on?" he shouted.

"Don't know," Razzy said, cell phone to his ear, breathing hard as he kept up a fast pace. "Somebody wantin' to put you down. Good thing their aim sucks."

Elaine said: "That woman we were with? She was hit?"

"Yeah. Christ!"

Parnell started to ask another question. Razzy held up his hand, silencing him, his face etched in concentration, the phone tight to his ear.

Parnell caught clips of Blanton's voice. Of course, he thought. The man who never sleeps. Blanton Miles—the supreme organizer—performing his administrative magic once again.

"You're gonna love this, Derek," Razzy said, putting his phone away and looking across the paved road at Spruce Tree Terrace, the people milling about. "The dudes takin' potshots at you an' Elaine are them arsonist pricks who've been in Durango lookin' for ya. Two of your guys tailin' 'em caught 'em."

"Great," Parnell mumbled, thinking: Spottswood and Delancey—two good men doing their jobs efficiently. He felt Elaine squeeze his hand.

Razzy lit up a smoke. Lipping the cigarette, he said, "They nailed a couple of innocent bystanders."

Parnell thought about Tico Samuels and Jerry Ray Allenson. How stupid could two men be? They had violated the terms of their probation by leaving the state of New York. They had murdered Willis Logan on the railroad tracks outside of Pittsburgh. They had come after Parnell thinking erroneously he had something to do with their incarceration. And just now they had tried to gun him down in a national park amid dozens of witnesses in broad daylight. All this after being given a *Get Out of Jail Free* card, avoiding long-term prison sentences.

Morons!

"So where are our gallivanting sharpshooters now?" he asked Razzy.

"Your guys have 'em in a van they rented. They gonna pick us up over at Sun Point View in twenty minutes. We need to hustle on over there. This place gonna be crawlin' with feds soon."

Parnell pulled Elaine along, trying to keep up with Razzy's hurried pace, wondering as he walked whether the Thorssen woman had set them up. Parnell recalled the extreme measures the petite Swede had taken to keep them separated from the tour group. But if she had set them up, why did she get hit? Were Samuels and Allenson incompetent shooters? Or had Thorssen just gotten in the way and ended up as collateral damage?

And then there was the troubling new possibility that Blanton had set up this attempted hit. Lady Thor's words flashed through Parnell's mind: *"Your trusted Blanton Miles is an extremely ambitious man. Oftentimes the number two man in a successful organization wants very badly to be number one, and will do anything to get there. Perhaps you shouldn't place so much blind faith in Blanton Miles."*

Outrageous. Parnell just couldn't buy into that scenario.

Equally outrageous was Jennifer Thorssen's claim that his daughter—Jennifer—was somehow still alive. Lady Thor claimed she had spoken with her face-to-face just last week. A complete Twilight Zone notion if ever there was one. And the mention of his extended family—Parnell's late wife Barbara's equally late first husband, Willis Logan, and the family on his side. Parnell had always done his best to avoid that clan, and knew very little about them. Why had Thorssen mentioned the Logans?

But as far-out as Jennifer Thorssen seemed to be, Parnell's gut told him she was no flake. Something about the woman's seriousness of purpose, the way she carried herself, the way she communicated, the way she doled out information and used it as currency. She was definitely an experienced operative. Parnell had dealt with many high-level intelligence agents, and he sensed this Thorssen woman could run with any of them. She had the right blend of moxie and intrigue, the aura of arrogance and mystery that came with the territory. He only wished he had more time to discover what she knew about his daughter. Parnell doubted he'd seen the last of her, however, since no money had exchanged hands yet.

Ten minutes later they stood at the side of the road near Sun Point View. An old U-Haul van rolled up, spewing exhaust. Kevin Spottswood sat behind the wheel. The rear doors swung open and Saul Delancey jumped out.

Delancey nodded at Parnell. "Hey, bossman," he said, scanning the immediate area.

Parnell helped Elaine up into the rear of the van, then climbed in behind her. The interior smelled like wet blankets and mildew and old furniture. Tinted windows on either side let in faint sunlight. The cargo area was cut off from the front; just a small Plexiglas window provided a glimpse into the front cab.

"I'm gonna ride shotgun," Razzy said. "Mistah Spottswood's gonna need a good navigator."

Parnell thought it was more about Razzy being able to smoke.

Delancey hopped up into the back of the van, pulled the doors shut.

In the dim light, Parnell saw two men sitting with their backs up against the opposite wall, their wrists handcuffed behind them.

"Whachu lookin' at, asshole?"

Parnell recognized Tico Samuels from photos Blanton Miles had sent him. Dusky Hispanic complexion. Shiny-shaved head. Pencil-thin beard running along a strong jaw line. Thick neck and heavily-muscled torso. Parnell shifted to Allenson, who remained slumped in a defeated posture, his Brillo-pad hair reminding him of a young Art Garfunkel.

"Well, well, well," Parnell said, looking back at Samuels, "if it isn't Frick and Frack. Or should I call you Sparky and Smoky?"

"*Besa mi culo, puto!*" Tico Samuels hissed.

Parnell ignored the barb by saying, "Nice to finally meet you after all these years, Tico . . . or is that *Freako?*"

"Fuck you!"

He watched Tico Samuels's beady eyes shining with arrogance and hatred. The man's defiant stare reminded him of rats he'd cornered in dark basements back in his exterminator days. Parnell wanted to kill this son of a bitch, right here and now, take him apart, limb by limb. He worked at controlling his breathing, tried to suppress his galloping rage.

He spoke to him. "You pinheads should have spent more time at the firing range. I've seen better shooting from drunks playing paintball."

Samuels said nothing, just sat there with his hands cuffed

behind him, square chin jutting out in a posture of superior insolence.

The van lurched forward. Parnell looked through the tinted
windows before turning to Saul Delancey. "Where are we headed?"

"Going back to your hotel so you folks can pick up your gear
and check out. Then we're headed to Utah. To the coal rail spur.
That's where you wanted these two mutts, isn't it? At your kill
site?"

Parnell nodded, smiling down at his two prisoners. "Absolutely."

Guardian of the Flame

HECKOUT AT THE HOTEL went quickly and they were back on the road within the hour. Kevin Spottswood used the time to switch the van's Colorado plates with Utah plates.

They made one other stop before hitting the road—the Home Depot in Durango—where Parnell bought a BernzOmatic propane torch kit. As the van motored toward Utah, Parnell began his interrogation in the rear cargo area. He twisted the propane knob on the canister, widening the diameter of the flame as he glared at Tico Samuels.

"Since you're an incurable pyromaniac, Freako, I'm sure you know torches like this one are used for soldering hard metals together. You need a scorching high heat for that. This little baby puts out a flame of thirty-five-hundred degrees Fahrenheit." He continued to adjust the torch, toying with Samuels, watching the guy's rodent eyes reacting to his every move. "That's close to the temperature of my house when you morons drenched it with accelerants and burned it to the ground. That's the kind of heat my wife and daughter were trapped in when you cremated them, Freako."

"We didn't kill nobody," Samuels said, his eyes wide as he kept a close watch on the flame. "The courts said so. Me and JR was cleared of any wrongdoin'."

"The courts are full of shit, Freako," Parnell said, the propane torch hissing in his hands. "All they're good at is putting losers like you two back on the street. The only real justice is out here in no-man's land. Out here is where things have a way of balancing out."

"I *told* you, we didn't kill nobody," Tico Samuels said. "I admit to settin' the fire. But there wasn't nobody inside when we did it."

Rage consumed Parnell. His hands shook. He felt lightheaded, the way he always did when the bloodlust started to overpower him. He wanted to set this creep on fire and watch him burn down to a pile of bony ash. After a long pause, he said, "The only thing I believe, Freako—the only thing I *know*—is that they pulled the charred bones of my wife and daughter out of the rubble."

Parnell reached out and torched Tico Samuels's cheek, smelling the sickly scent of burning flesh as he held the wand in place. Samuels screamed, a bloodcurdling cry. Parnell pulled the torch back and Samuels fell sideways, hitting his head against the floor as he whimpered in pain.

"Who was giving you your marching orders, Freako?"

Samuels lay inert, his breathing labored as he dealt with the searing pain in his cheek.

Parnell lengthened the flame, turned his attention to Allenson. He reached down and touched the wand to Allenson's pants leg. The cuff of his jeans caught fire.

"Goddamn! You're fuckin' loco, man!" Jerry Ray Allenson yelled, scrambling, flopping around on the floor like a hooked fish. He slammed his leg against the floor, squirming, cussing, trying to put out the fire that was eating up his pant leg. Tendrils of smoke wafted from his exposed calf, the skin on his lower leg puckering with bubbling blisters.

Parnell looked down at him, watched him writhe on the floor, listened to his moans that sounded like a mewling, dying cat. The van filled with hazy smoke and a putrid scent. Elaine coughed behind him.

"Stinks, don't he, E?"

"Terribly," Elaine said through her coughing jag.

"You're a sadist piece of shit!" Tico Samuels spat at Parnell, his jaw thrust out, clinging to his defiance in the face of great pain. "Real brave man, ain't ya? Torturin' us when we got our hands tied behind us. You got no *cojones* whatsoever, you yellow-bellied coward!"

Parnell opened the torch full bore, turned it on him, burning a blistering patch in his forearm that brought forth a wash of blood. Tico Samuels's screams rattled the walls of the van.

"Any more out of you and I'll burn your nuts off," Parnell said quietly, calmly. "Then we'll see who has the biggest *cojones*."

"You're a goddamned psycho!" Tico Samuels jeered at Parnell through gritted teeth.

"And you're very observant, Freako," Parnell said, kneeling, waving the torch in front of his captives' sweat-slicked faces. "I'm just getting started. I'm warming you gentlemen up for your grand finale. I've got a fun little thrill ride lined up for you two pyros. I call it The Rolling Inferno. You see, there're these abandoned mines in southern Utah where we're headed. Back in the good old days, the Hyacinth Corporation gouged a lot of coal out of those mines. At one time the company provided jobs for the area. Supplied the electrical grid in the region with energy-generating coal. But that was before greedy corporate execs and incompetent politicians mucked it all up. Before the pantywaist environmentalists stuck their self-righteous noses into it. Now the entire area is deserted. Ghost mines is what they are. Nothing but abandoned equipment left to rust. The wooden supports in the mines are rotting away, everything completely neglected and—"

"Save the history lesson, asswipe," Jerry Ray Allenson said.

"What was that?" Parnell said, looking down at him. "You a masochist or something, Allenson? Are you enjoying this?" He reached down with the torch and ignited the man's hair, the Art Garfunkel bush going up like a clump of dry sagebrush in a sweeping prairie fire.

More screams of anguish. More bouncing around on the floor as the two handcuffed men tried to snuff out Allenson's flaming hair without the use of their hands.

"Whew, you really stink, Allenson," Parnell said, reaching up with his free hand to pinch off his nose. "Nothing worse than the smell of burnt hair, don't you think, E?" He glanced behind him.

Elaine followed Parnell's lead. "Yeah, both of them stink. Our friends at the hobo camps are better groomed than these two."

Tico Samuels exploded. "Hey, eat shit! All three of you. Especially you," he screamed at Elaine, "you *pinche puta*! You think you're all high an' mighty, sittin' back there, judging us while your chickenshit cowardly girly-man tortures us. You ain't nothin' but a slutty *skonka*! And what's with that eye patch, bitch? You look like a pirate whore that maybe Blackbeard got the clap from!"

Parnell moved to lay the torch to Tico Samuels again, but Elaine beat him to the mark. She leaped up from her sitting position, pouncing on Tico Samuels, pinning him against the wall and pummeling his face with a wicked left-right-left-right combination. Samuels's head rocked side-to-side with each fierce blow. When the attack was over, Tico Samuels lay in a heap, stunned, his face bloody and battered, his nose shifted to one side. Elaine remained on top of him, her chest heaving as she gasped for air.

Parnell was impressed. He didn't think she had it in her.

He gave her a minute, then helped her up, making sure she

was okay. As he pulled her away, Elaine said to their captives, "I'm done being the victim, okay? I'm through with that shit. You two losers took potshots at us. I'm looking forward to watching both of you go down on Derek's thrill ride. I'll be in the front row, applauding, listening to your screams fade away as you plummet down that mineshaft."

"Yeah, let's get back to my thrill ride, shall we?" Parnell said, helping Elaine get reseated next to Delancey. "As I was saying, The Rolling Inferno will take you straight to hell. Should be nirvana for fire lovers like you bozos. You'll be strapped into an old wooden mining cart and sent plunging down the tracks, deep into the mine. To make your ride more thrilling, your mining carts will be doused in gasoline and set afire. The first leg of the journey will be hot enough, but the fun really begins when you hit those pockets of methane deep in the bowels of the mine. Methane gas plus coal ash plus fire equals one hell of an explosion. There won't even be a fingernail left of either of you. But then, you both know that. You're well versed in the properties of fire." Parnell gave them his most wicked grin. "Don't you guys just love science?"

"You're certifiable loony-tunes," Tico Samuels muttered.

"I'll give you that. And I'll also give you that you don't necessarily have to take that ride on The Rolling Inferno. I *do* have a heart, you know. All you have to do is cooperate. Answer my questions."

Samuels and Allenson looked at each other doubtfully.

Parnell continued. "First of all, tell me why you came out west, why you came after me."

Tico Samuels took the bait. "Because you dropped the dime on us."

"You're out of date, Freako. It costs a quarter to make a call nowadays."

"Whatever."

Parnell stared down at the two mutilated would-be assassins sprawled on the floor. They were sold on the erroneous idea he had ratted them out. He asked Samuels who had done the sales job on them. "Was it Willis Logan?" he asked.

"No. Logan turned us in so he could skate, but he didn't say nothin' about you."

"So who was it then? Who convinced you to come after me?"

Samuels and Allenson exchanged worried glances. Tico Samuels said, "They're dangerous, these dudes."

"Not as dangerous as the dude standing in front of you," Parnell heard Delancey say behind him. "The one who's gonna toast your gonads if you don't start talking."

"Listen to him, Freako," Parnell said. "He's a wise man." He waved the torch in front of Samuels's battered face. "Talk to me, Freako. Who put you up to trying to kill me?"

When Samuels refused to answer, Parnell turned the knob again. The flame shot out, singeing Samuels's left ear. The torch roared, the propane at maximum flow.

"Okay, okay, I'll talk for chrissakes," Tico Samuels yelped.

"I'm waiting. What was your deal with Willis Logan? You murdered him, didn't you?"

"Yeah, we murdered the asshole! He—"

"What're you doin', man?" Jerry Ray Allenson warned.

"Shut the hell up, JR. I can't take any more of that goddamned torch."

"Dude's gonna kill us anyway."

Parnell gave Allenson a warning look, pointed the wand at him. "I'll cremate your useless ass right here if you don't cooperate, *JR*," he said, putting an emphasis of absurdity on the man's initials.

Samuels started talking a blue streak. "Logan screamed like a little girl out there on them railroad tracks. That train came on him like a fuckin' tornado. Like *ten* tornados all whirlin' together. But we tied him to the tracks good. He wasn't gettin' away. No escape for that piece a shit. Willis Logan got squashed like a cockroach. Same way he squashed a lot of us who done business with him."

"What kind of business did you have with him?"

"Our specialty. Arson."

Parnell reached out and burned Samuels' lip.

"Shit-*damn*!" Samuels jerked backward. "What the hell was that for?"

"You got nothing to be proud of, Freako. Killing people isn't a fine art. It's murder."

"The only one we killed was Logan, and he deserved it. We didn't kill nobody else. These jobs we did for Logan were warehouse jobs. You know, torchin' places so his clients could collect on the insurance. At most there was just a night watchman or two at the places we hit, and they always got out."

"Of course. Insurance fraud," Parnell said. "I hear that's quite a lucrative industry."

The smile Tico Samuels showed reeked with greed. "Absolutely. Business has been great since the Crash."

"So you did Willis Logan after he fingered you."

"That's right. Bastard deserved everything he got."

"And he's the one who told you no one would be in my house the night you did your thing, correct?"

"Yeah. Logan did say that."

"And you believed him?"

"It kind of looked like Logan was tellin' us the truth. The house *seemed* empty."

"It *kind of looked like* Logan was telling the truth?" Parnell echoed, incredulous. "The house *seemed* empty? Are you jerking me around, Freako? Willis Logan was a crooked corporate exec, a high-roller investment banker. The truth is an alien concept to people like him. He wanted his ex-wife and my daughter dead. He knew arson to be a quick in-and-out crime. He knew you two wouldn't bother casing my house. He used you, and then when someone turned the heat up on his ass, he turned you. That's what people like Willis Logan do. Did your contract with him spell out the accelerants you used on my house? The acetone and carbon disulfide?"

The two men looked at each other.

"Talk to me!"

Allenson said, "No. Logan left all the details of the job to us. We had a lot of experience with those chemicals. We knew they were effective and untraceable."

"But they *did* end up being traceable, didn't they? The authorities found them in your basement, JR. How'd they know to get a search warrant for that, huh? How'd they know to look specifically for acetone and carbon disulfide?"

Parnell's two prisoners exchanged anxious glances.

"Talk to me, goddammit!"

Samuels said, "Logan didn't know about the chemicals. Didn't care."

"Who then?"

"Willis Logan's half-brother," Allenson said. "He told us you planted the chemicals in my basement, then led investigators there. He told us you were the one behind the search warrant approval and that you wouldn't be happy until you saw both of us behind bars for life. Or dead. After Tico and me got sprung, he told us you would track us down to the far corners of this earth to kill us—that we should get you first."

"Logan's half-brother?" Parnell said, thinking about that. He'd never heard any mention of a half-brother. "I need a name, JR. Give me some details."

Tico Samuels spoke up. "Dude's name is Shanks . . . Burton Shanks. Ain't somebody you wanna mess with. The dude's *muy malo*. He's high up in that wacko paramilitary group, the Liberty Dogs."

Parnell tried to hide his surprise at hearing that fringe group's name again.

"Yeah," Allenson agreed, "Shanks is an officer in that group. Guy's a real prick. The joke is he eats sticks of dynamite for breakfast. Not sure how much of a joke that really is. Anyway, he told us we had two weeks to kill you. Said if we didn't there wasn't no place on this planet we could hide from him."

"Christ," Parnell said. "You two really know how to make friends, don't you?"

They were interrupted by Saul Delancey's chirping cell phone. Del checked it, punched the connection and said, "Hey, Blanton." He listened for a beat, then looked at Parnell and said, "Yeah, he's here, holding court."

Parnell extinguished the torch and set it down on the floor, took the phone from Delancey and put it to his ear.

"I hope this is a good news call," he said, hearing his words echo on the cell.

"Not really. Are you all right?"

"Yeah. We're on our way to the Utah mines. I'm in the process of questioning our gang who can't shoot straight."

"Well, you'd better get what you need from them in a hurry."

"Why?"

"There were witnesses at the park. A couple on a picnic saw Spotts and Del round up your boys and drive away in the U-Haul. You need to ditch that van sooner than later. There's an APB out on your vehicle. Roadblocks are being set up at all the major Colorado border roads."

"Shit," Parnell muttered.

"Yeah, your friends who can't shoot straight ended up killing two, one of them a Mesa Verde park ranger. They wounded three others. You're running hot, Derek. Time to make yourselves scarce."

"Okay," Parnell said into the phone. His mind raced. "Listen, I need for you to dig up what you can on two names. The first is Jennifer Thorssen." Parnell spelled out the last name. "She's late-twenties, early-thirties, very small woman, pale and freckled Scandinavian skin, a slight accent that tells me she's spent some time in Sweden or Norway. Wide mouth with lips three sizes too large for her face. She was my contact at the park. She's an obvious intel veteran. She should be easy to find since she was one of the wounded."

"You got it. What's the second name?"

"Burton Shanks. He's allegedly Willis Logan's half-brother and some kind of high ranking officer in the Liberty Dogs organization. That's all I've got on . . ."

Parnell's phone conversation was cut short by the piercing whine of sirens. He moved to the back of the van and peered through the rear window. "Shit, Blanton, gotta go. We've got company," he said, seeing the two racks of flashing lights maybe a half mile back and gaining on them.

"What kind?"

"State patrol. Two cruisers hot on our ass."

"Keep your cool, boss. You need anything just give me a call."

He clicked off and handed the phone back to Delancey, looked around the cargo area, dismayed at the number of firearms scattered around them.

Over the eerie high wail of the sirens in pursuit, Parnell told Delancey to remove the cuffs from their prisoners while he and Elaine scrambled to pitch guns and ammo into the wheel wells.

The sirens increased to a painful volume.

He felt a pinch of dread in his gut as he heard the cruisers pull up near their rear bumper, an officer shouting amplified instructions to pull over as the frantic sirens continued to wail.

Spottswood, knowing there was no way this heap could hope to outrun a pair of Colorado state patrol cars, slowed, then pulled to the side of the road.

Close Encounter
on Navajo Trail

THE LATE AFTERNOON SUN blinded Parnell as he exited the back of the van. He lined up with the others along Route 160 West, a winding two-lane known to locals as the Navajo Trail. The two Colorado State Police cruisers sat on either side of the van, their bubbles throwing out kaleidoscopic swirls of color. Cop radios blared static; Parnell heard clips of disjointed police jargon. One officer stood with his gun drawn. Another checked IDs while the third pawed through the cargo area of the van, pulling out weapons and ammunition. Parnell kept his eye on the cop with the drawn pistol. He was young and jittery, brandishing a Smith & Wesson M&P .357.

The trooper in charge addressed Tico Samuels and JR Allenson as he checked their identification. "You two look like you just climbed out of a fryolator. Here, Jake," he said, handing the pair of wallets to the young cop with the firearm, "run a check on these two, will ya?"

Parnell didn't know why they bothered. They'd find both IDs to be bogus.

"It wasn't any fryolator got those two, Clayton," said the cop rummaging through the cargo area. "Looks like they got smoked with this blowtorch." He held up Parnell's BernzOmatic. "I also found these handcuffs."

From down the line, Tico Samuels pointed at Parnell and said, "Yeah, that son of a bitch cuffed us and then burnt the shit out of us."

Officer Clayton looked at Parnell from behind his dark Ray-Bans. "That true, partner?"

Parnell held his tongue. He knew it wouldn't take them long to make Samuels and Allenson as the Mesa Verde shooters. He also knew a sharp cop could nail him on charges of kidnapping, false imprisonment, and assault with a deadly weapon once all of the details about this little misadventure came out. Parnell was also painfully aware that if his Walther and Razzy's hogleg were linked to the slugs and shells found at the Chinle hunting shack, the best defense attorney in America wouldn't be able to get them off. Best to keep his mouth shut.

The trooper searching the van held up Elaine's painting of the evil-looking crossbow hunter. "And just what do we have here?" he asked.

"That's mine," Elaine said. "Be careful with it, will you? The paint's still wet."

Officer Clayton strutted to the back of the van and studied the painting. "Hmmmm. Strange the fascination people have with crossbow hunters these days, especially since those two were gunned down over in Arizona." He stared at Elaine. "You know anything about that, darlin'?"

Parnell was about to jump in and defend her when he heard Razzy say, "You got a warrant to search our vehicle, officer?"

Officer Clayton stepped in front of Razzy. He was a tall man who cast a long, thin shadow across the road. "You sure run your mouth a lot for a guy who doesn't carry any identification."

Razzy smiled. "Ain't no law 'gainst that, is there?"

"Only if you're involved in something illegal. But to answer your question, we don't need a warrant to stop and search a vehicle that's broadcast on an all points call. The plates have been switched, but we've got a confirmation from the U-Haul place in Denver. The VIN number matches the van rented by Mr. Spotts-wood three days ago. We've got witnesses at Mesa Verde Park who claim they saw four men enter a U-Haul van like this one a few hours ago, right after the shootings. Said two of the men were handcuffed and the other two were carrying rifles."

"What shootings?" Spottswood inquired.

Patrolman Clayton gave them the lowdown. Two dead, three wounded, a lot of pandemonium. "We've got more than enough to drag all of you down to HQ," he told them. "I think every one of you here knows about the Mesa Verde shootings, so don't bullshit me."

"We're just Boxcar Willies, officer," Elaine offered.

"Is that right? If you're hobos how come you're out here cruising Navajo Trail in a rental van full of enough weapons to take on the Taliban? Bums ride the rails, they don't rent U-Hauls. Especially vans spotted leaving the scene of a major crime." He walked up the line, searching each face, not getting any reaction.

"We're checking the weapons now." He glanced at the cop who was calling in the make and serial number of each gun. "My instincts tell me we might've stumbled on the mother lode here. Whaddaya think, Jake?"

The young cop known as Jake sat in the front seat of the cruiser, legs swung out the open door. He had Tico Samuels' and JR Allenson's rifles propped between his knees and nodded in response to the voice on the radio. Finally, he stood, held the rifles in front of him. "Yeah," he said. "The serial numbers have been scratched off both weapons, but they've been fired recently, and they match the bullets found in the victims at the park."

Elaine shot Parnell a worried look.

"So now it's just a matter of identifying the shooters," officer Clayton said. "Any of you want to fess up? It'll make things a whole lot easier in the long run."

Parnell spoke up for the first time, knowing they would all be booked if some truths weren't laid out. "There are your two shooters, officer," he said, nodding down the line at Samuels and Allenson. "The two burn ward patients. Jerry Ray Allenson and Tico Samuels. Allenson's the one with the charbroiled scalp. If you check, you'll find they both are in violation of their probation back in New York. You'll also find their prints all over those two Winchester rifles used in the shootings at Mesa Verde."

Officer Clayton scratched his head, looked at Parnell. "So if they're the Mesa Verde shooters, what were you doing with them? You the one who burned them?"

"Yeah," Parnell said, seeing no reason to lie. "We've got bad blood that goes way back, officer. It was me and my lovely lady here these two were trying to snuff at the park."

"You're a lyin' sack of shit, Parnell!" Samuels spat. He looked back at the cop. "The bastard's in this thing up to his neck with the rest of us."

Parnell smiled coolly at officer Clayton. "See, the man just confessed. Check it out, sir. You'll see I'm telling the truth here."

"He is indeed, officer," Razzy chipped in, followed by assurances from Spottswood and Delancey.

"They're all lyin' through their teeth, officer," said a very desperate Tico Samuels. "Derek Parnell is your shooter—that dude right there."

Officer Clayton sighed deeply. "Okay. Let's review what we have here. For starters, we've got stolen plates on the van. We've got a lot of firearms with no carry permits. Two of the rifles have had their serial numbers filed off, which is a federal weapons charge. We've got a bunch of folks here with no identification, all traveling in a vehicle wanted by authorities. We've got conflicting stories about what's going on. And since no one is forthcoming with any information, I'm gonna have to run you all in." He turned to the cop in the patrol car. "Jake, radio in and get a transport van out here. Enough room for seven and a large stash of weapons." Clayton turned back to the lineup. "We're going to have to take this little party down to the station to sort all this out." He turned to the cop searching the van. "Frankie, we got enough cuffs here for everyone?"

Parnell's mind raced. This was big trouble. If they were hauled in to state police headquarters, they would be detained indefinitely. And no telling what the authorities could dig up. He and Razzy would almost certainly be linked to the crossbow hunter murders. Then they'd dig deeper into his background and find other crimes in which he'd been involved. He knew they had to get out of this mess somehow. And quickly.

And then the scene turned hellish.

Tico Samuels—as though reading Parnell's thoughts—charged officer Clayton, tackling him around the knees, putting him down hard on the pavement. Parnell heard the sickening clunk of the cop's head hit the asphalt, saw the trooper's patrol hat bounce on its brim along the roadside.

Allenson went after the second cop's gun, pulling it from the officer's holster. The cop stood in stunned indecision as Allenson fired from close range, three shots that obliterated the cop's face.

Elaine screamed.

Shouts . . . confusion . . . bodies moving in all directions.

The young cop in the patrol car—Jake—tossed aside the radio mike and came out firing, hitting Allenson in the shoulder. Allenson spun around from the force of the impact, crying out as a second bullet caught him in the gut.

Tico Samuels retrieved the downed officer's gun and exchanged fire with the radio patrolman, both men going down as bullets ripped into flesh.

Everyone scrambled for their lives.

Parnell grabbed Elaine and shielded her as they ran. They rolled together down a slight ravine on the far side of the road, landing on a blanket of soft sand at the bottom of the drainage ditch. He kept her covered with his body as he listened to the rapid bursts of gunfire on the road above them.

And then there was silence.

A cool breeze wafted over them.

Parnell's ears rang from the concussive gunfire.

He kissed the top of Elaine's head. "Are you okay?"

"Yeah, I think so."

"It's been one crazy-ass day," he said, rubbing her arms. "It's all going to be okay, babe," he told her, wondering just how convincing he sounded.

Parnell waited for several long minutes, listening.

No sounds from up on the road.

He knew he had to go back up there to retrieve their backpacks and guns, maybe grab one of the cell phones. But heading back up that hill was a risk. One of the cops might be lying in wait. Or maybe Tico Samuels was alive and still armed. But he knew he had to chance it. It wouldn't be safe to travel without weapons. They needed their belongings and cash. They were going to have to hike inland and hitch another freighter, ride the rails.

Soon this area would be crawling with cops. He had to make his move.

Parnell instructed Elaine to head for the cover of the trees down the slope about a hundred yards, wait for him.

"No! I'm coming with you," she demanded.

"Listen to me, E. Things could get dicey up there. It makes no sense for both of us to risk it."

"But if something happens to you, I'd be lost out here. I'm no survivalist. No way I can make it without you."

"I'm just going up top to get our things. Then we'll catch a cannonball," he said, using hobo slang for hopping a fast freight train. "Try to relax, Lainey. I'll be back in five minutes. Keep the faith."

"All right," she nodded hesitantly. "*Please* be careful."

He kissed her again, squeezed her arms reassuringly, then cautiously made his way back up the hillside.

Dread soured his gut as he crawled the last twenty feet, scraping his knees and elbows on the cinder gravel. When he reached the top, he peeked up over the guardrail and saw what looked like a battlefield. Bloody bodies strewn everywhere. Glass shards from a shot-out windshield and brass shell casings were strewn across the road, glittering in the sunlight. Parnell scanned the area through the smoky haze, his heartbeat pounding in his temples.

Nothing stirred.

He made his way through the carnage, hearing the undecipherable static from the police radio cut through the quiet like a demented soundtrack. All three cops were dead. Tico Samuels and JR Allenson were slumped on the pavement, their blowtorched corpses riddled with bloody wounds. He found Saul Delancey's body near the U-Haul van. Parnell's employee had been shot in the back several times, apparently trying to escape. Parnell bent over the body, checking for a pulse.

Del was a goner.

Parnell knew he had to keep it together. Carefully, he checked the scene again. Razzy and Spottswood were nowhere to be found. Razzy's hogleg rifle was gone. Parnell grabbed his Walther and his ammunition, then jammed Elaine's pistol into his backpack, careful not to touch any of the other weapons.

He returned to Delancey's body, turned it over and pulled Del's cell phone from his pants pocket. He looked down on his longtime employee and saw the look of surprise frozen on his dead face. Such a wasteful, needless way to die. He knew he should try to move Del, take his body with them to get him away from this madness, to get him back to his family for a proper burial. But that wasn't possible. He'd have to leave him here, lying on a desolate stretch of Colorado highway with a spray of bullets in his back. What a cowardly way to kill somebody . . . what an undignified way to die, Parnell thought. He wanted to make somebody pay for it.

Sirens whined in the distance, bringing him back to reality. He heard the low groan of a truck engine and looked east, saw an 18-wheeler laboring around the bend, approaching slowly.

He wiped the tears from his face and scrambled down the hillside, the two backpacks slung across his shoulders. He gripped his Walther firmly in his right hand, ready for anything.

Running on Empty

THEY TREKKED INLAND, picking up the Santa Fe Burlington Northern headed southwest to Arizona. Along the route, helicopters buzzed the skies above them like angry steel mosquitoes. Parnell hadn't been able to see the chopper markings from their hiding place, but was sure they were law enforcement searching for the killers of the three Colorado State Police officers. Elaine suggested they turn themselves in, pleading innocence in the cop killings. Parnell silently cursed her naïveté, told her nobody would believe their story, that the authorities were after the four people who had escaped the murder scene and they wouldn't rest until they had them in lockup.

"So where are we headed?" she asked him.

He looked at her. Orange moonlight streamed through the railcar's Plexiglas skylight above, bathing her in a surreal spotlight. With her dark eye patch, ratty blouse, and disheveled raven hair, Elaine appeared as a sexy reanimated Anne Bonny in a fantastic erotic pirate dream. Christ she was hot! Parnell felt a stirring, a chemical rush. She had a way of doing that to him with just a look.

"Nowhere in particular," he said, trying to get his rampaging libido under control. "We just need to keep on the move for a while."

"For how long?"

"Until things cool down."

"Are you serious? That could be days . . . weeks . . . *months* even. They won't ever give up looking for us. You know that."

He sat there, Delancy's cell phone in his hands, concentrating on the touch screen, attempting to initiate a call.

"This is insane, Derek. Living like this."

"I can't argue with you there," he said absently, finding the dial pad on the cellular and tapping in Blanton Miles' phone number.

"We're going to have to face the cops at some point. The feds, too." She watched him bring the cell to his ear. "I thought you hated cell phones."

"I do. But right now this nasty little gadget is a necessity."

Parnell was relieved they'd finally gotten a connection after hours of tramping through the wilderness with no phone reception. He listened to the Locomotion Enterprises voicemail message kick in, then heard the beep. "Blanton, where the hell are you? It's me. E and I made it out okay. Del didn't. No sign of Razzy or Spotts. Call me on Del's cell." He punched off, put the phone in his pants pocket.

Elaine remained quiet. The wheels squeaked and rattled beneath them. The walls groaned, the floor vibrated. Finally she said, "We can't keep going like this, Derek. Running, running, running . . . dodging bullets. Sooner or later—probably sooner—one of those bullets is going to find us. I don't want to die out here the way Saul Delancey did. And I worry about you. I don't want to lose you."

He watched her wrap her arms around herself and shudder.

"Look, babe," he said, scooting closer and hooking an arm over her shoulders, "I don't like this any more than you do. I lost one of my best men today. And the sorriest thing is Saul died because of me. It's my fault he was gunned down. Del saved my life—*our* lives—at Mesa Verde and I let him down."

Elaine rested her head against his shoulder. "Those two arsonists tried to kill us. *They* murdered those cops. *They* were responsible for Saul's death, not you."

"Yeah. I only wish that I could have given them a final ride on the Rolling Inferno express straight to hell, the way I had it planned. *That's* what those two deserved."

Elaine snuggled closer. "You messed them up pretty bad with that blowtorch. That had to have given you some satisfaction."

"Not really. The whole time I was working those two over with the torch, I felt—I don't know . . . *shame*. Or guilt maybe. I think I might be losing my mojo, Lainey. I think I might be going soft. I felt like I was having an out-of-body experience, looking down on myself as I tortured them. I felt embarrassed. Tico Samuels might have been right. It *was* a cowardly act on my part."

"Nonsense. You were just giving them the same treatment they gave your wife and daughter. After all, they were trapped, too, when . . ." She paused, pulled her head off his shoulder and looked him in the eyes. "Shit, I'm sorry. I didn't mean to—"

"It's okay. You're right." Parnell leaned back, the cold steel wall against his spine making him shiver. "Let's just agree that it's complicated."

She rubbed his arm.

Parnell turned to her. She looked worn, beat-down, frazzled. She had undertaken so many risks to accompany him on this ill-fated trip. She had endured a lot of hardship just to be with him, and he loved her for her sacrifice. Elaine Leibrandt was beyond beautiful. Lainey was the only person in Parnell's life he'd ever been able to confide in. She was his alter-ego, his subconscious, his reason for going on. She was the only person in this god-forsaken life that he really cared about, the only person whose opinions mattered to him. So why had he persisted in leaving her behind in Flagstaff while he ventured out into this hellish world of deceit and danger the past six years? Why had he constantly risked his life riding the rails when he had such a special woman back home waiting for him, hungering for him? At the moment, his only conclusion was that he'd been a fool. For the first time in many years, Parnell felt the alien emotion of regret.

The moonlight illuminated Elaine's face with an ethereal glow. Her lips glistened. He reached out and caressed her cheek, bent in and kissed her, relishing the softness of her mouth, the playfulness of her tongue, the warmth of her breath.

When they came up for air, she smiled. "I know I asked for this, Derek. But this killing and death and violence—it's all too much. It's all so . . . unnatural. Ugly. Frightening. All I've ever wanted is a life with you. Whatever kind of life that is, I've been willing to accept it. It's funny. I remember my mother and several of my girlfriends warning me to stay away from you, that you were trouble. Strange thing is, I've never seen you as trouble. When I look at you, I don't see the man with the tombstone eyes. I don't see a dangerous killer with the incurable sense of wander-lust. I see behind all your bluster and—I don't know—*machismo*. Behind all that male bullshit is a very generous, sensitive man I love very much."

Parnell smiled, the first time he could remember smiling in days. "Just don't let that get out to the world or I might lose my advantage."

"Don't let it go to your head," she grinned. "Just accept it as one of my many character flaws."

They remained quiet, lost in their thoughts. Finally, Elaine said, "I just want to go home, Derek. I'm not built for the frontier life. But I'm not going home without you."

"I know, babe," he said. "I want to get back to Flagstaff as much as you do. But it's not safe to do that yet."

Elaine nodded, a reluctant admission. "You know, the time we spent together at my house before we left on this trip? Those were some of the best days of my life. Getting high, watching movies together, flying that goofy kite we built, eating dinner by candle-light with seductive jazz playing on the stereo, making slow and luxurious love in a comfortable bed, taking warm baths together. God, Derek, *that's* living. I was happy. Ecstatic even. I would give everything to live like that fulltime." She kissed him on the mouth, a lingering kiss. "I love you, baby, and I just want to be with you. That's all."

"I want to be with you, too, Lainey. And we'll get back to Flagstaff. But we can't right now. Every available federal agent in the Western U.S. is scoping out your house as we speak. If you think your first encounter with the fibbies was bad—"

"I think what you're trying to tell me is that we'll probably *never* be able to go back after what's happened."

"So, we'll start a new life together, somewhere else."

"Uh, by somewhere else, I hope you mean that retirement place you bought in Costa Rica and not a hobo camp."

Ever since Parnell had purchased the property on the Carib-bean side of Costa Rica a few years back, Elaine had given him grief about not taking her there to see it. She was right to do so, and he wished, for not the first time, he hadn't told her about it. But now that things had spiraled so far out of control here in the States, the little stilt house on the beach in Manzanillo seemed like the place to be.

"I just want to stop off at Shangri-La on our way south, and then—"

"Shangri-La? But that's a hobo camp, Derek."

"Let me finish. I just want to say goodbye to some of my friends and then we'll leave the country . . . head for the house in Costa Rica. The time for retirement is closer than you might imagine, Lainey."

She smiled at him. "Thank you, love. You're sweet." Elaine pulled him down on top of her, kissed him again.

Soon they were naked, entangled on the metal floor of the rail-car, showing how much they loved each other.

The Shadows of Shangri-La

D AWN APPROACHED. The eastern skies began to brighten behind the mountains overlooking the Petrified Forest. Parnell and Elaine—worn and bedraggled after a rough nighttime hike through northern Arizona backcountry—walked through the darkness of the drainage pipe entrance, and stumbled into Shangri-La.

An eerie calm hugged the hobo village.

Camp guard, Weasel Bethea, startled them, dropping out of a tree to greet them. He waved his sawed-off shotgun in front of Parnell. "Well if it ain't King Midas and another of his gorgeous twists." Bethea worked Elaine over with his eyes before turning back to Parnell. "I swear, you get more beautiful young women than Don Juan. Some dudes have all the luck."

Elaine looked at Parnell questioningly.

Before Parnell could defend himself, Weasel said, "Your nurse friend—Annie Finnegan—she's been a godsend around here the past few weeks."

"Oh? She's still around?"

"Yeah, Annie's done wonders for our miserable little commune. She took care of Crazy Walter after he got bit by a rattler. And she nursed the Ackworths back to health after they ate some bad mushrooms. Now she's lookin' after some wounded dude who got here a few hours ago. A young guy shot up real bad in the shoulder. Lost a lot of blood. Poor bastard's a mess. An old black cowboy with a funky hat and a scarred face brought him in. Strange guy. Goes by the name of Razzy."

"Razzy's here?" Parnell said, exchanging glances with Elaine. "Where?"

"Down near the river in the first aid tent Annie set up last week." Weasel pointed his shotgun down the hill. "That girl is plenty smart. One of the most spiritual people I've ever known, too. Some of us call her Doc, others, the Reverend. She's even started prayer groups. If Annie can't heal your body, she'll heal your soul. Like I said—a godsend."

"Glad to hear she's working out for you, Weasel."

Parnell pulled Elaine along with him toward the river, dreading the encounter with the girl he'd abandoned here a few weeks ago. As they approached, he saw a small canvas tent perched along the riverbank, a piece of cardboard with a crudely drawn red cross tacked to the side. He heard voices over the rush and gurgle of the Little Colorado River, and approached quietly, not wanting to alarm anyone.

"Hey, Derek," he heard a raspy voice call out behind him.

Parnell wheeled around, bumping into Elaine as he instinctively went for his Walther.

Razzy smiled at him, his eyes on the gun in Parnell's hand. "Ain't no need to do nothin' stupid, partner. We done had enougha that shit for a while."

"Amen to that, brother," Parnell said, taking a deep breath and sliding his pistol back in the holster. He hugged the big man to him. "You have a habit of showing up at the strangest times, Mr. Razzmatazz."

"Yeah," Razzy muttered, setting his rifle down. "Blanton Miles tol' me to get Spottswood here. Spotts is shot up purdy bad, Derek. Don't know if he's gonna make it, but the little nurse lady is doin' her damnedest."

"You talked to Miles?" Parnell said, thinking about the warning Lady Thor had given him about not trusting Blanton.

"Yeah. I talked with Miles right after everything went to hell. But I ain't been able to get hold of him since. Phone reception sucks out here."

"We haven't been able to get a hold of Miles either," Elaine said.

"Well, glad to see you two are okay. You are aren't you?" Razzy asked Elaine as he removed his dusty fedora, pulled her to him and hugged her.

Elaine nodded against Razzy's chest. "Yeah. we're all right, I guess." She stepped back from him. "So Kevin's in trouble, huh?"

"Yeah, 'fraid so. He ain't long for this world, I hate to say it."

Parnell noticed the bloodstains that darkened Razzy's left shoulder and shirtsleeve. "How'd you get him here so fast?" he asked him.

"After we escaped the shootout, I practically carried him to a nearby ranch. Lucky for me he ain't that big. I hotwired an old pickup truck and drove him to a place just offa Route 66 where Blanton arranged to have some folks from camp here help me out.

I thought we could save him, but now . . . I ain't so sure." Razzy returned his hat to his head, bent and picked up a stone, threw it into the river, a lazy, defeated motion.

"It couldn't have been easy," Elaine said to him.

Razzy turned to face them, the early morning sun giving his dark skin a purple sheen. "Kevin Spottswood is one of the most courageous men I ever knowed. An' I'm includin' all the brave fightin' men I knowed in Nam. A fine human bein' Spotts is. My reward is just knowin' him . . . getting' to spend time with the man. Come on, let's see how he's doin'."

They walked to the tent and rounded the corner where the flaps opened to the river. Parnell saw Spotts stretched out on a blood-soaked cot. Nurse Annie had her back to them, bent over the wounded man, applying fresh compresses, rinsing bloody towels in a bucket of river water as she dabbed at his shoulder. Spottswood grimaced in pain with each pat of the towel while Annie kept up a soft, one-sided monologue. Parnell couldn't hear her words, but judging by the tone and cadence, he figured it was Biblical scripture.

Kevin Spottswood's fevered eyes found Parnell. The wounded man tried to sit up, which resulted in a bark of pain. Nurse Annie gently pushed him back down on the cot and told him to relax. Spottswood closed his eyes and drifted off. He didn't look good at all. Parnell knew the Grim Reaper was close by. He almost expected to hear an owl in the woods.

Annie Finnegan turned to face Parnell.

"Well, if it isn't the long lost explorer," she said, snapping off her bloody rubber gloves and throwing them in a bucket. "Mr. Tombstone Eyes."

"Hey, look, I don't think—" Parnell began.

"Save it," Annie said, looking from Parnell to Elaine and back again, her green eyes alert and catlike. "You did me a favor, ditching me the way you did. I've found my true calling here at Shangri-La. These people need me. I'm home now and I have you to thank for it. In a roundabout way, of course."

"Well good . . ."

"That doesn't mean I wasn't pissed off at you. My first few days here I wanted to kill you. I thought you were the world's biggest jerk." She looked at him with a challenging stare. "But then I turned my anger into something productive."

"I'm glad, Annie."

"You should be. You should be *very* glad I have a forgiving nature."

Parnell glanced around the interior of the tent. Bloody rags were strewn everywhere. A Bible lay atop a battered wooden crate next to the cot. A rusty serving tray held silver surgical instruments and plastic syringes. A small Styrofoam cooler contained an array of glass vials embedded in half-melted ice—pain-killers and other assorted anesthetics, he figured. Parnell wondered where she got the medical implements and pharmaceuticals.

"How is he?" he asked, nodding at Spottswood on the cot behind her.

"Let's talk down by the river," she said.

He, Elaine, and Razzy followed Nurse Annie to the water's edge. She confirmed Parnell's worst fears as they stood looking out over the narrow bend of the Little Colorado. Kevin Spottswood would not make it despite her most valiant efforts to save him. She had been able to remove the slugs from his shoulder but couldn't stop the bleeding. The bone of his shoulder blade had been badly splintered. She didn't have the proper equipment or know-how to surgically repair his severed brachial artery. She had no blood-clotting drugs. It was just a matter of time until the man bled out.

Parnell shook his head sadly. "Can't we get him to a hospital in Winslow?"

Razzy said, "That was my first thought after the shooting. Almost took him to Winslow Memorial. I even discussed it with Blanton. But shit, Derek, we're fugitive cop killers. It wasn't really an option."

"*We* didn't kill any cops," Parnell said, but understood what Razzy was saying.

"I've done everything I can," Annie said, "but he was in bad shape by the time he got here. All I can do is try to keep him as comfortable as possible while he slips away. God wants him now. It won't be much longer until he rests in the arms of our Lord and Savior. I'm sorry, Derek."

Elaine wrapped her arms around Parnell where they sat on a smooth boulder, hugged him close. Razzy touched his shoulder, saying "We tried our best, partner."

Parnell felt a creeping sadness. All this blood and death and needless loss. Two of his best men gunned down, one gone and another perched atop the pearly gates. Three Colorado State

Policemen shot dead on a deserted stretch of highway. And all for what? Parnell's own personal vendetta against two clueless arsonists? Chasing down some vague promises presented by that Thorssen woman? Christ!

"You shouldn't beat yourself up over this, Derek," he heard Annie say, her tone compassionate. "Sometimes you just have to turn things over to God. You can't control everything and every-body, you know. Sometimes things just happen because God wants them to be that way."

"That's your response, Annie?" Parnell said, feeling his face burn in anger. "Six—no, make that *seven*—human beings dead after that incident on the highway. Two of my best men and three state cops among them. And all you can say is *things just hap-pen*?" He stood and walked to the river's edge, kneeled and dipped his hands into the cold water, rinsed his face. "None of this should have happened. It's all on me. All of this blood is on *my* hands."

Annie spoke to his back. "Some things are nothing more than destiny at play. They just happen and there's really nothing we can do about it. God pulls the strings and we dance. He has a plan for all of us."

"Sure, whatever you say, *Reverend*," Parnell retorted.

Elaine extended her arms, prompting Parnell to come to her. She took his hands in hers. "Listen to what Annie is saying, hon," she said. "Much of life *is* destiny and karma. Fate, if you will. We've talked about this before and you've always denied the presence of a higher power. Maybe it's time—"

Parnell let go of Elaine's hands and backed away, saying, "Look, I really don't want to discuss—"

"Destiny and fate can be positive things, too, Derek," Annie persisted. "Your destiny is intertwined with mine. Your fate led me to *my* destiny, and I was thankful. *Am* thankful. I never would have ended up here if it hadn't been for our chance meeting at the clinic in Albuquerque. And that meeting never would have hap-pened had you not been a macho stud idiot and gotten into that knife fight on the train and got your hand all sliced up. How is it, by the way? Your hand, I mean."

Parnell held his right hand out, examining it. "Fine. Almost completely healed. A little itchy where the stitches were . . . one finger is a little crooked, still some pain there, but you did an excellent job, oh wonderful nurse."

Annie let out a whispery laugh. "*Doctor*," she said. "I'm *Doc-*

tor Finnegan now. This is my calling. This and my preaching. The people of Shangri-La need me and appreciate me. My sunset prayer services are appreciated here. I give my new friends the spiritual enlightenment they are so starved for. I've converted one of the old port-o-lets up on the hill into an altar. It's become a popular meeting spot. And I have you to thank for all of this, Derek."

Parnell didn't know whether to laugh or cry, but he was happy for Annie Finnegan and her newfound sense of purpose. He just wished she could work miracles to save Kevin Spottswood. If only destiny and karma would lean in that direction.

Suddenly, they heard a raucous, caterwauling coming from the tent. Spottswood! They turned as one and rushed back up the slight ravine.

Kevin Spottswood had fallen off the cot, and lay face down in a pool of blood that darkened the hard-packed dirt.

Doctor Annie Finnegan determined he died before he hit the ground.

Revolutionaries in the Dog Pound

EXHAUSTION CONSUMED PARNELL. He sat at the river's edge, watching the clear blue water of the Little Colorado. Small whitewater rapids glittered like diamond clusters in the early-morning sun, mesmerizing him. Mallard ducks splashed in the shallows, their bright green heads rising and dipping like neon fishing bobbers. Cooking smells from Alice's lunch prep—fried wild onions and barbecued possum and coon—nauseated him even though he was famished. A stiff breeze whispered through the trees, bringing the sounds of Fingers Johnston's guitar from up at the base camp. Parnell listened to campers singing an out-of-tune chorus to "Turn! Turn! Turn!" which only depressed him more.

He looked out across the river, to the far bank, thinking about how these waters had traversed this same channel for thousands of years. This main tributary off the great Colorado River was eternal, a continuous living force, an immortal source of power and undiluted beauty. Too bad humans didn't possess this kind of long-term continuity. Parnell thought about Saul Delancey and Kevin Spottswood. They had died way too young. And for what? In a mere 24-hour period, Parnell had lost two men who had put their lives on the line to save him and Elaine. No matter how hard he tried to get past it, the guilt haunted him.

He opened his cell phone and tried Blanton Miles again. Straight to voicemail again. Angrily Parnell clicked off. He felt out in the cold, abandoned. Where was Blanton? Was there something to Lady Thor's warning? Was his right-hand man—the guy he had trusted all these years to run his operation—actually a traitor?

Parnell felt his carefully constructed organization coming apart at the seams. He felt helpless, out of touch, losing control.

He sat and watched the river, hypnotized by the powerful flow, listening to the incessant gurgle and babble of water rushing downstream. The whispery white noise worked on him like the relaxation audio tapes Elaine used to tame her chronic insomnia.

His cell phone beeped, the sound loud and alien. He checked the caller. Blanton Miles.

He answered, trying without success to keep the irritation out of his voice. "Well, well, well, if it isn't the great mute Sphinx of Egypt. Where the hell have you been, Blanton?"

"And a lovely good morning to you, too, boss."

Parnell was in no mood for Miles's sarcastic graciousness. "I'd watch it if I were you. You *have* been a little scarce lately, my friend."

"You're a fine one to talk, Derek—"

"Damn it! How many times do I have to tell you not to use my name over the phone?"

"Sorry, boss. I just—"

"Never mind," Parnell said, realizing he was letting his paranoia get the better of him. Now was not the time to get into it with Miles. "I'm a little stressed at the moment. Spottswood took the Westbound," he said, using the hobo term for dying.

"Oh, shit, no! Damn. I'm sorry. You and Elaine okay?"

"Good as can be expected, considering."

"So, you're at Shangri-La?"

"Yeah."

"Lucious still there?"

"Yeah, Razzy's here. He said he spoke with you right after our um, *entanglement* with the state cops."

"Yes. Lucious did everything in his power to save Spottswood."

"I know." Parnell felt a tightening in his gut. "It all went to hell fast, Blanton."

"That's what I hear. Lucious told me our two firebugs stirred things up."

"Yeah. Neither of those bozos had the sense God gave fresh roadkill. How big of a mess are we in?"

"Very little, actually. The only living witnesses to what happened out there on Navajo Trail Highway are you, Elaine, and Lucious. Nobody left on the law enforcement side to relate what went down out there, aside from a few garbled radio transmissions they caught on tape. The only way we're tied to this is Saul Delancey's body. He's a known employee of Locomotion Enterprises."

Parnell thought about that. "Has anybody questioned you yet?"

"We received a call from the Colorado State Police about an hour ago. That's how I found out about the recorded incident calls. I haven't gotten back with them yet. I wanted to talk with you first."

"Good. Tell them anything to keep them off our backs. But deny any knowledge of what Del was doing in the state of Colorado. Have you notified Saul's wife yet?"

"I plan to this morning. I guess I need to contact Kevin's family, too, now."

"Please do. Help them with funeral arrangements."

"His body is there? At Shangri-La?"

"Yeah."

"I'll get right on it."

"Have you been able to track down our wounded Lady Thor yet? Jennifer Thorssen?"

"Yes. Emergency Rescue took her to Mercy Regional in Durango after the shooting. Her full legal name is Genevieve Dahlberg Thorssen."

"She still there?"

"No. They released her last night. Turns out it wasn't serious— just a superficial flesh wound."

"We got any eyes on her now?"

"Unfortunately, no."

"Shit," Parnell grumbled, thinking he had lost a key contact. His *only* contact.

"What about that Madame Crystal fortune teller in Sedona? Did Grabowski get the goods on her?"

"Bad news there, too, boss."

"How so?"

"The woman disappeared. Grabowski said her house was dark. Said he talked to neighbors who told him the Madame was gone on her annual vacation in Europe, that she closes down her business for three weeks every year at this time."

Parnell huffed. "Funny how people take my money and run. What about this guy Burton Shanks? You get the scoop on him?"

"Yes. Burt Shanks is indeed Willis Logan's half-brother. Same mother, different fathers. The mother—Marianne—remarried a few years after her first husband, Christopher Logan, dropped dead of a heart attack. This was in the early 1980s. In 1984, she married her second husband—Warren Shanks, known to many as Wild Warren due to his rebellious, anti-government ways.

Vietnam draft dodger, member of the SDS and the Weathermen underground. Wild Warren was on many federal watch lists through the eighties and nineties as a serious domestic terrorist threat. He was a self-avowed enemy of U.S. foreign policy and worked to disrupt government activities every chance he got. Turns out Wild Warren was killed in a shootout with FBI agents in 1996 in a botched attempt to blow up an ROTC induction center. I know I'm digressing here, boss, but—"

"No, this is good, Blanton. Keep going."

"Okay. Well, early in their marriage, Marianne got pregnant. Burton Shanks came into the world July 20, 1985." Parnell heard Miles shuffling through papers. ". . . The first eleven years of his life he was subjected to his parents' hatred of the U.S. government. He grew up with all kinds of subversive types traipsing through his living room. The boy sat through many meetings where revolutionaries preached sedition as gospel and anarchy as the highest form of nobility. It was drilled into Burt from a young age that the U.S. government was the evil empire, that it was a festering bed of corruption that needed to be toppled."

Parnell let out a dry chuckle. "Sounds like the boy was wise beyond his years."

"The turning point was when eleven-year-old Burton witnessed federal agents shoot his father to death on the nightly news. Live televised event. It set the hook that has infected him to this day . . ."

Miles went on to explain that Burton Shanks spent his teen years in and out of juvenile detention homes. When Burt was seventeen, he was involved in a shooting where two U.S. Marshals were killed. He got off clean due to his minor status and the fact that they couldn't pin him as the shooter even though those in the know claim he was the trigger man. Five years later, Burt was implicated in another shooting. Not so coincidentally, the victim was one of the FBI sharpshooters who gunned down his father eleven years before. The fed had just retired. Tucson Police found him slumped over in his golf cart on the eighteenth green at Dove Mountain, both eyes shot out, execution style.

"What happened to Burt then?" Parnell asked.

"He disappeared . . . went underground. Joined up with the Liberty Dogs, which you know about. Worked his way up the organization. He's in his early thirties now, a lieutenant who runs the Colorado branch of the Dogs. Shanks oversees a weapons compound up in the Rockies. They're deeply embedded in a cave system they refer to as The Dog Pound. Cute, huh? Our sources tell us it's quite an impressive fortress. The feds know about the place. They keep an eye on it, monitor the group's Internet and cell phone communications . . . the comings and goings of shipments. But they don't stir up the hornet's nest."

"Probably because they're taking payoffs not to."

"That's doubtful," Blanton Miles said. The Liberty Dogs aren't all that well funded. Financially they're a rag-tag outfit. That's why they come after our agents. That's why they try to extort cash from groups like us."

"Yeah," Parnell agreed, knowing the Liberty Dogs had recently strong-armed two of their agents in Des Moines in an attempt to acquire a hundred grand. "Pettigrew and Carlson having any more problems with them lately?"

"No. We took care of that situation."

"How? You didn't pay them did you, Blanton?"

"Absolutely not. I simply relocated our guys."

"Okay, good," Parnell said, scratching his cheek, thinking, reviewing what he knew.

This Burton Shanks—half-brother to his late wife's first husband, Willis Logan—runs a weapons depot somewhere deep in the Rockies for the fringe militia group, the Liberty Dogs. Shanks somehow makes contact with Tico Samuels and Jerry Ray Allenson, the two arsonists who burned down Parnell's house. Shanks possibly gets Samuels and Allenson sprung from jail, and pressures them to kill Logan, which apparently they accomplish. The two firebugs then head west, coming after Parnell. Meanwhile, Parnell and Elaine are instructed to go to Durango to meet the mysterious Lady Thor, who claims that Parnell's daughter, Jennifer, is still alive. Samuels and Allenson, allegedly on orders from Shanks, take potshots at Parnell and Elaine in the national park at Mesa Verde, botching the job badly. Did Burton Shanks set all that up, or is someone else pulling the strings? Could it possibly be true that Blanton Miles is orchestrating all of this, as was hinted at by the puzzling Genevieve Thorssen?

"You still there, boss?"

"Uh, yeah, I am," Parnell said into the phone, wondering how much he should say to Blanton. "Just thinking . . . Lots of moving parts to my world lately. My head's spinning."

"Perfectly understandable."

"Seems to me Burt Shanks is at the center of everything that's gone down recently. Like he's trying to eliminate a trail that leads to him."

"I agree."

"So what are my chances of getting into the Dog Pound to pay him a visit?"

Blanton Miles emitted a tight chuckle. "Slim to none. You'd have a better chance of slipping into the Pentagon. But I think there might be a way."

"How?"

"I'm working on it as we speak, boss."

Parnell tried to keep the suspicion he felt out of his voice. "You say that a lot lately, Blanton."

"What's that?"

"That you're working on it. You seem to be juggling a lot of things lately."

"Just part of the job you pay me to do, partner."

"Yeah," Parnell said dully, wondering which job description Blanton Miles was working under.

Parnell sensed movement in the brush behind him. He turned, cell phone at his ear, watching Weasel Bethea come out of the woods, his ever-present shotgun out in front of him. A small group of people lagged behind him, but Parnell couldn't see them for the limbs and leaves of Gambel oak and alligator juniper.

"Hey, King Midas," Weasel announced. "Someone here to see you."

Parnell couldn't hide the shock on his face when he saw who stepped out of the shadows.

"Gotta run, Blanton," he said into the phone. "Something just came up."

The Lady and Her Pet Albino

LADY THOR, A.K.A., GENEVIEVE THORSSEN, stepped out of the woods trailing a huge man who had fluorescent pale skin and shoulder-length white hair that shone in the mid-day sun like platinum wire.

"I believe we have unfinished business," Lady Thor said to Parnell.

He checked out the gauze wrapping on her shoulder, which blazed as blinding-white as the man's hair and skin. "So we do," he said, looking over the big white guy. The man was as big as an Arizona butte with biceps thicker than Parnell's neck. "And who might you be?"

"This is Lars," Lady Thor said. "He's my bodyguard."

"I think that goes without saying. Didn't you used to play tackle for the Raiders?"

Genevieve Thorssen smirked at him. "Lars doesn't play games, Mr. Parnell. Unless you consider murder a game."

"Actually I *do* consider murder a game." Parnell looked up into the man's eyes, which were a strange shade of purple he found most unsettling. The guy was a card-carrying albino psycho.

"Lars is my protector," Lady Thor continued. "He messes up people who cross me. He's also my collector. He, um, *extracts* money from people who owe me."

"Well, I hate to break it to you, but I don't owe you any money. You haven't delivered anything yet."

"So true," Lady Thor said. "That's why I'm here. To deliver what I promised."

Parnell said to Lars, "So why weren't you at Mesa Verde yesterday protecting your princess?"

"Lars was busy with . . . shall we say, the collection side of things?"

Parnell never took his eyes off the big man. "Can't Lars speak for himself?"

"No, he can't. He's mute."

A *mute* albino psycho. Wonderful. "Can he hear?"

Lars nodded his head enthusiastically.

"Well then, listen closely, Lars. If you touch a hair on my head, my friend Mr. Bethea here will shoot you dead where you stand." He nodded at Weasel, who trained the deadly-looking sawed-off shotgun on the big bodyguard.

Genevieve Thorssen stepped between them. "No need for drama, Mr. Parnell. We're here to help you follow the money trail."

"What money trail?"

"The one that leads to Croesus. Surely you remember Croesus. Your mystery financier? The one who capitalized Locomotion Enterprises? That's the first part of my promise to you. The first of my services for which you will pay me dearly once I deliver."

The mention of Croesus piqued his curiosity. "What's the rest of these so-called services you're offering?"

Lady Thor frowned. "Don't you remember anything we discussed at Mesa Verde?"

"Um, things got a little dicey, if you recall. How's your arm, by the way?" he asked, nodding at the wrap encasing her left shoulder.

"It's fine," she said, touching the bandage. "Just a glancing shot. I got lucky. Two steps to my left and I'd be taking a dirt nap right about now. Funny how life is a game of inches."

"Yeah, *funny*," Parnell said. This was one tough broad, despite her petite, fragile appearance. "So let's get back to your services."

"Right, my services. If you remember, I also agreed to reunite you with your daughter, Jennifer. I'm a woman of my word, Mr. Parnell."

Parnell barked a sarcastic laugh. "Yeah, you're also crazy as a loon on a peyote high."

Lars took a step toward Parnell, but Lady Thor held him back. She said to Parnell, "Why don't you and your darling little girlfriend accompany Lars and I, and we'll show you just how crazy I am. What do you have to lose?"

"Oh, I don't know," he said, scratching his head in mock consternation. "My *life* maybe?"

"Seriously," she said, stepping up to him, "you need to get past your dramatics, Mr. Parnell. They'll give you ulcers. If you're that worried about it, you can bring your own bodyguard along . . . that Razzmatazz fellow you're so fond of."

"How do you know about him?"

"I've known about Lucious Razzy Jones nearly as long as I've known about you. The man has quite a reputation throughout the hobo world."

Parnell tried to digest that, make sense of it.

"So what do you say, Mr. Parnell? You ready to go meet Croesus?"

He turned his back to her, looked out across the river, thinking. He heard her say behind him: "The money trail to Croesus leads to the Yellow Brick Road, which leads to your daughter. Whaddaya say? Are we off to see the wizard?"

He remained silent, contemplating the situation. Six-plus years of riding the rails looking for the very things this slight Scandinavian woman was now promising him. A trail of mayhem and death and false leads that suddenly fed into a promising money trail leading to Jennifer? Of course it was a complete absurdity. Ludicrous. But then, he had nothing else. No other leads. No hope of any kind. Parnell remembered thinking this morning that his search had ended yesterday on the Navajo Trail, amidst the gunfire and smoke and deaths of the arsonists and cops. The tragic deaths of two of his own men. But maybe there was more. Maybe this petite, brassy woman would turn out to be his Dorothy and lead him to the Wonderful World of Oz.

"I don't have all day, Mr. Parnell. What's it going to be?"

He turned, tried to avoid the psychopathic burn in Lars's eyes. The guy really creeped him out. "All right," he said finally. "Let me make a couple of calls and round up Elaine and Razzy. If you tell me where we're headed I'll figure out the best train to hop."

"Absolutely not," Lady Thor said. "Do we look like tramps to you? We're not riding any foul-smelling, dirty boxcar. That's hobo class. We travel first class. We have a limo waiting for us. It's air-conditioned. Plenty of elbow room for everyone. Fully stocked bar with finger food and piped-in music. It's a long trip, so we want to be comfortable. You'll want to be well rested when you meet Croesus."

Parnell ignored her elitist crack about the hobo class. Best to see what this Thorssen woman was all about once and for all.

"Fine, then," he said."Let's hit the Yellow Brick Road."

Off To See The Wizard

P ARNELL SAT IN THE BACK OF THE LIMO, Elaine on one side of him, Razzy on the other. Facing them on the opposite bench seat were Lady Thor and Lars. The cloying smell of potpourri air freshener and leather interior reminded him of the conspicuous consumption he'd hated in his late wife, Barbara. Music blared at him through the surrounding speakers—the over-layered, syrupy sweet harmonies of ABBA. He felt trapped, closed-in by the bass-thumping bottom beat that came close to inducing concussions.

"Don't you have any *good* road tunes?" he shouted at Lady Thor over the pounding music.

"You don't like ABBA, Mr. Parnell?" she yelled back.

The song "Dancing Queen" started, and he groaned. "Oh for chrissakes, turn that shit off!"

Genevieve Thorssen angrily stabbed a button on her armrest, shutting off the music. "Are you for real?" she said, incredulous. "You have absolutely no taste in music. Not much class either."

"I agree with Derek," Elaine said. "ABBA sounds like the Mormon Tabernacle Choir on helium."

Parnell and Razzy broke out laughing.

Lady Thor tried to keep a handle on her composure. "Aren't *you* the witty one, Ellen," she said.

"It's *Elaine*."

"Right. Well, *Elaine*, where Lars and I come from, ABBA are rock royalty."

"Maybe in your country," Razzy chipped in, "but they sho' ain't exactly James Brown or Marvin Gaye or Aretha now, are they?"

The Thorssen woman turned indignant. "Arrogant Americans! And filthy hobos to boot! I give you luxurious transportation and you insult me? You question my musical tastes? Don't talk to me," she said, dismissing the three of them with a wave of her hand. "I can't take any more of your baseless opinions."

Parnell didn't care about Lady Thor's strange obsession with a washed-up Swedish pop band. He hit the mini-bar and poured himself a neat scotch, kicked back, sipped, took in the countryside through the tinted window. The view didn't help his foul mood. They passed through small towns dotting the Arizona high desert. He found the view depressing. So much real estate wasting away. He saw the same recurring theme from one town to the next: storefronts boarded up, their signage rusting or falling apart. Office buildings with no tenants; apartments sitting empty, void of renters. Home after home littered with foreclosure notices. Much of America had become a ghost town after The Second Great Wall Street Crash, which, of course, had led to this Second Great Depression. Parnell couldn't understand what was so "great" about crashes and depressions and why the media persisted in attributing the positive adjective to these deplorable conditions. The United States circled the toilet bowl on its final flush and most Americans remained in denial, even with all the evidence surrounding them.

Parnell figured it was inevitable. He knew his history. World superpowers—the ancient Greeks, the Roman Empire, Spain, Great Britain—ruled the planet for a period of about 200 years before they collapsed under the weight of greed and corruption and incompetence. America was overdue. Even the best systems of government and trade and social structure eventually caved under the quirks and temptations of humanity. It was America's turn. Somewhere along the line, both major political parties had jumped into bed with Big Business and Organized Religion, and this triad of strange bedfellows had raped the middle class into a state of utter destitution. The result was millions of wandering homeless, a barren landscape of dead and dying real estate, and a frightening sharp increase in hard crime. Five percent of the nation now possessed 85% of the wealth.

Parnell had seen this shift coming for decades. To him it had been like an epic train wreck unfolding in super slow motion. The decline of this once-great country saddened him, for he knew it didn't have to happen. He knew the whole mess could have been avoided with a little more government oversight and regulation. A little more separation of church and state, a lot less cronyism and bipartisan politics and unchecked greed. But what was done was done. Too late to undo it. It was the country's fate, the same cruel destiny that eventually cut every world power down at the knees. Riding in the luxury of this roomy sedan only added to his sadness. He felt guilty traveling in this ultra-expensive stretch limo with its wet bar and surround-sound stereo and rolling delicatessen when so many didn't have a roof over their heads and didn't know when or what their next meal would be.

Elaine leaned over, whispered in his ear, "Are you okay, hon? You seem far away."

"I am," he whispered back.

"Anything you want to talk about?"

"No, I just—"

"Listen, you two," Lady Thor's caustic voice cut into their whispers. "It's rude to carry on a private conversation in front of others."

Parnell pulled his head away from Elaine. "I thought you *didn't* want us talking to you. Jesus, make up your mind."

"I *have* made up my mind," Lady Thor said calmly as she studied him. "My sources warned me about you. About your mercurial nature."

"My mercurial nature?" Parnell laughed. "That's rich. Look, I didn't come on this trip to be ridiculed. Tell your driver to stop this overpriced tin can right now. This is where we get out."

Lars leaned forward, clenched his big fists, ready to take action.

"Come any closer and I'll make melon mush of your head," Parnell warned, feeling for the Walther in his waistband. He'd had enough of Lars and the way the big man kept staring at him with those freaky purplish-red eyes.

"Turn off the machismo, Mr. Parnell," Lady Thor said, flailing an arm out to restrain Lars. "Your act isn't as intimidating as you think."

"Let us out! Now!"

"Why? So you can hop one of your smelly freight trains? I'm beginning to think you're nothing but a damn fool. You're worth a small fortune and yet you persist in traveling the country as a tramp."

"Get your chauffeur to stop this shitbox right now! Time for us to hit the road."

"You're not going anywhere, Mr. Parnell. You know it and I know it. You've wanted to discover the identity of Croesus for more than six years. You're too close now to turn your back on it."

"*You* say we're close," Elaine said. "How can we be sure of that? So far you haven't delivered a damned thing."

"Trust me, girly. I'll deliver the goods," Lady Thor said.

Parnell asked, "So just who is this Croesus? Somebody I

already know?"

"You'll find out soon enough."

"Do you have a business relationship with him?"

Lady Thor snickered. "Of *course* Croesus and I have a business relationship. I'm a businesswoman extraordinaire, Mr. Parnell. My services are in great demand. He's paying me big money to bring you to him."

Razzy snatched a cigarette from his breast pocket and flicked his lighter, which caused Lady Thor to say: "If you light that in here, old man, I will give Lars permission to rip your arms off and shove them up your ass."

"And she calls *me* vulgar," Parnell said to Razzy.

Razzy placed the cigarette back in the pack and returned the pack and lighter to his pocket. "Bitch has too many rules, you ask me," he mumbled.

"Yeah," Elaine said. "I think she's still a tad pissed off about the ABBA thing."

"Shut up! All three of you."

"One last question," Parnell said. "Where are we headed? At least tell me that."

"We're going to the sandbox where most of the rich high rollers go to play. Las Vegas. Croesus has a penthouse at the Bellagio."

THE CULT
OF THE
HOSTILE TAKEOVER

Sin City

THREE HOURS LATER THEY ROLLED INTO VEGAS. Croesus had been expecting them. Their anonymous host had set them up with rooms at the lavish Bellagio. Quite an investment since their stay was booked through Sunday. Four days and three nights. What could Mr. Mysterious Moneybags possibly want with them for four days? Genevieve Thorssen knew but she wasn't saying.

They had the better part of an evening to kill before their first meeting with Croesus. Lady Thor informed them the great man didn't rise before midnight and rarely conducted business before one in the morning. This news didn't surprise Parnell. He knew Vegas operated on its own unique nocturnal biorhythms where the real movers and shakers only came out at night.

After a shower and nap that led to an intense round of love-making, Parnell and Elaine found themselves strolling through the Bellagio casino, hand-in-hand like a couple of love-starved country bumpkins, observing the curious assortment of nightlife while sipping watered-down booze.

Parnell had never been a fan of Sin City. This seeming oasis in the middle of the desert never failed to eat away at his psyche. To him, the ostentatious bright lights and glitz were little more than an impressive façade to camouflage the sleazy criminal element that lurked beneath. The big hotels lining the strip seemed gaudy and pretentious, the competing real estate moguls playing big-money one-upmanship games. He hated the noisy, boozy casinos with their one-armed bandits and rigged roulette wheels and slippery, sleight-of-hand blackjack dealers. It was an electronic jungle—everything movement, flash, and seduction, the predator-prey relationship constantly on display.

Back in the mid-1990s when he'd first set foot in Vegas, the town had just changed its sinful hedonistic image to a more wholesome representation in order to attract family-oriented business. For years that ploy worked, with profits soaring and hotel occupancy rates hovering near capacity. But then came the second "Great" Depression. And like a reformed alcoholic who has fallen off the wagon and started drinking again, Vegas returned to its old nefarious ways. Morals and ethics took a back seat to profit. Strictly a business decision. Catering exclusively to the pleasure-seeking rich and ultra-entitled brought in the money. *La dolce vita*, baby! Vegas laughed and carried on with its self-absorbed indulgences while the rest of the country suffered.

For Parnell, Vegas also stirred up memories of his father, a man whose life was snuffed at an early age over gambling debts, a man who never met a casino or bookie he didn't like. Parnell couldn't stand being around gamblers and their ilk. They were weak, foolish people—just like his late father—and he didn't want any of that undisciplined mindset to rub off on him. He suspected he already had the gambling gene, passed on by the old man's tainted blood, and he feared just being in a casino might bring it to the surface. As he and Elaine moved through the vast gaming room, he became more restless, wanting more than anything to escape the place. But he knew one of Elaine's favorite pastimes was people-watching, so he lingered with her, allowed her to do her thing, relieved that she showed no interest in joining the gambling festivities herself.

They passed by the baccarat and 3-card poker tables, the players hunched over their hands in concentration, then moved on to the Pai Gow tables, watching as the dealer expertly shuffled the dominoes and rolled the dice, then dealt out four dominoes to each player. This was an Asian parlor game that Parnell had not yet seen. He observed with interest, trying to figure the logic and the odds, watching the young female dealer's hands, trying to figure the scam.

"She shuffles dominoes better than I do cards," Elaine said into his ear.

Parnell watched as the bank won and the dealer raked in the players' chips. Groans and excuses were muttered around the table as the players took nervous gulps of their drinks and boldly slid more chips forward for the next hand.

Parnell leaned over, put his mouth to Elaine's ear. "Yeah, she's good," he said, nodding at the young Chinese dealer. "Old card dealer trick . . . the false shuffle. Makes it look like she's shuffling but she's not. Difficult to pull off with dominoes, but she's got quick hands and nimble fingers. She has the tiles lined up the way she wants them. She's in complete control."

"You got all that in what? A minute or two?"

Parnell nodded. "I've seen every parlor trick there is, Lainey."

"But look," she said, pointing down at the table where a burly man wearing a self-satisfied expression was raking in chips and stacking them in front of him. "Somebody just won a hand."

"That's just to keep the suckers at the table playing. It also keeps the suspicion off of her. Believe me, the dealer controls who wins and how much. But in the end, the house wins big. *Always*. Come on, let's go, I can't take much more of this."

They entered the cavernous Race and Sports Book Room, which was a beehive of activity. Hundreds of people sat at individual betting stations, intensely focused on small flat-screen monitors in front of them. A cacophony of noise roared in his ears as bettors waved their parlay cards and urged on their pari-mutuel picks—greyhounds and thoroughbreds sprinting around dirt tracks, jai alai players whipping the ball with their basketlike *xisteras* against open-walled frontons, soccer players running the pitch at international stadiums—the room was a frenzy of color and movement and sound. Parnell stood transfixed, fingers interlaced with Elaine's, taking it all in, mesmerized by the room's overpowering adrenaline.

He didn't know how long they'd been standing there when he felt a tap on his shoulder.

It was Razzy, lit cigarette dangling from his lower lip, the brim of his black fedora pulled down low. "Hey, ain't his place the balls?" he yelled over the noise.

"It has its moments," Parnell replied.

"I just got word," Razzy said before taking a deep drag on his smoke. "Our host, the rich dude? I never can say his name right. He's ready to see us now."

Croesus Cashes In His Chips

THEY WERE FRISKED FOR WEAPONS and wires at the door by one of Croesus's henchmen. Small, quiet guy with quick, deft hands who led them through the spacious penthouse to a well-appointed office in the back.

"So good to finally meet the esteemed King Midas," said a man dressed in a powder blue silk bathrobe sitting behind a gargantuan teakwood desk. "I'm John Dobkin, better known as Croesus. I must confess, I enjoy the irony of this meeting."

"How so?" Parnell said, thinking this wasn't the guy with the pencil neck and dark sunglasses and squeaky voice he'd met in the burger joint seven years ago.

"Do you know your ancient history? The relationship between Croesus and King Midas?"

"Can't say I do. Educate me."

"Historians claim that Croesus acquired his great wealth from King Midas's abundant gold deposits in the Pactolus River."

"Fascinating. So where's the irony?"

"The irony should be obvious, Mr. Parnell. In our case, the tables are turned. *You*—King Midas—have derived your great wealth from *me*—Croesus."

Parnell watched him get up, come around the desk to greet him. Short and stocky, a fire hydrant with limbs. Mid-to-late fifties with steely-silver hair. Gray eyes hooded by puffy lids and a thick brow. Jaded intelligent expression on a well-lined face darkened to a deep bronze by too much desert sun.

"I'm no king," Parnell said, shaking his hand.

"Sure you are," Dobkin said winking at Elaine. "Any man with a travel companion this beautiful is a king in my view." He took Elaine's hand and brought it to his lips for a quick, chaste kiss. "You must be Elaine Leibrandt."

"That would be me," she said, blushing.

"You are a most fetching woman. A man could get lost in those alluring eyes of yours."

Parnell thought: This guy is Vegas smooth. A real charmer. Surely Dobkin knew Elaine's left eye was glass.

The man who called himself Croesus turned to Razzy. "And certainly any man with a bodyguard this imposing has to be a king. You're Lucious Jones, correct?" he said, pumping his hand.

"Yessuh. My 'bo friends call me Razzmatazz, or Razzy for short."

"Razzmatazz," Dobkin said, seeming to mull this over as he returned to his seat behind the mammoth desk. "Is that Razzmatazz as in flashy with the intent to bewilder and deceive? Or Razzmatazz as in possessing ebullient energy?"

Razzy tipped his hat. "Take yer pick."

"Well, Razzy, you were very courageous out on Navajo Trail Highway yesterday. Shame you couldn't save Mr. Spottswood. But you tried. I commend you for your heroics."

Parnell spoke up. "What makes you so sure we've been anywhere near the Navajo Trail Highway?"

Dobkin let out a confident laugh, stared Parnell down with his hooded eyes. "Don't patronize me, Mr. Parnell. It's all over the news wires. Any time state cops get dusted it's an all-hands manhunt for the killers. All three of you are on their radar."

"Why would *we* be on their radar?"

"You can stop with the bullshit, Derek. May I call you Derek?"

"You can call me anything you like. But I don't like to be accused of something that—"

"Authorities dug slugs out of two of the bodies at the scene," Dobkin said, interrupting him. "They found shell casings that match the make and model of a rifle registered to one Lucious Corrigan Jones, last known address in Dearborn, Michigan. That would be you, wouldn't it, Mr. Razzmatazz?"

"That's my name, yes suh. But I ain't touched down in Dearborn in years. Besides, just 'cause they found ammo that mighta come from my hogleg don't mean I'm the shooter. Lotsa rifles shoot them kinda bullets."

"True," Dobkin said, nodding. "But those bullets came from your rifle, didn't they? You fired your own weapon."

Elaine said, "Is this some kind of interrogation? Are you a cop?"

"No, sweet buns. I'm just informing you that I know the score. There's even more incriminating evidence the authorities found in your rental van."

"Like what?" Parnell asked.

"A painting, signed and dated by Ms. Van Gogh here." Dobkin nodded in Elaine's direction. "The painting is of a very scary-looking crossbow hunter, which looks remarkably like one of the hunters murdered in Arizona. You're very talented, Elaine. You create an authentic sense of realism in your work. We did some checking and found that you have showings in a number of prestigious art galleries in Flagstaff and Sedona. I understand your paintings sell for decent money."

"Again, that ain't no proof of nothin'," Razzy said.

"Oh, you think not? That painting led the FBI to the hunting shack near Chinle, Arizona, where, guess what? They found more of your slugs and casings, Razzy. They also found slugs in one of the victims there I'll bet match that Walther automatic we lifted off you at the door, Derek. We're running a check on that weapon as we speak."

"The Fibbies accomplished all this in the past thirty-six hours?" Parnell said, a shadow beginning to darken his mood. This Vegas kingpin was thorough.

"They move fast when the trail is hot. Especially when state cops get blown away on a routine traffic stop. There's more, Derek. It implicates you directly."

"Oh yeah?" Parnell's stomach began to churn.

"Yes. They found your prints all over a propane torch, with two of the victims at the scene badly burned. Looks like you had some fun exacting your revenge. Did you enjoy barbecuing Tico Samuels and Jerry Ray Allenson?"

Parnell couldn't hide his shock. This guy seemed to have an inside line on everything. Elaine's painting and the slugs and shells tied them to two murder scenes, and this guy John Dobkin knew all about it. He even knew about the torture of Samuels and Allenson, which was information Parnell felt sure did not get released to the media. "Where are you getting this?" he asked him. "You work for the feds?"

"No. I have sources inside the FBI and many state law enforcement agencies. But I don't work for them. I'm independent."

"So who's your source?"

"Someone you are intimately familiar with."

"Oh yeah? Who?"

John Dobkin reached under the desk and opened a drawer, pulled out a glossy rosewood box—a humidor containing rows of thick cigars. He slid the plastic off one and removed the band, stuck it in the side of his mouth. "I know you and Elaine don't smoke, Derek, but maybe you would like one, Razzy? These are vintage *Cohiba Siglos*, one of the rarest of the Cubans," he said, lighting the cigar with a solid gold lighter he pulled from the humidor. "Most difficult to find in the States." Dobkin took a couple of deep puffs, smoke filling the room. "Here, take one, Razzy. You might want one, too, Derek. They do wonders for relaxing the nerves."

"I don't want a goddamned cigar," Parnell said, watching as Razzy took one and leaned over the desk, accepting a light from Dobkin. "Who is this source of yours you say I know intimately? Who thinks they know everything about our alleged where-abouts?"

John Dobkin smiled around the cigar. "I find that word to be fascinating—*alleged*. It's a defense attorney's favorite word. Fun-ny how often the guilty use it." Another deep puff and long exhale, Dobkin studying Parnell through the haze. "I know more about you than you'd ever dream. I know pretty much everywhere you've been the past seven years, the people you've *dealt* with. And I'm very impressed with the way you've built up Loco-motion Enterprises into a financial juggernaut. Not easy to accomplish in these tough times. You have a knack for it, and I admire that about you. But let's be honest here, Derek. Much of your empire has been built through illegal means, has it not?"

Parnell sat on the velvet divan between Elaine and Razzy, observing John Dobkin through the smoky curtain. After a long minute, he managed to say, "What is this? Persecute and implicate Derek Parnell day?"

"You've implicated yourself without my help."

"Well, then, if you want to turn me in—"

"I *don't* want to turn you in, Derek. I want to work *with* you, not against you. I'm no fan of the establishment, as I know you are not. We have that in common. When I say you built your empire through some illegal means, I say it with admiration. Do you really think I acquired all of this playing by the rules?" Dobkin said, waving his arm around the plush penthouse. "Do you think any of the robber barons of the nineteenth century acquired their wealth through legal means? Hell no. Jay Gould resorted to bri-bery at high levels of government to win control of railroads. Cornelius Vanderbilt defrauded the stock market to gain a mono-poly on the steamboat business and later to take over several large railroads. James Fisk was a stockbroker who made millions issuing phony Erie Railroad stock and working embezzlement schemes through the corrupt Tamany Hall Democratic party affiliate that controlled New York City politics. And then there's—"

"Look," Parnell interrupted, watching Dobkin puffing on his Cuban, an arrogant grin on his leathery face. "Everything I wanted to know about American history I learned in grade school."

"Hey, no need to get testy, my friend. I'm just trying to make a point here."

"Which is?"

"That rules are for fools. Not too many wealthy folks got that way without resorting to illicit undertakings. You're no different. With what I know about you, I could put you behind bars for decades if I had a mind to. But I don't play that way." John Dobkin offered his guests a sinister smile. "I'm a lot of things, but I'm no snitch."

"Then what are you?" Parnell asked. "*Who* are you? You're not the Croesus who met me in the burger joint back east."

"Of course not. He worked for me. I use couriers, the same as you."

"So how can I be sure I'm talking to the real deal? The guy who financed my company?"

Dobkin picked up a pen and scribbled several lines on a pad of paper, turned the pad around and slid it across the desk to Parnell.

"So what am I looking at here?"

"I think you'll recognize the top three lines as the account numbers of your largest offshore bank accounts—financial institutions I wired money to once upon a time. I believe all three are still active accounts. The bottom lines are PIN logins for three of the ATMs you visit most often. I believe your wanderlust lifestyle calls for mobile banking, does it not?"

Parnell was astounded and a bit fearful. All this off the top of the man's head. "Okay, you've sold me. Let's get back to your source you say I know so intimately."

Dobkin answered without hesitation. "Blanton Miles."

"Miles?" Parnell said, feeling like he'd been slammed in the chest. "How do you know Blanton?"

"I've known Mr. Miles for years."

"Before I hired him to run my company?"

"No. *After* he started working for you."

Parnell felt as if the oxygen had been sucked from his lungs.

"Oh don't give me that look, Derek. Everybody has their price. You know that." Dobkin chewed on his cigar, watching his guests.

Parnell felt like he was tumbling over the edge of reality. Lady Thor's words rattled through his brain: *"Your trusted Blanton Miles is an extremely ambitious man . . . Perhaps you shouldn't place so much blind faith in Blanton Miles."*

"Relax, Derek. It's not what you think."

"Isn't it?"

"No. Believe it or not, Blanton Miles has your best interests in mind."

"How so?"

"We'll get to that in due time."

Parnell's head spun. "What about Genevieve Thorssen and her Nordic muscleman? Are they on your payroll, too?"

"Yes. I've known Thor and Lars for a long time. Eleven years ago I was on a vacation in Stockholm and happened to cross paths with them. They tried to run a sting on me. I didn't fall for it, of course, but I was impressed with their creativity and organization. I offered them jobs and they've been with me ever since. Genevieve is one of my best operatives. She and Lars make a great team. I told them if they got you here safely, they would both get cash bonuses and a month off with all expenses paid."

"Such a generous employer," Parnell said, the sarcasm evident.

"I try."

Elaine said, "What about Madame Crystal?"

"Who?"

"Madame Crystal. The gypsy fortune teller in Sedona who put us in touch with Ms. Thorssen."

"I don't know her," Dobkin said. "Must be someone Genevieve contracted herself. " He stubbed out his cigar in a big marble ashtray, studied his guests with a pensive expression, his eyes coming back to rest on Parnell. "We have much to discuss, Derek. First, I'll tell you who I am and the nature of my interest in you. Then I'll tell you what I want from you and how I want you to go about it."

Parnell didn't like the man's assuming nature. "Something you want *me* to do for *you*?"

"That's right."

"What if I don't agree to it?"

"You don't have any say in the matter," Dobkin said with a cold gleam in his eye. "You owe me. Without me, Locomotion Enterprises would never exist. King Midas wouldn't exist. You'd still be living in the one-bedroom apartment in Millford, Pennsylvania, whoring yourself out as a lowly exterminator. You never would have come west and met your lovely lady friend here. And let us not forget that I'm the only thing standing between you and a long stretch in prison. I think you knew this day would come sooner or later. It's time for me to cash in my chips. That's how we roll in Vegas, my friend."

Parnell stared at Dobkin. The man's arrogance was daunting. "What about my daughter?"

"What about her?"

"The Thorssen woman claims Jennifer is still alive and that you can lead me to her. Any truth to that ludicrous rumor?"

Dobkin produced a malevolent grin. "It's not ludicrous, nor is it a rumor."

"How about a few details, then? Something specific."

"I'll get to your daughter in due time. First I need to tell you a few things about myself. That's the only way you'll be able to fully grasp what's happened to your Jenny."

The Man Behind the Curtain

P ARNELL, ELAINE, AND RAZZY sipped drinks brought up by room service and listened in rapt fascination as John Dobkin told them his story.

Thirty-two years ago, after graduating from the United States Naval Academy, Dobkin entered George Washington University where he earned a Master's degree in International Affairs. Over the next dozen years he worked for a succession of rear admirals who served as directors in the Office of Naval Intelligence. There he cultivated his most valuable contacts in the upper echelons of the National Security Agency. His associations within the uber-secretive NSA provided him with information about key foreign diplomats and hidden spy networks embedded deep within strategic American embassies.

Working with the NSA, Dobkin learned how to collect valuable data and play it at precisely the right time. He came to understand that a well-executed sense of timing was everything in the intelligence trade. He also came to appreciate the filament-thin ethical line that separated the gathering of incriminating legal evidence from the practice of using it for financial gain through blackmail and extortion. Several of his morally-challenged superiors preached that anything you didn't get caught at was legal. The young John Dobkin followed that wayward pronouncement as if it were gospel. He came to know the confidential information game as a dark currency that never lost its value.

After twelve years of building detailed dossiers, accumulating mountains of incriminating data, and acquiring an impressive list of friends in all the right places, Dobkin left Naval Intelligence and Bethesda behind. He moved west to Nevada, where he hung his shingle for a private investigative service. Of course, Dobkin himself was not qualified to be a private dick, nor did he have any interest in such penny-ante shenanigans. The big money was in dealing confidential information, and he went after it aggressively.

He opened Dobkin Investigative Services of Henderson, Nevada. The firm posed as a front for his domestic intelligence operation, and was comprised of six detectives licensed to practice in the state of Nevada.

Soon, the investigative firm outgrew the offices in Henderson. John Dobkin picked up stakes and moved the operation into Las Vegas proper, renting a suite of offices on South Rainbow Boulevard to be closer to the action. The Vegas location paid huge dividends quickly. Sin City was a 24-7 party, a surreal landscape populated by loose cannon high rollers with swaggering egos who guzzled alcohol and recklessly threw their money around. To capture more of this lucrative free-floating information, Dobkin added three beautiful women to his payroll—high society escorts, call girls with class. Amazing what powerful men would reveal when stunning ladies catered to their every need. Dobkin had accumulated some of his most incriminating intel through his three female operatives. Parnell and Razzy chuckled like pubescent schoolboys when Dobkin told them what he called his trio of high-class hookers—The Three Lustketeers.

"You would make an enticing Lustketeer, my dear Elaine," Dobkin said, winking at her through a cloud of cigar smoke. He sat back in his chair, licking his lips as he tapped the ash off his cigar. "I know many men who would pay big money to fulfill their female pirate fantasy with that eye patch you wear."

Parnell clenched his fists in his lap, felt his throat muscles tighten up. Real asshole move, coming on to his woman in front of him like this.

Elaine saved him from doing something stupid by saying to Dobkin, "I've got all the man I'll ever need right here." She scooted closer to Parnell and grabbed his hand, caressed his knuckles.

"How romantic," Dobkin said.

"What the hell do you know about romance?" Parnell said.

"Apparently not much," Dobkin answered with indifference. "My four ex-wives are testament to that."

Elaine said, "How do you know about my eye patch?"

"Oh, I know all about your eye condition, sweetcakes. Real classy boyfriend you had there in Jessie Waltham."

"So just what is it you want with me, Dobkin?"

"Patience, Derek. I'm getting to that. And please, call me *John*. You're among friends here."

"I think that might be a matter for debate."

"You have to trust me here, Derek. I'm not going to turn you in. The only reason I know so much about your, shall we say, *misdeeds*, is that it gives me a certain amount of control. You'll thank me for that control once you understand what all this is about."

Room service brought up more liquor and sandwiches and the conference continued, with John Dobkin doing the talking.

He told them that shortly after the move into Las Vegas, he was approached by several of his government contacts. They were interested in his firm doing clandestine research on anti-government paramilitary groups operating in the Western U.S. These research projects were well funded and profitable, basically easy information-gathering work. The incoming revenue stream hit numbers that Dobkin himself had a hard time believing. The agency prospered. He quadrupled his payroll. Things were rolling along in unprecedented fashion.

And then, eight years ago, Dobkin's firm was asked to start compiling intel on an emerging domestic threat, a fringe militia outfit known as the Liberty Dogs, with operations in Colorado, Iowa, and Montana. Of primary interest to the government were the group's munitions bunkers hidden deep within the bowels of the Rocky Mountains, and one of the Dogs' arcane lieutenants, Burton Shanks. Through shrewd and sophisticated electronic eavesdropping and infiltration of their camps, Dobkin's organization collected gigabytes of intelligence on the operation. They had everything from recorded phone conversations to still photographs of massive weapons bunkers to onsite video footage of several of their key personnel in action. The federal government continued to pay handsomely. The Dobkin Investigative Services coffers swelled.

As Dobkin paused to light up another cigar, Razzy asked, "So your operation is some kinda independent covert thing, then? Working with the feds, only independent? A private contractor, maybe like Blackwater or Halliburton?"

"Not really. The only similarity is that we're all private consultants working for the U.S. government on a contractual basis. There're hundreds—perhaps *thousands*—of these operations doing work for the feds. Blackwater operates more on the military side of things, the execution of strategic defense, mostly overseas. Halliburton is more involved in the corporate sector—drilling rigs, oceanic exploration, geothermal energy—more on the scientific side than military, though they do dip their toes in military waters, so to speak, doing work for the Navy and Coast Guard. My outfit, on the other hand, is mainly about information collection and analysis—more like a smaller, more mobile domestic CIA. And, as opposed to the CIA, we harvest and manipulate intelligence for profit. We've done it well for a long time, and have been rewarded with some unbelievable contracts."

"So what does this Liberty Dog operation have to do with me?" Parnell asked. "What's *any* of this got to do with us?"

"Well, through our research on the Liberty Dogs we discovered a connection."

"What kind of connection?"

"One between you and Burton Shanks."

"And that would be?" Parnell asked, not liking where this was going.

"Christ! Are you really going to play this game with me? We know that Shanks is Willis Logan's half brother. And Willis Logan was your late wife Barbara's first husband. Shanks set up the hits on both Logan and your ex, Barbara. The feds really want to pin those murders on Burton Shanks, and they were about to before you stepped in and mucked everything up by whisking away Shanks' muscle after the shootings at Mesa Verde. Thanks to you, Tico Samuels and Jerry Ray Allenson are now dead and can't testify against Shanks."

An indignant heat washed over Parnell. "The stinking feds are the very ones who let those two ass clowns skate in the first place!"

"Maybe so. But you silenced them forever."

Parnell stared down John Dobkin across the smoky room. "Samuels and Allenson got what they deserved."

"Maybe," Dobkin said, sucking on his stogie. "*Probably.*"

"Who the hell *are* you?" Parnell said. "Why are you so deep into my shit?"

"I told you, Derek. I'm calling in my chips to realize a return on my investment. Seven years ago I laid out a healthy sum of money to finance your future."

"Why me?"

"I found out about you through our network. We were investigating big-time New York banking executive, Willis Logan, and through that, we stumbled onto your story. That's how you came under our radar. But really, you were more of a footnote until the night of the fire. You thought you'd lost your wife and daughter. You were devastated. I would like to say my financial generosity was a sympathetic gesture on my part—a humanitarian donation—

and in a way, it was. But there was more to it. Much more.

"We already had Logan fingered for a number of illegal activities—bribery, check forgery, SEC violations, to name just a few—so he was in play. We knew he was a bad stretch of road that we could use to our advantage. Even better, we learned that Logan was the half-brother of the Liberty Dogs munitions militant, Burton Shanks, who we'd been investigating for a year or more. It all came together for us, fell in our laps like manna from heaven. A multipronged plan started to come together.

"I knew you were hell-bent to find your wife's killers and so I figured if I threw a substantial amount of money your way, you would use it to chase down Shanks, helping us to build a more incriminating case against him. The government had us on a huge cash retainer to provide them such information, anything they could get to hang this Shanks and his radical cronies. I figured you could help us do some of the legwork. You did your part up to a point. You got close when you picked up Samuels' and Allenson's scent. But that's where the trail went cold out there on Navajo Trail Highway with the shootout. You never got to Shanks the way we hoped you would. I finally had to get Miles to tell you about him. You disappointed me greatly, Derek. You made my investment look bad, and as a businessman, I don't like that."

Parnell was getting his head around the fact that Blanton Miles was the one who told him about Shanks when Razzy spoke up. "The deal with them two arsonists wouldn't never a happened if they didn't try to plug us up there at them cliff dwellings."

Dobkin shook his head. "It *would* have happened in due time. Mr. Parnell here was so intent on revenge, so focused on eliminating the two scumbags who incinerated his house, he failed to see the big picture. He failed to discover the identity of the master puppeteer, the man pulling all of the strings in this thing—none other than Burton Shanks. Shanks got the two arsonists to torch your house, then manipulated them into killing his half-brother, Willis Logan. Shanks and Logan hated each other—no love lost there between the half-brothers. Then Shanks sent Samuels and Allenson to you by putting a bounty on your head, letting you know well in advance they were on their way west to hunt you down. Shanks knew how you'd react, and knew you were more skilled in the art of killing than they were. He knew if it came down to a confrontation, you would emerge the victor. It was his crowning achievement. Shanks accomplished all of this without leaving his mountain retreat and without getting a drop of blood on his hands. And now he's got you running for your life. The man is brilliant. In a depraved, warped way, of course."

Parnell thought about this, remembering Samuels and Allenson in the van, telling him about Shanks. Samuels: *"Shanks ain't somebody you wanna mess with. The dude's muy malo . . ."* Allenson: *"Guy's a real prick. The joke is he eats sticks of dynamite for breakfast. Not sure how much of a joke that really is. Anyway, he told us we had two weeks to kill you. Said if we didn't there wasn't no place on this planet we could hide from him."*

Parnell said to Dobkin, "You said Shanks let me know Samuels and Allenson were on their way west, coming after me. But it was Blanton Miles who told me they'd been released from Broome County Correctional and were coming to find me."

"Precisely," Dobkin said with a knowing grin.

A sudden realization came over Parnell. "No, that can't be," he said, the feeling of betrayal building. "Blanton Miles working with Burton Shanks of the Liberty Dogs? *My* Chief Operations Officer Blanton Miles?"

"Absolutely true. Blanton has been my liaison with Shanks for a few months now. We're working on a big sting operation that, if successful, will bring down the Liberty Dogs once and for all."

"So let me get this straight," Parnell said, trying to keep his rampaging emotions in check. "My number one guy, Blanton Miles, has not only been supplying you information behind my back, but he's also been dealing with this soldier of fortune, Shanks?"

"That about sums it up, yes. But before you start condemning Blanton, you'd best know he is doing this for your benefit as well as his own."

"Yeah, you've alluded to that before, but I fail to see—"

"Blanton has found your daughter, Derek. Jennifer is alive, and while she is a little worse for the wear, she is healthy."

"What?" Parnell said incredulously, stealing a look at Elaine. "Blanton Miles has been—?"

"Yes, it's true. Blanton has been doing what he can to lead you to her without blowing our cover on this sting operation we've got in play."

Parnell studied Dobkin, searching the man's leathery face for any sign of bullshit.

"You don't believe me, do you, Derek?"

"No, I don't. You have to admit that after seven years of searching—"

"I've got something here you should see." Dobkin pulled a laptop computer close to him, opened the lid and began tapping the keyboard. "What I'm about to show you might be a little hard to take, Derek," he said squinting at the monitor in front of him as his fingers worked the keys. "There," he said. He turned the laptop around so his guests could see the screen. "Have a look."

It was a streaming Webcam video. The lighting was dark and murky, the camera a little unsteady, but the young woman's face filling the screen was crystal clear.

Parnell felt as if his brain had been zapped by electroshock treatment.

It was his long-presumed-dead daughter, Jennifer.

Her eyes were jittery, her mannerisms nervous. She silently kept looking off to the side as if waiting for instructions. No doubt about it. She was indeed older, on the cusp of womanhood, but it was his Jen-Jen, Parnell was certain. Her hair was darker now, a shade between auburn and brunette, worn longer than she'd worn it as a kid. But her facial features were the same. Pert upturned nose, expressive hazel eyes framed by long lashes, the same sunken cheeks and narrow mouth that made her look thinner than she really was. The fleshy upper lip that overlaid the bottom, the mole on the bridge of her nose. The delicate cleft in her chin. It was her, all right. But she looked cheaper. Harder. *Violated.*

She spoke to the camera: "This Webcast is for you, Dad. I've really missed you and I want to come home. At first I didn't understand why you didn't come for me. My first couple of years here I was scared all the time. I felt like I was living with that mean old toad from Thumbelina, that ugly old toad who upset my beautiful little tulip world. I thought you'd deserted me . . ."

She paused, momentarily confused. Looked away. Parnell checked the date/time stamp in the bottom corner of the screen— last week, very recent if it was to be believed. He heard a man's voice off-camera: "Keep to the script, bitch!"

She turned back to the camera, more frightened now. "But I understand everything now, Daddy. I really do. I know now that you've been searching for me for a long time. These men here, they've been, um . . ." She looked off-screen again, "they've been good to me. They really have." She returned her vacant gaze to the camera. "But I want to come home and be with you. I want to be in a family again, Daddy. A *real* family . . ."

Suddenly a pair of hairy arms swooped in and pulled Jennifer away with a bit of a scuffle. The screen went dark.

Quick as a lightning flash, Parnell leaped off the divan and dove across the desktop, grabbing the collar of Dobkin's bathrobe. The laptop and ashtray full of cigar butts crashed to the floor as Parnell squeezed Dobkin's neck in a vise-grip. "Where is she? I swear to Christ you don't tell me where she is right now you're a dead man!"

Just as quick, two burly bodyguards stormed into the room and pried Parnell's hands from their boss's throat, yanked Parnell away from a gasping John Dobkin and muscled him out of the room.

Elaine and Razzy remained seated on the divan through the scuffle, looking at each other in stunned silence.

The Long, Crooked Road

AN HOUR LATER PARNELL, ELAINE, AND RAZZY sat in plush leather chairs in a game room of the suite, gathered around John Dobkin, now dressed in an expensive Italian suit, shirt collar open at the neck. Parnell could see two angry red welts on Dobkin's throat where he'd choked him.

A digital clock above the horseshoe bar displayed the time—3:21 AM. A Bellagio nightclub comedian fired his one liners in a live performance piped into the room on a flat-screen TV. Uproarious laughter followed well-timed punch lines. The hilarity bothered Parnell. It seemed wrong somehow, too light and out of place after the heaviness of the evening.

He heard the sharp crack of billiard balls as the two bodyguards worked their way around a snooker table, biceps straining their short sleeves as they made their shots. Parnell still seethed over being roughed up, but knew he wouldn't get anywhere with another violent outburst. If he lost his shit again, those two wouldn't hesitate to beat him to a pulp.

There remained much he didn't understand. Was this Jennifer-Parnell-is-alive-and-well thing just a huge con being played on him? He'd heard it from Lady Thor and he'd heard it from Madame Crystal. Samuels and Allenson claimed they'd torched an empty house, even though Parnell knew firemen had pulled two charred female bodies from the rubble. And then there was the Webcam clip that hit him with equal parts hope and dismay. He wanted to believe his Jenny was still upright and breathing—*goddamn* how he wanted it more than he'd ever wanted anything. But he refused to buy into it, knowing he'd be setting himself up for crushing disappointment when he found it was all a big Vegas illusion, some kind of David Copperfield magic act employing a very skilled actress who bore an eerie resemblance to what his daughter might now look like at age eighteen.

He addressed Dobkin. "So I'm supposed to believe my daughter miraculously survived that fire seven years ago, and after all these years, you've found her?"

"Partially right. I didn't find her. Blanton Miles did."

"Right, Blanton again. So then, you would have me believe that my Jenny just waltzed out the door of our burning home and never contacted me?"

"Not exactly that way, no. Surely you remember the two bodies pulled from the ruins were burned beyond recognition. No chance for DNA matches."

"Yeah, so?" he said, casting a glance at Elaine.

"Your wife was finally identified through dental records. The young girl's body, however, couldn't be positively identified. Same age and bone structure as your daughter, but the body was too far gone to be ID'd properly. Couldn't get a dental match on the girl due to excessive trauma to the mouth and jaw. Medical examiners determined the young female victim in your house had suffered a brutal beating just before the fire."

Parnell knew this to be true. The teeth on the girl's body were badly broken and mangled; her skull was crushed, her jaw separated. Death had occurred pre-fire, probably more than twenty-four hours earlier.

"The body of an eleven-year-old girl was pulled from your destroyed house, Derek. But it wasn't your Jennifer."

Parnell felt Razzy and Elaine staring at him, but he kept his eyes trained on Dobkin. He did know these facts very well. The post-mortem findings had shifted the case from simple arson to malice murder. But after the initial suspects were cleared, and no murderer found, the case dried up. There had never been proper closure. Investigators had left the case behind, needing to move on to other homicides and growing court dockets. The question had lingered for seven long years: Who could that second victim of the house fire have been if not his Jennifer? Through his long years of drifting, Parnell had clung to the desperate hope that his daughter had survived the fire somehow. But if so, why hadn't she tried to contact him? Parnell was forced to live with the fuzzy verdict: the second victim of the fire was Jennifer Anne Parnell, 11-year-old daughter of Derek and Barbara Parnell of Binghamton, New York. But still he'd kept on, riding thousands of miles of railhead, visiting the hobo camps, asking questions of everyone he met. Had they seen Jennifer? Heard anything about her? He'd followed up on every lead he got, no matter how miniscule the possibility. But as the years passed and the miles accumulated, Parnell's hope diminished to a tiny flicker, a flame that was nearly snuffed out. But in the past few weeks, that small flame had flared back to life.

He remembered Lady Thor discussing the consensus that his daughter was still alive: *"Where there's smoke, there's fire. Pardon the pun."* Now this guy John Dobkin had shown him what was purported to be video evidence of Jennifer's survival.

He decided to get to the bottom of that video clip. "So where is she, Dobkin?"

John Dobkin studied Parnell for a long moment, then said, "Your Jennifer is with Burton Shanks in the Dog Pound. She's been there since the day after the fire."

"Huh?" Parnell didn't know what he expected to hear, but it wasn't this. "How is that even remotely possible?"

"I'll tell you if you promise not to attack me again."

Parnell gave him his *don't be ridiculous* look, held up his hands in the surrender position. *No attack forthcoming* his body language said.

Dobkin began. "Okay. Burton Shanks has a thing for young girls. I mean *really* young. He has a large harem of girls up there in his mountain bunker, ranging in age from nine to seventeen. Shanks and his revolutionary cowboys take extreme liberties with them. Most of these girls were kidnapped, many taken from hobo camps where people disappear all the time and no questions are asked. Your daughter Jennifer is an exception. She was plucked out of a wealthy household by someone she knew quite well."

Parnell felt Elaine take his hand and squeeze gently. "Who?" he said.

"Willis Logan."

"What the—?"

"It's true, Derek. Your wife's first husband kidnapped your Jennifer just before the fire was set. Then he got on a plane with her and they flew to Colorado together. Logan delivered her personally to Burton Shanks."

Parnell shot a confused glance at Razzy, then Elaine. "I'm not sure I follow."

"I told you earlier that Shanks and Logan hated each other. Lots of jealousy between those half-brothers. All kinds of dark sibling rivalry going on there. Either one of them would have been happy to see the other dead. Shanks had the goods on Logan that would have gotten Logan thirty years in Sing Sing, and he was threatening to turn state's evidence on him. Shanks worked a deal with authorities to set up Logan, and then he played his half-brother into a trap. Logan, wanting to save his own ass, agreed to

Shanks' demands. Shanks wanted a quarter of a mil—seed money for the Liberty Dogs. Easy enough for Logan. The banker had all kinds of illicit funding channels set up. But Shanks also wanted something else. He wanted young Jennifer. That's where Shanks screwed up. He got bad information. He mistakenly thought Jennifer was Willis Logan's biological daughter."

"Why would he think that?" Parnell asked.

"Well, because Logan advertised her that way to Shanks. So did Barbara. Your wife falsified custody paperwork in order to get continuing child support for Jennifer. Barbara and her legal team forced Willis Logan into signing on the dotted line, claiming him to be Jennifer's biological father. The fudged legal papers made you the adoptive parent. Logan knew Jennifer wasn't his and fought it at first, until he realized your daughter could be a valuable commodity in his ongoing war against his half-brother. He figured the child support payment he made faithfully to Barbara each month was a good long-term investment in keeping his dangerous brother at bay. Jennifer Parnell became one of Willis Logan's many trump cards. He played her when the time was right. No skin off his ass. It wasn't his flesh and blood he was peddling. He also did it to screw you over. Are you telling me you know nothing about this?"

"No, nothing," Parnell said, feeling like an uninformed rube as he caught Elaine's sympathetic look. He felt like a stooge, seeing how all of this might have come together the way Dobkin explained it, and having no clue that anything like it had occurred. "I kind of checked out on family affairs back then," he said, knowing it sounded weak as he said the words. "All any of them cared about was money and possessions, and I'd had an ass-full of the entire bunch of them by then. All I cared about in those days was Jennifer. I would have given my life for her. The rest of them could burn in hell for all I cared. Barbara and me? We stayed together for Jennifer's well being. Lotta good that did, eh?"

Dobkin cleared his throat and continued. "So Logan agreed to bring Shanks your daughter. He certainly had no problem getting to Jennifer. He was a frequent visitor to your house. Jennifer was used to seeing him around. All Logan had to do was get her in his car. Promise to take her for an ice cream or to buy her some jewelry or new clothes or something."

Parnell felt a slow burn coming on. "My Jen-Jen *never* would have gone anywhere willingly with Willis Logan. She was afraid of him."

"Maybe so. Perhaps he took her by force."

Parnell thought for a moment, then said, "And the girl's body they found in my house?"

Dobkin said, "Maybe a girl from Shanks' harem who'd fallen out of favor. At last count, he had twenty-six girls, all minors, each of them conditioned to cater to the most twisted whims of the men under his command. But since Shanks doesn't like to give up his youngest prizes, the body found in the ruins was more likely some unfortunate girl hustled out of one of the hobo camps. Probably not pretty enough to be one of his chosen."

"Get back to the night of the fire," Razzy said. "Whaddaya know 'bout that shitstorm?"

"Well, we have no idea what Derek's wife was doing that night, but I doubt she was involved. Somehow Logan had to get the body of our Jane Hobo into the house. It's doubtful that Barbara—as duplicitous as she was—would have implicated herself in it. Too many questions." Dobkin looked at Parnell. "My guess is Logan used chloroform on your wife and then got the Jane Hobo body in the house before he grabbed Jennifer. As he was fleeing the area, he made the call to his torches—Tico Samuels and JR Allenson—who were waiting for the green light."

"You knew about this all these years?" Parnell said, a quivery edge in his voice.

"No. We just uncovered this a couple of months ago when we got one of our guys inside. Look, I realize all of this must be difficult for you to—"

"This prick Shanks knows about me? That I'm Jennifer's father?"

"Yes. He's been trying to make contact with you the past few weeks but you're like smoke in the wind, Derek. You're a hard man to find. Surely you've been briefed about Liberty Dog operatives contacting your field agents."

"I have. But we thought they were strong-arming us for money . . . to finance their fry-brain revolution."

"That's *exactly* what they've been doing. But their first priority has been to find you. Shanks wants to sell your daughter back to you. For a hefty price tag, of course. He figures money is no object when it comes to Jennifer. You are, after all, King Midas."

Parnell stared at Dobkin, dumbfounded.

Dobkin continued. "As I said, Shanks likes them young. Your

daughter just turned eighteen. She's legal now. That means Jennifer no longer packs a thrill for him. He's gotten all he wants out of her; she's used goods to him. The only value your Jennifer has to Shanks now is how much she can fetch on the international sex trade market. Shanks has a pipeline to Asia set up and he's been shipping 18-year-old girls to the Far East for a decade or more. Rich Chinese men pay dearly for his product. There is a big demand in Asia for beautiful young American women who are eager to please. And Shanks has trained these girls to be *very* eager . . ." Dobkin stopped, seeing Parnell's expression. "Why are you looking at me that way, Derek? Surely you're not so naïve to think this kind of thing doesn't go on."

"I just find human nature to be insanely pathetic at times."

"No argument from me on that."

Parnell felt his homicidal blood beginning to rise. "And now this pervert has had enough of my little girl and he wants to sell her to me?"

Dobkin nodded slowly.

"How do I get at this low-rent piece of shit?"

"Funny you should ask," John Dobkin said with a ghoulish grin. "That's part of the work I need you to do for me. I'm going to get you inside the Dog Pound for a face-to-face with him. Day after tomorrow."

"Really? What's to stop me from just knocking down the door to his cave? Going in and taking my daughter back and then snuffing the slimy bastard?"

Dobkin frowned at him. "This is no time to play comic book hero. I know you're upset but—"

"*Upset?*" Parnell boomed. "I'm not even sure Shanks has my daughter. But if he does, *upset* won't even begin to cover it."

"Look, you need to work with us on this, Derek. First, you don't have a clue where the Dog Pound is. We do. Second, we have an appointment set up with him. You don't get in for a face-to-face with someone like Burton Shanks without connections and an appointment."

"You set up the appointment for me?"

"I didn't," Dobkin said. "Your guy, Blanton Miles did."

"Blanton again, huh? He's been a busy little beaver behind my back," Parnell said with disgust. Lady Thor's words taunted him once again: *Mr. Miles knows a lot more than what he's been telling you.* "And Blanton is the connection?"

"Yes, Miles has architected this entire thing. For obvious reasons, we've stayed out of it. We've worked in the far background, performing as a liaison between Locomotion Enterprises and various branches of the federal government. Blanton Miles has been the point man in negotiations with Shanks and the Liberty Dogs."

Parnell couldn't believe what he was hearing. His trusted, right-hand man, the guy who had almost singlehandedly run Parnell's company and made it the success it was, had gone rogue on him. Blanton Miles had sold him out for a bigger piece of the pie.

"He's a two-faced Judas! I'll kill that traitorous scum!"

"Cool it, Derek. Miles is doing you a huge favor. He's accomplished what you've been chasing for seven long years. He's taken some daring steps to get you back with your daughter. You should be thankful, not vengeful."

"So why all the secrecy then? Why has he left me in the dark about all this?"

"Because we couldn't risk anything that would compromise the success of our sting operation. You're out gallivanting around the country, talking to who-knows-who about who-knows-what. With all due respect, you're seen as an off-the-grid loose cannon. We couldn't have you out there running around with your hobo friends, talking this thing up, having it get back to Shanks and his tin soldiers. It's my job to ensure we have a failsafe operation. We've all worked too hard on it to watch it implode now."

The crack about being a loose cannon pissed him off, but Parnell held it in check. Instead he said to Dobkin, "So how did Shanks find out Jennifer was my daughter? Was that Blanton Miles, too?"

"No. Miles had nothing to do with that. It was Willis Logan. The night Samuels and Allenson lashed him down to those train tracks outside of Pittsburgh, Logan sang for his last supper, so to speak. He spouted anything and everything he thought might save his skin. One thing he told them was that Jennifer was not his biological daughter. Logan informed them she was *your* daughter. Of course, this knowledge didn't make a bit of difference to Samuels and Allenson with regards to snuffing Logan. But they did think it might have some pull with the big man, so they reported it to Shanks."

Razzy said, "Yeah, that's the other thing ain't makin' no sense to me, man."

"What's that?"

"If this Shanks dude wants to make a deal with Derek, why'd he have the torch men try to gun us down at Mesa Verde?"

Dobkin spoke to Parnell. "If Samuels and Allenson had ended up killing you, Shanks knew he could still sell your Jennifer overseas and make good money on her. You would have been eliminated and the two firebugs would have been on death row. Shanks would still be in for a nice payoff and all of his ties to Logan would be severed. It was a win-win situation for him."

"And since they failed to knock me off?" Parnell said, "How does Shanks see me now?"

"As a means to an end."

"You mean the payment I make to him for Jennifer?"

"Yes."

"So how much are we talking here, Dobkin? Six figures? Seven?"

"No. There won't be any cash payment. Payment will be in another form. You're going to make a delivery to help us pull off our big sting. You and your trusty sidekick here," he said, nodding in Razzy's direction.

"Oh yeah? How?"

"You know anything about suitcase nukes?"

The question was from so far out of left field that Parnell felt himself flinch. "Suitcase nukes? As in *nuclear weapons*?"

Dobkin's tan face softened into that creepy smile again. "Excellent. We understand each other."

"Uh, I don't think I understand anything at this point," Parnell said, exchanging worried glances with Razzy. "What *about* suitcase nukes?"

Suitcase Wars

DOBKIN EDUCATED THEM ABOUT mobile nuclear weaponry. He talked about how a single strike from a suitcase nuke was capable of decimating a 100-square-mile area, vaporizing a major metropolitan city and its suburbs with its blast. He informed them the Liberty Dogs had been trying to secure one of these little dirty bombs for quite some time, with plans to annihilate Washington D.C. and surrounding areas. The radioactivity would drift in virulent clouds for days afterward, killing millions.

"We have finally secured one of these dastardly little bastards and I want you to deliver it to Shanks personally."

Parnell let out a feeble laugh. "Yeah, sure. You're telling me with a straight face you actually have one of these in your possession?"

"We do, indeed."

"And you want me and Razzy to tap-dance into a paramilitary munitions bunker populated by a bunch of anti-government wackjobs and hand it over to them?"

"Yes."

"So they can make the White House and Pentagon go boom?" Razzy said.

"That's the idea, yeah."

"Look," Parnell said, "I'm all for blowing up the politicians. It'd go a long way in improving our political system. But that doesn't mean I care to be a part of it. And me and Razzy? You think somebody like Shanks is just going to let us walk away from a transaction like that knowing what we know? Might as well paint targets on our backs."

"We've got that covered. Shanks will have to let you walk away."

"How do you figure?"

"First of all, they don't have anyone inside with any expertise on nuclear warheads. Oh, they know what to look for on a physical inspection—a pair of neutron generators, a firing tube and detonation unit, the existence of plutonium and uranium—but they can't exactly test it. What our contractors have built will certainly pass.

Right size and weight. Nuclear materials are very dense. Makes it a heavy little sucker—seventy-seven pounds to be exact."

"Wait a minute. You're sending us in with a *fake* suitcase nuke?"

"Would you rather it be *real*? Do you want to be at the center of a nuclear blast should something go wrong? Relax, Derek. Of *course* it's fake. It's a real bomb but not a nuke. For your information, the whole idea of suitcase nukes is pure mythology as far as anyone knows. Pure fantasy stuff best left to Hollywood action movies. Years ago, rumor was that the Soviet Union had a few dozen of these miniature nukes, but there's never been any real proof behind it. Truth is, it's practically impossible to build a nuclear warhead inside of something as small as Samsonite luggage. I think that rumor was a product of Cold War bravado, back when Big Bad Boris and Uncle Sam were engaged in a pissing contest. Those rumors only grew when word started circulating that terrorists had gotten their evil little paws on a few of them. Again, pure speculation and no factual evidence. But people like Burton Shanks? They're the first to believe those kinds of rumors. They *want* to believe them and so they do. Shanks and his cronies live in a fantasy-prone world up in their mountaintop hideaway. They're completely sold on this suitcase nuke idea. We've thought this thing through. We've created some of our own completely unimpeachable mythology behind the origins of this bomb you're going to deliver for us. We've examined every potential scenario very thoroughly. It's going to be a bang-bang play. You deliver the suitcase device in exchange for your Jennifer. Then all of you are whisked out of the Rockies in a helicopter and flown to your new lives."

"New lives?" Elaine said. "What does that mean—*new lives*?"

"You'll go into a government-sponsored witness protection program, all three of you. It's known as WITSEC."

Razzy came to life. "Why the fuck we need protectin'?"

"Once you're on the helicopter and safely away from the mountain, we plan to detonate the bomb through remote control. No more Burton Shanks. No more Dog Pound. There'll still be plenty of life left in the Liberty Dogs. You're damaging their main weapons depot. It's like chopping off the tail of a snake. Does some real damage but it won't kill them. They'll go all out trying to find you. You won't be safe anywhere in the States. Believe me, you're going to need protection."

Parnell thought about that. He wondered how anyone in the Liberty Dogs would know he and Razzy were involved if everyone in the Dog Pound was to be eliminated, and he asked Dobkin about that.

"The upper echelon of the Liberty Dogs know the suitcase nuke is being secured through your company, Derek. Locomotion Enterprises is the seller of record."

Parnell stared at Dobkin, the realization of how he had been played beginning to take root. "I thought *your* organization was handling those negotiations."

"Oh no," Dobkin said with a impatient huff. "We have to remain invisible in this thing. Shanks and his minions don't know anything about us and we have to keep it that way. *Your* company is the go-between on this suitcase nuke deal. Your guy Miles set it up and has done all the work with the defense contractors getting the stand-in bomb built to specs. He's a brilliant man, your Blanton Miles. Scarily so."

Parnell realized he had been manipulated by a mastermind. John "Croesus" Dobkin's entire sting was coming together in his mind now, and Parnell had to admit he had been played to perfection. For the past seven years, Parnell had been maneuvered like a pawn in an elaborate chess game that had crisscrossed the U.S., and they had now arrived at the end game. This guy John Dobkin had Parnell's balls in a vise and was tightening the clamps. And even though Parnell was feeling the squeeze, he couldn't help but admire the audacious genius it took to plan and execute what he surmised to be that end game.

Razzy said, "So what's to keep 'em from snuffin' us right then and there once we hand over the bomb?"

Dobkin smiled lazily at Razzy. "I like you, Mr. Razzmatazz. Always Johnny on the spot with the right questions. They'll let you live because there's a detonation code to set the timer. Shanks knows he won't get that code until you delivery agents are safe. One of our big stipulations in this deal is your safety. They want this miniature warhead so bad they can taste it. The Liberty Dogs want to make their mark on history. I guarantee you they will bend over backwards ensuring you return to civilization safely."

"So tell me more about this bomb we're delivering," Parnell said.

Dobkin offered a devious grin. "Our bomb isn't nuclear. It contains just enough radioactive material to be convincing. But it *will* pack a heavy knockdown punch. Enough of a wallop to set off whatever weapons are stored nearest the flashpoint of the blast. Too bad it won't set off the rest of their arsenal up there—the skids of grenades and rockets, the surface-to-air missiles, all the ammo they're sitting on. But it will cause a massive cave in. Once that thing detonates, no one gets out alive. We'll finally be exterminating the rats in their holes. You remember that, don't you, Derek? Killing rodents where they sleep and fornicate? Very satisfying work, wouldn't you agree?"

The comment annoyed Parnell, especially delivered the way it was, with a smarmy, elitist smile.

Elaine spoke up. "What about the girls in Shanks' harem? What happens to them?"

Dobkin's smile evaporated. "In any war, there will always be collateral damage, my dear. You have to accept that."

"Spoken like a true mercenary," Parnell said, still irritated by Dobkin's exterminator remark. "You saying there's no way to get those girls out of harm's way?"

"Believe me, Derek. We've looked at that from all angles. The girls are spread out through the network of caves. It would be impossible to round them all up and get them out safely. Like I said, this has to be a quick in-and-out."

Parnell doubted that Dobkin and his people had looked at the situation from any angle other than their own. "Why do you feel the need to blow up anything at all? Why not just deliver a dud and leave them holding the bag while the ATF and FBI move in to round them up? Seems like a less messy way to handle it. That way there's no collateral damage."

"Jesus, Parnell, you're too good for your own good. Always looking out for your fellow man, aren't you? That kind of compassion will get you killed some day. Surprised it hasn't already. How about you let us handle our business and you just take care of your own ass for once."

"Because I'm involved, that's why. Look, why don't I just pay you back the money I owe you—with interest, of course—and the three of us will be on our merry way."

Dobkin shot him a skeptical look. "You have no interest in getting your daughter back?"

"I'm still not convinced she's alive."

"Oh, but she is. Jennifer is very much alive. You saw the Webcam footage."

"Yeah. That I did," Parnell said, thinking about high-tech, special effects tricks that might be possible with digital camera technology. After all, if they could come up with a passable suitcase nuke, how difficult would it be to create a reasonable video facsimile of his grown daughter?

He decided to keep those thoughts to himself. One thing remained that he wasn't quite sure about and he took the plunge by asking Dobkin, "So how am I supposed to run my company if I'm sequestered away in a WITSEC program someplace?"

"You don't need to worry about Locomotion Enterprises anymore."

Bingo, Parnell thought, but played ignorant. "What're you talking about?"

"Well, you've never really *run* the company, Derek. You set it up and hired Blanton Miles, which was a brilliant move on your part. That's always been one of your strong suits—your insight into people. But Blanton's handled all the day-to-day business while you've been out joyriding the rails. He's the one who's taken your modest little startup into the big leagues. We both know you're more hobo swashbuckler than corporate exec, let's be honest here. Blanton Miles is a genius businessman. You're a Boxcar Willie cowboy . . . a rich vagabond who champions the cause of his fellow hobos everywhere. You're *King Midas*. It's admirable what you do, but let's not dive too far into self-deception. There would be no Locomotion Enterprises today were it not for Blanton Miles."

"That might well be true. But the last time I looked, I was President and CEO of the company. I have the final say on all business decisions."

John Dobkin gave Parnell a sad look. "You've been away too long, Derek. You're out of touch. Things have changed. It was official a couple of weeks ago. Locomotion Enterprises is now a subsidiary of Dobkin Investigative Services. Blanton Miles and our attorneys have taken care of all the necessary paperwork and legal requirements. You've been in absentia long enough to qualify Miles as proxy chief executive officer. Blanton has complete control with fully authorized signoff privileges. All nice and tidy. All by-the-book legal. And now with your criminal activities coming to light, well . . . let's just say it would be next to impossible to run your company from prison."

Parnell pretended to be shocked.

Dobkin said, "Look, I know this must be hard for you to take. But let's look at this situation in a clear light, shall we? We're keeping you out of prison. We're offering you a new life and identity someplace safe—British Columbia to be precise. We're reuniting you with your long-presumed-dead daughter. And all you have to give up is Locomotion Enterprises—which you've never really owned anyway—and deliver a fake nuclear bomb to a bunch of cavemen. Sounds to me like you're getting the best of the deal in this exchange."

Parnell locked stares with Dobkin, seething inside with the knowledge he'd been manipulated and humiliated the past seven years. He felt things shifting deep inside, his emotional platelets rearranging themselves. He could feel his life changing course like a freight train being rotated onto adjacent rails in a switching yard.

He said to him, "You are one smooth son of a bitch, Dobkin. A real cool customer. No detail escapes you, does it? Tell me something. There's one thing you haven't been real honest with me about, isn't there? You knew Blanton Miles long before he hooked up with me, didn't you?"

Dobkin's hardnosed expression softened, changing to one of respect. "You got me, Parnell. Very good. Yes. Miles came to work for me about two years before his first interview with you. He was a plant."

"What if I hadn't hired him?"

"There was no way you *weren't* going to hire him. We made sure of that. I seem to recall how impressed you were with Blanton's knowledge of you and your situation, the way he knew you had checked up on him through the Chester County Pennsylvania court system. You were blown away by the fact that Blanton Miles the job candidate seemed to be plugged into some sophisticated information channels. You wanted that kind of intel connection for Locomotion Enterprises. That information channel was us, Derek. In reality, your company has always been a subsidiary of Dobkin Investigative Services. You have been in my employ since the day you accepted the startup money from my courier."

"All that just for the remote possibility of getting at Burton Shanks," Parnell said, more statement than question.

"Absolutely. In my line of work we look into every nook and crevice no matter how dark or cramped. No matter how remote the possibilities. We figured you to be a pretty safe bet, being close to Willis Logan's family the way you were. I'm surprised, however, that you didn't know anything about Shanks."

"Logan's family didn't interest me much."

"Obviously," Dobkin said, standing.

The meeting appeared to be over. Parnell looked at Razzy and Elaine as everyone stood. He said to Dobkin, "Just one last thing. If you're planning any funny business with this bomb delivery ruse . . . if by some chance that's not really my daughter Jenny up there in the Rockies, you'd best believe I will hunt you down and kill you."

Parnell felt a chill traverse his spine as Dobkin stared through him. The look was one of a cold-blooded killer. Parnell had stared into eyes like those before.

Finally Dobkin said, "You'd best be careful about who you threaten, Parnell." He turned on his heel and walked away, saying over his shoulder, "I've spent quite enough time on this project. We'll meet tomorrow to discuss the logistics of the operation."

Dobkin's two bodyguards followed him out the door like obedient puppy dogs.

Ghosts In the Shadows

P ARNELL COULDN'T SLEEP. He tossed and turned in the luxurious Bellagio bed, unable to shut down his mind. Too many things coming at him the past few days. Too much to get done before The Big Delivery.

Elaine had finally fallen into an exhausted slumber. Parnell knew her deep, slow breathing rhythms meant she would be out for some time. He quietly got dressed and went down to the casino, picking up a tail as soon as he stepped off the elevator. Same guy in the tweed jacket and low-slung watch cap he had noticed earlier when he and Razzy sat in the hotel bar discussing their plans. To Parnell, this shadow was overkill. Dobkin didn't need to keep this close watch over them. The Vegas kingpin had threatened them, that if Parnell and Razzy were to get "happy feet" and skip town before making the delivery, the FBI and ATF would take them into custody and charge them with the hunting shack murders and their involvement in the cop killings on the Navajo Trail Highway. Parnell knew enough about John Dobkin to assume it was no idle threat.

Instead, he and Razzy had made post-suitcase-nuke-delivery plans. No way did either of them want to spend the rest of their lives in a government sponsored witness protection program. Parnell smiled when he thought of Razzy's take on WITSEC: "We'd be like coyotes caught in steel traps. I ain't gonna gnaw off one of my legs for freedom, nosiree! I ain't givin' up my mobility for the man, you can forget 'bout that shit."

Parnell stopped at an ATM just off the hotel lobby. He entered his PIN and the maximum withdrawal amount. His request was declined, which is more or less what he'd expected. He watched the text scroll across the LED screen: THIS ACCOUNT HAS BEEN CLOSED OUT AND DISABLED – YOUR TRANSACTION CANNOT BE PROCESSED AS ENTERED.

He tried a different account set up through another bank. Same result.

A third attempt, this one set up through his most secure off-shore financial institution. A bank in Belize. Impossible that Dobkin had these login credentials.

Rejected again.

The bastard had tapped out his three biggest Locomotion Enterprises business accounts. The guy had brass balls and the knowhow to do serious damage.

A bold, audacious act, for sure. But the theft didn't faze Parnell much; he had stashes of cash in other places—his rainy day money, which he figured a man in his position would need someday. Sure, the quick theft of high six-figure capital stung, but it didn't bother him near as much as the blow to his personal pride. He'd been played for a fool the past seven years, and that crushed him more than anything. Dobkin's humiliation of him was what stuck in Parnell's craw. The asshole even had the sack to dethrone him from his kingdom in Elaine's presence, Dobkin doing his best to emasculate him in front of his woman. That lack of masculine respect got to Parnell, and he hoped to be able to repay Dobkin with some similar disrespect someday soon.

And then there was Blanton Miles, Parnell's right-hand man, the go-to guy he had trusted with his life the past six-plus years. Miles had been in on it from the beginning, doing his part to pull off the hostile takeover of Locomotion Enterprises. Parnell had been screwed and tattooed by his own operations officer. Worse, he hadn't seen it coming, didn't even know it was going on. What a damned fool he'd been.

Attempts to reach Blanton proved unsuccessful. The man had vanished. Parnell tried calling Miles on the private line they'd used for years, but was informed that the number was no longer in service. A call to the Locomotion Enterprises main number was forwarded to Dobkin Investigative Services, where a vivacious young female voice told him there was no one named Blanton Miles worked there.

Parnell also tried getting in touch with several of his employees, his field agents, the ones who'd been the most loyal over the years. Same result. They had turned into ghosts in the shadows. Nowhere to be found. Dobkin had left no stone unturned. The intelligence guru had completely assimilated Parnell's company and all of his employees. It was a masterful brushstroke across a bizarre canvas. He wondered how long Dobkin and Miles had worked to pull it off.

King Midas? What a humorless joke! The royal title mocked him now, adding to his disgrace.

He left the hotel, donning his sunglasses as he walked out into the bright late-morning sunlight. The streets were nearly deserted, just a few industrious Yellow Cabs and food service delivery trucks spouting their exhaust. A lone car horn beeped. Mammoth neon billboards appeared faded and tired in the daylight. He passed several bleary-eyed souls on the sidewalk, looking like zombies in their exhausted state. This was dead time in Vegas, a nocturnal town that went into hibernation during daylight hours.

He stopped at a Starbucks, where he indulged in a Caffè Americano espresso and an apple fritter. After eating, he paid a woman $100 to rent her laptop for forty-five minutes. She shrieked joyously, carrying on like she'd just hit a slot machine jackpot.

Parnell sat near the front window and logged into the store's proprietary Wi-Fi network. He began researching northern Colorado rail routes, scratching out notes on Starbucks napkins. Dobkin had given him a general location for the Dog Pound—along the Continental Divide in the heart of the Routt National Forest, nestled in a pass cutting through Mount Zirkel. Dobkin described the area as "beyond God's country . . . more like Satan's playground with the Liberty Dogs roaming the area." Parnell studied a couple of the topographical maps he'd pulled up on the laptop screen. The location was indeed remote, an area in which he'd never before set foot. Approximately 30 miles south of the Wyoming border, the Little Snake River flowing parallel to a major rail line. More research revealed a connecting hub in northern Utah with which he was familiar, rails he'd ridden before that led south through Arizona to Nogales and the Mexican border. Perfect! Parnell committed to memory a primary and secondary escape route.

Several times he looked up from his work to see the man in the tweed jacket and watch cap walk slowly past the front window. He could have reached through the glass and touched him. The third time Parnell saw him, he waved, letting the guy know he knew he was being watched. Incredibly, the guy waved back. No secrets between warring factions here.

Parnell returned the laptop to its rightful owner and left Starbucks. He walked to a pawn shop where he purchased several untraceable, easily concealable guns with ammo. He also bought a Garmin GLONASS GPS handheld unit designed for use in deep canyons and heavy wilderness areas, a Silva Ranger compass, a pair of hinged police handcuffs, and four canisters of pepper spray designed to look like tubes of women's lipstick. The slim cylinders of pepper spray brought back memories of Nurse Annie Finnegan riding the rails with him a few weeks back. That boxcar ride across northern New Mexico seemed like a few *years* ago now.

After paying for the merchandise, Parnell laid out four additional twenties on the worn countertop and told the pawnbroker, "This is for keeping your mouth shut. Comprende?"

"Certainly," the clerk said, scooping up the bills greedily and stuffing them in his shirt pocket.

Parnell exited the shop and started his walk back to the hotel. He had gone about a block when he saw the man in the watch cap following him. He didn't worry Parnell any. He knew the man's job was merely to keep an eye on him. The only way Dobkin's crony in the tweed jacket would take action was if Parnell decided to skip town suddenly.

Arriving back at the Bellagio, Parnell took the elevator up to the room and entered.

The room was dark, the heavy drapes closed. The bathroom door was open a crack, throwing a yellow stripe of light across the floor. His eyes quickly adjusted. He spotted the glint of Elaine's glass eye, the sweep of her dark hair. She was crouched behind the bed, both hands on the small pistol she had trained on him.

"Is that you, Derek?" Panic in her voice.

"Jesus, Elaine! Of *course* it's me! Who else would it be?" Parnell switched on the overhead light, set his bags down in one of the easy chairs. "Put that damned thing down before somebody gets hurt."

Slowly she stood, tossed the gun on the bed like it was poison. She rushed to him and he pulled her into his arms. He felt her trembling against his chest.

"It's okay, Lainey," he whispered into her hair. "Everything's going to be okay, baby. I'm here with you now."

"I know," she said, half sobbing. "I woke up and you weren't here. My mind started going crazy. Insane scenarios, like a bad dream but I was awake. I was terrified for what might have happened to you."

He realized he hadn't left a note for her. "I'm sorry, Lainey," he said, rubbing her arms. "I wasn't thinking, babe."

"Please don't leave me alone again," she said, gripping him with an intensity that startled him.

"I won't, baby, I won't," he said, stroking the back of her

head.

"I just don't know what to expect anymore, Derek. It could have been anybody coming through that door the way things have been going."

"I know. Everything's gone to shit. But it'll all be over Sunday."

"How can you be so sure?"

Parnell knew their room was most likely bugged. He went to the desk on the far wall and opened a drawer, grabbed a pen and several sheets of hotel stationery, wrote:

Keep talking but keep it meaningless. They're listening.

Elaine nodded her understanding and started babbling about how beautiful the weather was for this time of year.

Parnell wrote:

After Razzy and I deliver Dobkin's little American Tourister Trojan Horse, we'll have the rest of our lives together, you and me.

Elaine kept up her rambling monologue as she grabbed the pen and wrote:

How do you know they'll keep us together under federal witness protection?

Parnell wrote:

Screw WITSEC! The feds won't have a clue where we are.

Elaine wrote:

But wouldn't witness protection be an easy life for us?

And back and forth it went, both of them keeping up an inane dialogue as they took turns writing out their real conversation.

Parnell: You obviously don't know much about witness protection. They monitor you, keep you under constant surveillance. And you can't go anywhere without asking their permission. I've had enough of Big Brother myself. Time to break free and fly like eagles, Elaine. Just you, me, and my Jen-Jen.

Elaine: What about Razzy?

Parnell: He wants to stay Stateside. Says he's too old for changes, wants to take his chances someplace he knows rather than start over in a foreign country. Says he got enough of that shit in Nam.

Elaine: But the feds will lock him up and throw away the key.

Parnell smiled at her as he wrote: Razzy's his own man. He won't go down without a fight.

Parnell leaned in and whispered to Elaine, "I'm getting writer's cramp. Let's go outside."

They left their room, locking the door behind them. When

they were alone in the elevator, Elaine said, "So you think that's really your daughter we saw on the Webcam?"

"Yeah, I think so. She made a reference to the mean old toad from Thumbelina. My young Jen-Jen loved for me to read her the fairy tale of Thumbelina. The mean old toad used to give her nightmares, but she never tired of the story. I think Shanks has been holding Jennifer captive up there in the Colorado mountains the way Dobkin described it. I don't see any way they'd know about the Thumbelina connection if she wasn't up there in the Dog Pound. That young girl on the video was a ringer for Jennifer—eyes, mouth, hair, mannerisms, voice. I have a strong gut feeling that my Jenny—my little Thumbelina—is waiting for me up there on Mount Zirkel."

"You don't think this is a trick to get us somewhere where the feds can pick us up?"

"Naw . . . too much trouble. It'd be a lot easier to pick us up here at the hotel. They would have if that was their plan. I think the feds and Dobkin's organization are working together to put an end to the Liberty Dogs, and they're using us to start that war. They've got us in a position where we can't refuse. And I'm not about to turn my back on my daughter. I absolutely have to believe Jennifer is being held against her will at the Dog Pound."

The elevator doors opened to the expansive lobby and they walked out into the cavernous room.

"I can tell you really loved her," Elaine said, walking slowly. "Your eyes light up and there's a hopeful lilt in your voice when you talk about her. It's nice."

"She was the center of my universe for eleven years, Lainey. We were a team, Jen-Jen and me. Jennifer got me through some rough patches, and I got her through some tough growing-up years. After she, um . . . well . . . after the fire, I completely lost my shit. I felt like my soul had been carved out." Parnell felt his eyes welling with tears as visions of the smoking ruins of his house and the two shrouded bodies being wheeled out on gurneys rolled through his mind. "You can't begin to know what that fire did to me—"

"Oh, I have a pretty good idea," she said, moving closer to him and touching his face, kissing the tip of his nose.

"I've been lost, Lainey. I mean *really* lost. I've been full of rage, confused and . . . shit, I don't know. I've done a lot of horrible things. Things I'm not proud of."

"You've done a lot of *good* things, too," she said. "You've helped a lot of people who needed help. Me, for one. All your friends in the camps. The charities you've contributed to." They stopped next to a row of slot machines and she hugged him tightly. "You're too hard on yourself."

She tried to get him to look at her, but he kept his head turned, embarrassed by the tears in his eyes.

"Maybe. But I've spent years wandering the country in a daze, looking for justice, looking for peace of mind. Searching for ways to correct wrongs. I see now that you can't ever really change things that have happened. You can only learn from them. And the fact that my baby girl might actually still be alive and all grown up gives me hope for the first time in what feels like forever. I guess I always thought that if I found Jennifer I'd be able to recover the part of me that's lost."

"Well, then, let's go find her," Elaine said, reaching up and turning his face to her, planting a tender, lingering kiss on his lips.

Into the Belly of the Beast

A T 7:00 AM THE MORNING OF THE NUKE DELIVERY, Parnell, Elaine, and Razzy were packed and ready to go as instructed. Two thickset men in expensive suits escorted them to a black stretch limo and accompanied them on the short ride to Henderson Executive Airport. At Henderson, they boarded a twin-prop Cessna for the twenty-minute flight to northern Nevada and a small air field—Battle Mountain Airport. During the flight, Parnell mentally reviewed the plans they had made, going over all the failsafes they'd discussed in the event that something should go wrong. He felt prepared yet apprehensive now that the big day was underway.

After a bumpy landing at Battle Mountain, the suits took them to a large concrete helipad. Dobkin told them they would be flying to Mount Zirkel and the Dog Pound in a military helicopter. A Sikorsky Blackhawk waited for them, its four overhead rotor blades whirling, whipping up dust and blowing tumbleweeds across the tarmac. As they approached, Parnell was stunned by the logo emblazoned along the fuselage in bold text: **LOCOMOTION ENTERPRISES**.

"What's that?" he yelled to one of the suits over the engine noise.

"It's a helicopter. What the hell does it look like?"

"No, I mean the logo. What's with that?"

The suit shouted, "Mr. D says this deal has to look like it's going through your ex company. Dressing up this chopper was the least of our worries."

His *ex* company. Another reminder of Parnell's fallen status. It fed his determination to pull off his plans today.

They boarded the chopper and stowed their gear. A couple of young men dressed in Army fatigues showed them the fake nuke suitcase placed in the cargo area in a heavy lead-lined trunk. The trunk was just a precaution, Parnell was told. Not much chance for a radiation leak since the bomb package contained just enough plutonium and uranium to make believers of the Liberty Dogs.

This did nothing to reassure Parnell, and in fact, only added to his growing anxiety.

Ninety minutes later they were flying over Routt National Forest along the Continental Divide in northern Colorado. Nearly two miles up and the change in altitude and whipping of the rotors overhead caused a pressurized pain in Parnell's ears. Elaine complained, too, but Razzy remained stoic, quiet, seemingly hypnotized by the lush green carpet of forest below. The pilot maneuvered the Blackhawk up and over a snow-capped ridge several times in wide sweeping arcs, repeatedly bringing the craft back around to the western side of the mountain. Finally, on a fourth pass, Parnell saw a green light flash three times from within a nest of fir trees, and the chopper began its descent.

They landed in a small clearing, the turbo shaft engines deafening in the tight space. Razzy leaned over and said to Parnell, "This guy knows his shit, bringin' this thing down in here."

"Scared the crap outta me," Elaine said, her hands tightly clenching the bench seat.

The overhead blades and tail rotor shut down, the instant quiet overwhelming. Parnell heard voices outside the chopper. One of the suits told him and Razzy to file out, but for Elaine to remain on board. As Parnell got up from his seat, Elaine grabbed him by the arms and kissed him hard.

"We'll be back soon, E," he told her, his lingering look conveying confidence as well as unspoken instructions to be ready.

A wave of chilly mountain air slapped Parnell and Razzy as they exited the chopper. Parnell was glad they had dressed for the cold weather. They had also packed additional cold weather gear knowing they'd need to be prepared for what lay ahead.

He stood at the rear of the chopper, took in an invigorating breath of frosty air and looked around, calculating their odds. There was the pilot, the two suits employed by Dobkin, a pair of federal agents connected with WITSEC, one a late-40s male, the other a young woman. Five in all. They were all to wait with Elaine in the chopper while he and Razzy met with Shanks and his soldiers to deliver the nuke. The plan that Dobkin had negotiated with Shanks through Blanton Miles called for a quick in and out— a fast exchange of the dirty bomb for Parnell's daughter. It should only take as long as it took Shanks' men to inspect the nuke. If they were inside any longer than 30 minutes, Parnell was to radio out that there was trouble, and Dobkin was to be notified.

A pair of Liberty Dogs introduced as Bosworth and Kittridge frisked him and Razzy for weapons. As he was being searched, Parnell said to Bosworth, "Don't you find it odd to be looking for guns and knives when right here in this chest we have a weapon that can take out millions of people?"

"Keep quiet," Bosworth said, checking out Parnell's agreed-upon shortwave radio, satisfying himself it wasn't a recording device.

"Okay, maybe odd is the wrong word choice. Ironic is probably more apt."

"Shut your face, asshole," said the Dog named Kittridge, who inspected the exterior of the lead trunk. "Is this our nuke?"

"Yep," Parnell said. "Amazing what this little package is capable of." He nodded at Razzy. "Professor Milton Luke here will answer any questions. The professor has done consulting work with some of the top nuclear physicists in the country. Did a stint at Los Alamos a while back, isn't that right, Doctor Luke?"

"That I did," Razzy said with assurance. "I'm proud to say I worked on the highly-classified West Eden Project. That's where we got the plutonium for this she-devil." He pointed a gnarled finger at the heavy chest.

They had planned for this. With his Nam demolitions experience, Razzy was intimately familiar with explosive devices and the lexicon, even if he did have to wing it through the nuclear talk. Dobkin had Blanton Miles sell the Liberty Dogs on Razzy being the independent specialist who had secured the suitcase nuke for them. Parnell felt more assured. Razzy was expertly off and running in his new role.

"Okay, men," Kittridge said to his two cohorts, "let's get this thing inside and check it out."

Carefully, they loaded the nuke into the back of a military Jeep and piled in, five of them. Bosworth drove while Kittridge sat in back with Razzy. Kittridge asked Razzy rapid-fire questions about their newly-acquired weapon of mass destruction as Bosworth negotiated the Jeep through several tight bends. Parnell spotted two good escape paths leading into the woods along the route, both wide enough to accommodate this Jeep. As they made their way to the Dog Pound caves, Razzy skillfully recited facts and figures about nuclear fusion weaponry—plutonium synthesis, thermal ignition, neutron combustion rates, cordite detonation systems, remote-controlled firing protocols. Razzy had done his homework well. More importantly, Kittridge seemed convinced that Razzy was the Real Thing.

Good so far.

They arrived at a well-camouflaged cave entrance. Bosworth and the third Dog—a tall slender man they called Slamdunk—jumped out and moved a wall of foliage to the side, revealing a twenty-foot-high steel door. From the Jeep, Kittridge punched in numbers on a control pad mounted on the dash. Slowly the big door squeaked open, sliding back on a track like a huge garage door.

They drove into the womb of the cave, past two armed guards and a parked transport truck. The guards wore helmets and camouflage, arm bands bearing likenesses of bulldogs with blood dripping from their teeth. Comical overkill. Wanna-be soldiers is what Parnell was thinking. All dressed up and no place to go. Pure amateurs. These guys would crap in their pants if they ever faced a real battle.

The air smelled of stale gunpowder, granite dust, and Jeep exhaust. They rode to an exposed wire cage lift and entered, thick cables jerking taut overhead as the cage descended. Down they went, one level . . . two. Sodium vapor lights mounted on the rock walls cast a wavering yellow glow over everything. Shadows danced in the crevices as the cables squeaked and groaned overhead. The second sublevel was obviously a munitions storage area, with a hodge-podge of crates and plastic-wrapped skids bearing logos from U.S. military branches. Parnell saw high-explosive fragmentation grenades, rocket propelled grenades, M4 carbine and M16 rifle ammunition, shoulder-fired Stinger surface-to-air missiles, and pallets of other various armaments marked DANGER–HIGHLY EXPLOSIVE and HIGHLY FLAMMABLE – KEEP COOL AND DRY. Christ, Parnell thought, this bunch has Armageddon in mind. And a holocaust they would get, too, once Dobkin's bomb went off down here. As they descended to the third sublevel, he became concerned about their escape plan. How deep were they going? What if he and Razzy got detained down here and all this shit went up? It would be hell on earth.

The cage jerked to a stop three levels down. A small group of soldiers stood in a semicircle, chattering excitedly. Bosworth drove out of the cage, stopped, shut off the engine. A tall athletic man with rigidly erect posture came around to Parnell's side of the Jeep. He wore a U.S. Army general's uniform and light-tinted aviator sunglasses. Parnell recognized him immediately as Burton Shanks. He bore a striking resemblance to the late investment banker, Willis Logan, Shanks' half-brother.

"So we finally meet. You're a difficult man to pin down, Mr. Parnell. I'm General Burton Shanks, Commander-in-Chief of this operation. Welcome to the Dog Pound." Four silver stars gleamed from Shanks' lapel. The moron actually fancied himself as a four-star general.

Parnell climbed out of the Jeep and said, "Where's my daughter?"

"We'll get to your little princess soon enough," Shanks said. "I want to check out the merchandise first. Is that it?" he said, pointing to the trunk in the back of the Jeep.

"Yeah, it is," Parnell said, looking around at the men gathered there, doing a quick evaluation of his and Razzy's chances for escape. He noticed with a bit of surprise that Shanks and Kittridge were the only ones armed. Shanks had some kind of semi-automatic in his shoulder holster. Kittridge had a Beretta 9 millimeter semiautomatic on his hip. Apparently the rest of them felt safe deep in the bowels of the Dog Pound without weapons. More likely, Shanks didn't trust his own men.

"Carlisle and Renfro," Shanks boomed, "help Bosworth and Slamdunk get our new investment down to the lab for inspection."

Two men broke ranks and moved to the trunk. Parnell grabbed one of them, pushed him back into the other. "Our delivery isn't going anywhere until I see my daughter. That was the deal, Shanks."

"It's *General* Shanks to you, Parnell. Show some respect."

The comment infuriated Parnell. He imagined all the perverted liberties this scumbag had taken with his little Jen-Jen over the years—years when his daughter was underage—and he wanted to kill the rat bastard where he stood.

"*Respect?*" he said, getting in Shanks' face. "Respect is the last thing you'll get from me! You kidnap my daughter and hold her prisoner up here in your twisted underground hell. You use her for your sick fantasies, all the while letting the world think she died in a house fire, and you want *respect*? You're a coward and a pedophile, Shanks—a mountain hillbilly rapist. The U.S. government will crush you like the cockroach you are and I can't wait to see it happen."

A couple of Dogs moved in closer to protect their leader, but

Razzy stepped between them and Parnell.

"Real hard-ass, aren't you?" Shanks said, remaining nose-to-nose with Parnell. "I've heard that about you. Hard as nails and bloodthirsty. Cut your own mother's throat to get ahead. They told me to be careful with you. But now I see you're nothing but a skuzzy hobo. Just another commoner riding the rails in search of your next meal. And you dare to come into my place of business and threaten *me*? I should put a bullet in your brain right now." Shanks yanked the gun from his shoulder holster.

Parnell felt like he'd tumbled down the rabbit hole and was facing the Mad Hatter. "Go ahead," he said. "Shoot me and you'll never get the code to activate the nuke. Your bomb will pack all the punch of a Tijuana firecracker. Now I'm giving you five minutes to produce my daughter. You knew that was the deal so where is she?"

After a long, tense staring match, Shanks turned and said, "Kittridge and Bosworth, go fetch the slut."

"What did you call her, Shanks?"

"Are you hard of hearing, Parnell? I called her a slut. That's exactly what your little darling is." The self-professed general returned the gun to his holster and looked at Kittridge. "Go get the slut, I said. What the hell's keeping you?"

Dutifully, Kittridge and Bosworth scrambled to the Jeep. Bosworth jumped behind the wheel and started it up.

"Wait a minute," Parnell yelled as he stepped in front of the Jeep. "The trunk stays here until I have Jennifer."

Shanks let out a deep sigh. "What the fuck, Parnell."

"I mean it. Get it out of the Jeep. Now!"

Hesitantly, Shanks nodded at Slamdunk, who recruited a couple of Dog soldiers to help him. Once the heavy trunk had been lifted from the vehicle and set on the ground, Bosworth and Kittridge roared off, allegedly to get Jennifer.

Shanks turned back to Parnell. "Let me tell you about your daughter. Jenny's learned her lessons well. She's given us years of pleasure, isn't that right, gentlemen? We're all going to miss her, aren't we?"

A chorus of grumbled acknowledgment.

Parnell could only imagine the hell Burton Shanks had put his Jenny through, the psychological damage he had inflicted on her, the living nightmares he had caused for so many young girls like her. He turned away, unable to look at him a moment longer.

Parnell's insides churned with acidic rage. He tried to control his breathing as he thought about the pleasure he was going to get from snuffing this vile creep.

"What's the matter?" Shanks said to his back. "Can't take the truth? Your Jenny is a beautiful girl in a hard, skanky kind of way. She's got a tight little pussy and a very eager mouth . . . and oh how she *loves* to give it out!"

That's all Parnell needed. He clenched his fists and turned to take a swing at Shanks, but Razzy jumped in to restrain him.

"Be cool, Derek," Razzy said into his ear. "Let's just take care of business an' get out, okay?"

"Yeah, sure," Parnell said, trying to harness his anger.

"Listen to your good professor, Parnell. He's smarter than you." Shanks grinned at him. "Let's face it. What else could your little Jenny have been? She came from the womb of that bitch wife of yours. Barb was a runaround gold digger. She used Willis for his money. Only reason my brother put up with her was because she was hot. A real trophy wife, at least when she was young. But after she got some mileage on her Willis dumped her. She convinced the courts she deserved a big settlement for having to live with a prick like Willis Logan all those years. Barbara was a money whore. She loved the easy life, the life of wealth and affluence. You know that as well as I do. She was a real cunt, and with genes like those, what chance did your daughter have? What else could she have been but a cheap slut? Just like her mother."

It took all of Parnell's strength and reserve not to murder Shanks right here and now. He tried to keep his voice even as he said, "So you killed Barbara."

A flush of anger darkened the faux general's face. "I did no such thing."

"Let me rephrase that. You *arranged* to have her killed."

Shanks thought for a minute, then said, "The world is better off without people like her."

"And your brother, Willis? Is the world better off without him, too?"

"Absolutely. I despised that arrogant tightwad. Always rubbing his success and wealth in my face. Always trying to prove he was better than me. I finally had enough."

"But it was more than that, wasn't it? Logan wouldn't help fund your revolution, would he?"

"You got it. Willis could've helped us out. He had the means and the connections. But he refused. Even after I threatened him. He just ignored me. Like I was a nobody."

"So you arranged to have him murdered, too. Had him tied to the tracks south of Pittsburgh and run over by a freight train."

Shanks nodded proudly. "That's right. Nothing I did was too harsh for that dipshit."

Parnell shook his head in disgust. "Christamighty. And here I thought *my* family was dysfunctional."

Razzy intervened in a calm voice. "Look, I hate to interrupt this heartwarming family reunion talk, but this isn't getting us anywhere."

You're right, it's most unproductive," Shanks agreed. "How about I give you the grand tour while we wait for your daughter, Parnell."

"I'm not a tourist," Parnell said. "We'll wait right here. And I'd better see my Jennifer soon."

Razzy said to Shanks, "I'm sure you must have quite a few questions about the nuke."

Shanks' expression changed as he gazed lustily at the steel chest. Razzy bent and unlatched it, threw the lid open, began his rehearsed presentation of the technical aspects of the bomb. Shanks listened attentively.

As time passed, Parnell got increasingly restless. He didn't trust Dobkin and whoever had their finger on the activation button for the bomb in the trunk not five yards away from him. What was to prevent them from setting it off before they got out? He recalled Dobkin's answer to Elaine when she had asked him about getting all the young girls out: *"In any war, there will always be collateral damage, my dear. You just have to expect that."*

This was taking way too much time. Parnell realized that they could all be blown to smithereens. Every passing second brought greater risk.

Where the hell was Jennifer?

Parnell was beginning to think he'd been duped again, that they'd been set up. He heard Shanks speaking now, talking about his justification for setting off a suitcase nuke in D.C.

". . . and for years they've been stealing huge sums of money from the American people through taxation and Ponzi schemes like Social Security and Medicare. It's time for the crime syndicate that is the Washington corporate-political-military complex to burn in hell. Time to vaporize the imperialist pigs once and for all and—"

"Nice speech, General Patton," Parnell said, cutting him off. "Real inspiring stuff, but where's my daughter?"

As if on cue, Parnell heard the low-pitched moan of an engine. From around the bend in a cloud of dust came the Jeep. A girl in a light blue halter top sat in the backseat, her long brunette tresses blowing in the wind. As they got closer, Parnell could see that it was his long-lost Jennifer.

They hadn't lied to him.

His precious Jen-Jen had not perished in the house fire seven years ago.

As the Jeep approached, father and daughter made eye contact. Parnell experienced an emotion of elation and joy that literally lifted him off his feet. He found himself running to the Jeep, his eyes never leaving Jennifer, fearing her face might fragment and scatter like the waking remnants of a wonderful dream if he looked away.

He heard her yell out, "Dad?" several times, questioning, her voice a lower timbre now than what he remembered, but unmistakably his Jennifer's voice.

He watched her leap from the Jeep as the vehicle began to slow. She ran to him and they grabbed on to each other, their bodies locked together in a wild emotional tangle of hugs and kisses.

They held each other tight, embracing in the weird yellow light of the sodium lamps in this depressing underground sanctum, tears flowing freely. Jennifer buried her face in the crook of his arm and sobbed with joy, "Oh Daddy, Daddy, Daddy . . . you're here . . . you're really *here* for me! This is freakin' unreal! Gawd how I've missed you!"

Parnell's heart took flight. Tears rolled down his cheeks.

He didn't want to let go of his little Thumbelina ever again.

Escape From Hades

"HOW TOUCHING. A father and daughter reunion. We have us a genuine Hallmark moment here."

Parnell wanted to slaughter Shanks for daring to speak, but he realized his job now was to get them out of here safely. He knew he had to focus.

He let go of Jennifer and nodded at Razzy, who touched the bill of his fedora in answer. This is where their planning had to be pinpoint accurate. Everything had to be split-second as there was little margin for error. The element of surprise was an advantageous weapon, and they had to use it expertly.

Razzy jumped Shanks, who emitted a startled gasp as Razzy yanked the gun from the general's shoulder holster and stuck the barrel in Shanks' ribs. Parnell charged Kittridge and knocked him to the ground, wrestled the Beretta from him.

Jennifer let out a shriek.

Pandemonium ensued.

Several Liberty Dogs moved in.

Parnell jumped to his feet, pointed the pistol at them. "Stop right there!" he warned. "One more step and I'll put every last one of you down!"

"You're making a huge mistake, Parnell," Shanks said from the back of the Jeep where Razzy had him covered. "What the hell do you hope to gain from this idiotic move?"

"We're leaving this shithole and you're coming with us."

"Hah!" Shanks huffed. "Fat chance of that."

"Daddy, what are you doing?" Jennifer yelled out. "This man is dangerous! He'll freakin' hurt you!"

"No, he won't, honey. Come here and stand behind me. Stay quiet and let me handle this." With his free hand Parnell pulled the shortwave transmitter from his pocket and called up to one of the suits in the helicopter. "Hey, mission accomplished. We're on our way up." Parnell glanced at Razzy as he returned the transmitter to his pocket. Both of them knew the call to the surface was Elaine's signal to take action.

"You're crazed, Parnell," Shanks said. "This will never work."

"Won't it?"

"No, it won't. For one, I'm not going anywhere with you. Two, you'll never get out of here alive."

Parnell gave Shanks a sly smile. "Wrong on both counts."

"Dad?" Jennifer said, looking at him strangely. "There's no need for this. They told me—"

"I don't know what you've been told, Jenny, but I'm sure it wasn't the truth. Now please keep quiet and come stand behind me."

Jennifer took a leery sidelong glance at Shanks, then dutifully moved behind Parnell.

Parnell addressed Shanks. "Now get behind the wheel and take us topside. Now! Do it!" he barked.

"I'm not going anywhere with you, asshole. You might as well shoot me right here and now."

"That's very tempting. It would be a hell of a lot easier to put a couple of slugs in you and leave your useless carcass here. But you're coming with us. I'm not done with you yet. Now get your ass in the Jeep!"

"Not a chance."

This was going to be difficult. Shanks was being obstinate, not convinced they meant business. Parnell had to do something quick to persuade him otherwise. He noticed movement to his left—Kittridge getting to his feet and side-stepping his way out of his peripheral vision. "Stay where I can see you," he yelled out. "I mean it."

He saw a blur of churning arms and legs coming at him—Kittridge charging like an enraged bull. Parnell turned and squeezed the trigger repeatedly, the initial spray of automatic gunfire taking Kittridge's legs out from under him, the final spray of shots striking higher—*splat-splut-splat*—the man's head exploding like an overripe melon hitting pavement from fifteen stories up.

"Daddy! Oh-my-gawd! Oh-my-freakin' gawd!" he heard Jennifer screaming behind him.

"I'm sorry you had to see that, honey," he said, reaching behind him to grab her hand and pull her to the Jeep. "Get behind the wheel, Shanks. Take us topside and make it fast," he said, moving with Jennifer toward the general.

Shanks, showing fear for the first time, had his hands up over his head in a gesture of surrender. "Okay, okay . . . I'm going," he said in a feeble voice, glancing at Kittridge's mangled body sprawled on the dusty floor. "You've made your point. Jesus!" He carefully got into the driver's seat of the Jeep and turned over the ignition.

Razzy jumped into the passenger seat, sweeping his gun over the stunned Liberty Dogs, who looked down in abject horror at the bloody, tattered corpse of their fallen comrade. Parnell could tell from the shocked reaction that none of them had ever witnessed a kill-shot.

He helped Jennifer up into the rear of the Jeep and climbed in behind Shanks. He pointed the Beretta at Bosworth and said, "If any of you try to come after us, the professor will detonate your little suitcase nuke, and every last one of you losers will be vaporized. So best to be good little boys and stay put."

They rose the three levels in the lift, slowly, oh-so-achingly slow. Too much time, Parnell thought as he listened to the groaning pull of the cables overhead and the distant hum of generators. His heartbeat raced triple time. He kept the gun to the back of Shanks' head, surprised at the way the shots from the little hand-held pistol had echoed through the caves like cannon fire.

The lift cage pulled up to ground level. One of the gate guards met them with gun drawn and serious intentions, a bit of confusion on his face causing him to hesitate. Razzy didn't waste time with subterfuge, just dropped the man with a well-placed shot between the eyes.

"Oh-my-gawd, Daddy! This is too freakin' much! Please make this be over, Dad! Please!"

"See how much you're upsetting your little princess, Parnell?" Shanks said as he drove the Jeep out of the cage.

Parnell clubbed him hard in the back of the head with his fist. "Open the front gate!"

"I can't do that," Shanks said, rubbing his head as he drove.

"You *can* and you *will*," Parnell said. "From the dash. I saw your guy Kittridge do it on the way in. Now do it!" He clubbed Shanks again, this time with the butt of the gun.

Shanks cursed Parnell, but did as he was instructed, leaning over and punching in the gate code on the keypad mounted on the dash. They rounded a turn. Parnell saw sunlight as the big door ahead crawled open. The lone guard on duty flailed his arms in a panic.

"If he gets in our way, run him over," Razzy yelled sidelong from the passenger seat.

"Like hell," Shanks protested, taking his foot off the accelerator.

"It's either you or him," Parnell said, burying the barrel of the gun deeper into the back of the general's skull. "Make like it's the Indy 500. Now!"

They pitched forward, the engine grinding furiously as they picked up speed. A look of shocked surprise stretched across the guard's face as he realized the Jeep wasn't stopping, that his commander was ignoring his frantic signals.

The Jeep hit the guard head-on with a sickening thud. A thick streak of blood sprayed across the windshield. Jennifer screamed in Parnell's ear: "Oh-my-gawd . . . Oh-my-gawd . . . This is not freakin' happening! . . . Oh-my-gawd!"

They burst out of the cave at a rapid clip, bottoming out as they hit the front gate track. They jounced over the rough terrain, the big tires doing little to absorb the jolts.

They had gone a couple of hundred yards when Shanks tried to wreck the Jeep. The Liberty Dogs General yanked the steering wheel hard left trying to dump it. The vehicle rode precariously on two wheels.

Everyone held on.

Shouts and screams.

Curses.

The Jeep swerved in a wide arc, sideswiping a huge boulder before righting itself, bouncing back down on all four tires.

Parnell grabbed Shanks around the neck from behind, squeezed tightly. "Stupid move, shithead!" he shouted in his ear. "Stop this thing. Now!"

Shanks braked, a cloud of dust enveloping them.

"Razzy, take us the rest of the way." Parnell directed Shanks to get in back with him, told Jennifer to move up front in the passenger seat. After they were all resituated, he pointed the Beretta at Shanks and said, "Try anything else and I'll splatter your guts all over this back seat."

They rode on, Razzy driving the Jeep along the twisty, deeply rutted dirt road As the helicopter came into view, Parnell could see Elaine had done her part. The two feds were on the ground, writhing in agony. One of Dobkin's men leaned against the fuselage, puking, the other on his knees, hands to his face. The pilot slumped over in the cockpit, rubbing at his eyes. Elaine stood at the rear of the chopper, a rifle in the crook of her arm, her black eye patch and do rag giving her a dangerous, on-the-edge pirate look. She had their backpacks lined up and ready to go. Parnell saw Razzy's hogleg rifle propped up against one of the heavy-duty shock oleos of the landing skids.

Lainey had pepper-sprayed them to perfection, taking all five of them out. Parnell had never loved Elaine Leibrandt more than he did at that moment.

Razzy brought the Jeep to a stop and jumped out. Per their plans, Elaine tossed the handcuffs to him, who proceeded to bind Shanks' hands behind him. Shanks squirmed and yelled, hoping someone would help him, but no one did. No one *could*. They were all incapacitated.

"Let's go!" Parnell barked as he shouldered his backpack. "Razzy, Lainey, grab your stuff and let's hit it. Follow me."

Parnell jogged to a trail he'd spotted on the way in. Jennifer did her best to keep up with him. Razzy prodded the handcuffed Shanks along behind them with the long barrel of his hogleg.

Parnell dug through his backpack as he entered the heavy woods, pulling out his Silva Ranger compass and handheld GPS device. Checking his coordinates, he saw they were headed west down the mountain.

The Freedom Trail

THICK STANDS OF WHITE-TRUNKED ASPEN and pesky conifer scrub made the hike down the mountain difficult. A crisp, cool breeze brought the sweet scent of Engleman spruce and Douglas fir, but the thin high-altitude air made breathing a chore. The five of them labored through the woods, their breaths coming in elongated gasps.

Parnell led them through the path of least resistance, cutting back brush with his Bowie knife and navigating around tumbled boulders and fallen trees. He stopped to get a compass reading and to check GPS coordinates. He was pleased. They should make it to the Little Snake River by late afternoon. The plan was to cross the river and hop a Union Pacific freighter heading west into Utah, then catch a southbound at the Provo switching yards.

"Why are we running like this?" Jennifer asked, winded, bent over, hands on knees, trying to catch her breath. "And why is *that* monster with us?" she said, pointing back over her shoulder at Shanks.

"We'll talk about it later, Jen, after we're riding the iron."

"Riding the iron? Could you, like, speak English, please?"

Parnell stopped and turned to his daughter, bringing the small caravan to a halt. "Riding the rails. We're taking a train into Utah."

"Utah?" Shanks chimed in. "Nothing in Utah but a buncha crazy Mormons. Nothing but wife-swappin' scumbag rapists in Utah."

Parnell moved past Jennifer and Elaine, positioned himself in front of Shanks. The ridiculous Army officer uniform annoyed him, made him want to vomit. It was an insult to real military generals, the warriors of genuine courage who had earned the right to wear a decorated uniform. Burton Shanks was no warrior. He wasn't even a soldier. He was a war reenactment fool, a weekend military junkie. Worse, he was a nasty pedophile child molester. And had Parnell heard him correctly? Shanks was accusing *Mormons* of being wife-swapping rapists? Jesus! What did this creep see when he looked in the mirror?

Parnell reached out and ripped one of the small silver stars from the left shoulder of Shanks' military blazer. Tossed it to the ground. Shanks flinched, moved back a step. Parnell reached in again and stripped the remaining stars—the three on the left shoulder, then the four on the right—one by one, tossing them into the dirt at his feet as punctuation for his words to the faux general. "Utah also has some really cool crematoriums, Shanks. These stars won't do you any good at the one you'll be visiting."

Shanks looked down, aghast as he watched his precious silver stars tossed to the ground like so much chicken feed. "You think you're so fucking clever, but you'll never get away with this."

"I already have," Parnell said. He unsheathed his Bowie knife and handed it to Razzy. "Here . . . if he opens his mouth again, cut his tongue out!"

"Dad, what's happened to you?" Jennifer implored. "I don't understand. You've like, *really* changed."

Parnell looked at her, noticing for the first time the purplish bruises on her left arm, the ugly scabbed-over wound on her right shin. "I don't have time for explanations right now, sweetheart."

"But they told me we'd be flying home. They told me Mom couldn't wait to see me. Why're we running through the woods like freakin' escaped convicts. Why're we taking a *train* to Utah? How come we're not flying back to New York?"

Christ, Parnell thought. She thinks her mother is still alive. Jennifer doesn't know anything about the house fire or Barbara's murder. Shanks had kept her completely in the dark. Parnell gave Shanks a contemptible look, and the general merely shrugged his shoulders in a belligerent *What the hell did you expect?* response.

Parnell turned back to his daughter, realizing how terrifying all this must be to her after seven long years of imprisonment. The only one she knew was Shanks, and he frightened her for obvious reasons. He wished he could take her in his arms and tell her everything would be okay, explain to her the horrible events of the past seven years that had resulted in the ragged vagabond who stood before her now—her father, the vigilante killer with the tombstone eyes. He wanted to comfort her, to let his daughter know how much he loved her, and that he and Elaine and Razzy were her friends, that they would protect her with their lives. But he couldn't. There wasn't time for explanations now. There wasn't time for the love Parnell knew he needed to show his Jen-Jen. They had to get to the Little Snake River before nightfall.

"Look, sweetie," he said to her, trying to keep the pity and sadness he felt out of his voice, "I know this is very confusing to you right now. I promise I'll catch you up on everything once we're on the rails. But right now we have to keep moving."

Parnell turned and continued his progress through the woods.

Jennifer watched his back, crossed her arms and sighed, looked at Elaine questioningly.

"Come on, Jen," Elaine said to her, taking her by the elbow. "Your father is right. We've got to stay on the move."

Jennifer pulled her arm free. "Excuse me, but who the hell're *you*, anyway?"

Hearing this, Parnell stopped and turned, saw the look of helplessness on Elaine's face as she struggled for an answer. "Sorry we haven't had time for proper introductions, Jenny," he said, walking back toward the two women. "This is Elaine Leibrandt, better known as E or Lainey. She's a very good friend of mine."

"I see," Jennifer said, her blank expression indicating she didn't understand at all.

Parnell pointed at Razzy. "And that there is Mr. Lucious Jones. His 'bo handle is Razzmatazz, or Razzy for short."

" 'Bo handle?" Jennifer said.

"Yeah, you know, a hobo nickname. It's how we 'bos refer to each other."

"Hobos? I don't get it, Dad. What's happened to you?"

"I promise I'll tell you everything when we're on the freighter. But I'm serious. We have to get down off this mountain. Now."

He did an abrupt about-face and disappeared into the thick brush. Jennifer shook her head and mumbled, "Whatever," before falling in behind him.

The other three followed, Razzy bringing up the rear with the barrel of his Winchester hogleg planted firmly in Shanks' spine, just above the cuffed hands.

Twenty minutes later, they heard the low *thump-thump-thump* of an approaching helicopter.

"Everyone down!" Parnell shouted. "Take cover!"

Instinctively, he grabbed Elaine and Jennifer and fell on top of them, Jennifer complaining he was hurting her. Razzy shoved Shanks under some low-lying branches with his rifle and dove in behind him.

Through a break in the overhead canopy, Parnell saw the chopper, the familiar LOCOMOTION ENTERPRISES logo getting larger as the craft approached.

"Keep your heads down," he instructed as the big Blackhawk rumbled overhead, its rotor blades beating the air with a thudding frenzy, the aspen leaves fluttering in the downdraft. He thought they might have been spotted as the chopper hovered nearby. But then, thankfully, a few long minutes later, the Blackhawk veered off and disappeared over the horizon. The forest returned to its previous calm.

"How'd your company ever get hold of a Blackhawk helicopter, Parnell?"

Shanks' irritating voice was like a knife slicing through Parnell's brain. "I told you to keep your mouth shut and I meant it," he said. "Razzy, keep the moron quiet, will you?"

"Sure 'nuff, Derek."

They continued on, Parnell keeping alert for approaching aircraft. The feds would have a search party out soon. He knew they had to stay under cover as much as possible now.

Ten minutes later, a rumbling concussive *whump* seemed to suck the air from the side of the mountain. The earth shook violently. Elaine and Jennifer went down hard. Razzy managed to keep Shanks covered as they slammed into a rock outcropping.

"What the hell was that?" Shanks said when calm had returned. "An earthquake?"

"That was no earthquake," Parnell said, realizing that Dobkin and his crew had triggered the explosive device. He shuddered as he recognized that the bomb had probably been set on a timer all along, hence Dobkin's repeated message to get in and out as quickly as possible. "That was the beginning and end of your revolution . . . the official closing of The Dog Pound. Your suitcase nuke went off, Shanks. Your precious military bunker has been blown to shit. The general just lost his army."

"Bullshit. That was definitely an earthquake," Shanks said, desperation in his voice.

Razzy jabbed Shanks in the ribs with his rifle. "It's the way we planned it, motherfucker. You should be countin' your lucky stars you weren't down in them caves when all that shit went off. I'm sure it was hellfire down there . . . body parts flyin' ever which way. All your sad sack cronies just got buried."

A look of dismayed understanding crossed Shanks' face. "You fucking pieces of—"

"Careful, dude," Razzy said, waving the Bowie knife in front of him. "You value your tongue, don't you?"

"I wish someone would freakin' tell me what the hell's going on," Jennifer said from her seat on the ground.

Little Snake Getaway

THE LITTLE SNAKE RIVER coiled through northwestern Colorado in a serpentine slither. Parnell and his troop arrived at water's edge a little past four-thirty. Low-angled sunlight reflected off slick, river-smoothed stones. A calm breeze rippled the surface of the water as they cleaned up and refilled their canteens. Refreshed, the five of them followed the meandering river to where the Little Snake narrowed and they could cross.

Parnell consulted his GPS as they negotiated the rocky, rugged terrain another ten miles. There they came upon the much bigger Yampa River—the feeder for the Little Snake. They followed the wide, rushing Yampa to where it intersected with the rail line, finding themselves at the bottom of a culvert along the muddy shore, staring up at the train tracks spanning the river on a trestle a thousand feet or more above. Impressive white canyon walls rose on both sides of the river.

"Let's go," Parnell told the others, walking toward what looked to be a deer trail. "Up to the top. Freighters always slow before crossing bridges. Easier to catch on before the train hits the bridge."

"We're going up *there*?" Shanks said, incredulous. "Why don't we just forge the damned river like we did a while back?"

"Because I'm not real fond of drowning, pinhead," Parnell said. "And the train runs *over* the river, not *through* it. I don't want to have to tell you again—keep your legs moving and your yap shut."

Exhausted after their daylong hike down Mount Zirkel and trek along the river, it took them 45 minutes to make the arduous climb up to the trestle. The late afternoon sunlight shone bright up here. They drank from their canteens and gazed out across the bridge, the tracks rolling out across the steep gorge on a narrow platform, the river a precipitous drop below.

Parnell leaned against a concrete abutment and wiped his brow. "We'll head back up the tracks a hundred yards or so, give us a running start to catch on. Hafta be careful. If you're not onboard before the train is out there, chances are you're going into the drink. It's a long way down."

Elaine said, "Jesus! Quit trying to scare us, Derek."

"Just stating the facts. If it makes you feel any better, I'll make sure all of you are aboard first. I'll be the last to hook on."

Burton Shanks bristled. "How the hell do you expect me to hop a train with my hands cuffed?"

Parnell glared at him. "What'd I tell you about keeping your mouth shut?" He nodded at Razzy. "Give General Custer here another reminder that we mean business."

"Gladly," Razzy muttered, sliding the Bowie knife from its leather sheath, letting the sunlight shimmer off the big blade before pressing it to Shanks' throat. "One more word outta you an' I'll gut ya like a fresh-killed deer. Got it?"

Shanks backed away from the blade and Razzy moved with him, keeping the knife at his throat. Shanks said, "I knew damn well you weren't any nuclear physicist. You don't know shit about suitcase nukes, do you?"

Razzy gave Parnell a slow smile. "The man's pretty quick, ain't he, Derek?"

"Very. Must be related to Albert Einstein. Theory of relativity and all."

"Fuck both of you!" Shanks snarled.

"Can I slice him up, Derek?" Razzy said eagerly. "*Please* say yes."

"No, I don't want blood all over our boxcar."

"Look!" Jennifer cried, pointing across the river to the butte towering above the far bank.

They looked to where she pointed, saw a pair of bighorn sheep, their racks remarkable bony plumages atop their heads.

"Male rams," Razzy said, putting the knife away and lighting up a smoke. "Mighty impressive animals. Used to be more of 'em out in these here parts. But the bears an' wolves an' cougars have cut 'em down."

"They're beautiful," Jennifer said dreamily. "Look how graceful they are along the edge of the cliff."

They watched the sheep work their way along the canyon rim. Parnell saw the animals suddenly come to a stop and remain still, heads up, on alert. A second later they scampered off. Something had spooked them.

He moved to the tracks, bent at the knees and placed his hand on the steel rail, could feel the faint vibration of a far off train.

That's what had alarmed the bighorns, he thought. "Come on let's move it," he told the others. "Our ride is approaching."

As they scurried up the tracks for a better catch-on point, Parnell heard a faint thumping sound, rhythmic and familiar. He stopped and turned back, listened.

A helicopter.

They had not encountered any aircraft on their journey down Mount Zirkel since the initial flyover of the Blackhawk hours ago.

Only one reason for a chopper to be out here in this no-man's land.

Great timing, Parnell thought, hearing the unmistakable *thump-whump-thump* sound of rotor blades increasing in volume. He wondered if it was the feds. He looked overhead, distressed that their catch-on run didn't have much tree cover. They'd be in the open as they ran alongside the train.

A train whistle blew in the distance, weak but urgent. Parnell hurried the others along. He looked over his shoulder, saw the chopper now hovering in over the trestle, flying along the elevated tracks, coming up behind them quickly. Shit! It was the Blackhawk, the blue LOCOMOTION ENTERPRISES logo gleaming in the sun.

The train whistle again, closer. The unique steamboat chimes of the Union Pacific freighters so familiar to Parnell.

He instructed the other four to get in position alongside the tracks, to stay bunched close together but to be careful not to trip each other up. The five of them crouched beside the rails, the big railroad ties stinking of asphalt and sun-baked steel.

Parnell pulled the handcuff keys from his pocket and grabbed Shanks from behind, unlocking the cuffs. Shanks brought his hands out in front of him, shook them rigorously, trying to get the feeling back. Parnell jammed the cuffs in his pants pocket and warned him, "I'll be right behind you, Shanks. You hop this train when I say. You try anything funny and I'll push you under the wheels. You'll become track lubricant. Not at all a pleasant way to die."

"What's the difference?" Shanks whined. "You're gonna kill me anyway."

"Yeah, but it's so much more humane the way I do it. Not quite as messy."

The big locomotive roared into view, a monstrosity of clanking steel and chugging pistons. The steam whistle blew again, earsplitting at this close distance.

Parnell glanced back down the rails. The Blackhawk had cleared the trestle, flying in a straight line down the tracks directly at them, a football field away.

The immense locomotive blew past them in a pounding, punishing roar. A cyclone of wind ripped Razzy's fedora from his head and sucked it up under the wheels. It was a long freighter, at least fifty cars. The first dozen cars were flatbeds hauling containers. Parnell shielded his eyes from the swirling gravel and dirt, looked down the line, saw several empty livestock cars a ways back, their side doors open to air them out. He counted to make sure the car he targeted wasn't the thirteenth in line. Very bad hobo voodoo to hop the thirteenth car of a freighter. Last time he made that mistake he got jumped by three tramps.

Another glance back at the helicopter. Close enough to make out the pilot's face through the tinted bubble. Same pilot who had flown them to the top of Mount Zirkel and the Dog Pound. Quick decision time—stay hunkered down out of sight of the Blackhawk and wait it out for the next freighter, or make their move now and take their chances with the chopper. He knew trains ran on an infrequent schedule out here. Quite possible the next train would not come through for another day or two. And it might not be hauling any easy-access cars.

They had to risk it now.

"Okay . . . move!" he shouted. Elaine took his cue and began to sprint alongside the train, Jennifer following her lead as though she had been a 'bo-ette train-jumper her entire life. Razzy fell in behind, running with arms flailing in a lumbering gait along the gravel berm that lined the tracks. Parnell shoved Shanks. "Let's go, Cap'n Crunch! Remember what I told you."

The first of three louver-sided livestock cars thundered beside them and Elaine caught on expertly, pulled herself up and in. Quickly she reached down and extended her hand to Jennifer, locked onto her wrist and tugged her up and aboard. Razzy loped alongside and timed his leap, heaving himself up and on with an agility that defied his age. He was old, yes, but he had ridden the rails for many years, and like any experienced Boxcar Willie, his timing was perfect. Parnell ran behind Shanks as they kept pace with the clanging livestock car. Above the din, he could hear Elaine screaming out his name, yelling for him to hurry.

Above them, the helicopter dipped and turned in a wide arc,

doubling back around to follow them, rotor blades spinning furiously. Parnell heard tiny pops through the commotion—the unmistakable sound of gunfire. Bullets pinged off the railcar's aluminum siding. Shanks awkwardly grabbed hold of one of the vents and pulled himself up and on. Parnell stole a glance at the Blackhawk as he ran, saw two guys propped against the beams of the open doors, pointing rifles at them and firing indiscriminately. Their shots were wild and inaccurate, their aim affected by the chopper's unstable flight as it tried to keep pace with the train.

Parnell turned back to the railcar, saw that he had lost a few steps. He picked up his pace though his legs felt like melted rubber. Stray shots kicked up sprays of gravel and plinked off the metal siding as Parnell prayed for just five more seconds. Adrenaline coursed through his arms and legs as he saw the pilings of the trestle fast approaching.

Fifty yards . . . forty . . .

He saw Elaine stretched out on her belly, smartly reducing her target size, her hand draped over the side of the car, waving so he would see it. Shots thudded all around him. Razzy's return fire caused the helicopter to bob and weave erratically alongside the chugging train. As he ran, Parnell could hear both Elaine and Jennifer urging him on.

Thirty yards . . . twenty . . .

He grabbed hold of Elaine's hand and pulled himself up just as the chopper lifted sharply to clear the bridge framework.

Ten yards . . .

Their car rolled out onto the trestle platform. The ground dropped away abruptly. The sound of wheels meeting the rails shifted from a low roar to a higher, more precarious pitch.

The Blackhawk dipped and came at them again, the snipers shooting through the suspension struts of the bridge. Razzy returned fire while the others remained safely out of harm's way—Elaine huddling with Jennifer at the rear of the car, Parnell keeping Shanks cornered, making sure he couldn't get at the two women. Razzy knelt, reloaded quickly, came up firing again, shouting curses with each shot. The chopper turned in slightly, trying to get a closer angle on the bridge. Razzy zeroed in on the pilot through the magnified scope of his hogleg, pulled the trigger twice. Parnell saw the Plexiglas bubble spider web as it shattered, then saw the pilot's forehead rupture in a fountain of blood.

"Gotchya, ya cocksucker!" Razzy yelled in triumph, watching

as the chopper careened out of control, dumping the two snipers out the open side, sending them to a long screaming descent to the river below.

Parnell rushed to Razzy's side to view the spectacle. Both watched as the helicopter tried to right itself, but then quickly lost control again, losing altitude and spinning erratically before slamming into the sheer cliff wall on the far side of the Yampa River. A thunderous explosion rocked the gorge.

Parnell opened his mouth to congratulate Razzy when he heard, "Dad! Watch out!"

Jennifer's warning shout was just enough to make him turn and move out of the way as Burton Shanks charged, tackling a surprised Razzy and taking him out the door with him into the rushing wind. Parnell saw Razzy's hogleg rifle clear the bridge struts. The entangled men slammed violently into a crossbeam before dropping a thousand feet into the Yampa River.

Parnell stood there, stunned, looking out at the burning wreckage of the helicopter, wind buffeting his face. He could smell the sickly scent of burnt helicopter fuel. He traced the outline of the handcuffs in his pocket. They felt extremely heavy. His first thought was: This wouldn't have happened if I secured Shanks to one of the interior beams right away. His second thought was overwhelming grief for the inexcusable loss of a man who had protected Parnell and saved his life on several occasions, a man who had become the closest thing Parnell had to a friend in recent years.

It had all happened so unbelievably fast.

Behind him he heard Elaine say, "Holy shit!"

"Oh my freakin' gawd!" Jennifer exclaimed.

Parnell felt arms snaking around his waist from behind. He turned to see Elaine staring at him, tears rolling down her dazed face. He pulled her close and hugged her to him, noticed Jennifer standing nearby, looking lost, in complete shock. He motioned for her to join them.

The three of them held on to each other as the train rumbled through the forests of northwest Colorado and on into Utah.

Last Stop On the Gypsy Train

T HEY ROLLED INTO THE PROVO SWITCHING YARDS just after midnight. It had been a quiet trip as the three of them, exhausted and beaten down by shock, drifted in and out of restless sleep.

Parnell ached to the marrow of his exhausted bones. He felt grungy, the sweat and trail dirt clinging to him like a second skin. Just nine hours ago they'd freshened up in the Little Snake River. Seemed like nine *days* ago. The fatal events on the train trestle unspooled in his mind, playing over and over like a jumpy 8 milli-meter film loop—all of the events taking three, maybe four, minutes. So much death and destruction in just 240 seconds. Parnell obsessed over what he could have done—*should* have done—differently to change the outcome. Could he have saved Razzy's life? His conscience weighed heavily on him.

The train slowed on the outskirts of the yard. He sat with his back against the wall, the multicolored lights of the switching station washing over him. He observed the two sleeping forms next to him and felt an overpowering tug of contentment. Elaine and Jennifer, the two women in his life. The muted light filtering through the slats of the railcar softened Jen's features, reminding Parnell of the little girl who used to fall asleep in his lap after he'd read her bedtime stories. She always looked so peaceful when she slept. He reached out and gently brushed a lock of hair away from her eyes. She moaned and shifted where she lay, but remained in a deep slumber.

Elaine stirred beside Jennifer. She opened her good eye and, seeing him fuss over his daughter, smiled at him knowingly. Par-nell returned Elaine's smile, feeling like the luckiest man on the planet.

Elaine sat up, yawned, pulled her patch down over her dam-aged eye socket, leaned back on an elbow. "Where are we?" she asked groggily.

"The Provo yards," he said to her in a low voice.

"We getting off here?"

"Soon." He looked at her through the dim light. "You did

good work today, Lainey,"

"You mean getting everyone on the train?"

"Yeah, that, but mostly I meant back up on the mountain, with the pepper spray."

"My part was easy. Just point and spray."

"You're too modest, E. Your timing was spot-on. You were the key to us getting out of there alive."

Elaine looked out the open railcar siding, her gaze far away. "Well, I'll admit, it was crazy," she began. "All the chemicals in the air . . . all the confusion and chaos. My throat closed up at one point. I thought I was going to suffocate and I panicked. One of those feds fought me, tried to wrestle the spray away from me. But I finally managed to get a direct hit on him and he went down hard. He squealed like a little girl."

"Yeah, well, you did great, Elaine. I'm proud of you."

She continued to stare out at the night. The clank of coupling railcars sounded in the distance. They heard shouts—instructions barked by switchyard personnel. Finally she said, "But I couldn't save Razzy. I couldn't save those poor people in that helicopter. Damn, that was horrible to watch."

"Those *poor people* in the helicopter were shooting at us. They were trying to kill us."

"I know, but—"

"But nothing, Elaine. Razzy gave them what they deserved."

"Nobody deserves to die like that, Derek."

"Nobody deserves to die the way *Razzy* did. He deserved better. It was us or them."

Jennifer came awake and sat up, scooted back against the wall, looking confused and fearful. "Is Shanks really dead or was that just a dream?"

"Yes, he's really dead."

"And so is the other guy? The old black dude?"

"Razzy? Yes, he's, um . . . he's gone, too."

"He was your friend, wasn't he?"

"Yes, honey. Actually he was more than just a friend. He saved mine and Lainey's life more than once."

She thought for a minute before responding, "So, he was like a guardian angel or something?"

Parnell exchanged looks with Elaine, then said, "Yeah, I guess Razzy was something like that."

Elaine placed her hand on top of Jennifer's. "You know, we

all need a guardian angel at some point. Your father has been mine."

Jennifer glanced down at Elaine's hand cradling hers and looked up questioningly. She started to say something then stopped, thinking better of it, and pulled her hand away.

"Look, sweetie," Parnell interjected, picking up on Jennifer's trampled emotions, "a lot has happened since you've . . . well, since you've been, . . . away—"

"It's okay, Dad, really. I understand. A lot *has* happened. A whole freakin' shitload of stuff. You're right about that. One thing you should know—I'm not your sweet, innocent little girl anymore. That monster who flew off the bridge with your guardian angel Razzy made sure of that. Burton Shanks was a twisted pervert—a freakin' animal! He stole my childhood from me. He stole my *life* from me. The things he made me do . . . oh my gawd! The things he made *all* of us girls do for him and his men. I'm glad the sick fuck is dead! My only regret is that I didn't get a chance to kill him with my own hands . . ."

He let Jennifer rant, seeing the anger and hurt and violation come out of his hardened adult daughter in waves. He wanted to reach out and comfort her, to let her know what a miracle it was that they were together again, to let her know that yes, both had been severely wounded by the extreme events of the past seven years, and against all odds, they were together. Alive and well. But he kept quiet, let her go on. She had remained fairly quiet on the hike down the mountain and along the river, and it was good that she was finally getting all of this out. Parnell also refrained from mentioning that he, too, was disappointed that he hadn't been able to kill Shanks with his own hands. He'd planned to take the faux general to the abandoned Hyacinth coal mines in southern Utah and send him plunging to a fiery death on his Rolling Inferno mine car contraption. But it wasn't meant to be. Fate had intervened once again. Burton Shanks, just like the two arsonists before him—Tico Samuels and Jerry Ray Allenson—had escaped Parnell's amusement park ride to hell.

". . . I'm sorry your Mr. Razzy had to die, Dad. My guardian angel was killed, too. I know what it feels like."

Elaine said, "Your guardian angel? Who was that, Jen?"

"There was a man in the Dog Pound who was nice to me. He took a shine to me, looked out for me. He brought me extra food and protected me when he could. I mean all the girls had certain men they learned to manipulate to their advantage, but this was different. This guy was really sweet. I think I might have even loved him. At least I think that's what I felt . . . I was only sixteen when we met. I think he felt the same way about me. His name was Russell. Not sure if that was a first or last name, but I called him Russ. About a month ago, Russ confessed to me he wasn't one of the Liberty Dogs. He told me he was working for the government in an undercover sting operation and that something big was in the works, something that involved you, Dad. He said he was working for a man named John Dobkin. I know it was hard for him to tell me those things, and I still don't quite know why he did, except that I think he loved me and was looking out for my best interests. Russ was my guardian angel. He made my last couple of years in that shithole underground prison bearable. So when we were making our way down the mountain and we heard the explosions going off in the caves, my heart shattered, because I knew I had lost Russ . . . my guardian angel."

"I'm so sorry, Jennifer," Elaine whispered.

Parnell said, "Wait a minute. This guy Russ, he told you he was a fed working for John Dobkin?"

"Yeah, why?"

"You're sure that was the name of his boss? John Dobkin?"

"I'm positive, Dad. Why're you so freaked over that?"

Parnell avoided looking at Elaine though he could feel her staring at him. "I'm not freaked, Jen," he said, wondering whether Dobkin was coldblooded enough to sacrifice one of his own informants in his attempt to kill Shanks and take down the Dog Pound. Would he and Razzy also have been sacrificed down in the caves if they hadn't made their move fast enough?

"You sure look freaked to me, Dad."

"No, no . . . I'm fine. Just thinking about a John Dobkin I used to know."

Elaine said, "Maybe your guardian angel Russ made it out of the caves before the explosions, Jen."

Jennifer shook her head sadly. "No, I don't think so. He was with me until about twenty minutes before they came to get me."

"Well," Parnell said, "that's time enough if he knew what was coming."

Jennifer stared at him, quiet, unmoving, an awkward silence filling the railcar. Finally she said, "I don't really know you at all, Daddy dear. I get the feeling that you're, like . . . keeping a lot from me. I think I deserve some answers. I deserve to know what's going on."

"You're right, Jen. You *do* deserve an explanation," Parnell said.

"You told me you'd fill me in once we were on the train."

"I know. You deserve to hear the entire unvarnished truth of what's happened the past seven years. But it's long and complicated and there isn't time to do it justice here and now. We need to keep on the move, honey. I promise I'll catch you up on everything after we get to where we're going. We all need some rest. I want a clear head when I tell you the story."

She mulled this over for a long moment, then said, "So where are we headed?"

"To my safe house in Costa Rica."

"Safe house?" Jennifer asked. "Why do we need a safe house?"

Elaine said, "Because we're wanted felons in at least three states."

"Actually," Parnell said, "we're wanted by the FBI and quite a few of the other federal alphabet agencies."

"Holy shit!" Jennifer blurted.

"Jen, I know I said I would tell you everything, and I will. But you've got to pay attention right now. When this train stops moving, we need to slip off quietly and keep on the lookout for bulls—"

"Bulls?"

"Railroad cops," Elaine explained. "They'll lock us up if they catch us."

"Lainey's right about that, Jen," Parnell said. "We have to be careful. So, when we come to a stop you ladies will follow me and we'll hook onto a southbound here in Provo. It'll be a couple of days to Nogales and the Mexican border. Once we cross the border, we'll charter a plane to Sixaola in southern Costa Rica, then head to my place in Manzanillo. It's my own little slice of paradise on the Caribbean coast."

"You have a house on the Caribbean?" Jennifer said, incredulous.

"Yeah, I do. On the beach. You girls are going to love it."

Jennifer turned to Elaine. "You haven't been there?"

"No. I've seen photos, but I haven't had the pleasure. Two years ago when Derek bought it, he told me it was a retirement home. He keeps promising to take me, but—"

"Well, I'm taking you now, aren't I?"

"Yeah, now that it's a *safe house*."

"Retirement home . . . safe house. It's just semantics, Lainey."

Parnell was now counting his blessings that he'd had the foresight to purchase the house in Costa Rica with cash, and that he had kept the transaction under the radar. He had supplied one of his hobo friends fake identification and paid him well to make the trip south to secure the property. John Dobkin and Blanton Miles couldn't steal the beach house from him since they knew nothing about it.

"How are we gonna get across the border?" Jennifer asked. "I don't have any ID."

"No worries, Jen," Parnell said. "I've got friends on the Border Patrol at Nogales Station. They owe me a few favors. I set it all up when we were in Vegas."

"Jesus, Dad, you've like turned into this really badass dude or something."

Elaine laughed. "Oh, if you only knew the half of it, sweetie. If you only knew."

The freighter chuffed and squeaked to a complete stop.

"Come on, ladies," Parnell said. "Get your things. Time to turn into beach bums."

EPILOGUE
10 MONTHS
LATER

MANZANILLO, COSTA RICA

PARNELL SAT WITH ELAINE on the glassed-in deck at the rear of their Manzanillo stilt house. She sipped a Mai Tai while he drank from a bottle of Bavaria Gold beer. Piped-in music played over the stereo system—clanking steel drums and plinking marimbas—true island reggae-beat Calypso.

He swigged his beer, his eyes sweeping the sugary-platinum sand that unfurled like a cotton blanket out to a turquoise sea. Parnell loved this remote paradise, a place of tranquility tucked in the crook of Costa Rica's southern Caribbean shore. The sleepy fishing village of Manzanillo was the end of the line, the last gasp of civilization before Costa Rican paved roads gave way to dense jungle and the Panama border.

The elevated house offered unobstructed views of pristine ocean on one side and rugged jungle on the other. The relentless hiss of Caribbean waves licking the shore competed with the croaking vocalizations of howler monkeys high in the treetops. Huasteco parrots, tropical kingbirds, and keel-billed toucans threw vibrant splashes of color against the verdant green curtain of rain-forest. Swift-footed iguanas darted to and fro. Manzanillo was a whole new universe, one that he and Elaine had embraced with open arms upon their arrival ten months ago. It was home now, and Parnell often wondered why it had taken him so long to bring Lainey here.

Elaine had been first to integrate, joining a sea turtle rescue organization. Twice a week she traveled 80 miles up the coast to Barra del Pacuare in Tortuguero to work with an oceanography conservationist group. Lainey had become quite taken with endangered sea turtle species such as the Ridley, loggerhead, leather-back, and green hawksbill. She and her like-minded Tortuguero friends worked to stop poachers and changes in habitats from deci-mating turtle populations. Poachers were the toughest battle. Turtle meat is considered a delicacy in many parts of the world, and in Mexico, turtle eggs are thought to be an aphrodisiac, sub-sequently bringing big money on the black market.

The work seemed to make Lainey happy, which in turn, fed Parnell's sense of well-being. She always returned from her turtle sojourns in an upbeat mood, feeling she was contributing some-thing valuable to the world. She talked excitedly about her new friends—Martha Turnbull and Denise Allicotti—two American widows who had retired to Costa Rica to pursue careers as marine conservationists. And so, though Parnell missed Elaine terribly and worried when she was away, he was glad to see her reconnecting with life through her volunteer save-the-sea-turtle work.

Parnell, being a lone wolf, didn't mix with locals the first three months. Then, on a marlin fishing trip, he met Vance Toohey, charter boat captain and owner of Toohey and Son's Sportsfishing Excursions. Casual conversation revealed that Captain Vance shared Parnell's passion for model trains.

Vance Toohey—a rugged outdoorsy type in his early sixties had light cocoa skin derived from Irish-Jamaican parentage and spoke a lilting Patois Jamaican-English—an engaging Creole-inflected Irish brogue that Parnell never tired of hearing. The skipper had grown up on cruise ships where his Dublin-born father had been a facilities manager and his Jamaican mother a house-keeping supervisor. When Vance was a young boy living aboard the *Montego Queen*, his father had introduced model trains to the passengers, an attraction that became a huge hit with adults and children alike. Toohey told Parnell he'd been smitten the first time he'd taken the controls of that Lionel set, and his father would have to repeatedly run him off so the paying passengers could have their turn with the miniature trains.

In turn, Parnell felt comfortable enough with the easygoing fishing guide to share his own childhood model train experiences. He'd told Toohey about how a similar Lionel set had bonded him and his father for a short time. He also told the captain about the impressive model train layout he'd built back in the States, but didn't get into the reasons why he hadn't brought it with him to Manzanillo. Toohey never pursued it further. Parnell liked that about the skipper—the man knew how to keep his curiosity in check. They soon became inseparable. When Captain Vance wasn't on the water guiding his customers to choice fishing spots, the two men spent a lot of time together at Toohey's place, drinking beer and playing with the captain's elaborate train setup. *Just a pair of Peter Pans playing with your toys,* is how Lainey teased him about the relationship.

His reverie was interrupted by Elaine. "You're very quiet today," she said over the music.

"Just thinking. This place has a way of pulling me into my thoughts. *Good* thoughts."

"I know. It's beautiful here. Makes you think of positive things. We should have come here years ago."

Parnell looked out over the endless sea, watched a tanker scudding across the horizon where the blue-green Caribbean met sapphire sky. "You think things would be different if we had?"

"Well, we could have avoided a lot of trouble."

He turned to look at her. Her skin had darkened to a deep bronze from all the time she spent on the beach. The Costa Rican sun had brought out the scars on the left side of her face, like finely-etched cracks in copper-painted pottery. But even this pigmentation defect could not detract from her natural beauty. Elaine still took his breath away, and she always would.

"We might have avoided certain troubles," he said. "But we wouldn't have Jenny. Jen was worth every minute of trouble to me."

Elaine sipped her Mai Tai, dabbed at the corner of her mouth. "She's really a very special girl, your daughter."

"Of *course* she is. She's a Parnell."

Elaine laughed. "One thing you've never lacked is self-confidence."

Parnell shrugged his shoulders, letting her know she was stating the obvious.

"Jenny's been through so much."

"We all have, Lainey."

"True, but Jen survived a horrific ordeal that lasted half her childhood. Not many of us would be strong enough to deal with something like that. Especially at her age. Quite a few of those girls Jennifer told us about didn't make it."

Parnell mumbled, "Yeah. Those girls never had a chance. It was tragic what happened to them."

He retreated back into his thoughts. The first few months here were absolute hell. Jennifer had suffered terribly from post traumatic stress syndrome. All three of them had. But Jenny had been hit the hardest. She'd had screaming nightmares, her wails drowning out those of the howler monkeys in the jungle. They had discussed getting her professional help, but quickly discarded the idea. Southern Costa Rica wasn't exactly rich with qualified psychologists and shrinks. And seeing how Parnell and Elaine were on the FBI's Most Wanted List back in the States, it wouldn't be smart to have Jennifer relating their story to perfect strangers, no matter how mental health professionals vowed to maintain doctor-patient confidentiality. Parnell knew that any and all information was available for a price, and he didn't want an unscrupulous money hungry doctor taking advantage of his unstable daughter.

And so, in the end, he and Lainey decided it best to work through it themselves. The three of them bared their souls to each other in open, frank discussions. Parnell laid everything out for Jennifer, leaving no detail uncovered, no matter how bloody or twisted. He told her about meeting the mysterious courier known as Croesus and how the man had inexplicably set him up with great wealth, how the money trail eventually led to John Dobkin in Vegas. He told Jenny about her late mother, Barbara, and the fire that had taken her life. About how they'd met Lucious Razzy Jones and had brought him on as a trusted bodyguard. About the crossbow hunter murders near Chinle and the shootout on Navajo Trail Highway. He told her about the two arsonists and how he'd tortured them with an acetylene torch in the getaway van. They discussed how all of these events and more had changed Derek Parnell from loving, doting father into a cold-blooded killer—the happenings that led to his transformation into the man with the tombstone eyes. Parnell and Elaine described to Jennifer the way they met, the truth behind Lainey's blinded left eye, and the way Parnell had dispatched of Lainey's attacker, Jessie Waltham.

And they, in turn, listened to Jenny talk about her long years as a sex slave in the Dog Pound. She described to them in great detail her life in the Liberty Dog hellhole caves that she and the other girls referred to as "the anus in the earth." The things those men made Jenny and countless other underage girls do shocked even Parnell. Often, Elaine had to leave the room as Jenny related the worst of it to them. Her horror stories sent Parnell into paroxysms of fury, making him want to return to Colorado to dredge Burton Shanks' body from the depths of the Yampa River and kill him all over again.

Anything went in that underground prison atop Mount Zirkel, anything to scratch the malevolent itch of those depraved predators—bondage and discipline, lesbian orgies, psychosexual humiliation, sadomasochism and torture, gang rape . . . even branding and bloodletting. Jenny talked about all of it in excruciating detail. Hearing the descriptions of these contemptible acts trip off the tongue of his daughter sickened Parnell, the inhumanity of it almost too overwhelming to take. As these sessions continued, there were many tears, many hugs, many screaming rants followed by soft, caring words of support and understanding. The three of them teetered on the precarious edge of emotional breakdown for several months. But they got through it, tough as it was. They each seemed to realize the importance of it, understood that the sessions brought them closer together, that the unburdening release of confession provided a steadfast bond that cemented their relationships. Talking about it seemed to help Jennifer deal with the aftermath and heal from the nightmarish psychological fallout. And after every one of these intense sessions, Parnell thanked the gods of fate that those evil pricks who had violated his daughter and so many other innocent young girls had perished in the blast that had decimated the Dog Pound.

His only regret was that many innocent young girls had also been buried by the explosions. Parnell wished there had been some way to rescue them. Jen talked about one of her friends she'd lost—Luanne Solton—whom she missed dearly. Luanne had been plucked from her family at age ten from one of the hobo camps in Wyoming. Jennifer told them she and Lulu had been planning to escape together and go to the authorities. They'd planned to start up a business together when they got free. Fashion design is what they thought they wanted to do, since fashion was something they could only fantasize about during their captivity. Jenny cried every time she brought up Lulu Solton, saying it wasn't fair that someone should have to die such a horrible death at the tender age of sixteen.

No it wasn't fair, Parnell thought. But then life never would be a thing of perfect justice. He thought about how the U.S. government had hung the whole Dog Pound bombing on them— himself, Elaine, and Razzy. All three of them had made the Federal Bureau of Investigation's Most Wanted List. They were wanted on 47 counts of first-degree, premeditated murder. They had done the government's dirty work for them and then were made the fall guys. Parnell knew that's the way the government agencies rolled, but when he saw this kind of thing in action, it shocked and surprised him that "trusted" elected officials could make the wheels turn in such an underhanded, deceitful manner. This was the work of high level politicians. Self-serving bullies and cowards, every last one of them. The United States would never get back on track with their breed at the helm.

The screen door to the patio squeaked open behind him. Parnell turned to see Jennifer standing there, clutching a large suitcase. Her face was made up and she smelled sweetly of soap and perfume. She wore a dark blue skirt with a white silk blouse.

"Hi, Dad . . . Elaine," she said, nodding in Lainey's direction.

Parnell knew at once this was the day he'd been dreading. He felt like he'd been slammed in the chest as he said, "Hey, sweets, what's with the luggage?"

"Well, um . . . I know it's short notice and everything, but, well . . ."

"Just say it, dear," Elaine said.

Parnell looked at Elaine, knowing from her reply and body language that she and Jenny had already discussed this.

"Okay," Jennifer said haltingly. "I guess I'm, uh . . . leaving for a while."

Parnell had tried to prepare himself for this moment, but now that it was staring him in the face, he couldn't handle it. He couldn't form any words. His mouth and tongue refused to cooperate. He just sat there like an idiot, staring at his daughter.

"Look, Dad," she said, setting the suitcase down and coming to him, touching his shoulder. "This is just something I have to do, okay? You have been unbelievably good to me—and so have you, Elaine—but . . . well, I'm nineteen now, and I need to move on with my own life. This place you brought me to is absolutely gorgeous and everything, but I have to, well . . . I have to confess—I sorta feel trapped here. It feels like a dead end to me. I mean, you two have each other and I'm a little embarrassed to say it . . ." She took a deep breath. "Wow, okay, I'll just say it—I'm, like, really *envious* of the relationship you guys have. I'm jealous if you want the truth. It's awesome how loving and natural and . . . *real* your love is for each other. There I said it." She looked through the floor-to-ceiling sliding glass doors, at the expansive ocean. "I don't really know why that was so hard to say after all the other shit we've confessed to each other. Anyway, you both like, *inspire* me when I see you together. I want the kind of relationship you have. But I'm not going to find it here. No way, no how. I don't want a life with a wrinkled-up old fisherman or a banana farmer. There's nobody here for me to even think about dating. Like I said—dead end. There's an entire universe out there just waiting for me," she said, sweeping her arm in a wide arc. "I think it must be that restless Parnell blood in me, Dad. You know—unable to stay in one place for very long. Always curious to see what's over the next mountain. The road not taken . . . or in your case, what's on the rails around the next bend. You know what I'm saying? It's the restless and inquisitive Parnell hobo blood."

He tried to hide his smile, but couldn't. *Restless and inquisitive Parnell hobo blood?* She had worked on that line for a while. "Yeah," he said, sneaking a peek at Elaine, "I believe I do understand that, Jen. So where are you going?"

"To live with Russ."

"Russ?"

"Yeah, you know. My guardian angel? The guy who looked out for me when I was in the Dog Pound?"

"Oh, *that* Russ," Parnell said, thinking about the man's ties with John Dobkin. "But I thought he—"

"Remember I told you that he left me about a half hour before you showed up on the mountain?" Jenny said.

"Yeah, I know you said that, but—"

"Well, Russ got out before the explosions. He knew it was coming and that you were the one bringing the bomb. He stuck around long enough to be sure you would be able to get me out safely. Then he had to protect himself. I've told you this before, Dad."

"I know, but he's been missing all this time and you thought he was—"

"Dead, I know. But he's not. Russ had to go into hiding. Deep under cover. But he's recently resurfaced and contacted me. He's alive and I'm going to be with him!"

"That's wonderful, honey," Elaine said.

Parnell wasn't so sure. The last thing he needed was for his daughter to be cavorting around with one of John Dobkin's employees—a key player in the Liberty Dog suitcase nuke sting— while he and Elaine were evading capture by the American feds for that very crime.

"I think you're getting yourself into a dangerous situation, Jen. You barely know this guy," he said, sorry to have to piss on Jennifer's obvious happiness.

"I know him plenty well. Believe me, I have learned to read what's in the minds and hearts of men—at least the few males who actually have minds and hearts—and I know this man to be good and kind. He loves me, Daddy, and I love him."

Jesus, Parnell thought. Bad enough she wants to leave after all he and Lainey and Razzy went through to rescue her, but *this*?

He got up to turn off the stereo, grabbed another beer from the mini-fridge. "So how did he contact you?" he asked as he twisted the cap off the bottle, took a gulp.

"We found each other on Facebook and I'm—"

"Facebook?" Parnell exploded. "Are you out of your ever-loving gourd, oh sweet, naïve daughter of mine? Do you have any idea just what—?"

"Derek," Elaine said, getting up from her chair and stepping between father and daughter. "I don't think you understand what—"

"You stay out of this, E!" he said, brushing her aside. But before he could get another word out, he felt the cold hard slap of Jennifer's hand across his face. Stunned, disbelieving his daughter had actually struck him, he rubbed his cheek and stared at her.

"Look, Dad," she said, chest heaving, face flushed in anger, "I really appreciate all you have done for me over the past year and I love you probably more than I've ever loved another human being. But you can be one of the most stubborn, selfish, pain-in-the-ass people I've ever known. You're suffocating me. You lord over me and control my every waking minute. You won't even let me work a part-time job. I can't take it anymore." Suddenly she seemed embarrassed by what she had just blurted. "I hope you can, like, *understand* that," she said to him, her voice softer, sympathetic.

Parnell glanced at Elaine, whose knowing expression told him she agreed with Jennifer. He thought he'd done a good thing. Jennifer didn't have to work. None of them needed to work since he'd had the prudence to bury $250,000 in a waterproof casket deep in the jungle when he'd bought this beachfront property. The quarter-million was Parnell's little retirement nest egg, money he'd siphoned from the Locomotion Enterprises accounts through creative bookkeeping. The cost of living was cheap here in Costa Rica. That stash would go a long way. He thought he'd been doing all three of them a favor by taking care of their financial future, and he had. But he'd also lost sight of the fact that he'd been keeping Jennifer planted too firmly under his thumb.

"I do appreciate what you're saying, honey," he said, turning back to Jenny, rubbing his jaw where she had smacked him. "But I'm worried about you and this Russell fellow and communicating through Facebook—"

"You must see me as a freakin' imbecile, Dad. Do you think for a second that I would jeopardize yours and Elaine's safety by taking a stupid security risk?"

"I don't know, Jen. I know how you young folks are with your

Facebook socializing, and—"

"I signed up for my Facebook account using my new identity," Jenny said, her face flushed in anger. "I'm Jessica Cooper. And don't worry, the few times I've referred to you or Elaine online, I've used your aliases as well."

"That's good, Jen, but you're forgetting one disturbing fact."

"What's that?"

"Since this Russell guy was in on our Liberty Dogs sting operation, he knows all about me and my old company, Locomotion Enterprises and that we were the ones who delivered the bomb that brought down the mountain."

"Obviously. So what, Dad?"

"*So what, Dad?* Have you forgotten there is a huge price on mine and Lainey's heads? An informant could retire on what the feds are offering for information to our whereabouts."

Jennifer went back to her luggage, grabbed the handle. "You are so freakin' paranoid."

"That's the main reason I'm still alive, Jenny."

She looked at him appraisingly. "You just won't give me any credit, will you?"

"How do you mean?"

"I mean you treat me like I'm some dumb hick kid who doesn't know enough to get out of my own way. You think I'm a young damsel in distress, damaged and all kinds of messed-up in the head. I'm some of those things, yes. We're all crazy fucked-up in the head—you, me, Elaine—how could we not be after the crazy shit we've been through? But I've discovered some things about myself along the way. Mostly that I'm strong and intelligent and self reliant. What I've been through has toughened me up. I can take care of myself. And you know what?"

"No, what?" Parnell said.

"I have you to thank for most of it."

"Huh?"

"It's true. You've taught me to be independent and to think for myself. You taught me how to be tough and how to hang in there when the world is throwing you impossible odds. I thank you for that and I love you for it, Dad. But let's not kid ourselves. You're far from perfect. In fact you're, like, really flawed. Seriously. You jump to conclusions about things. About people. You still really don't know me. You think you do, but you don't. I'll tell you this right now . . . If you think I would ever endanger you and Elaine, then you don't know shit about me.

"Russell Holt—*my* Russ—isn't interested in turning you and Elaine in to the authorities. Just the opposite, really. He was royally pissed off at the way the whole thing at the Dog Pound went down, the way it was handled. Too many innocent people were killed, my friend Luanne Solton being one. And Russ figured out that Dobkin was trying to kill him, too, to take out a key witness to the crimes that went on there. Russ is planning to turn state's evidence against Dobkin and some of the rogue federal agents who were involved. After he testifies, he's going into protective custody. He's entering the federal witness protection program and I'll be with him the whole way. So you see, Dad, Russell Holt—*my* Russ—is a good, decent man who wants to see justice done. He wants to take the blame off you and put it where it belongs. He wants to see the right people do prison time. I want to help him get that done."

She kneeled and opened her luggage, pulled out a small scrap of paper. "Here, Daddy," she said, standing and handing him the paper. "I'm flying up to Vancouver tonight to meet him. Here is where I'll be staying until the whistle blowing starts."

"Vancouver?" Parnell said. "In British Columbia?"

"Yeah, where else is there a Vancouver?"

Parnell looked down at the slip of paper she had given him. The Vancouver address and phone number were written out in Jen's looping, feminine handwriting, clear and precise. At the bottom she'd written: *I'm going to miss you, Daddy. I promise to stay in touch. Don't worry. I'll be fine.* He remembered Dobkin telling him British Columbia was where he, Elaine, and Razzy were supposed to start their new lives in WITSEC. Coincidence? He thought not.

He looked back at Jennifer, thinking that she was so young and impressionable, no matter what kind of grownup front she was trying to present.

"I'm really worried about you, sweetie," he told her. "I think you might be heading into a trap. A very *dangerous* trap."

"I can take care of myself," she said, defiance in her stare.

A car horn sounded out front, shrill and urgent.

"There's my cab," Jennifer said, tears clouding her eyes. She closed up her suitcase. "Call me any time, day or night. Or you can contact me on Facebook. I love you guys."

"This is uh . . . this is awfully fast, Jen," Parnell said, hating the whiny desperation in his voice. "You should give some more thought to this."

The horn beeped again.

"I have to go," Jennifer said, hugging Parnell and Elaine and kissing both on the cheek before leaving.

From the open front door, they watched the cabbie stow her single piece of luggage in the trunk and Jennifer get in the back seat. They watched the taxi pull away, Jenny waving goodbye through the rear window before the cab turned the corner and was gobbled up by the thick jungle.

After several minutes of listening to the howler monkeys chatter from the treetops, Parnell felt Elaine take his hand and say, "Are you okay, babe?"

"Yeah, I think so," he responded with a shaky voice. "My little Thumbelina's all grown up now, Lainey."

"Yes, she is."

"Obviously you've known about this for a while," he said.

"Yes, I have. Are you mad at me?"

"I could never be mad at Karen Cooper."

Elaine laughed. "What about Elaine Leibrandt?"

"She's another story," he said, stuffing the paper slip in his shirt pocket and looking at her. "The Leibrandt woman makes me very angry."

She held his stare. "Jen came to me a few weeks ago and told me all of this. She didn't think she could face you with it. She wanted to leave you a note instead of discussing it with you. I told her I thought that was a bad idea."

"Good advice," Parnell said dully.

"She thought her leaving would break your heart."

"It does, Lainey. It also worries me."

"I know, Derek. But she's a grown woman now. She has to make her own way in the world, and you have to let her do that."

"Yeah, I suppose. I just hope she doesn't come to a bad end."

Elaine noticed his befuddled, anxious expression. "Please tell me you are not going after her, Derek. You wouldn't happen to be getting the hobo hotfoot, would you?"

"Why would you ask that, my dearest Mrs. Cooper?"

She smiled at his alias reference and said, "Because you're getting that far-off vagabond look in your eyes I haven't seen in a while. Must be the restless and inquisitive Parnell hobo blood."

Parnell laughed. "That was quite a line Jenny threw on me

there, wasn't it?" he said. "You helped her with that one didn't you, Lainey?"

"I plead the fifth," she said, holding up her free hand.

"Well, I promise, I'm not planning on going anywhere anytime soon."

"Does that rule out a trip to the bedroom?"

"That's a very different kind of hobo hotfoot, my lovely lady," he said with a wide grin.

He lifted her off the floor and kicked the front door shut. Elaine giggled like a little girl and planted kisses along his neck as he cradled her in his arms and carried her back to their bedroom.

But her kisses barely registered. He was thinking about the promise he'd made to her. The one about not going anywhere. He knew damn well there would come a day in the not too distant future that he would have to return to the States to see justice done. John Dobkin and Blanton Miles had cleaned him out, financially and emotionally. They had deceived him and stolen his company, used him as an unwitting pawn in a federal government sting operation. They had humiliated him and emasculated him. They had forced him to kill or be killed. And then they had framed him and hung the indictments on him to where he had to flee his own country. Both men would pay, oh yes they would. Jennifer could put her youthful trust in the U.S. Justice Department and naively count on them to mete out appropriate penalties for those who deserved it, but Parnell knew how it would play out. Privilege and money and connections always won over true justice. If left up to the U.S. government, both John Dobkin and Blanton Miles would skate away clean.

And that's when Parnell would take action.

Dobkin and Miles had generated a lot of negative karma. One fact Derek Parnell was absolutely sure of—karma was the ultimate judge and jury.

And sometimes karma had to be helped along a little.

Acknowledgements

It has been stated many times before that no author is an island, that no literary creation is solely the work of a singular writer. This is certainly true with this book. Many wonderful people have helped me through the multiple rounds of drafts and the seemingly endless process of taking a story from concept to completion.

I would like to thank the following for their greatly appreciated input and feedback. First, my wife Cheryl, proofreader extraordinaire, partner in life and all things creative. She possesses the eyes of a hawk and the heart of an angel, and helped breathe life into the Elaine Leibrandt character. Tracy Rud, whose keen story editing and blunt honesty helped me keep the story on the tracks at all times. Jedwin Smith, for his friendship and mentoring over the years, and for letting me know when and where to cut back on the longshoreman dialogue. A writer could not hope for a more inspirational influence than Jedwin. My thanks also goes out to Mike Jimison, an early reader who made sure I had the helicopter stuff right. Heywood and Pattie Gould provided an abundance of friendship along the way . . . thanks for the cool cover blurb, Heywood! To my son, Ira, who, along with my lovely wife Cheryl, designed the kick-ass train cover—my most heartfelt thanks and love go out to you both for being the best family a guy could ask for, and for your graphical genius. Everyone knows the old adage is true: "A book is only as good as its cover." Thanks guys.

Other folks I would like to thank for their support of *King of the Hobos* and my first novel, *The Wisdom of Loons*: Susan Jimison, Mike Jimison, and George Scott of Peerless Book Store . . . Doug Robinson, Charles Robinson, and the rest of the sales gang at Eagle Eye Book Shop . . . My fellow creative scribes in the Fictioneers . . . The foxes at FoxTale Book Shoppe—Karen Schwettman, Jackie Tanase, and Ellen Ward . . . Thanks also to Mother Mary, who instilled in me a love of reading and story. . . and last, but certainly not least, thanks to anyone and everyone who has ever purchased (and enjoyed) one of my books.

Jeff Dennis
Norcross, Georgia
August 2012

About the Author

JEFF DENNIS lives in Norcross, Georgia with his wife, Cheryl. He is the author of the dark fantasy short-story collection, *When the Sandman Meets the Reaper*, and the paranormal romance novel, *The Wisdom of Loons*.